Vengeance from the S

A Tale of Redemption and

C000064006

BY SHAVONNE BULMER

COPYRIGHT

Instagram @makeroomforyourself07

TikTok @makeroomforyourself07

Dedication

In the pages of this enchanting book, you'll find a tale born from the depths of my own life story, one I call 'Get Out and Stay Out.' As I embark on this literary journey, my heart brims with gratitude and love for the extraordinary man who is my husband.

My dearest, you've been my unwavering anchor, loving me through every imperfection and illuminating the path to love and joy beyond the shadows of abuse. In your arms, I've discovered a love that transcends time itself, and I am endlessly thankful for everything you've bestowed upon me.

Within these pages, where reality intertwines with fantasy, I hope to extend a hand of solace to those grappling with their own pain. Remember, you are inherently deserving, capable of reshaping your destiny, no matter the formidable trials you encounter!

Please be aware that the events within these fantastical pages draw inspiration from my own journey, but they have been artfully embellished for the sake of fantasy. Here, you'll uncover a blend of horror, fantasy, and the intoxicating allure of romance. Proceed with a heart open to wonder and adventure.

[Trigger Warning: This content contains depictions of violence, abuse, and sexual assault.]

Table of Contents

The Serpents Constriction

The castle's ominous facade stood as a grim testament to its sordid past, its towering walls adorned with grotesque gargoyles that seemed to mock the desolate land below. A sinister, ivy-clad aura clung to its ancient stones, as if nature itself recoiled from the malevolence harbored within. The woods surrounding the castle held an equally foreboding air—a twisted labyrinth of gnarled trees and thorny undergrowth, where even the bravest souls dared not tread, haunted by the echoing cackles of witches and the menacing snarls of wolves. The trees whispered ancient incantations, their contorted branches weaving eerie silhouettes against the moonlit sky.

Count Malachi's name spread dread and infamy across the realm, synonymous with wickedness and depravity. He was rumored to conspire with dark forces, invoking vile spells under the shroud of night and making unspeakable sacrifices to his infernal masters. His very presence seemed to poison the land, transforming once-fertile fields into barren wastelands, where only skeletal trees and poisonous thorns thrived, and the sweet scent of flowers turned to the stench of decay.

Amidst this abyss of darkness and despair, a glimmer of hope emerged from an unexpected source—the kingdom's highborn families. Confronted with the looming menace of Count Malachi and the impending darkness he brought, the nobles devised a desperate plan for peace. In a heart-wrenching decision, they chose one of their own, a highborn daughter, to be sent to live with the malevolent count, hoping to quell his insatiable thirst for power and darkness.

The maiden chosen for this sacrifice was none other than Lady Seraphina, a name steeped in the annals of highborn lineage. She bore her family's crest—a fearless horse galloping across a majestic field, symbolizing strength, determination, and courage. Seraphina, with her auburn tresses and piercing emerald eyes, embodied the grace and nobility of her lineage.

Yet, beneath her beauty, beat a heart filled with unwavering resolve and a fierce determination to free her kingdom from the clutches of evil.

Draped in her most resplendent gown, a vision of opulence and elegance, Lady Seraphina's attire underscored her elevated status at the medieval court. Woven from the finest silk, the dress glowed in pristine white, a symbol of purity and grace. Its fabric cascaded gracefully, forming a train that flowed behind her like a shimmering river.

The gown's bodice featured intricate embroidery, delicate patterns of silver threads and pearls that seemed to dance across the fabric. These embellishments framed her figure, accentuating her slender waist and regal bearing. The neckline, modestly cut, offered a glimpse of her fair collarbone, while long, fitted sleeves added an air of sophistication.

But what truly set this gown apart were the jewels that adorned it. Precious gemstones and pearls were intricately sewn into the fabric, creating a breathtaking display of opulence. Sapphires, emeralds, and rubies sparkled like stars in the night sky, their vibrant colours contrasting with the pure white silk. Strings of pearls encircled her waist and neckline, their lustrous sheen reflecting the light.

The gown's skirt was generously embellished with diamond-like crystals that caught and scattered the light, casting a mesmerizing, ethereal glow. As Lady Seraphina moved, the jewels seemed to come alive, creating a captivating play of colours and reflections that enraptured all who beheld her.

Completing the ensemble was a flowing, sheer veil of the finest gossamer, delicately embroidered and studded with jewels to match the gown. It cascaded from an ornate diadem adorning her head, further enhancing her regal presence in the shadow of impending sacrifice.

The selection of Lady Seraphina was a painstaking process that unfolded during a solemn council meeting held in the grand chamber of Castle Ravenshadow, the ruling seat of King Alaric's realm. The highbred families, driven by the urgent need to appease the malevolent Count Malachi and safeguard their kingdom, gathered with heavy hearts and determined spirits.

The grand chamber, bathed in the warm glow of flickering torches and furnished with tapestries depicting the kingdom's storied history, bore witness to the gravity of the situation. The air was thick with tension as the nobles took their seats around a massive, intricately carved oak table. Each noble's countenance bore the weight of the kingdom's destiny, their eyes reflecting a mix of fear, determination, and resolve.

At the head of the table sat Lord Cedric, the eldest among them and the voice of reason in these dire times. He was a man of wisdom, with a flowing white beard that spoke of his many years of experience. His eyes, however, gleamed with a fierce determination as he addressed the assembly.

"Ladies and gentlemen," Lord Cedric began, his voice carrying the weight of authority and concern, "we stand on the precipice of a dark abyss, with Count Malachi's ominous shadow looming over King Alaric's realm. We have convened here to make a grave decision—one that may be our only hope for peace."

A heavy silence settled upon the chamber as all eyes turned to Lady Isabella, the matron of the highbred families. She was known for her grace and composure, but today her gaze held a hint of sorrow as she spoke, "We have unanimously agreed that a sacrifice must be made to appease the malevolent count. It is our duty to choose one among us who will bear this burden."

Lady Seraphina's name had already been whispered throughout the kingdom as a potential candidate, given her lineage and noble qualities. She had distinguished herself in court, not only with her beauty but also with her intelligence, kindness, and unwavering dedication to King Alaric's realm.

Lord Cedric continued, "We have considered the qualities required of the chosen maiden: courage, purity, nobility, and, above all, a heart filled with love for King Alaric's kingdom. Lady Seraphina embodies these virtues."

Lady Seraphina sat with a solemn grace, her eyes glistening with a mixture of trepidation and determination. She knew the gravity of the situation and the burden she would bear.

Lady Seraphina's parents, Lord Maximus and Lady Elena, were pillars of honour within King Alaric's realm. Their dedication to the kingdom and unwavering commitment to its values were well-known throughout the land. They had raised their daughter, Seraphina, with the same principles of nobility, courage, and self-sacrifice that had been passed down through generations of their family.

In the face of the council's solemn decision to send Lady Seraphina to Count Malachi's castle, Lord Maximus and Lady Elena bore a profound sorrow. They had always dreamed of a bright future for their beloved daughter, filled with joy and prosperity. However, they understood the dire circumstances that had compelled the highbred families to make this painful choice.

With heavy hearts and tears in their eyes, Lord Maximus and Lady Elena stood by Lady Seraphina's side, providing her with unwavering support and guidance. They knew that their family's honour and the safety of King Alaric's depended on their daughter's courage and sacrifice. While their sorrow was profound, it was tempered by the knowledge that their family had always been driven by a sense of duty and loyalty to their kingdom.

A murmur of agreement rippled through the assembly, but not without dissent. Lord Alistair, a stern and imposing figure, raised his voice, "Are we certain that this is our only course of action? Must we sacrifice one of our own?"

Lord Cedric, unyielding in his resolve, replied, "Count Malachi's power grows with each passing day, and our lands wither in his malevolent grasp. We have exhausted all other avenues. This is our last chance to save King Alaric's realm."

The council's decision was reached, and Lady Seraphina accepted her fate with a grace that left no doubt about her courage and resolve. The council pledged their unwavering support, vowing to do everything in their power to ensure her safety and eventual return.

In the weeks that followed, preparations were made for Lady Seraphina's departure. The kingdom's best scholars and sorcerers provided her with knowledge and protections against the dark forces she would face. The people of King Alaric's realm rallied, offering their prayers and support for her journey into the unknown.

In the days leading up to Lady Seraphina's departure, Lord Maximus and Lady Elena found strength in their family's traditions of honour and selflessness. They shared stories of their ancestors who had made similar sacrifices for the realm's well-being, instilling in Lady Seraphina a deep sense of purpose and determination. Together, they upheld the legacy of their family, which had always placed the kingdom's needs above their own desires.

As the day of her departure neared, Castle Ravenshadow's grand chamber was once again filled, this time with a somber procession. Lady Seraphina, resplendent in her gown of opulence and elegance, stood at the center, a symbol of sacrifice and hope. Her auburn hair shone like a beacon of courage, and her emerald eyes blazed with determination.

With tearful farewells and heartfelt blessings, Lady Seraphina embarked on her perilous journey to the castle of Count Malachi, her noble heart and radiant spirit ready to confront the darkness that threatened King Alaric's realm.

As Lady Seraphina set out on her perilous journey to Count Malachi's castle, her parents watched with hearts heavy with sorrow but also bursting with pride. They knew that their daughter embodied the very essence of their family's honour, and they believed in her ability to face the darkness with the same unwavering resolve that had defined their lineage for generations. Lord Maximus and Lady Elena's love for Lady Seraphina was matched only by their love for King Alaric's realm, and they accepted the weight of the sacrifice required to protect it.

Lady Seraphina's journey to Count Malachi's castle was a day's ride, filled with both trepidation and determination. As she rode her horse through the rolling hills and winding paths that led her out of King Alaric's Kingdom, the breeze played a gentle symphony in her auburn hair. It whispered secrets of hope and courage, soothing her restless spirit.

The breeze was Seraphina's gentle companion, offering a comforting presence amid the uncertainty of her path. Its gentle caress carried with it the scent of wildflowers and the distant fragrance of pine trees, mingling with the sweet nostalgia of her homeland. It was as though the very air conspired to reassure her, to remind her of the love and support she carried with her in her heart.

Yet, as Seraphina followed the prescribed path that would take her deeper into Count Malachi's realm, the landscape began to change. The once lush and fertile fields of King Alaric's Kingdom gave way to desolation and decay. Barren stretches of land stretched out before her, a stark contrast to the vibrant, flourishing kingdom she had left behind.

The transformation of the fields was a chilling reminder of the malevolence that Count Malachi had brought upon the land. It was as if his very presence had sucked the life from the earth, leaving only a lifeless wasteland in its wake. Seraphina's heart ached for her people, and she felt a renewed determination to confront the darkness that had enveloped this once-thriving land.

The path led her deeper into a dark and eerie forest, where gnarled trees seemed to reach out with twisted branches that twisted and contorted, as if corrupted by evil forces. The forest was a labyrinth of shadows and secrets, and the very air was heavy with an unsettling silence. The whispered enchantments of the trees filled the air, their sinister murmurs echoing in Seraphina's ears.

With every step deeper into the forest, Seraphina's resolve grew stronger. She knew that this eerie place was the threshold to Count Malachi's realm, and she had to press on. The forest was a test of her courage, a test she would not fail. She whispered words of encouragement to her steed, urging him to carry her forward through the ominous woods.

Emerging from the forest, Seraphina found herself in yet another barren field, a desolate expanse that stretched out before her like a vast, lifeless canvas. At the far end of the field, perched atop a hill that seemed to rise ominously from the earth, stood Count Malachi's castle.

The castle was a formidable sight, its towering spires and imposing walls casting long shadows over the desolation below. It was a fortress of darkness, a symbol of the malevolent power that Count Malachi wielded. Seraphina's heart raced as she gazed upon the castle, knowing that her destiny lay within its foreboding walls.

With a deep breath and a silent prayer, Seraphina urged her horse onward, up the hill toward the castle that loomed like a sinister sentinel. The journey had been arduous, and the challenges had tested her courage and resolve. But she was determined to face whatever awaited her within the castle, for the fate of King Alaric's realm depended on her strength and unwavering determination.

The castle doors were towering high and wide, carved from rich, dark wood and reinforced with iron embellishments. They were a testament to the imposing nature of Count Malachi's fortress, with their sheer size and weight seeming almost insurmountable. The ironwork, meticulously crafted into intricate patterns, depicted coiled serpents, the very crest of Count Malachi, which seemed to mockingly await Lady Seraphina's arrival.

As Lady Seraphina approached the entrance, the castle guards, all dressed in dark black armour adorned with serpent furnishings, stood sentinel-like and motionless. Their presence added to the foreboding atmosphere, and they watched her with cold, unyielding stares. There was an unsettling silence, and no one among them interacted with her. Lady Seraphina, resplendent in her white, jewel-encrusted dress, felt increasingly out of place in this eerie setting.

The white dress she wore was not merely clothing; it was a masterpiece of craftsmanship, a symbol of her noble lineage, and a testament to her family's opulence. Originally intended as her wedding gown, it had now become a sacrificial garment meant to secure the safety of the Kingdom. Her family had hoped that the dress's exquisite beauty would sway Count Malachi to spare her life within his castle.

Lady Seraphina had journeyed to Count Malachi's castle alone, accompanied only by her trusted companion, Sir Sterling. He was a magnificent white stallion, a vision of grace and power combined. Standing tall with a proud and noble bearing, he commanded attention wherever they went. His pure white coat was immaculate, glistening as if touched by celestial hands, and it felt soft and silky to the touch, a canvas of pristine brilliance.

The bond between Lady Seraphina and Sir Sterling was unbreakable. He was not merely a horse but a loyal companion, her steadfast protector, and a symbol of their shared journey. He understood her on a profound level, recognizing her every nuance and unspoken wish. When their eyes met, an unspoken language of trust and devotion passed between them.

As Lady Seraphina stood before the imposing castle doors, she couldn't ignore the sense of unease that permeated the air. Sir Sterling's restlessness communicated danger, and she knew they had to complete their task together to safeguard the Kingdom. With a silent understanding, she dismounted and led him to the stables, ensuring his comfort before she ascended the stairs to the castle's entrance, where the carved serpent crest seemed to leer in anticipation of her presence.

As Lady Seraphina crossed the threshold into the count's ominous domain, the oppressive atmosphere of centuries of malevolence seemed to bear down upon her. It was as though the carved serpent, which adorned the entrance, threatened to constrict her, making each breath a struggle. She couldn't escape the realization that her destiny was intricately tied to this accursed place, and every step she took would be fraught with peril and shrouded in darkness.

The halls and corridors that stretched before her were no less foreboding. They appeared to have witnessed the passage of time itself, with their stone walls bearing the weight of history, both dark and enigmatic. Dimly lit torches flickered along the passage, casting eerie, dancing shadows that seemed to whisper secrets long buried within these ancient walls.

The air was heavy with an otherworldly chill, and the silence was broken only by the faint echoes of Lady Seraphina's footsteps. It was a labyrinthine maze of passages, each one seemingly leading deeper into the heart of Count Malachi's enigma. Intricate tapestries, faded with age, draped the walls, depicting scenes of forgotten legends and haunting tales of lost souls.

As Lady Seraphina ventured further into the castle's depths, she couldn't shake the feeling that these corridors held secrets of their own, waiting to be uncovered. Every turn revealed another twist in the labyrinth, and she found herself ensnared in the unsettling ambiance of Count Malachi's domain, where danger lurked in every shadow, and darkness clung to every stone.

The castle's ancient halls echoed with the cries of past tortured souls, almost as if they tried to wail warnings to the souls who entered. Its walls seemed to pulse with a sinister energy that caused one's hair to stand up on the back of one's neck. Lady Seraphina felt the sorrow of the past souls through the soles of her feet as she slowly walked through the halls towards what seemed to be an opening. The dim light barely shone through the halls as she came to a thorn garden with black roses and poison ivy, surrounded by an eerie stillness. She looked up at the grey, cloudy sky where even the sun seemed to dismally fight to shine through.

"My Lady!" She heard in a deep, dark voice, and Lady Seraphina spun around to look upon who addressed her. There stood Count Malachi, still within the darkness of the hallway, bowing slightly at the waist while gazing upon her with hungry eyes.

Count Malachi's appearance was as foreboding as the castle itself. He was a tall, slim man whose imposing presence contrasted starkly with his lean physique. His bald head gleamed ominously in the faint light, adding to his unsettling aura.

Count Malachi possessed distinctive facial features that contributed to his imposing presence. His nose was a commanding element of his visage, featuring a straight, prominent bridge that exuded an air of aristocratic refinement. It gradually sloped down to a well-defined, finely chiseled tip, adding to the sharpness of his overall appearance. While not overly large, his nose had a regal quality, symbolizing his authority and dominance.

Beneath his nose, Count Malachi's chin was strong and well-defined, with a subtle cleft that added character to his face. It provided a solid foundation for his facial structure, lending him an air of unwavering determination and resolve.

His jawline was impeccably chiseled, with sharp angles that accentuated his facial symmetry. It framed his face with a sense of strength and purpose, showcasing his unwavering confidence and unyielding character. The combination of his nose, chin, and jawline created a harmonious and formidable countenance, making Count Malachi a figure of both mystery and authority, capable of captivating and unsettling those who encountered him.

His eyes, like twin pools of inky darkness, held a captivating intensity that seemed to pierce through the very soul of anyone who met his gaze. They were eyes that hid a multitude of secrets and hinted at a mind that was always calculating and scheming.

Count Malachi was cloaked in an ensemble entirely shrouded in deep black, a colour that absorbed light and exuded an aura of foreboding. His outer garment was a long, flowing black cape made of heavy, rich fabric that billowed dramatically as he moved. The cape was embellished with intricate, silver-embroidered patterns that seemed to writhe like serpents, hinting at his cunning and deceitful nature.

Beneath the cape, he wore a tailored black doublet, embellished with dark, metallic accents that gleamed ominously. The doublet was fastened with silver clasps that resembled the eyes of predatory beasts, adding to his sinister appearance. The fabric was rich and textured, hinting at a hidden wealth amassed through nefarious means.

Count Malachi's trousers were fitted and black, leading down to polished black leather boots that rose to just below the knee. The boots had subtle, wickedly pointed toes, a subtle nod to his cunning and deceit.

Around his waist, he wore a thick black leather belt embellished with a silver buckle in the shape of a twisted, serpentine creature, symbolizing his manipulative and treacherous nature. A dagger with a hilt furnished in onyx and silver dangled ominously from the belt, a silent reminder of his capacity for cruelty.

His hands were clad in black leather gloves that fit like a second skin, concealing any hints of vulnerability. These gloves were furnished with silver filigree patterns that appeared to crawl like creeping vines, adding to the overall aura of malevolence that surrounded Count Malachi.

"Your Grace!" She responded back with a slight curtsy, remaining weary of his movement as she watched him pace the circumference of the throned garden.

"I see you have found the castle courtyard," smirked Count Malachi as he started to pace towards Lady Seraphina. His tone was taunting, and a sardonic glint danced in his eyes. "But, my dear Lady, I'm afraid it is not much of a courtyard. You see, gardens are meant to have life, vibrant and colourful, while here, well..." He gestured to the black roses that surrounded them, their petals dark as night.

Lady Seraphina, bewildered by the eerie sight of the flowerbed, couldn't help but voice her confusion, "Why are the roses black?"

Count Malachi's lips curled into a twisted smile, and his voice dripped with a mix of sinister amusement and chilling sincerity. "Ah, each black rose that blooms in this sanctuary serves as an emblem for a life I have taken," he explained tauntingly. "Their souls are trapped by the thorns within this castle, their anguish echoing through these ancient walls. And when the moon reaches its peak in the sky at night, you will hear them cry out to the heavens."

Lady Seraphina's heart raced; her fear palpable as she struggled to comprehend the gravity of his words. She was torn between believing his macabre explanation or dismissing it as a sick and twisted sense of humour. Count Malachi's enigmatic nature left her bewildered, unsure of how to respond to the chilling revelation.

"I shall arrange for a tour of the castle and for you to be shown to your chambers," Count Malachi announced with a wicked glint in his eyes. He savored the moment, relishing in the fear he had instilled in Lady Seraphina. His voice dripped with a sinister charm that sent shivers down her spine. "You will, of course, have a lady-in-waiting to attend to your every need."

With a theatrical flourish, Count Malachi executed a deep, mocking bow, his cape dramatically billowing behind him like the wings of a dark angel. It was as though he were performing for an audience, and Lady Seraphina was the unwitting spectator of his malevolent play.

As Count Malachi made his exit from the courtyard, the echoes of his footsteps seemed to taunt Lady Seraphina, and the ominous swishing of his cape added an eerie final note to the unsettling encounter. Lady Seraphina, still paralyzed by fear and confusion, could only watch in silence as the enigmatic count disappeared from her sight. She was left in the courtyard, trembling and unable to move or speak, a captive in the web of Count Malachi's dark and foreboding world.

It was in this moment of profound unease that a rustling sound disrupted her thoughts. Turning her head ever so slightly, Seraphina's terror was momentarily forgotten as she beheld an unexpected sight. A lady in waiting was approaching her, emerging from the shadows as if summoned by the darkness itself. The lady was of diminutive stature, her figure twisted and deformed, like something out of a nightmare. Her hunched back curved in a grotesque arch, and her gnarled limbs ended in claw-like fingers. Her face was a patchwork of deep creases and scars, and her eyes, while disconcerting, held a glimmer of warmth and kindness.

Her attire was equally remarkable, a stark contrast to the bleakness of the castle. She wore a gown that seemed to defy the very essence of the place as if it had been plucked from a different realm entirely. The gown was a cascade of vibrant colours, a tapestry of rich purples, deep blues, and emerald greens, all interwoven like a painter's palette brought to life. It was as though she wore the very essence of a lush and enchanted forest as if the leaves were feathers of peacocks.

"Welcome, Lady Seraphina," the lady in waiting spoke her voice a soothing melody that contrasted with the eerie silence of the courtyard. "I am Lady Isolde, and I am here to offer my assistance during your stay at Count Malachi's castle."

The shock of Count Malachi's ominous presence still lingered in Seraphina's mind, but she found herself drawn to the lady's kind eyes and gentle demeanor. With a gracious nod, she managed to curtsy politely. "Thank you, Lady Isolde. Your dress is simply extraordinary, like a breath of fresh air in this forsaken place."

A soft smile graced Lady Isolde's lips, and she offered a small curtsy in return. "I'm glad you find it pleasing, Lady Seraphina. If you will follow me, I shall lead you to your chambers and then offer a tour of Count Malachi's castle."

Lady Seraphina, her curiosity piqued, fell in step beside Lady Isolde as they ventured further into the heart of the sinister fortress. As they passed through dimly lit corridors and climbed winding staircases, Lady Isolde began to share tales of the castle's dark history, each story more chilling than the last.

They explored rooms decorated with macabre artwork, depicting scenes of despair and torment, and chambers where the very walls seemed to whisper with unsettling secrets. Seraphina couldn't help but shudder at the eerie ambiance that permeated the castle, but Lady Isolde's presence provided a sense of comfort amid the unsettling surroundings.

As Seraphina and Lady Isolde continued their exploration of the eerie castle, they soon found themselves standing before a corridor unlike any they had encountered thus far. The passageway stretched ominously ahead of them, its walls draped with faded tapestries and lit only by flickering torches that cast long, unsettling shadows. At the end of the corridor stood two imposing, dog-like statues, their eyes gleaming with an otherworldly malevolence.

The air grew colder as they approached, and Seraphina couldn't help but feel a shiver run down her spine. The statues, with their solemn gazes, appeared to stand as sentinels guarding a pair of colossal wooden doors that loomed ahead. These doors, carved with intricate and cryptic symbols, seemed to pulsate with an unsettling energy, drawing her closer with an irresistible allure.

Lady Isolde turned to Seraphina, her expression grave, her voice a mere whisper amidst the eerie silence that enveloped them. "This, my dear, is Count Malachi's corridor," she breathed, her words carrying the weight of forbidden knowledge. "It is a realm forbidden to all within the castle, and with good reason."

Curiosity and trepidation mingled within Seraphina as she fixed her gaze on the foreboding entrance. She couldn't resist the temptation to inquire further. "Why is it off-limits? What mysteries lie behind those formidable doors?"

Lady Isolde's eyes bore into Seraphina's, caution and concern etched across her features. "Legend has it that those who dare to tread down this corridor are swallowed by its shadows, never to return. Count Malachi, they say, conducted unspeakable experiments within these very walls, and the very air here is tainted with dark magic. It is a place that harbours unimaginable horrors."

The flickering torchlight seemed to flicker in agreement with Lady Isolde's foreboding words, casting eerie, dancing shadows upon the walls. Seraphina swallowed hard, her heart beating wildly in her chest. An overwhelming sense of fear washed over her, like a chilling wave.

Standing before the enigmatic doors, Seraphina couldn't help but notice the intricate carvings adorning them. Twisted, grotesque faces contorted in agony, and serpentine patterns snaked across the surface. The doors themselves seemed to pulsate, as though they were alive, breathing in the malevolence that emanated from within.

Lady Isolde's gentle hand on Seraphina's shoulder brought her back to the present. Her voice was low, urgent. "You must understand, my dear, Count Malachi is a man consumed by unspeakable darkness. His thirst for power knows no bounds, and the atrocities committed in this castle are beyond human imagination. It is said that he delved into forbidden arts, seeking to unlock secrets that should have remained hidden."

Seraphina nodded; her eyes fixed on the sinister doors. The weight of history pressed down upon her, suffocating and inescapable. "But why keep it off-limits?"

Lady Isolde's gaze remained unwavering, fixed on the doors that held so many sinister secrets. "The malevolence that dwells within these walls does not die; it lingers, festers, and waits for any unfortunate soul who dares to tread here. Those who have ventured down this corridor in the past have vanished without a trace, their fates sealed by the malevolent forces that reside here."

A chill wind seemed to sweep through the corridor, extinguishing one of the torches with a ghostly hiss. Seraphina's breath trembled as she considered the grim tales and Lady Isolde's ominous warning. The atmosphere itself seemed to press upon her, suffocating and laden with an impending sense of doom.

As they turned away from the cursed corridor, Seraphina couldn't help but cast one last glance back at the doors. She knew she would never forget the palpable darkness that surrounded them or the unsettling stories that shrouded Count Malachi's legacy. In that moment, she understood the wisdom in heeding Lady Isolde's advice, leaving the corridor to its sinister secrets.

The remainder of their exploration of the castle was fraught with tension, the memory of that chilling corridor and the whispered tales of Count Malachi's atrocities etching themselves into Seraphina's psyche. It was a stark reminder that some doors were better left unopened, and some secrets were best left undisturbed in the shadowy depths of a castle steeped in macabre history and unspeakable horrors.

Finally, they arrived at a set of heavy wooden doors that led to a corridor lined with guest chambers. Lady Isolde opened one of the doors with an air of grace, revealing a chamber that was both opulent and eerie. The walls were draped in shadowy tapestries, and the bed, while sumptuously appointed, seemed to exude an unsettling aura. "It's... unique," Seraphina said, her voice filled with a mixture of admiration and unease.

Lady Isolde nodded with a serene smile. "I'm pleased you appreciate it, Lady Seraphina. If there is anything you require during your stay, please do not hesitate to summon me."

As she stepped into the room, the first thing that struck her was the oppressive atmosphere that seemed to seep through the walls. The air was heavy as if carrying the weight of centuries of secrets. The chamber was bathed in dim, filtered light, casting long, wavering shadows that danced eerily along the walls. The windows, framed with heavy, velvet drapes in a deep shade of crimson, were mostly covered, allowing only a sparse stream of light to penetrate the room. The few rays of sunlight that managed to pierce the gloom painted a faint, ghostly pattern on the cold stone floor.

The walls were decorated with dark tapestries that depicted scenes of sorrow and despair—figures shrouded in shadow, twisted, and tormented; their faces contorted in anguish. These grim artworks seemed to tell a haunting tale, and their presence added to the unsettling ambiance of the room. The centerpiece of the chamber was a four-poster bed, its intricately carved wooden frame bearing the weight of heavy, velvety curtains that cascaded down to the floor. The curtains, much like the drapes, were a rich crimson colour, but they seemed to absorb the little light that filtered in, creating an eerie cocoon around the bed.

The bed itself was furnished with sheets of dark silk, and a canopy overhead was draped with deep, blood-red fabric. It appeared both inviting and ominous, with its promise of comfort and the lingering suggestion of something more sinister lurking beneath. A mahogany writing desk stood in one corner of the room, covered in a layer of dust as if it had not been used in years. An ornate mirror hung on the opposite wall, its surface tarnished and spotted with age, casting distorted reflections that added to the room's unsettling atmosphere.

A flickering candle in a tarnished silver holder was placed on a small table beside the bed, providing a feeble and wavering light source. Its flame seemed to dance to an unknown melody, casting eerie, shifting shadows that played tricks on the eyes.

Lady Seraphina's belongings, carefully arranged on an antique dresser, added a touch of familiarity to the otherwise eerie chamber. Her dresses, each one a vibrant contrast to the room's darkness, hung neatly on a wooden rack. A collection of delicate porcelain figurines adorned a nearby shelf, their fragile beauty contrasting sharply with the room's foreboding aura.

Despite the unsettling atmosphere, Lady Seraphina could not help but feel a sense of curiosity and intrigue about her chambers. They reflected the castle itself—dark, enigmatic, and shrouded in mystery. It was a place where secrets whispered in the shadows and where every corner seemed to hide a story waiting to be uncovered.

As Lady Seraphina settled into her unusual surroundings, she couldn't help but reflect on the strange and haunting beauty of her chamber. It was a room that defied expectations, a place where darkness and opulence were interwoven in an unsettling dance. And as she lay beneath the crimson drapes, with the echoes of the castle's secrets all around her, she knew that her time in Count Malachi's castle would be an experience she would never forget, her mind was a whirlwind of thoughts and emotions. The castle was even darker and more foreboding than she had imagined, and the encounter with Count Malachi had left her shaken. But Lady Isolde's presence had offered a glimmer of solace, a rare kindness amid the cruelty that hung in the air.

Over the days that followed, Seraphina and Lady Isolde forged an unexpected bond. The lady-in-waiting's gentle nature and unwavering support during Seraphina's diplomatic negotiations with Count Malachi became a source of strength for her. They spent hours conversing about everything from the castle's enigmatic history to their shared hopes and dreams, and Seraphina found herself feeling an ever-deeper connection to Lady Isolde.

As the days turned into weeks, the bond between Lady Seraphina and Lady Isolde deepened in the eerie depths of Count Malachi's forbidding castle. They became inseparable, sharing secrets and dreams amidst the shadowy corridors and dimly lit chambers. Seraphina, drawn to Lady Isolde's gentle nature and unwavering support, found solace in their burgeoning friendship.

One evening, after they had retired to Seraphina's dimly lit chambers, Lady Isolde's gaze seemed to linger on a particularly haunting tapestry that adorned the room. The scene depicted a solitary figure, a forlorn soul engulfed in darkness, with a twisted and tortured visage.

Seraphina, sensing Lady Isolde's contemplative mood, gently inquired, "Lady Isolde, is something troubling you?"

Lady Isolde hesitated, her kind eyes shimmering with unspoken pain. Finally, she took a deep breath and began to speak in a voice heavy with sorrow. "There is something I must share with you, Lady Seraphina. Something that has been a burden upon my soul for far too long."

Seraphina listened intently, her heart aching as Lady Isolde's story unfolded. "Many years ago," Lady Isolde began, "my family lived in a peaceful village not far from here. We were humble folk, living a simple life, until Count Malachi cast his malevolent shadow over our lives."

Lady Isolde's voice trembled as she continued. "One fateful night, he and his dark minions descended upon our village, wreaking havoc and causing unspeakable horrors. They took the lives of my parents and siblings, leaving me as the sole survivor."

Tears glistened in Lady Isolde's eyes, and Seraphina reached out to place a comforting hand on her shoulder. "I am so sorry for your loss, Lady Isolde. What happened next?"

Lady Isolde's voice grew even softer as she recounted the grim fate that had befallen her. "Count Malachi spared my life, but he placed a curse upon me, one that twisted my appearance and left me forever marked by his malevolence. He decreed that I was to serve him in this castle for the rest of my days, a constant reminder of the darkness he had brought upon my family and our village."

Seraphina was filled with a mixture of sympathy and anger at the cruel fate that Lady Isolde had endured. "That is a most terrible curse, Lady Isolde.

How have you managed to bear such a burden?" Lady Isolde sighed, her eyes heavy with the weight of her suffering. "I have tried to find solace in the beauty that still exists in this world, in the kindness of those like you, Lady Seraphina. Our friendship has been a beacon of light in this darkness, and for that, I am truly grateful."

Seraphina's heart swelled with compassion for her friend. "You are a remarkable person, Lady Isolde, and your strength in the face of such cruelty is inspiring." Lady Isolde offered a small, sad smile. "Thank you, Lady Seraphina. I have found purpose in our friendship, and for that, I am grateful. But I long for the day when Count Malachi's hold on me is broken, and I can be free of this curse."

Seraphina's determination burned brightly as she grasped Lady Isolde's hand. "We shall find a way, Lady Isolde. I will do everything in my power to help you break this curse and bring an end to Count Malachi's tyranny." Lady Isolde's eyes shone with hope, and for the first time in many years, she felt a glimmer of possibility. "Thank you, Lady Seraphina. Your friendship and your pledge mean more to me than words can express."

From that pivotal moment, Lady Seraphina and Lady Isolde embarked on an arduous journey, one that was fraught with peril and shrouded in mystery. Their mission was to unravel the intricate web of secrets surrounding Count Malachi's dark magic and to discover a means of breaking the malevolent curse that bound Lady Isolde to the castle's haunting corridors. They were determined to liberate her from the sinister clutches of their oppressive host.

Together, they delved deep into the castle's ominous history, poring over ancient tomes and scrolls, seeking out cryptic clues hidden within the shadowy confines of the fortress. The history of the castle, they discovered, was a tapestry woven with threads of darkness and despair, and it was riddled with cryptic references to ancient spells and incantations.

In their relentless pursuit of knowledge, Seraphina and Isolde sought the counsel of wise sages and knowledgeable mystics who were rumoured to reside in hidden enclaves far beyond the castle walls during their afternoon rides. These wise elders were revered for their profound wisdom and their deep understanding of the arcane arts. Seraphina and Isolde hoped that these sages might possess the key to unraveling the dark enchantment that bound Lady Isolde to her cursed existence.

They ventured through dense, ancient forests where the trees seemed to whisper secrets and along winding, treacherous mountain paths where the wind howled like a mournful spirit. At every turn, they faced challenges that tested their resolve and their bond as friends. Yet, Seraphina's unwavering determination and Isolde's quiet courage saw them through each trial. They pressed onward, guided by their shared hope and the knowledge that they were each other's greatest source of strength.

Finally, after what felt like an eternity of searching, they reached the hidden enclave of the wise sages. These ancient beings, with their long, flowing robes and eyes that seemed to hold the wisdom of ages, welcomed Seraphina and Isolde with a solemn nod. The sages listened intently as the two women recounted the harrowing tale of Count Malachi's curse and their quest for a solution.

With a profound understanding of the dark forces at play, the sages began to share their own knowledge and insights. They spoke of ancient rituals, long-forgotten spells, and the delicate balance between light and darkness in the world of magic. Together, they delved into the intricacies of the curse, seeking the one chink in its armour that could lead to its undoing.

Days turned into weeks as Seraphina and Isolde worked tirelessly alongside the wise sages, their shared determination unwavering. They performed intricate rituals, conducted experiments with ancient artifacts, and deciphered cryptic runes etched into the castle's very walls. Each step brought them closer to unlocking the secrets of the curse and the means to break its cruel hold.

As they delved deeper into their research, the bond between Lady Seraphina and Lady Isolde grew stronger with each passing day. Their friendship became a source of unwavering support, a beacon of light that cut through the darkest of nights. Together, they navigated the treacherous labyrinth of Count Malachi's castle, facing the eerie and unsettling challenges that lurked around every corner.

But amid the shadows and the gloom, a glimmer of hope emerged. The wise sages had uncovered a rare spell, a long-forgotten spell said to have the power to sever the bonds of the curse. It was a perilous undertaking, fraught with danger, but it offered a chance—a chance to free Lady Isolde from the torment that had haunted her for so long.

The day of the ritual arrived, and Lady Seraphina and Lady Isolde stood before the wise sages in a chamber bathed in a dim, ethereal light. Candles flickered, casting dancing shadows upon the ancient symbols etched into the stone floor. The air was thick with anticipation as the sages' chanted spells passed down through generations.

The moment of truth had come, and Lady Seraphina and Lady Isolde joined hands, their eyes locked in a shared resolve. As the spell reached its crescendo, a surge of magic enveloped Lady Isolde, and the curse's malevolent grip began to weaken.

But with the release of such potent magic came an unexpected consequence. The very foundations of Count Malachi's castle quaked, and the fortress itself seemed to rebel against the breaking of the curse. Walls shifted, and eerie echoes filled the corridors as if the very soul of the castle protested its imminent liberation.

Amid this tumultuous upheaval, Seraphina and Isolde clung to one another, their bond, and their shared hope a beacon of strength amidst the chaos. The spell reached its zenith, and with a blinding flash of light, the curse was not lifted! Puzzled by the outcome, it was back to research to find a way to set Lady Isolde free!

Lady Seraphina and Lady Isolde returned from their exhilarating ride on Sir Sterling. The ride had been a much-needed respite from the relentless pursuit of knowledge and magic. The cool breeze had ruffled their hair, and the spirited gallop of the horse had filled their hearts with a sense of freedom they had not known within the castle's foreboding walls.

As they dismounted and led Sir Sterling back to the stables, their faces flushed with exhilaration, they exchanged knowing glances. Though they had made significant progress in their quest, they were acutely aware that their actions needed to remain concealed. Count Malachi's malevolence ran deep, and they couldn't afford to arouse his suspicion.

In the sanctuary of Seraphina's chambers, they carefully concealed the artifacts and knowledge they had acquired during their afternoon excursions. Ancient scrolls were hidden within the intricately carved wooden chest, and cryptic symbols were carefully obscured beneath a velvet-lined drawer. Their secrets were safeguarded against prying eyes.

Their moments of respite were fleeting, for they knew that they had little time to prepare for the evening's dinner with Count Malachi. As Lady Isolde assisted Lady Seraphina in choosing an appropriate gown, they whispered in hushed tones about the events of the day, ensuring that their words could not be overheard.

Seraphina's chosen attire was a breathtaking creation, a gown of sapphire blue that shimmered like moonlight on water. It was finished with delicate lace and intricate embroidery, a masterpiece of craftsmanship that enhanced her natural beauty. Her hair was elegantly styled, cascading in gentle waves down her back.

With Lady Isolde's guidance, Seraphina was ready for the evening's dinner, and together, they made their way to the grand dining hall. The hall itself was a testament to Count Malachi's opulence and his taste for the macabre.

The dining hall was an expansive chamber, its stone walls adorned with dark tapestries that depicted scenes of battles and suffering. A massive fireplace dominated one end of the room, its roaring flames casting flickering shadows that danced along the walls almost for a moment giving shadowed figures to the souls trapped within the castle. The air was filled with the scent of burning wood and the faint aroma of exotic spices.

The long dining table was a marvel of dark wood, polished to a gleaming sheen. It stretched the length of the room, and its surface was set with gleaming silverware, crystal goblets, and fine porcelain dishes. The table settings were exquisite, with intricately designed plates and ornate silverware that gleamed in the firelight.

The meal itself was a feast fit for a king, a testament to Count Malachi's extravagant tastes. Platters of roasted meats, rich sauces, and exotic fruits were arranged in a tantalizing display. The centerpiece was a magnificent roast boar, its skin crispy and golden, surrounded by an array of side dishes and vegetables.

As Seraphina and Isolde took their seats at the table, they were acutely aware of Count Malachi's watchful gaze. He sat at the head of the table, his dark eyes assessing their every move. It was a tense and foreboding atmosphere, one that seemed to suffocate the very air in the room.

The dinner began in silence, punctuated only by the soft clinking of silverware and the crackling of the fire in the grand fireplace. Seraphina and Isolde exchanged cautious glances, their hearts racing as they navigated the treacherous waters of Count Malachi's suspicion.

It was during the meal that Count Malachi finally broke the uneasy silence. His voice, smooth as silk but laced with an underlying menace, addressed Lady Seraphina. "Lady Seraphina, I have noticed a change in your behaviour of late. You and Lady Isolde have been spending a great deal of time together, often away from the castle. I find this... curious."

Lady Seraphina, her heart pounding in her chest, tried to maintain her composure. "Count Malachi, we have been seeking to explore the castle's history and its many secrets. Lady Isolde has been an invaluable guide in this endeavor."

Count Malachi's dark eyes bore into her, and for a moment, it felt as though he could see through the facade she had carefully constructed. "Indeed," he murmured, his voice a dangerous whisper. "And what, pray tell, have you discovered in your explorations?"

Lady Seraphina's mind raced, and she could feel the weight of his scrutiny pressing down upon her like a vice. She needed to divert his attention, to quell his suspicions without revealing the true nature of their quest. It felt as though a serpent was constricting around her, squeezing the breath from her lungs.

With a carefully measured smile, she replied, "We have uncovered some fascinating insights into the history of your castle, Count Malachi. The tales of its previous inhabitants and the secrets it holds are truly intriguing." Count Malachi's eyes narrowed, and a sinister smile tugged at the corners of his lips. "Ah, my dear Lady Seraphina, it is true that this castle holds many secrets. But some are best left undisturbed."

The tension in the room was palpable, and Seraphina could feel the weight of Count Malachi's scrutiny intensifying. As they continued to dine in silence, she knew that their quest to break Lady Isolde's curse had placed them on a precarious precipice. The delicate balance between secrecy and survival had never been more treacherous, and the serpent of suspicion threatened to tighten its grip with every passing moment!

It became clear to Lady Seraphina that, in the complex dance of alliances and rivalries that defined their world, keeping Count Malachi appeased would be a crucial aspect of ensuring her own survival, even as she remained unwavering in her commitment to the forces of light and harmony. The question is how far will she allow Count Malachi to push his boundaries of appeasement and pleasure?

The Haunting

Lady Seraphina and Lady Isolde had become inseparable during their time in the dark and gloomy Count Malachi's castle. Their friendship was the making of legends, an unbreakable bond forged through countless shared secrets and stolen moments. They were more than friends; they were sisters of the heart.

Count Malachi had begun to harbour a deep suspicion about their closeness. He watched them closely, his eyes filled with jealousy and intrigue, unable to comprehend the depth of their connection. After all, he was a man who valued power and control above all else, and the thought of someone else having a claim on Lady Seraphina troubled him greatly, after all, she was only a lady-in-waiting where he was a Count, how could she be more favourable in Lady Seraphina's eyes?

Count Malachi stood on the ornate balcony that overlooked the grand courtyard of his opulent estate, hidden in the shadows of the towering columns. His finely tailored clothing did little to ease the discomfort that churned within him as he observed the scene below. Lady Seraphina and Lady Isolde, two women who had entered his life as mere acquaintances, now laughed, and giggled together in a way that filled his heart with envy and bitterness.

The morning had started innocently enough, with a walk the ladies taking their morning walk in the barren courtyard. Count Malachi had invited Lady Seraphina to accompany him on his morning walk. She had, of course, accepted his invitation, her delicate smile and graceful demeanor hiding any hint of reluctance. Little did he know that morning would take a turn that would gnaw at his very core.

As they returned from their walk, Lady Isolde was waiting in the courtyard for Lady Seraphina with their sewing and embroidery kits ready. Count

Malachi allowed them to have access to the finest materials, so they could engage in more elaborate and decorative sewing projects. They would create intricate embroidery, tapestries, and clothing embellished with intricate patterns, often using precious materials like silk and gold thread.

Excitedly, Lady Seraphina excused herself from Count Malachi's presence and happily frolicked to Lady Isolde. The two women stood together near a glistening fountain, bathed in the soft glow of sunlight as the day was still awakening. Their laughter was infectious, carrying across the courtyard like a sweet serenade. Count Malachi watched them, his eyes filled with an emotion he struggled to define—a potent mixture of jealousy and intrigue.

Lady Seraphina, with her auburn hair cascading like a waterfall of fire, wore a gown of shimmering blue silk that clung to her every curve. Her eyes sparkled with amusement, and her laughter was like a crystal chime. Beside her, Lady Isolde was only too happy to share stories with her about her village and the comical baker who used to live not too far from her and her family.

Count Malachi found himself transfixed, unable to tear his gaze away from the enchanting duo. Lady Seraphina, his sacrifice who should have been at his beck and call, was now immersed in the company of another, and it troubled him greatly. How could Lady Isolde, a lady-in-waiting, command so much of Lady Seraphina's attention and affection? It was a question that gnawed at him, and he couldn't find a satisfactory answer.

As the day passed, Count Malachi's envy grew more palpable. He watched as Lady Seraphina and Lady Isolde shared whispered secrets; their heads bent close together. Their laughter became more infectious, and their bond seemed to strengthen with every passing moment. Count Malachi's clenched fists tightened even more as he saw Lady Seraphina's hand brush lightly against Lady Isolde's arm—a gesture of intimacy that sent a pang of jealousy coursing through him.

In that moment, Count Malachi couldn't help but reflect on his own desires and ambitions. He was a man who valued power and control above all else, and the thought of someone else having a claim on Lady Seraphina troubled him greatly. After all, she was his sacrifice, and he was a Count of considerable influence and wealth. How could Lady Isolde, lady-in-waiting, be more favourable in Lady Seraphina's eyes?

The happiness between the two women only deepened Count Malachi's sense of isolation. They danced together in the sunlight, twirling gracefully as if they were the only two people in the world. Their laughter and smiles were genuine, and it was clear that their connection was not fleeting but rooted in something profound.

Count Malachi's jealousy had now transformed into a burning desire to possess what he believed was rightfully his. He wanted Lady Seraphina's undivided attention, her laughter, and her affection. He yearned to be the one who controlled her smile, that radiant smile, to be the one who controlled her physical affections.

But as he continued to watch from the shadows of the balcony, he realized that his desire for control had blinded him to the true nature of Lady Seraphina's happiness. It was not something that could be coerced or demanded; it was a gift freely given to those who touched her heart. Lady Isolde had managed to do just that, and Count Malachi had to grapple with the fact that he couldn't simply claim Lady Seraphina as his own.

In the courtyard below, Lady Seraphina and Lady Isolde continued to revel in each other's company, oblivious to the turmoil they had stirred in Count Malachi's heart. Their laughter rang out like a melody, a testament to the genuine bond they had forged. As the day passed, Count Malachi knew that he had a choice to make—whether to let go of his envy and allow Lady Seraphina to find happiness in her own way or to cling to his desire for control and power.

As he stood on the balcony, Count Malachi couldn't help but feel the weight of his own choices pressing down upon him. The envy that had consumed him had shown him a mirror to his own insecurities and shortcomings, and he knew that he had much to learn about love and happiness, lessons that Lady Seraphina and Lady Isolde had already embraced with open hearts. He asked himself if he really cared because learning about such things meant a change in his path.

That fateful afternoon, as the sun hung low in the sky, Lady Seraphina and Lady Isolde prepared for their usual ride through the sprawling castle grounds. The barren meadows and enchanted forests surrounding the castle provided them with a sanctuary away from the prying eyes of the court. But on this day, Count Malachi's jealousy reached its peak, and he hatched a sinister plan.

As they prepared to mount their horses, Count Malachi appeared, his face a mask of feigned concern. "My dear Lady Seraphina," he said with a tone that sent shivers down her spine, "I'm afraid Lady Isolde cannot accompany you on your ride today. She is needed here in the castle."

Seraphina's heart sank at the prospect of riding alone, but before she could protest, Count Malachi took Lady Isolde by the arm and started to guide her to the castle, "Enjoy the ride My Lady!' as he peered over his shoulder while walking back to the castle with Lady Isolde firmly within his grip. "I shall be alright my Lady, I shall await your return," said Lady Isolde as she looked back at Lady Seraphina while being guided to the castle. Seraphina thought the quicker she went and got back the better it would be for her friend, so she and Sir Sterling galloped away with great speed! Once Malachi entered the courtyard of the castle he turned to Lady Isolde and with a swift, cruel motion, he drew a dagger from his belt and slit Isolde's throat! Lady Isolde, startled by what had just happened, grasped her throat to try and keep life from escaping her.

Blood spurted from Lady Isolde's neck, staining the ground crimson. Her body crumpled, and she lay still, her eyes vacant and her life seemingly drained away. Count Malachi, his face betraying no emotion, walked away from the gruesome scene. He wiped his dagger clean with a flick of his cloak and then, with an air of detachment, shouted out a command to the servants who had witnessed the horrifying act.

"Remove the body before Lady Seraphina returns!"

The servants, their faces aghast, hurriedly moved to obey Count Malachi's orders. The urgency in his voice was evident, and a heavy silence hung over the courtyard, broken only by the sound of shuffling footsteps and hushed whispers.

Lady Seraphina had returned shortly before dusk from a refreshing ride, the wind tousling her auburn hair and the rhythmic clip-clop of Sir Sterling's hooves beneath her creating a soothing melody. She dismounted with grace; her heart filled with anticipation at the thought of reuniting with her beloved friend. The loyal steed had carried her through the twisted forests and open barren fields, forging a connection that ran deeper than words.

As Lady Seraphina led Sir Sterling to the stables, she couldn't help but notice the unease that seemed to emanate from him. His noble head was held high, his nostrils flaring with each breath, and his dark, expressive eyes darted around, scanning the surroundings of the castle grounds. It was as though he could sense something amiss, something that stirred a primal instinct within him.

"Thank you, my dear Sir Sterling," Lady Seraphina whispered, her voice a soft, soothing murmur as she patted his sleek neck. She knew her loyal companion was more than just a horse; he was a trusted confidant, a silent listener to her deepest thoughts. The bond they shared was undeniable, and she valued it above all else.

But this evening, something was different. Sir Sterling remained on edge, his powerful muscles tense, and his ears flicking back and forth, as though he were attuned to every rustle in the nearby trees or the faintest whisper of the evening breeze. Lady Seraphina could feel his restlessness, and it troubled her. She couldn't fathom what had unsettled her faithful steed so profoundly.

With gentle reassurance, Lady Seraphina led Sir Sterling into the stables, her fingers running through his silken mane. She murmured soothing words, trying to calm the magnificent creature's racing heart. As she brushed him down and provided him with fresh hay and water, she couldn't shake the feeling that something was wrong.

Their bond had always been one of trust and understanding, and Lady Seraphina trusted Sir Sterling's instincts as much as she trusted her own. She knew that horses possessed an uncanny ability to sense danger, their keen senses attuned to even the slightest shifts in their surroundings. It was a survival instinct that had been honed over centuries, and Sir Sterling was no exception.

After ensuring her beloved steed was comfortable, Lady Seraphina kissed him gently on the forehead. "Rest well, my faithful friend," she whispered, her heart heavy with worry. She couldn't shake the feeling that the unease she sensed in Sir Sterling was a forewarning of something she could not yet comprehend.

With a heavy heart, Lady Seraphina made her way back to the castle, her footsteps echoing through the stone corridors. The fading light of the day cast long shadows, and the flickering torches lining the walls added an eerie ambiance to the ancient castle. The unease she had felt from Sir Sterling seemed to linger, tainting the air with a sense of danger.

As Lady Seraphina briskly walked through the entrance and made her way through the dimly lit halls, her thoughts were consumed by the unsettling atmosphere. She longed for the comforting presence of her friend, Lady Isolde, whose laughter, and companionship had always been a source of solace.

But her journey was abruptly halted as she reached the castle's courtyard. Her heart skipped a beat, and her breath caught in her throat as she beheld a sight that sent shockwaves through her very being. There, amidst the stone flagstones, was a crimson circle of blood, stark and unmistakable against the pale stone.

Lady Seraphina's hands trembled as she approached the gruesome scene, her mind racing to comprehend the horrifying sight before her. The bloodstain seemed to form a macabre sigil, an omen of darkness that defied explanation. Her thoughts whirled, and a sense of dread settled over her like a shroud.

Lady Seraphina could only stand and watch in silent horror, frozen with disbelief, as her heart shattered like a fragile glass falling to the ground. The brutality of the scene before her had rendered her speechless, her mind struggling to process the nightmare that had unfolded. Count Malachi, lurking in the shadowy corner of the courtyard just out of sight, relished the sight of her torment. His lips curled into a wicked smile as he moved with deliberate slowness, his malevolence etched into every step. He walked past the pool of Lady Isolde's blood, leaving behind her scarf as a cruel and chilling memento of his unspeakable cruelty.

The courtyard, once a place of serenity and shared laughter, had been transformed into a haunting tableau of horror now mirroring the garden of black roses, thorns, and poison ivy. Lady Seraphina's gaze remained fixed on the pool of crimson that marred the cobblestones, a stark reminder of the life so brutally extinguished. The courtyard's atmosphere seemed to close in on her, the weight of the tragedy bearing down on her chest like an iron vise.

As Count Malachi disappeared, Lady Seraphina's trembling legs finally gave way, and she crumpled to her knees amidst the chilling silence. Her hands, stained with Isolde's blood, hung limply by her sides as she stared, unseeing, at the scarf. Tears welled up in her eyes, but they refused to fall. The pain that coursed through her heart was too immense, too overwhelming to be expressed through mere tears.

Her chest heaved with an agonizing emptiness as if her very soul had been torn asunder. The realization that Isolde, her dearest friend, and confidante, was gone forever gnawed at her with relentless cruelty. It was a pain that went beyond the physical, a pain that cut deep into the core of her being that made breathing hurt.

With great effort, Lady Seraphina managed to rise to her feet, her limbs heavy with grief. She staggered away from the pool of blood and slowly made her way back into the castle. Every step was a struggle, each breath a painful reminder of the life that had been stolen. Her vision blurred as she climbed the winding staircase leading to her chambers.

Once inside her room, Lady Seraphina's composure finally crumbled. She threw herself onto her bed, burying her face in her pillow to muffle her cries of anguish. The pain that had been building inside her burst forth like a torrential storm. Her cries were heart-wrenching, a sound that resonated with the very depths of despair.

The howl that escaped her lips was a haunting lament, a raw and guttural cry that echoed through the stone walls of the castle, like the howling wind on a stormy night. It was a sound that defied words, a sound that spoke of a grief so profound that it threatened to consume her entirely. Her cries were a symphony of sorrow, a dirge for the lost friendship that had meant everything to her.

The pain was relentless, a constant ache in her chest that refused to abate. Lady Seraphina clutched at her heart as if she could physically hold the shattered pieces together. She longed for the embrace of Lady Isolde, the laughter they had shared, and the warmth of their friendship.

But now, all she had were memories! The world outside continued to turn, oblivious to her anguish, as Lady Seraphina's cries of heartbreak reverberated through the castle, a mournful requiem for a sister's love lost to the darkness.

As the days stretched into weeks, the haunting presence of the black roses in the castle's courtyard remained an ominous reminder of the life that had been violently extinguished and the souls trapped within the castle's oppressive walls. The once-vibrant garden, before Count Malachi's evil, now held a multitude of these dark blooms, each representing a lost soul, their beauty twisted into a macabre spectacle.

Lady Seraphina, burdened by grief and guilt, found herself drawn to the courtyard every morning. She couldn't resist the allure of the black roses, their velvety petals seeming to absorb the very essence of the darkness that had descended upon the castle. With a heavy heart, she stepped onto the stone pathway that led to the courtyard, her footsteps echoing with the weight of her sorrow.

The first rays of dawn cast a pale, ethereal glow on the garden, illuminating the rows of black roses that stretched before her. Each one was a somber sentinel, a testament to the tragedy that had befallen within the castle. Lady Seraphina knew that these flowers, once vibrant symbols of life and love, were now forever tied to the memory of lives lost within this castle. Since Lady Isolde's passing a new black rosebud had formed.

As Lady Seraphina approached the black rosebud, she hesitated for a moment, her trembling hand reaching out to touch the inky petals. The sensation was surreal as if she were contacting Lady Isolde's very essence. The black rose was cold to the touch, its beauty marred by the darkness it represented.

Tears welled up in Lady Seraphina's eyes as she whispered a heartfelt apology to Lady Isolde, a promise to never forget the precious moments they had shared as friends. Lady Seraphina felt a growing determination within her, a need to bring justice to Lady Isolde's memory.

With a heavy heart, she continued her morning ritual, moving from one black rose to another, each one a reminder of the pain that had engulfed the castle. The weight of her grief pressed down upon her, threatening to consume her entirely. Lady Seraphina couldn't help but blame herself for not being there to protect Lady Isolde, for not sensing the danger that had lurked in the shadows.

As she moved through the garden, her steps grew slower and heavier. The weight of her sorrow was almost unbearable, but Lady Seraphina knew that she couldn't turn away from the truth. She couldn't let Lady Isolde's death go unanswered, for the black roses demanded justice as much as her heart did.

Weeks turned into months, and Lady Seraphina's resolve did not waver. She tirelessly investigated every corner of the castle, seeking answers, and unraveled the dark secrets that had been hidden in its depths for centuries.

Lady Seraphina's rides, which had once been a source of solace, had become increasingly fraught with dread. Each return to the castle left her more devastated than the last, the memory of that fateful afternoon an ever-present specter in her mind.

Sir Sterling had also been profoundly affected by the spectral presence that haunted the castle. He, too, bore witness to the ethereal spirits that roamed the darkened corridors, their mournful whispers echoing in the stillness of the night.

Though unable to vocalize his unease, Sir Sterling was keenly attuned to the supernatural forces that lingered. His ears would twitch, and his powerful frame would quiver in response to the unseen entities that crossed his path. The stallion's eyes, once full of fire and vitality, now held a haunted, knowing look, as if he could perceive the souls trapped in the castle's shadows.

Lady Seraphina could sense Sir Sterling's unease, for their bond transcended words. She would often find him standing vigil in the courtyard, his gaze fixed on the fading black roses. The stallion's presence was a silent testament to the enduring trauma that had taken place within these stone walls.

As she moved through the courtyard each morning, Sir Sterling would accompany her, his large form a protective shield against the lingering malevolence. His presence was both a source of strength and a reminder of the darkness they had faced together.

The castle, once familiar and comforting, had transformed into a place of uncertainty and fear. Lady Seraphina couldn't shake the feeling that she was never truly alone, that unseen eyes watched her every move.

One evening, as she made her way down a corridor, she felt an abrupt drop in temperature, a chilling cold spot that sent a shiver racing down her spine. The air around her seemed to thicken, heavy with an unseen presence. She glanced around, her heart pounding in her chest, but there was nothing to be seen—just the oppressive darkness of the castle.

Another day, while she was sitting in the library, poring over old books in search of answers to the castle's mysteries, she heard it—a series of faint but distinct knocks, coming from the walls themselves. Her breath caught in her throat as she strained to listen, but the knocks ceased as suddenly as they had begun.

The knocks continued, sporadic and unpredictable, throughout the days and nights that followed. Lady Seraphina couldn't explain them; they seemed to come from within the very stone and mortar of the castle. Each time she ventured closer to the source of the sound, it would move, as if taunting her, leading her deeper into the labyrinthine halls.

Fear gnawed at her, but her determination to uncover the truth pushed her forward. She began to research the castle's history in earnest, seeking any mention of the strange occurrences that now plagued her. It was during these late-night investigations that she often heard Lady Isolde's voice, guiding her with whispered insights.

As each day passed, the malevolent presence within the castle seemed to intensify, as if the tortured souls of the departed were growing more desperate to communicate with Lady Seraphina. Their whispers in the night, the inexplicable knocks on the walls, and the eerie figures darting at the corners of her vision all became more pronounced, a relentless chorus of voices yearning for release from their eternal torment.

Lady Seraphina's life within the castle had grown increasingly grim. Count Malachi, consumed by his jealousy and desire for control, had become ever more domineering and malevolent. He seized every opportunity to assert his power over her, reveling in her grief and despair. His whispered promises were laced with cruelty, each word intended to tighten his grip on her heart and soul.

"You are mine now," he declared one evening, his voice dripping with possessiveness. "I will not share you with anyone ever again!" His words hung in the air like a dark omen, a chilling reminder of her captivity.

Count Malachi's control over Lady Seraphina had become all-encompassing. He assigned guards to watch her every move, turning her home into a prison. Even her most private moments were no longer her own; her solitude was a luxury she could no longer afford. Guards stood vigilant outside her chamber doors, their presence a constant reminder of her captivity.

As Lady Seraphina moved through the castle's corridors, Count Malachi's watchful eyes followed her every step. The once-spacious hallways now felt suffocating, the stone walls seemingly closing in around her. She longed for the freedom she once had, for the carefree rides through the castle grounds with Lady Isolde, and for the laughter that had filled her days.

The guards, handpicked by Count Malachi for their unwavering loyalty, monitored Lady Seraphina even during her solitary moments. They took note of her every action, her every whispered word, and her every thought. Nothing escaped their scrutiny.

Lady Seraphina's distress was palpable, her spirit crushed by the relentless control exerted by Count Malachi. She could no longer express herself freely; her words were stifled, and her thoughts were guarded. The weight of her captivity bore down on her like a leaden cloak, and the once-bright light of her spirit had dimmed.

As the days turned into weeks, Lady Seraphina's transformation extended beyond her emotional state to her physical appearance. The vibrant, flowing gowns that had once adorned her figure were replaced by garments of muted colours and modest design. Gone were the rich silks and ornate embroidery that had celebrated her femininity and spirit. In their place were somber fabrics that hung loosely, concealing her form, and betraying no hint of her radiant beauty.

The transformation of her wardrobe mirrored the stifling environment in which she now found herself. Count Malachi's control over her had left her feeling like a caged bird, stripped of her ability to soar freely. Her once-lustrous hair, which had cascaded like a waterfall of auburn silk, was now pulled back into a severe bun, a symbol of the restraint imposed upon her.

Each morning, as Lady Seraphina moved through the castle's dimly lit halls, her footsteps were muted by the soft fabric of her unassuming attire. Her gait, once graceful and confident, had become hesitant and measured as if she were constantly walking on eggshells. The vibrant colours that had once adorned her had been replaced by dull, inattention-grabbing tones that allowed her to blend into the background, invisible to the world outside.

Yet, beneath the surface of her subdued appearance, a spark of resilience still smoldered. Lady Seraphina's spirit, though dimmed, was far from extinguished. In the secret chambers of her heart, she nurtured her dreams of freedom and justice, knowing that one day she would break free from the oppressive grasp of Count Malachi.

As she moved through the castle's opulent chambers, she couldn't help but recall the vibrant young woman she had once been. Her reflection in the ornate mirrors revealed a stark contrast to her former self. The glow of youth had given way to a weariness that etched lines upon her face, and the light in her eyes had dimmed to a mere flicker.

Sir Sterling, her loyal companion, had not been spared from the transformation that had swept through the castle. The magnificent stallion, once a symbol of strength and vitality, now bore the weight of the oppressive atmosphere. His white coat, which had once gleamed with health, seemed dull and lackluster, mirroring the subdued palette of Lady Seraphina's attire.

Yet, despite the changes that had befallen them both, Lady Seraphina and Sir Sterling remained bound by an unbreakable bond. The stallion, though diminished in appearance, still stood as a symbol of her strength and determination. His presence provided solace in the face of Count Malachi's tyranny, a silent reminder that they would endure, no matter the odds.

In the quiet hours of the night, Lady Seraphina would steal moments of respite, tending to Sir Sterling's needs with a tenderness that transcended words. She would brush his mane and whisper soothing words to him, a promise that their spirits would one day soar free once more. It was in these stolen moments that the spark of hope within her heart burned brightest.

Lady Seraphina's transformation, though marked by the constraints of her captivity, did not diminish the fire of her resolve. She remained committed to the pursuit of justice, her spirit undaunted by the darkness that surrounded her. Count Malachi's control over her had brought about changes in her appearance, but it had failed to extinguish the indomitable spirit that lay beneath the surface.

As the days turned into months, Lady Seraphina's journey toward freedom and justice continued. She knew that she would reclaim her vibrant spirit and the colours that had once defined her. Until then, she and Sir Sterling would stand as symbols of resilience and unwavering determination, ready to face the trials that lay ahead.

The castle had become a labyrinth of torment. The oppressive atmosphere seemed to conspire against her as if the very walls held her captive along with the restless souls that yearned for freedom. The black roses in the courtyard, dark as the abyss, stood as a testament to the anguish that permeated the castle.

Lady Seraphina's every attempt to seek answers or solace was thwarted. Count Malachi's sinister influence extended even to the castle's library, where books that might contain clues to their predicament had mysteriously disappeared. Her inquiries were met with stony silence, and the servants, cowed by Count Malachi's malevolence, dared not speak of the castle's secrets.

Count Malachi's malevolent grip extended beyond the physical realm. Lady Seraphina's dreams were filled with haunting visions, her sleep tormented by nightmares of Lady Isolde's death and the suffering of the trapped souls. She would awaken in a cold sweat, gasping for breath, only to find herself still ensnared within the castle's walls.

But amid the darkness that had enveloped Seraphina's life, a glimmer of hope emerged. Lady Isolde returned to her as a ghost, every midnight when the castle lay shrouded in darkness. The first time it happened, Seraphina was terrified. She had retired to her chambers, her heart heavy with grief, and the room seemed to whisper with a chilling presence.

As the witching hour approached, strange things began to occur. Objects in her room shifted of their own accord, her candle flickered and danced as if moved by unseen hands, and a haunting chill settled in the air. Seraphina huddled beneath her covers; her eyes wide with fear as the room filled with an otherworldly glow.

Then, she heard it—a soft, ethereal voice, like a distant echo. It was Lady Isolde's voice, a gentle and soothing melody that called out to her. At first, Seraphina was too terrified to respond, but as the voice grew closer, she recognized the familiar cadence, the warmth that had always defined Isolde's presence.

Summoning her courage, Seraphina whispered, "Isolde? Is that you?"

The room seemed to shimmer with an otherworldly light, and there, before her, stood Lady Isolde's ghostly figure. She was pale and radiant, her eyes filled with a sorrowful longing, but her physical form was that of her body before she was cursed. Short but slender with beautiful soft features. Seraphina's fear gave way to overwhelming relief as she reached out to touch her friend. Her fingers passed through Isolde's form like mist, but there was no denying the connection that still existed between them.

Tears filled Seraphina's eyes as she embraced the ghostly figure of her dear friend, feeling a faint, ethereal presence envelop her. Isolde's spirit had not abandoned her; it had found a way to return. She was there to comfort Seraphina, to remind her of their unbreakable bond.

In the nights that followed, Seraphina eagerly awaited Isolde's ghostly visits. They spoke of cherished memories, whispered shared secrets, and reaffirmed their friendship. The darkness that had consumed Seraphina's heart began to recede in the presence of her dear friend. Isolde's voice became a soothing balm, and her gentle laughter filled the room.

Isolde shared with Seraphina the tragic truth of their predicament. As long as Count Malachi remained alive, she and all the souls who had lost their lives within the castle would be unable to find peace. They would remain trapped, their spirits bound to the castle's darkened halls.

In the castle of secrets and shadows, where betrayal and jealousy had taken root, the love and friendship of Lady Seraphina and Lady Isolde endured, transcending the boundaries of life and death. The haunting presence of the black rose served as a solemn reminder of the price they had paid, but it also symbolized the unbreakable bond that not even Count Malachi's malevolence could sever.

Determined to free Isolde and the tormented souls of the castle, Lady Seraphina made a solemn vow. She confided in Isolde one night, her voice filled with determination, "I promise you, Isolde, one day I will find a way to bring peace to your soul. I will find a way to break the curse that binds us all to this wretched place. You will be set free, and the darkness that plagues this castle will be lifted."

Isolde's ghostly smile was filled with gratitude, and she whispered, "I believe in you, Seraphina. With your strength and our unbreakable bond, we will find a way to end this torment." Their shared resolve forged a newfound determination in Lady Seraphina's heart. She knew that they were facing an arduous battle against the malevolent force that held them captive within the haunted castle, but she was ready to confront it, uncover its secrets, and set the tormented souls free.

The morning sun cast a soft, golden glow over the castle's courtyard, where Lady Seraphina had once walked with Lady Isolde, blissfully unaware of the darkness that now pervaded their lives. Today was different; it carried an air of purpose and defiance.

As Lady Seraphina made her way to the courtyard, she was dressed in a flowing gown of deep emerald green, a colour that symbolized her determination and hope. The dress, with its intricate lace details and delicate embroidery, billowed around her like a vibrant forest, a stark contrast to the oppressive atmosphere that hung over the castle.

Unbeknownst to Lady Seraphina, her choice of attire had not gone unnoticed by Count Malachi, who had been closely monitoring her every move. From his vantage point high in the castle, he had observed her descent into the courtyard with a mixture of curiosity and intrigue. Count Malachi was a man who valued power and control above all else, and the sight of Lady Seraphina in the emerald dress had piqued his interest.

In his twisted perception, Count Malachi believed that Lady Seraphina had adorned herself in the resplendent green gown as a token of her devotion to him. He fancied himself the object of her affections, and the emerald dress, in his mind, was a testament to her desire to please him. His vanity knew no bounds, and he reveled in the idea that he held such sway over her.

As Lady Seraphina reached the courtyard, her steps were measured and purposeful. She moved with a grace that seemed to defy the heaviness of the air around her. The emerald dress flowed like a river of hope, its vibrant colour a stark contrast to the somber backdrop of the castle's oppressive walls.

Count Malachi, hidden in the shadows, could not tear his eyes away from the sight before him. He watched Lady Seraphina's every movement, convinced that her attire was a silent declaration of her devotion to him. In his twisted fantasy, he imagined that she had dressed for him and him alone.

Unable to contain his self-importance, Count Malachi vainly pronounced an instruction to the guards stationed nearby, his voice dripping with false humility. "See to it that Lady Seraphina is given every comfort and assistance," he declared, his words laced with a smug satisfaction. "She has dressed for a special occasion, and I would not want her to be disturbed."

The guards, ever obedient to their master, nodded and followed his orders without question. In their eyes, Lady Seraphina's attire was indeed a sign of her devotion to Count Malachi, and they were eager to cater to her every whim. Little did they know that her emerald dress was not a gesture of love for their lord but a symbol of her determination to bring light to the darkness that had plagued the castle.

As Lady Seraphina moved through the courtyard, her emerald dress seemed to cast a radiant glow upon the withered black roses that had once dominated the garden. It was as if the gown itself held the power to banish the malevolent spirits that had tormented the lost souls within.

Count Malachi, though deluded by his own vanity, could not deny the transformation that seemed to take hold of the courtyard. The once-oppressive atmosphere began to lift, replaced by a sense of renewal and hope. The emerald dress had unwittingly become a symbol of Lady Seraphina's indomitable spirit and her commitment to bringing justice to those who had suffered.

The breakfast table had been set up in the very spot where Lady Isolde had tragically lost her life. It was a solemn reminder of the past, but Lady Seraphina refused to be shackled by the castle's history. The table, draped in a pristine white cloth, was adorned with fine China and polished silverware, a stark contrast to the darkness that had plagued the castle.

The morning's fare was a bountiful spread. Plates of freshly baked pastries and delicate finger sandwiches were arranged with care. Fruits glistened with dew, and the fragrance of freshly brewed tea filled the air. It was a breakfast fit for a queen, a stark contrast to the haunting presence that loomed in the background.

Seated at the table was Count Malachi, his stern expression betraying the unease that had settled within him. His dark eyes darted about as if he could sense the gathering storm, though he remained oblivious to the true source of his discomfort.

Lady Seraphina took her place at the head of the table, her emerald gown flowing around her like a cascade of leaves. She maintained an air of composure, her determination hidden behind a serene facade. Beside her, Lady Isolde's ghostly figure appeared in her presence, a reassuring reminder of their shared purpose, but only Lady Seraphina could see her.

As the breakfast unfolded, Isolde decided to play a trick on Count Malachi. Her translucent form moved with ethereal grace, and she discreetly manipulated his fork, causing it to slide off the table each time he attempted to use it. Count Malachi's temper was already frayed, his paranoia mounting with each passing day. The continuous movement of his fork pushed him to the brink.

With a sudden clatter, Count Malachi's fork tumbled to the ground once again, leaving him with nothing but a frustrated scowl. His face turned crimson with anger as he slammed his hand on the table, causing the fine China to rattle.

"What is the meaning of this?" he thundered, his voice echoing through the courtyard.

Lady Seraphina maintained her composure, her gaze steady. "Count Malachi, it seems there are unseen forces at work here," she replied calmly, her voice carrying an underlying strength.

Count Malachi's temper flared, and he rose abruptly from his chair, his face contorted with rage. "Unseen forces?" he spat, his eyes narrowing at Lady Seraphina. "Do not mock me, Seraphina! This is your doing, isn't it?"

Lady Isolde's ghostly figure remained poised and enigmatic, her ethereal presence a stark contrast to Count Malachi's escalating fury.

"I assure you, Count Malachi, I had no part in this," Lady Seraphina replied firmly, her green gown swaying gently in the morning breeze. "Perhaps it is the restless spirits within these walls, yearning to make their presence known."

Count Malachi's anger reached its zenith, and he stormed away from the breakfast table without even finishing his meal. His departure left the courtyard in an eerie silence, broken only by the faint rustling of leaves and the distant cawing of crows.

Lady Seraphina turned her attention to Lady Isolde's ghostly form, a knowing look passing between them. Isolde's playful trick had served its purpose—it had rattled Count Malachi and disrupted the oppressive atmosphere that had held them captive for so long.

With renewed determination, Lady Seraphina and Lady Isolde continued their quest to uncover the castle's secrets and free the tormented souls within. The path ahead was treacherous, but they would face it together, with hope in their hearts and the strength of their unbreakable bond. The emerald dress, symbolizing their resolve, billowed in the morning breeze, a testament to their determination to bring light to the darkness that had plagued the haunted castle for generations.

As Lady Seraphina and Lady Isolde ventured deeper into the labyrinthine corridors of the castle, they felt the oppressive weight of the malevolent spirits that held sway over the ancient stones. Shadows seemed to dance in the corners of their vision, and the air grew heavy with an eerie chill. Lady Isolde, once a vibrant and ethereal presence, had become a flickering specter in the dimly lit hallways.

It was during one of their treks through the castle's labyrinth that Lady Isolde, with a voice that echoed with a haunting sorrow, spoke to Lady Seraphina. "My dearest friend," she whispered, her form wavering like a mirage. "I fear that this may be the last time I am able to manifest to you in this way."

Lady Seraphina's heart sank at Lady Isolde's words, her eyes brimming with tears. "No, Isolde," she pleaded, reaching out to touch the ethereal figure of her dear friend. "We cannot let them win. We must free you and the others."

Lady Isolde's gaze was filled with a mixture of longing and resignation. "I wish it were that simple, my beloved Seraphina," she replied, her voice fading like a distant melody. "The dark spirits that hold power over this castle have noticed my energy. They are closing in, and it will not be long before they trap me further."

Lady Seraphina's emerald dress, once a symbol of their resolve, now felt like a weighty shroud of sorrow. She clung to Lady Isolde's fading presence, her fingers passing through the insubstantial figure as if grasping at a wisp of smoke. "We cannot give up," she implored, her voice trembling with emotion. "We will find a way, Isolde. I will not rest until you are free."

A flicker of hope ignited in Lady Isolde's eyes, a glimmer of her former self. "You have a strength and determination that knows no bounds, my dearest friend," she said, her voice growing fainter. "Promise me that you will carry on, even in the face of darkness. The souls trapped within these walls need you, now more than ever."

Lady Seraphina nodded solemnly, tears streaming down her cheeks. "I promise, Isolde. I will not falter. We will uncover the truth, and we will set you free."

With those words, Lady Isolde's spectral form began to fade, like a fragile memory slipping away into the depths of the castle's haunted history. Lady Seraphina stood alone in the dimly lit corridor, her heart heavy with grief and determination.

From that moment forward, Lady Seraphina's resolve burned brighter than ever. She would not let her dear friend's sacrifice be in vain. She would unravel the castle's secrets, confront the malevolent spirits that hold sway, and bring an end to the torment that had plagued the souls trapped within its ancient walls.

The emerald dress, though dulled by the shadows of the castle, served as a symbol of her unyielding determination. With every step she took, every secret she uncovered, Lady Seraphina drew closer to the truth. The path ahead was fraught with danger and uncertainty, but she would face it with the strength of her unbreakable bond with Lady Isolde and the unwavering promise to set her friend's spirit free.

As Lady Seraphina ventured deeper into the heart of the castle's darkness, she knew that the road ahead would be fraught with challenges and sacrifices. Her determination burned like a steady flame, casting light upon the shadows that threatened to consume her. With every step she took, she was guided by the memory of Lady Isolde, a cherished friend whose spirit remained bound within the castle's ancient walls.

The winding corridors seemed to stretch endlessly, and the air grew heavy with an ominous presence. It was during her explorations that Lady Seraphina stumbled upon a concealed chamber, its entrance hidden behind a heavy tapestry adorned with symbols that sent a shiver down her spine. The flickering light of her torch revealed a dark, foreboding space that seemed to defy the very essence of the castle.

Upon entering, Lady Seraphina was met with a chilling sight. The chamber was adorned with symbols of dark worship and witchcraft, the walls covered in inscriptions and drawings that hinted at unspeakable rituals. At the center of the room, a massive pentagram had been meticulously etched onto the stone floor, its lines gleaming with an eerie, otherworldly glow. Carefully placed candles surrounded the pentagram, their flickering flames casting dancing shadows upon the chamber's walls. She couldn't help but notice the extremely pungent smell of rotten eggs in the air which made it very difficult to concentrate.

Lady Seraphina's heart raced as she realized the malevolent nature of the chamber she had stumbled upon. It was clear that dark rituals had taken place here, and the presence of such maleficent symbols sent a shiver down her spine. She approached the pentagram cautiously, her torchlight revealing the intricate details of the sinister design.

As she stood next to the pentagram, a palpable darkness seemed to envelop her. The air grew thick with evil, and a malevolent spirit made itself known. He materialized before her, his form a grotesque distortion of humanity. His eyes burned with malevolence, and a wicked grin twisted his lips.

"Ah, Lady Seraphina," the evil spirit hissed, his voice a chilling whisper that echoed within the chamber. "You have stumbled upon a place of great power, a place where the boundaries between worlds grow thin."

Lady Seraphina recoiled in horror, her heart pounding in her chest. She had not anticipated encountering such a malevolent entity within the castle's depths. "Who are you?" she demanded, her voice trembling with fear.

The evil spirit's laughter echoed through the chamber, a chilling sound that sent shivers down Lady Seraphina's spine. "Call me Mephistopheles," he replied, his eyes gleaming with malice. "I am but one of many who dwell within these cursed walls, but I am the one who holds the key to power beyond your wildest imagination."

Lady Seraphina's curiosity warred with her fear as she regarded Mephistopheles. "Power?" she echoed, her brow furrowing in confusion. "What power do you speak of?"

Mephistopheles stepped closer to her, his presence a suffocating force. "Count Malachi," he hissed, "he possesses great wealth, power, and influence, does he not?"

Lady Seraphina nodded, her thoughts racing. Count Malachi's rise to prominence had always been shrouded in mystery, and she had often wondered about the source of his wealth and authority.

Mephistopheles grinned, revealing jagged, yellowed teeth. "Count Malachi has sold his soul to the Devil himself," he whispered, his words dripping with malevolence. "In exchange for his riches and power, he has pledged his allegiance to darkness. But you, Lady Seraphina, you could have it all. You could be the queen of darkness, with power and riches beyond your understanding."

Lady Seraphina's blood ran cold as she comprehended the extent of Mephistopheles's proposition. The realization that Count Malachi had made a sinister pact with the Devil filled her with a sense of dread. She had always sensed that there was something unholy about the Count's rise to power, but now the truth lay bare before her.

"I would never make such a bargain," Lady Seraphina declared, her voice resolute. "I will not sell my soul to darkness, no matter the temptations it may offer. I worship the one true God!" Her words rang out with unwavering faith, a fervent belief in the benevolent force that guided her heart and soul.

Mephistopheles, the malevolent spirit, recoiled at the mention of her faith. He sneered with a wicked grin, his voice dripping with contempt as he taunted her, "Ah, the God of light and love, you say? It seems your God has forsaken you, my dear Lady Seraphina. Where is He now when you stand on the precipice of darkness and despair?"

Lady Seraphina's faith did not waver in the face of Mephistopheles's taunts. She clung to her belief with unwavering conviction. "My faith in the Lord is unshakable," she declared, her voice unwavering. "Even in the darkest of times, His light guides me, and His love sustains me. I will not be swayed by the temptations of darkness."

Mephistopheles's laughter echoed through the chamber, a mocking sound that reverberated in the air. "We shall see, Lady Seraphina," he hissed. "Your faith may be strong, but the darkness that surrounds you is far more potent. It will not be long before you realize that your God cannot save you from the depths of despair that await you."

Lady Seraphina's heart sank as she absorbed the depths of Count Malachi's malevolence. The realization that he had crossed a spiritual threshold that no one should ever dared to tread upon left her mortified and disgusted. The very thought of harnessing the powers of malevolent spirits for his dark ambitions sent shivers down her spine. She had witnessed the dark tendrils of Count Malachi's influence spreading, and the corruption it wrought was an affront to the purity and harmony she had sworn to protect.

With those chilling words, Lady Seraphina turned away and fled from the chamber, leaving Mephistopheles behind, his malevolent laughter trailing after her like a haunting refrain. She knew that her faith would be tested in the trials that lay ahead, but she remained resolute, determined to confront the malevolent spirits, and bring light to the haunted castle, no matter the cost. The battle against Count Malachi had become not only a clash of earthly and spiritual realms but also a test of her unwavering commitment to goodness and her courage to face the darkest depths of malevolence.

She knew that her faith would be tested in the trials that lay ahead, but she remained resolute, determined to confront the malevolent spirits, and bring light to the haunted castle, no matter the cost.

Seraphina's Resolve

Lady Seraphina, determined to uncover a way to weaken Count Malachi's grip on the castle and the malevolent forces that served him, devoted herself to long hours in the castle's library. She scoured ancient tomes and manuscripts, searching for clues, hidden knowledge, or any mention of Count Malachi's unholy pact with darkness.

Her relentless pursuit of answers led her to a discovery that sent a shiver down her spine. Among the dusty books and scrolls, she found references to dark rituals and blood sacrifices. According to the texts, every drop of blood shed by Count Malachi served as a twisted offering to the devil, strengthening the malevolent forces that surrounded him. It became clear that to weaken Count Malachi, she would need to disrupt these dark rituals and sever his connection to the unholy pact.

With this newfound knowledge, Lady Seraphina's resolve only grew stronger. She knew that Count Malachi's hold on the castle was a direct result of his malevolent alliance. She also realized that confronting him head-on would not be enough. She needed allies, a force that could stand against the darkness that had consumed the Count.

Continuing her research, she delved into accounts of the crusader armies of old, noble warriors who had fought under the banner of God against the forces of darkness. These accounts spoke of righteous battles waged in the name of faith and justice, and Lady Seraphina felt a glimmer of hope. Perhaps the remnants of such an army could be summoned to aid her in the struggle against Count Malachi.

As she poured over the texts, she came across references to relics and artifacts that were said to possess the power to ward off evil and strengthen the resolve of those who fought in the name of God. Lady Seraphina remembered the countless artifacts she and Lady Isolde had discovered on their rides together. These objects, gathered from ancient ruins and hidden caverns, could hold the key to her salvation.

Lady Seraphina returned to her room, where the artifacts were carefully stored. She began to examine each one, seeking any sign of their hidden power or connection to the divine. As she handled a golden amulet, her fingers brushed over the engraved cross, and she felt a surge of warmth and strength. It was a sign that this relic, at the very least, held the blessing of faith.

Days turned into weeks as Lady Seraphina tirelessly researched, gathered relics, and formulated a plan. Her room became a makeshift command center, filled with maps, books, and the artifacts that would aid her in her quest to weaken Count Malachi. The weight of her mission bore heavily upon her, and the darkness that pervaded the castle threatened to consume her spirit.

Amidst the chaos of her preparations and the constant tension within the castle's walls, Lady Seraphina found solace in her afternoon rides with Sir Sterling. Those moments on horseback allowed her to escape the oppressive atmosphere of the castle and breathe in the fresh air of the countryside.

One fateful evening, as she pored over a particularly ancient tome, the door to the library swung open with a force that made her jump. Count Malachi stood in the doorway; his eyes filled with a malevolence that sent a shiver down her spine. She had expected confrontation, but she had hoped it wouldn't come to this.

Count Malachi's voice was a venomous hiss as he approached her, his anger and frustration evident. "You think you can defy me?" he sneered, his hand reaching out to grip her arm with a bruising force.

Lady Seraphina winced in pain but refused to show fear. "I will not yield to your darkness," she declared, her voice trembling but resolute.

In a fit of rage, Count Malachi raised his hand and struck her across the face, the force of the blow sending her sprawling to the floor. She tasted blood in her mouth, but her spirit remained unbroken.

"I will not allow your defiance to continue," Count Malachi spat, his voice filled with malice. "You will submit to me, or you will suffer even more."

As he advanced on her, Lady Seraphina's hand instinctively reached to try and shield herself from Count Malachi. He pushed her over the table, and the weight of his body pinned her down. Her heart pounded in her chest as fear coursed through her veins. Count Malachi, his face contorted with malice, drew his dagger, its cold steel pressing against her throat. Lady Seraphina trembled uncontrollably, her voice quivering as she pleaded for him not to hurt her. Tears welled up in her eyes as she prayed within her thoughts and spirit for deliverance from the darkness that threatened to consume her.

"Now I shall take what is mine, I shall make you surrender!" snarled Count Malachi like a wolf licking his chops before it was about to eat its prey. "No, please Sir, please, I am untouched!" Those very words ignited a fire in Count Malachi's eyes, a desire Lady Seraphina had never witnessed before, "It will not take long, it will hurt a little, but you will begin to enjoy it!" he whispered in her ear while licking her ear almost lizard-like, this sent a shiver of revulsion down Lady Seraphina's spine.

Lady Seraphina now frozen from fright for her very life lay as still as possible allowing Count Malachi to feed on her body like a starving vampire awakened from centuries. The dagger remained at her throat while he traced her body with his free hand to lift her dress and undo his trousers, he then proceeded to thrust himself inside her sending spiking pain through Lady Seraphina's body as it felt her pelvic areas were being torn through by a knife. She could feel blood start to drip down her legs and her back started to pain from the pounding onto the table because of Count Malachi's savage-like thrusts.

Lady Seraphina was in so much pain it felt like she was unable to breathe, unable to cry, and unable to think while Count Malachi continued to treat her body as a feast now using the dagger to rip her corset open exposing her breasts to his delight.

Lady Seraphina had tears running down her cheeks as she cried silent tears during the nightmare that was happening to her. She tried to focus on something within her immediate sight surroundings to help her focus until this horror came to an end. She realized that above her was a bronze cross hanging against the library wall, something could focus on to help her to the end.

Finally, Count Malachi let out a whelping screech of pleasure as he finished, and he retracted from Lady Seraphina leaving her lifeless on the table. "You were delicious, I shall ensure to have more of you more often!" With that, he exited the room leaving Lady Seraphina collapsing to the cold stone floor curling into a tight ball so she may recover to find the strength to walk to her chamber.

Lady Seraphina lay on the cold stone floor, her body trembling with a mixture of fear and revulsion after the terrifying encounter with Count Malachi. The echoes of his malevolent words still lingered in her mind, and the weight of his presence felt like a sinister shadow that clung to her.

Summoning every ounce of strength, she managed to push herself up from the ground. Her limbs felt heavy, and her heart ached with an overwhelming sense of despair. Bruises from the encounter marred her skin, and her clothing was tattered and soiled. She had to escape to the safety of her chambers, where she could find solace, if only for a moment.

With unsteady steps, Lady Seraphina stumbled down the corridor, her vision blurred by tears. The castle's oppressive atmosphere seemed to close in on her, and she felt as though the very walls were watching, bearing witness to her suffering.

As she continued, her presence did not go unnoticed by the castle's maid servants. They watched her with sympathetic eyes, their hearts heavy with the knowledge of the horrors she endured. They longed to offer her solace, to lend a helping hand, but they knew all too well the consequences of crossing Count Malachi's path.

The unspoken understanding among the servants was that they must not address Lady Seraphina in any way or attempt to assist her in her fragile state. The fear of invoking Count Malachi's fury kept them silent and motionless, even as their empathy for her plight tugged at their souls.

Lady Seraphina's earlier cries for mercy had nearly swayed the castle guards, their hearts moved by her torment. They teetered on the edge of intervention, their humanity clashing with their loyalty to Count Malachi. Yet, they did not intervene, bound by the unspoken rules of the castle, their unwillingness to provoke further wrath from their malevolent master.

Finally, Lady Seraphina reached the sanctuary of her chambers. With trembling hands, she closed and locked the door behind her, shutting out the prying eyes and oppressive presence of the castle. Her room, once a refuge, now felt tainted by the darkness that had invaded her life. She couldn't bear to remain in her soiled clothes any longer. Stripping them off, she discarded them in a heap on the floor.

Exhausted and emotionally drained, Lady Seraphina politely asked the servants to drew her a bath, filling the tub with warm water. As she sank into the soothing embrace of the water, she couldn't help but feel that no amount of scrubbing could cleanse her of the contamination she felt deep within her soul. The water, though comforting, seemed to mock her, as if it too knew the horrors she had endured.

With a trembling hand, she reached for a bar of soap and began to wash her body, scrubbing furiously as if trying to wash away not just the physical stains but also the emotional scars that had been inflicted upon her. Each stroke of the soap against her skin felt like an act of defiance, a desperate attempt to regain control over her own body.

But no matter how hard she scrubbed, she couldn't rid herself of the feeling that Count Malachi's touch still lingered, that his darkness had left an indelible mark on her and that his violation of her body he somehow managed to scrape her soul to pieces. She sobbed softly, the tears mixing with the bathwater as she continued her futile efforts to cleanse herself wishing she could peel her skin off from her!

Hours passed as Lady Seraphina remained submerged in the water, her body and spirit exhausted from the ordeal. The water in the tub had grown cold, and her fingers were pruned from the prolonged soak. She finally emerged from the bath, wrapping herself in a robe and sitting by the window, her wet hair clinging to her shoulders. The castle's oppressive presence still loomed, but for a brief moment, in the silence of her chambers, she found a sliver of respite from the torment she had endured.

The moonlight streamed into the room, casting a silvery glow that illuminated the tear stains on her cheeks. Lady Seraphina felt a deep sense of despair and vulnerability that she had never known before. The encounter with Count Malachi had stripped away her sense of safety and control, leaving her exposed and broken.

She knew that the battle against the darkness that had consumed the castle was far from over. Count Malachi's malevolent presence still loomed, and the malevolent forces that served him were relentless. Lady Seraphina would need to find the strength to confront her fears and continue her quest for justice and redemption.

With a heavy heart, she leaned against the windowpane, gazing out at the moonlit night. The tears had stopped, but the ache within her remained. Lady Seraphina knew that she couldn't allow herself to be defeated by the darkness that threatened to consume her. She would rise from this moment of despair, stronger and more determined than ever to bring light to the haunted castle and release the tormented souls within.

In the dark and oppressive months that followed Count Malachi's initial attack, Lady Seraphina found herself trapped in a nightmare from which there seemed to be no escape. Count Malachi's cruelty knew no bounds, and he took pleasure in tormenting her both physically and emotionally continuously filling the corridors with her screams and cries!

As each day passed, Lady Seraphina went into survival mode, her spirit battered but unbroken. She learned to endure the mistreatment, to hide her fear and vulnerability behind a mask of stoicism. She had to bide her time, waiting for the right moment to strike back and reclaim her dignity and freedom.

Count Malachi's abuse took many forms. He would subject her to cruel taunts and verbal degradation, seeking to break her spirit. He would deny her food and basic comforts, forcing her to rely on her inner strength to endure the physical hardships. He would physically and sexually abuse her to enforce the mindset upon her that he controls her, and he is powerful. Lady Seraphina's once–vibrant spirit was slowly eroding under the weight of the darkness that surrounded her.

Yet, in the depths of despair, she found pockets of resistance. She would steal moments to be alone with her thoughts and to gather information about the castle and its secrets. She couldn't let Count Malachi's cruelty defeat her. She had a mission to accomplish, a mission to weaken his grip on the castle and free the tormented souls within.

One of the few respites she found was in the company of Sir Sterling, her loyal stallion. He had become her silent protector, a steadfast companion who seemed to sense the danger that surrounded her. Whenever she was near him, she found solace and a glimmer of hope.

It was during one of their stolen moments together in the stables that Count Malachi's cruelty reached a breaking point. Lady Seraphina had been trying to soothe Sir Sterling, who had become increasingly agitated by the malevolent forces that lurked in the castle. His restlessness mirrored her own.

Count Malachi, perhaps sensing the bond between Lady Seraphina and her stallion, seized the opportunity to exert his dominance. He entered the stables with a malicious glint in his eye, his intentions clear. As he approached Lady Seraphina, his voice dripped with venomous mockery.

"You seem to have a peculiar fondness for this beast," he sneered, his gaze shifting between Lady Seraphina and Sir Sterling. "Perhaps I should teach you a lesson in obedience."

Lady Seraphina's heart pounded in her chest as she tried to stand between Count Malachi and her beloved stallion. She knew that any act of defiance would come at a great cost, but she couldn't bear to see Sir Sterling suffer.

As Count Malachi reached for her, Sir Sterling reared up, his massive form standing between them. His eyes blazed with fierce determination as he let out a deafening neigh, a primal declaration of his loyalty and protection. With each thud of Sir Sterling's hooves hitting the ground, the vibrations seemed to command Count Malachi to retreat! The stallion's head swung side to side, his flaring nostrils emitting snorts of defiance that filled the air with a palpable tension. It was a moment of silent communication between Lady Seraphina and her beloved companion, a warning to Count Malachi that he had crossed a line he could not retreat from.

Count Malachi, taken aback by the stallion's unexpected defiance, reacted with anger and fear. He drew his swords, brandishing them with deadly intent. In a swift and brutal motion, he struck out at Sir Sterling, cutting a deep gash in the horse's shoulder.

The stallion let out a pained cry, his eyes filled with agony. Lady Seraphina's heart shattered as she witnessed the cruelty inflicted upon her loyal companion. She knew that she had to act, that she couldn't let Count Malachi's brutality go unanswered.

In a desperate attempt to defend herself and Sir Sterling, Lady Seraphina spotted a pitchfork leaning against the stable wall. With trembling hands, she grabbed it and advanced on Count Malachi, her eyes burning with determination.

Count Malachi, though momentarily surprised, soon regained his composure and let out a malevolent chuckle. He seemed to revel in the confrontation as if the pain he had inflicted on Sir Sterling had only fueled his sadistic desires.

"You think you can defy me, little lady?" he taunted, his swords poised for a counterattack. "I will break you!"

Lady Seraphina's grip on the pitchfork tightened as she raised it, ready to defend herself and Sir Sterling. She knew that she couldn't allow herself to be broken and that she had to find the strength within her to endure and resist.

As Count Malachi advanced, she thrust the pitchfork forward, aiming to disarm him. In the ensuing struggle, she managed to knock one of his swords from his grasp. But Count Malachi, fueled by his malevolent determination, refused to relent.

In a desperate move, Lady Seraphina aimed the pitchfork at Count Malachi's chest, narrowly missing a fatal blow. He staggered back, clutching his wounded side, his expression a mix of pain and anger. It was a moment of opportunity.

Breathing heavily and shaking with fear, Lady Seraphina knew that she had to act decisively. She couldn't allow Count Malachi to regain the upper hand. With all her strength, she lunged forward and managed to disarm him completely, sending his remaining sword clattering to the ground.

Count Malachi, now defenseless, stumbled backward, his face twisted with rage. He glared at Lady Seraphina, his eyes burning with hatred. "You will regret this," he hissed, his voice filled with venom.

But Lady Seraphina didn't waver. She knew that she had stood up to the darkness that had plagued her for far too long. With a deep breath, she turned to Sir Sterling, who stood trembling from his wound.

Tears filled Lady Seraphina's eyes as she addressed her loyal stallion. "Go, my friend," she whispered, her voice breaking with emotion. "Flee from this place, find safety."

At first, Sir Sterling hesitated, unwilling to leave her side. But Lady Seraphina, with a mixture of sorrow and determination, shouted at him to run. With a final glance back at her, the stallion turned and galloped away, his powerful form disappearing into the night.

Lady Seraphina, now alone and emotionally shattered, collapsed to the stable floor. She wept not just for her own suffering but for the pain she had been forced to witness in her beloved companion.

As Sir Sterling galloped away from the oppressive darkness of Count Malachi's realm, his powerful hooves carried him further and further from the malevolent forces that had tormented him and Lady Seraphina. The night air was cool and crisp, and the moon cast a gentle glow on the twisted trees that marked the boundary of the enchanted forest.

With each stride, Sir Sterling put more distance between himself and the horrors he had witnessed. The pain from the wound Count Malachi had inflicted on his shoulder was a constant reminder of the violence he had endured. But as he neared the enchanted forest, an inexplicable sense of calm began to wash over him, as if the very air was filled with magic and healing.

The enchanted forest was unlike any place Sir Sterling had ever encountered. The trees stood tall and majestic, their leaves shimmering with an otherworldly light. The ground beneath his hooves was soft and mossy, and the air was filled with the sweet scent of wildflowers. It was a place of peace and serenity, untouched by the darkness that had plagued the lands beyond.

As Sir Sterling ventured deeper into the enchanted forest, he sensed a presence watching him. Ethereal figures, lithe and graceful, began to emerge from the shadows of the trees. They were the elves of the enchanted forest, beings of ancient magic and wisdom who had guarded this realm for centuries.

The elves were a sight to behold, their appearance a testament to their connection with the mystical energies of their enchanted home. Both male and female elves possessed an otherworldly beauty that seemed to radiate from within. Their features were delicate and finely chiseled, with high cheekbones, pointed ears, and almond-shaped eyes that sparkled with an ageless wisdom.

The males of the elven race stood tall and slender, with a natural grace that made their movements appear effortless. Their hair, which could vary in colour from moonlight silver to forest green, cascaded in long, flowing locks down their backs. They often wore their hair loose, allowing it to catch the dappled sunlight that filtered through the canopy of leaves.

Elven males were often adorned with intricate jewelry made from materials found in the forest—delicate silver bracelets, necklaces of sparkling gemstones, and ornate circlets that rested upon their brows. These adornments were not merely decorative but held significance, symbolizing their connection to the natural world and the magic that flowed through it.

Their clothing was both practical and elegant. They wore tunics and trousers crafted from fine fabrics that seemed to shimmer with an otherworldly luminescence. Earthy hues, such as moss green and deep azure, were common among their attire, blending seamlessly with the natural surroundings of the enchanted forest. Cloaks made from the leaves of the forest's unique flora completed their ensembles, allowing them to blend effortlessly into their woodland home.

Elven females, like their male counterparts, possessed a timeless beauty that captivated all who beheld them. They, too, were tall and slender, with graceful, lithesome forms that moved with an almost ethereal fluidity. Their hair, which ranged in colour from silvery white to rich chestnut, cascaded in long waves down their backs, often adorned with delicate flowers and vines.

Elven females were known for their affinity with nature, and they often wove elements of the forest into their attire. Gowns made from shimmering silk and adorned with intricate leaf motifs were a common sight. Their clothing was designed to allow freedom of movement, perfect for traversing the forest's lush terrain.

Adornments played a significant role in elven female fashion. They wore tiaras and crowns made from woven vines and delicate blossoms, which symbolized their connection to the cycles of nature. Necklaces made from polished stones and crystals captured the forest's mystical energy, while bracelets of intertwined vines and leaves added a touch of elegance to their ensembles.

The elves' footwear was crafted from soft leather and designed to be both functional and elegant. Elven boots were often embellished with intricate embroidery and leaf-shaped patterns, reflecting the flora that surrounded them. These boots allowed them to move silently through the forest, leaving no trace of their passage.

Both male and female elves had a natural grace that was enhanced by their attire, making them appear as though they were an integral part of the enchanted forest itself. Their clothing and adornments were not mere fashion statements but expressions of their deep connection with the natural world and the magic that flowed through it.

As Sir Sterling found himself in the presence of these ethereal beings, he marveled at their beauty and grace. He could sense the ancient wisdom that radiated from them, a wisdom born of centuries spent in harmony with the enchanted forest. It was clear that these elves were not only its guardians but also its living embodiments, embodying the magic and wonder of their mystical home.

The elves approached Sir Sterling with a mixture of curiosity and concern. They recognized the stallion as the companion of Lady Seraphina, a human they had occasionally glimpsed near the boundary of their forest. They had watched her from afar, intrigued by her presence so close to the border between their enchanted realm and the twisted, evil forest beyond.

Upon seeing the wound on Sir Sterling's shoulder, the elves knew that he had suffered greatly. With gentle hands, they began to tend to his injuries, using their knowledge of herbal remedies and ancient magic to ease his pain. As they worked, they sang soft, soothing melodies that seemed to resonate with the very heart of the forest.

Sir Sterling felt a deep sense of gratitude and trust toward these mystical beings. He allowed them to care for him, knowing that they held the power to heal not only his physical wounds but also the emotional scars he carried from his time with Lady Seraphina in Count Malachi's cruel grasp.

The elves, sensing the connection between Sir Sterling and Lady Seraphina, decided to send a small group of their own kind to investigate the borderlands and discover what had become of the human they had observed. They were determined to reunite the loyal stallion with his beloved companion.

Meanwhile, back in the dark and haunted castle, Lady Seraphina continued to endure Count Malachi's relentless mistreatment. Each day seemed to blur into the next as she struggled to maintain her resilience and determination. The memory of Sir Sterling's brave intervention in the stables provided her with a sliver of hope, a reminder that she was not entirely alone in her fight against the darkness.

But as the days turned into weeks, Lady Seraphina's spirit grew increasingly fragile. Count Malachi's cruelty showed no signs of waning, and the castle's oppressive atmosphere continued to suffocate her. She knew that she had to find a way to escape, to break free from the chains that bound her to this malevolent place.

It was during one of her stolen moments of solitude that Lady Seraphina stumbled upon a hidden passage in the castle, a long-forgotten tunnel that led deep into the heart of the evil forest. The tunnel was dark and foreboding, its walls covered in strange symbols and runes that seemed to pulse with a malevolent energy.

Despite the risks and the foreboding darkness that loomed ahead, Lady Seraphina was determined to take her chance and escape from Count Malachi's oppressive grip. She had meticulously planned her escape, waiting for the cover of night and the safety of the witching hour when Count Malachi would retire to his chambers, leaving the castle in an eerie silence.

In preparation for her daring escape, Lady Seraphina had chosen attire that would not draw undue attention. She dressed in a simple, dark gown made of unremarkable fabric that would blend into the shadows. It was a stark contrast to the opulent and vibrant dresses she had once worn, but she had learned that subtlety would be her greatest ally in this treacherous journey.

Her hair, once carefully coiffed and adorned with jewels, was now pulled back into a simple braid to keep it out of her way. She carried with her only the essentials—a small leather satchel containing some provisions, a flask of water, and a dagger she had taken from the castle armoury. It was a weapon of last resort, but Lady Seraphina knew that in her quest for freedom, she might encounter dangers that required her to defend herself.

As the witching hour approached, Lady Seraphina's heart pounded with a mixture of fear and anticipation. She had spent countless hours studying maps and diagrams of the castle to ensure that she knew the path to the hidden tunnel. Her knowledge of the castle's layout was her key to escaping undetected.

With each step she took through the darkened hallways, Lady Seraphina's senses were on high alert. The castle seemed to hold its breath as if aware of her intentions. She moved silently, her footsteps barely making a sound on the cold stone floor. Every creak and groan of the ancient building sent shivers down her spine, but she pressed on.

Finally, she reached the entrance to the tunnel, a nondescript door hidden in a forgotten corner of the castle. With trembling hands, she pushed it open and stepped into the blackness beyond. The tunnel was narrow and suffused with an oppressive chill, but Lady Seraphina's determination kept her moving forward.

As she stepped into the tunnel, her heart pounded with fear and determination. She could hear the faint whispers of the trapped souls that lingered within the castle, urging her onward. The tunnel seemed to stretch on endlessly, its darkness swallowing her whole.

Back in the enchanted forest, the elves had not been idle. They had sent scouts to investigate the borderlands, and their efforts had borne fruit. The scouts had discovered the hidden passage that led from the evil forest into Count Malachi's realm, and they had seen Lady Seraphina venture into it.

Realizing the danger she faced, the elves decided to act. They summoned their most skilled trackers and warriors, a group of elves who were well-versed in navigating the treacherous terrain of the evil forest. Their mission was clear, to find Lady Seraphina and bring her back safely to the enchanted realm.

The elven warriors chosen for the mission were a formidable group, known for their unparalleled combat skills and their unwavering dedication to protecting their realm and its inhabitants. They stood apart, even among their kind, as the elite guardians of the enchanted forest.

These elven warriors were characterized by their heightened agility and strength, traits that made them formidable adversaries to any who dared threaten the peace of their realm. Their training began at a young age, honing their natural talents and instilling in them a deep sense of duty. Each of them had undergone rigorous trials to earn their place among the forest's protectors.

The attire of these elite warriors reflected both their martial prowess and their connection to the enchanted forest. They wore suits of armour made from materials found within their mystical home—armour that was as resilient as it was graceful. The armour consisted of interlocking plates crafted from the bark of ancient trees, enchanted to be both lightweight and impenetrable. These plates covered their chests, shoulders, and limbs, providing protection without hindering their agility.

Beneath their armour, the warriors wore garments of fine elven silk, woven with enchantments to enhance their natural abilities. These garments were designed to move with them, allowing for swift and fluid movements in combat. The colours of their attire were often a reflection of their affinity with the forest—shades of deep green, earthy browns, and the occasional touch of silver or gold.

Elven warriors were known for their skill with a variety of weapons, and their choice of armament was as diverse as their individual strengths. Some favored longbows, carved from the ancient trees of the forest, and quivers filled with arrows tipped with enchanted blades. Others wielded finely crafted swords, their blades imbued with the forest's magic, while a select few favored the grace and precision of dual daggers. The warriors' footwear was specially designed for agility and stealth. They wore boots made from supple leather, reinforced with woven fibers from enchanted vines. These boots allowed them to move soundlessly through the forest, their steps barely leaving a trace on the forest floor.

In addition to their weaponry and armour, the elven warriors were adorned with symbols of their rank and status. Intricate pendants hung from their necks, crafted from precious stones that captured the essence of the enchanted forest. These pendants were both symbols of their elite status and sources of protection, offering blessings from the forest's ancient energies.

As the group of elven warriors embarked on their mission to rescue Lady Seraphina from the clutches of the evil forest, their appearance and attire spoke volumes about their dedication and resolve. They were not just protectors of the enchanted realm; they were its living embodiment, defenders of the mystical magic that flowed through every leaf and branch of their beloved home.

With their skills, their unwavering commitment, and their attire that blended seamlessly with the enchanted forest, they ventured forth to face the perils of the evil forest and bring Lady Seraphina safely back to the realm of ancient magic and wonder.

As they ventured into the evil forest, the elven warriors encountered unspeakable horrors. The trees twisted and contorted, their branches reaching out like skeletal fingers. The very ground seemed to writhe with malevolent energy, and strange creatures lurked in the shadows.

But the elven warriors were undeterred. They pressed on, following the trail left by Lady Seraphina. Their determination and unity were their greatest strengths, and they knew that they had a duty to protect the human who had ventured so close to their enchanted forest.

Meanwhile, Lady Seraphina's journey through the tunnel was fraught with peril. The further she ventured, the more she could feel the darkness closing in around her. Whispers of ancient curses and tormented souls echoed in her ears, and a sense of dread gnawed at her heart.

Finally, after what felt like an eternity, Lady Seraphina emerged from the tunnel into the heart of the evil forest. The sight that greeted her was a nightmare come to life. Twisted trees loomed overhead, their branches covered in thorns and dripping with a noxious, black ichor. The very air seemed to pulse with malevolence.

As she cautiously made her way through the dense underbrush, Lady Seraphina could feel the eyes of unseen entities watching her from the shadows. She knew that she had to stay vigilant, that the evil forest held many dangers. The very air seemed to be charged with malevolent energy, and the eerie silence was broken only by the occasional rustling of leaves and the distant, haunting cries of creatures that lurked in the darkness.

The evil forest was a twisted, nightmarish place where the laws of nature seemed to have no meaning. The trees, their branches gnarled and contorted, seemed to reach out hungrily, their bark bearing grotesque faces and twisted forms. The ground was uneven and treacherous, making each step a potential hazard. Vines and thorns seemed to conspire to impede her progress, snagging at her clothing and clawing at her skin.

Lady Seraphina's journey through the evil forest was not just a physical trial; it was a test of her mental fortitude as well. The oppressive atmosphere weighed heavily on her as if the very air was thick with despair. The twisted, gnarled trees seemed to close in around her, their branches forming a canopy that blotted out the sky. The dim, eerie light that filtered through the dense foliage cast eerie, shifting shadows that seemed to dance with malevolence.

Fear gnawed at her heart, and doubt crept into her mind. In the midst of this unnatural place, she couldn't help but question her decision to flee the castle. The familiar oppressive walls of Count Malachi's stronghold suddenly seemed like a sanctuary compared to the terrors that surrounded her now.

Lady Seraphina's mind was filled with haunting thoughts and unsettling memories. She remembered the torment she had endured at the hands of Count Malachi, the violence and cruelty that had become a daily part of her life. At times, she wondered if the castle, with all its darkness, had been a twisted kind of refuge compared to the horrors of the evil forest.

But deep within her heart, she knew that she couldn't turn back. The memory of Sir Sterling and the hope of reuniting with him drove her forward. She also couldn't ignore the knowledge she had gained in her research—the revelation that Count Malachi's power was tied to bloodshed. She was determined to find a way to weaken him, to end his reign of terror, and to bring justice to Lady Isolde.

As Lady Seraphina pressed on, she came across strange and unsettling sights. Grotesque, malformed creatures slithered and skittered through the underbrush, their eyes gleaming with malevolence. Unnatural, glowing mushrooms sprouted from the decaying roots of ancient trees, casting an eerie luminescence that seemed to beckon her further into the darkness.

The very flora and fauna of the evil forest seemed to conspire against her. Thorned vines reached out to ensnare her limbs, and noxious, choking fumes wafted from twisted, carnivorous flowers that lined her path. It was a constant battle to free herself from the clutches of the malevolent vegetation.

Despite the overwhelming fear and the physical toll, the forest exacted on her, Lady Seraphina refused to give in to despair. She clung to her determination and the flicker of hope that burned within her heart. She didn't know that she was not alone in her quest—she had the support of the elven warriors who had ventured into the evil forest to find her, and the unbreakable bond she shared with Sir Sterling.

With each step, she whispered words of encouragement to herself, reminding herself of the injustices she had suffered and the horrors she had witnessed in the castle. She knew that she had to be strong, not just for herself but for Lady Isolde's memory and for all those who had suffered at the hands of Count Malachi.

The journey through the evil forest continued to be a harrowing trial, one that pushed Lady Seraphina to her limits. Her heart raced with every shadow that moved and every eerie sound that echoed through the trees. Yet, she pressed on, driven by the hope of freedom and justice, and the knowledge that she was no longer willing to be a pawn in Count Malachi's twisted game.

As the darkness of the evil forest closed in around her, Lady Seraphina felt a growing determination within her. She would face whatever horrors lay ahead, confront the malevolent forces that lurked in the shadows, and bring an end to the reign of terror that had plagued her life for far too long. The castle may have been a place of darkness, but she would be the light that banished the shadows, no matter the cost. Back in the enchanted forest, the elven warriors drew closer to their destination. They could sense Lady Seraphina's presence growing stronger, her aura of determination and hope leading the way. They knew that they were drawing nearer to the human they had vowed to protect.

Finally, the elven warriors reached the border of the evil forest, where the twisted trees gave way to the enchanted realm. They could see Lady Seraphina in the distance, her figure a beacon of light in the darkness. With a surge of relief and determination, the elven warriors pushed forward, their hearts filled with the knowledge that they were on the brink of reuniting Lady Seraphina with her loyal companion, Sir Sterling.

As they drew closer, Lady Seraphina's form became more distinct. She staggered through the underbrush, her gown now tattered and dirtied from her arduous journey through the evil forest. Her face was etched with exhaustion, and her eyes were filled with a mixture of relief and disbelief at the sight of her rescuers.

The elven warriors wasted no time. With swift and graceful movements, they closed the distance between them and Lady Seraphina. As they approached, they spoke softly in their melodious elven tongue, words of comfort and reassurance that she was safe now.

Lady Seraphina weakened and overwhelmed by the emotional and physical toll of her ordeal, collapsed to her knees as the elven warriors reached her. Her body shook with a mixture of exhaustion and relief, and her hands trembled as they grasped at the grass beneath her. Tears welled in her eyes as she realized that her rescue was not a dream, but a reality.

The elven warriors knelt beside her, their expressions filled with empathy and kindness. One of them, a tall and graceful elven maiden with luminous silver hair and eyes like pools of liquid moonlight, gently placed a hand on

Lady Seraphina's shoulder. Her touch was soothing, a balm to the weary soul.

In hushed, melodic tones, the elven maiden introduced herself as Lirael, the leader of the rescue party. She spoke of their mission to find Lady Seraphina and bring her back to the enchanted forest, where she would be safe from the malevolent forces of the evil forest.

Another warrior, an elven archer with auburn hair and emerald-green eyes, introduced himself as Thalion. He spoke of the determination that had driven them to venture into the heart of darkness to rescue her and the unbreakable bond they shared with the enchanted forest.

The remaining warriors, both male and female, stepped forward to introduce themselves as well, each bearing a unique name and story. They were a diverse group, united by their unwavering dedication to their realm and their desire to protect those who sought refuge within it.

With their introductions completed, the elven warriors gently lifted Lady Seraphina from the ground, cradling her in their arms as if she were the most precious of treasures. She was too weak to protest, too overwhelmed by their kindness and the enormity of her rescue.

They carried her with the utmost care, their steps light and graceful as they made their way back to the enchanted forest. The journey was swift, and the oppressive darkness of the evil forest gave way to the vibrant and magical realm that lay beyond.

As they crossed the border into the enchanted forest, Lady Seraphina felt a palpable shift in the atmosphere. The air was filled with the sweet scent of blossoms, and the leaves of the trees seemed to shimmer with an inner light. It was a stark contrast to the malevolence of the evil forest, and Lady Seraphina couldn't help but feel a sense of wonder and awe.

The elven warriors continued to speak soothing words of reassurance to Lady Seraphina, telling her of the healing properties of their enchanted realm and the restorative powers it held. They assured her that she would find solace and safety within its boundaries.

As they began to reach the heart of the enchanted forest, Lady Seraphina's weariness began to lift, replaced by a newfound strength and hope. She gazed around in wonder at the ethereal beauty of her surroundings—the towering, ancient trees, the crystal-clear streams, and the delicate, luminescent creatures that flitted through the air.

Finally, they arrived at a secluded glade, where a small, enchanting cottage nestled among the trees. It was a place of serene beauty, a sanctuary within the enchanted realm. The elven warriors gently set Lady Seraphina down on a soft bed of moss and leaves, ensuring her comfort.

Lirael, the elven maiden who had been her first comforter, approached Lady Seraphina once more. She spoke of their desire to help her recover from her ordeal, to offer her the healing magic of the enchanted forest. Lady Seraphina nodded, gratitude welling up in her heart.

The elven warriors worked in unison, their gentle ministrations and the magic of their realm aiding Lady Seraphina's recovery. They cleansed her of the dirt and grime from the evil forest, soothing her aching body and providing nourishment to replenish her strength.

As Lady Seraphina rested, enveloped by the tranquility of the enchanted forest, she couldn't help but feel a profound sense of gratitude and wonder. She had escaped the clutches of the evil forest and found herself in the care of beings of unparalleled kindness and grace.

In the days that followed, Lady Seraphina would learn more about the enchanted realm, its secrets, and its ancient magic. She would come to understand the bond that connected the elven warriors to their forest and how they had dedicated their lives to preserving its beauty and protecting those who sought refuge within its boundaries.

But for now, as she lay in the heart of the enchanted forest, surrounded by the elven warriors who had rescued her, Lady Seraphina allowed herself to heal and begin the process of rebuilding her strength and her hope. She knew that her journey was far from over and that the challenges that lay ahead would require her newfound resilience and the support of her new friends.

With each passing day, she would feel her spirit rekindling, and the spark of determination within her grow stronger. She would be ready to face whatever trials awaited her, armed with the magic of the enchanted forest and the unwavering support of the elven warriors who had become her protectors and her allies.

The morning sunbathed Count Malachi's castle in a golden glow as its first rays pierced through the heavy curtains of his bedchamber. Count Malachi stirred; his sleep interrupted by a gnawing sense of unease. It was as if the very air had changed overnight, carrying a foreboding message that something was amiss.

With a sense of urgency, Count Malachi rose from his bed, his bare feet sinking into the lush, velvet carpet that furnished the chamber. He strode to the window, pulling back the heavy drapes to reveal the view of the courtyard below. His eyes narrowed as he scanned the scene, searching for any signs of Lady Seraphina.

But the courtyard was empty, save for a few servants going about their morning duties. Lady Seraphina was nowhere to be seen.

Fury coursed through Count Malachi like a torrential storm. His face contorted with anger as he realized the truth—Lady Seraphina had escaped. She had slipped through his grasp under the cover of night, leaving behind the confinement and torment he had subjected her to.

Count Malachi's hands clenched into fists, and he let out a guttural roar of rage that echoed through the chamber. It was a sound that sent shivers down the spines of those who heard it, a primal expression of his fury and frustration.

He stormed out of his bedchamber, descending the grand staircase of the castle with a thunderous presence that sent servants scurrying out of his way. The news of Lady Seraphina's escape had already reached the ears of his loyal guards, and they stood at attention as he approached.

"Find her!" Count Malachi barked, his voice a venomous hiss. "Find Lady Seraphina and bring her back to me! I want her alive, but I don't care in what condition!"

The guards exchanged nervous glances but dared not question their master's orders. They knew the consequences of failure all too well.

Count Malachi's rage burned like wildfire, consuming everything in its path. He was not accustomed to being thwarted, to having his will challenged. Lady Seraphina's escape was a slap in the face, a defiance that he could not tolerate.

With a wave of his hand, Count Malachi dispatched his guards to scour the castle and its surroundings in search of Lady Seraphina. He himself would join the hunt, his determination to recapture her driving him forward.

The day wore on, and the search for Lady Seraphina intensified. Count Malachi's anger only grew as the hours passed without any sign of her. He interrogated servants and questioned every soul within the castle, but it seemed that Lady Seraphina had vanished without a trace.

As the sun began to dip below the horizon, Count Malachi returned to his bedchamber, his exhaustion matched only by his simmering fury. He knew that Lady Seraphina could not have escaped without help, and he would make whoever had aided her pay dearly.

In a fit of rage, Count Malachi ordered the guards who had been on duty the previous night to be brought before him. He accused them of negligence and complicity in Lady Seraphina's escape, their pleas of innocence falling on deaf ears.

Without hesitation, Count Malachi condemned them all to death. He ordered that they be hung at dawn, their lives forfeit for their failure to prevent Lady Seraphina's flight.

The guards were dragged away to their grim fate, their faces etched with fear and despair. Count Malachi watched them go, a cruel smile playing at the corners of his lips. It was a small measure of satisfaction, a way to vent his pent-up anger and frustration. However, his satisfaction was short-lived, for the news of Lady Seraphina's treacherous actions weighed heavily on his mind.

Count Malachi had been suspicious of Lady Seraphina for some time now. She had always been a secretive woman, and her recent behavior had raised more than a few red flags. Rumors had reached his ears that she had been gathering information, maps, and artifacts, all without his knowledge or consent. It was clear that she was planning something, something that could jeopardize his power and authority.

Unable to contain his curiosity any longer, Count Malachi had ordered his most trusted advisors to search Lady Seraphina's chambers for any incriminating evidence. What they discovered sent shockwaves through his veins. Her chambers were like a treasure trove of forbidden knowledge. Hidden maps of the kingdom's defenses and vulnerabilities, research on ancient spells and rituals, and a collection of valuable artifacts that should never have been in her possession.

Count Malachi's palpable anger stemmed from Lady Seraphina's clandestine accumulation of knowledge that posed a grave threat to his power.

In a fit of anger, Count Malachi ordered for all of Lady Seraphina's belongings to be brought to the courtyard, including the resplendent jewels adorning her garments. With an unsettling desire in his eyes, he coveted those precious gems, yearning for them to be pulled off and forged into a weapon that would bear a grim testament to his dominance.

The courtyard became the stage for a macabre display of his wrath and obsession. Her clothes, once symbols of her grace and nobility, her personal possessions, and the jewels that had adorned her with elegance—all were ruthlessly thrown into the roaring flames.

As the inferno blazed, the flames danced and crackled, consuming everything in their path. The jewels, once a part of Lady Seraphina's regal attire, melted and fused together, taking on a sinister form as they transformed into the hilt of a menacing sword. Count Malachi's dark ambition was etched into every twist and curve of the blade.

This act was more than a mere act of destruction; it was a twisted ritual, a declaration of his intent to break Lady Seraphina's spirit and reclaim absolute power and control over both her life and the remnants of her existence. The fire raged on, casting an ominous glow over the courtyard, a reflection of Count Malachi's malevolent desire to bend all that he touched to his will.

Count Malachi, devoid of any capacity for sorrow, was the epitome of a villainous character. To him, Lady Seraphina had merely been a pawn in his power game. As the flames devoured the remnants of her belongings, Count Malachi stood there with a face twisted by a cocktail of emotions—anger, disappointment, and a sinister curiosity. Lady Seraphina had once occupied a role as a trusted confidant, perhaps even a semblance of friendship, or so he had believed. Now, however, all that remained in his perception was the looming figure of a traitor. His thoughts were consumed by questions about her motivations, driven to understand what had led her down this treacherous path. What were her ambitions in collecting such forbidden knowledge?

Count Malachi knew that he needed to act swiftly and decisively. The information Lady Seraphina had gathered was a potential threat to his rule, and he couldn't afford to underestimate it. He called for his council of advisors and generals, and together they devised a plan to strengthen the kingdom's defenses and counter any potential threats that might arise from the stolen knowledge.

As the days passed, Count Malachi's anger began to give way to a cold determination. He would not allow Lady Seraphina's treachery to undermine his rule. He would do whatever it took to protect his kingdom and maintain his grip on power. The events of that fateful day in the courtyard served as a stark reminder that even those closest to him could be harboring dangerous secrets, and he would be vigilant from that moment on. The burning of Lady Seraphina's belongings marked the beginning of a new chapter in his reign, one where he would leave no stone unturned in his quest for security and control.

But deep down, he knew that Lady Seraphina's escape was a far more significant blow than the punishment of a few guards. She had eluded him, slipping through his fingers like a wisp of smoke. And in her absence, Count Malachi could feel the castle's oppressive walls closing in on him, their silence mocking his impotence.

As the night descended and Count Malachi retired to his bed, his mind raced with thoughts of vengeance and retribution. He would not rest until Lady Seraphina was back in his clutches until he had broken her spirit and reclaimed the power and control, he so desperately craved.

But for now, he could do nothing but seethe in the darkness, his anger festering like a wound that refused to heal. Lady Seraphina had escaped, and in her absence, the castle seemed to whisper its secrets, secrets that threatened to unravel his carefully constructed world of dominance.

As the dark clouds of treachery and betrayal loomed over Count Malachi's thoughts, he found himself descending further into the abyss of malevolence. The discovery of Lady Seraphina's covert activities had not only awakened his wrath but also ignited a sinister curiosity. His thirst for power and control knew no bounds, and he believed that the answer to achieving absolute dominion lay in embracing the darkest forces imaginable.

Count Malachi had always been willing to do whatever it took to maintain his hold on power, but now he crossed a line he had never dared tread before. He began to engage in more sinister rituals, evoking the ancient and malevolent spirits that dwelled in the shadows. With each ritual, he bartered with the devil, offering pieces of his soul in exchange for unfathomable power.

As he delved deeper into the occult, a palpable transformation overcame him. His appearance altered; his once refined countenance now marred by a haunting malevolence. His eyes, once a piercing shade of cobalt blue, now gleamed with a malevolent, fiery crimson. His voice, once commanding and eloquent, grew harsh and guttural as if it were forged in the depths of hell itself.

Count Malachi's demeanor also changed, becoming more erratic and unhinged. He became obsessed with amassing forbidden knowledge, consulting ancient tomes filled with spells and curses that would make a sane person shudder. His advisors and generals watched in fear and awe as their leader transformed before their very eyes, from a shrewd and calculating ruler into a demonic figure driven by an insatiable lust for power.

With each new ritual, Count Malachi grew more demon-possessed, less human, and more volatile. His appetite for darkness was insatiable, and he reveled in the terror he instilled in those who served him. His laughter, once warm and hearty, now sent shivers down the spines of those who heard it, as it echoed with the madness that had consumed him.

Fear and despair gripped the hearts of his subjects as they witnessed the malevolent transformation. The very land seemed to wither and decay under his dark influence even further, as crops failed, rivers ran black, and the skies remained eternally shrouded in ominous clouds.

Yet, despite the horrors that unfolded, Count Malachi's grip on power seemed unassailable. He had become a force of nature, a living embodiment of the malevolent spirits he had consorted with. His demonic visage struck terror into the hearts of all who dared to oppose him, and his power continued to grow with each sinister pact he made.

In the end, Count Malachi's insatiable thirst for power led him down a path from which there was no return. He had sacrificed his humanity, his soul, and his kingdom in his relentless pursuit of dominion. The once calculated but cruel ruler had become a cautionary tale, a testament to the dangers of unchecked ambition and the seductive lure of the darkness that dwells in the hearts of men.

Count Malachi, driven by his insatiable hunger for power, recognized the profound significance of the sword adorned with the jewels of Lady Seraphina. It was not merely a weapon of great beauty, but a symbol of her connection to the enchanted realm and the embodiment of all that was good and pure. Knowing the sword's significance, he had devised a sinister plan to harness its potential for his own nefarious purposes.

With each dark pact made with malevolent spirits and the devil himself, Count Malachi channeled their otherworldly energies into the jeweled sword. The jewels, once radiant symbols of Lady Seraphina's grace, began to glow with a malevolent light. It was a transformation that mirrored the corruption of Count Malachi's soul, as the sword gradually became a source of control and influence over Lady Seraphina herself.

As the sword's power grew, so did Count Malachi's ability to manipulate and manipulate Lady Seraphina's emotions and decisions. The once harmonious connection between her and the enchanted realm became tainted, as the sword served as a conduit through which Count Malachi could exert his dark will. The very essence of Lady Seraphina's purity was under siege, and she would face the greatest challenge of her existence in confronting the corrupted power of her own sword.

Echoes of Betrayal

Lady Seraphina awoke in a secluded glade within the heart of the enchanted forest, where ancient trees stretched majestically towards the sky, their leaves aglow with ethereal light. It felt like a dream, but as her senses sharpened, the reality of her surroundings became clear. She had been separated from her beloved stallion, Sir Sterling, for what had felt like an eternity. The bond between them was unbreakable, forged through countless adventures and unwavering loyalty. The memory of the danger he had faced in the clutches of Count Malachi still haunted her.

The elven warriors who had guided her to this tranquil place had ensured her comfort. In this hidden glade, a small, enchanting cottage nestled among the ancient trees, offering a sanctuary within the enchanted realm. The soft bed of moss and leaves upon which she lay was a testament to the elves' care for her.

As Lady Seraphina adjusted to her surroundings, her thoughts turned to Sir Sterling. It had been a perilous journey to reunite with him, fraught with danger and suffering. The abuse she had endured at the hands of Count Malachi had left her weakened and bruised, her spirit a mere shell of its former self. She had fought to preserve her determination, her hope, her love for her faithful companion.

She began to rise from her makeshift bed, her mind heavy with thoughts of the recent past. All she desired was a leisurely walk to savor the fresh forest air and find solace amidst nature's embraces. Just as she was about to step outside, fully unaware of the surprise that awaited her, she heard a familiar sound—soft, rhythmic hoofbeats approaching the cottage.

With a mixture of disbelief and joy, Lady Seraphina hurried to the cottage's entrance. There, emerging from the surrounding foliage, was none other than Sir Sterling himself, her noble steed and dearest friend. Tears welled up in her eyes as she rushed forward to embrace him, her arms wrapping around his strong neck. Sir Sterling nuzzled her cheek affectionately, his eyes reflecting relief and happiness.

It was as though he understood the suffering she had endured in his absence. Their reunion was a moment of pure, unbridled joy, a testament to the unbreakable bond they shared. Lady Seraphina whispered words of gratitude and love to Sir Sterling, who responded with a soft nicker, as though reassuring her that he would always be there for her.

As she examined her beloved stallion, Lady Seraphina's fingers gently traced a healed but still visible scar on Sir Sterling's shoulder—a mark left by Count Malachi's cruelty. Yet, the elves, with their innate connection to nature's magic, had dressed the scar with delicate mother-of-pearl stones, creating a symbol of Sir Sterling's bravery and resilience.

Their reunion felt like a triumph, a moment of hope rekindled in the heart of the enchanted forest. The forest itself seemed to come alive with their happiness. Birds of every colour and size flitted through the trees, their songs forming a symphony of joyous welcome. Each bird contributed its unique tune, creating a mesmerizing harmony that echoed through the woods.

The air was filled with floating glittering orbs, manifestations of the magic that pulsed through the forest. These luminous spheres, like floating stars, danced around Lady Seraphina and Sir Sterling, casting a gentle, ever-changing light upon them. It was as if the very essence of the forest rejoiced in their reunion, celebrating the enduring love and bond between human and steed.

As the glittering orbs of enchantment swirled around them, Sir Sterling, with an air of purposeful grace, knelt down before Lady Seraphina. His obsidian eyes held a knowing glint, as if he had something extraordinary to share with her in the heart of this enchanted forest. Lady Seraphina, her heart filled with a sense of wonder and curiosity, couldn't resist the silent invitation.

With a graceful motion, she swung her leg over his back and settled herself comfortably on Sir Sterling, riding him bareback as they ventured deeper into the forest. Her fingers lightly brushed his silky mane, and she could feel the warmth of his powerful body beneath her. The bond between them was palpable, a connection that transcended words and transcended the trials they had faced.

Sir Sterling moved with an effortless grace through the ancient woods, his hooves barely making a sound as they tread upon the mossy ground. It was as though he knew the way, as though he was leading Lady Seraphina to a destination of great significance. The forest around them seemed to come alive, its secrets whispering through the leaves and branches.

As they continued their journey, Lady Seraphina couldn't help but marvel at the magical beauty of the forest. The air was filled with a soft, otherworldly light that bathed the surroundings in an ever-changing, iridescent glow. The leaves of the ancient trees above them shimmered like a thousand emeralds, and the fragrant scent of blooming flowers filled the air.

The forest's inhabitants, including mischievous fairies, graceful elves, and various other magical creatures, watched in awe as Lady Seraphina and Sir Sterling passed by. They recognized the significance of this union between woman and steed, an unbreakable bond that had endured the trials of darkness and adversity. The creatures of the forest joined in their silent celebration, adding their own enchantment to the journey.

Sir Sterling's strides became purposeful, leading Lady Seraphina deeper into the heart of the forest. The soft hoofbeats of their journey echoed like a soothing rhythm, a testament to their unbreakable connection. Lady Seraphina sensed that they were drawing closer to their destination, a place that held profound meaning.

As they rounded a bend in the forest path, a breathtaking sight came into view. Before them lay the tranquil pond, its waters shimmering with a captivating, ethereal radiance. Luminous flowers adorned its banks, casting a soft, otherworldly glow that bathed the area in a gentle, ever-changing light. It was the very same pond she had read about in her extensive research. This pond was renowned for its mystical and extraordinary properties, believed to possess the power to heal those who bathed in its waters. It was said to be a place of rejuvenation, where the natural magic of the forest manifested in a tangible way, offering solace and healing to those who sought it.

Lady Seraphina had long been intrigued by the legends surrounding this remarkable pond, but it was her extensive research that uncovered the most treasured secret of all—the source of its unparalleled healing powers. The ancient texts and folklore she had diligently studied spoke of a legendary artifact, a golden amulet, that lay somewhere at the bottom of the pond's crystalline waters.

This golden amulet held a story steeped in history and sacred significance. It was said to have once belonged to one of the most revered saints in the annals of time, a holy figure blessed by God with the extraordinary gift of healing. His touch could cure the gravest of illnesses, mend the most grievous of wounds, and bring solace to troubled hearts. It was by God's divine intervention through him that countless lives had been transformed and restored.

When the saint reached the end of his earthly journey, he left behind a legacy of compassion and healing. In his final moments, he imparted his wisdom to his students, instructing them to continue his work and share the gift of healing with the world. But he also had one last request, one that held profound significance for the generations to come.

With a voice filled with divine serenity, the saint instructed his students to take his golden amulet—a relic believed to be imbued with the very essence of God's grace—and cast it into a sacred pond hidden deep within the enchanted forest. He explained that this act would be a testament to his unwavering faith and devotion to the Creator, a way to ensure that the gift of healing would continue to bless mankind and all the creatures of the world.

The students carried out their master's final wishes with solemn reverence. They journeyed to the heart of the enchanted forest, guided by ancient maps and the whispers of the forest itself. After much searching, they discovered the hidden pond, its waters shimmering with an otherworldly light. It was here that they fulfilled the saint's directive, releasing the golden amulet into the depths of the pond.

As the amulet descended into the waters, it seemed to be enveloped by the very essence of the pond—the same essence that bestowed upon it the power of healing. The waters embraced the amulet, and it became an integral part of the pond's magic, a source of divine energy that would shape its destiny for centuries to come.

Over time, the legends surrounding the pond and its golden amulet became intertwined, a testament to the deep spiritual connection between the enchanted forest and the healing gift of God bestowed on the saint. The pond's reputation as a place of miraculous healing grew, drawing people from far and wide who sought solace, restoration, and transformation in its sacred waters. The mystical creatures were the perfect guardians as they had no desire for power and naturally were incredibly connected to nature.

Lady Seraphina's research unveiled the sacred history of the pond and the profound role the golden amulet played in its healing properties. The stories were handed down through generations, and her meticulous exploration of ancient manuscripts had brought her to this moment—a moment of profound revelation.

As she approached the pond with Sir Sterling he could sense she wanted to dismount, so he gently knelt down for Lady Seraphina to gently side off. Lady Seraphina couldn't help but feel a sense of awe and reverence. The air was filled with an undeniable sense of tranquility, a testament to the extraordinary properties of the place. The waters of the pond glistened with an ethereal light, casting a serene and inviting aura.

She had learned that the pond's healing powers were believed to be linked to the ancient magic of the forest itself as well. The waters were said to be infused with the essence of the enchanted realm. It was this unique combination of magical energies that made the pond a place of profound healing.

Lady Seraphina recalled the detailed descriptions in her research. It was said that when one immersed themselves in the pond's waters, a remarkable transformation occurred. Aches and pains would melt away, wounds would mend, and weariness would be replaced by newfound vitality. But the healing did not stop at the physical level; it extended to the depths of one's soul, offering solace and emotional restoration.

The pond's waters were believed to be imbued with an ancient wisdom that could discern the ailments of those who sought its healing embrace. It was said that the waters had the ability to draw out toxins, both physical and emotional, and replace them with a sense of well-being and renewal. People would emerge from the pond feeling rejuvenated as if a heavy burden had been lifted from their shoulders.

Lady Seraphina, with a deep sense of curiosity and longing, approached the pond's edge. She could feel the magic in the air, a tangible presence that whispered promises of healing and renewal. She dipped her fingers into the cool, luminescent waters, and a soothing sensation washed over her. It was as if the pond itself was extending a gentle invitation, urging her to experience its miraculous powers.

She looked to Sir Sterling, her loyal companion who had stood by her side through thick and thin. His eyes held a sense of understanding, as if he too recognized the significance of this moment. With a deep breath, Lady Seraphina made her decision. She disrobed, letting the forest's natural beauty surround her, and stepped into the pond.

The moment her body was submerged, Lady Seraphina felt a wave of warmth and comfort wash over her. The waters seemed to embrace her, their touch gentle and soothing. Aches and pains that had plagued her from her trials at the hands of Count Malachi began to dissipate, leaving behind a sense of relief she had longed for.

But it wasn't just physical ailments that were addressed; the pond's healing powers delved into the depths of her soul. Lady Seraphina's heart, burdened by the scars of her past and the emotional toll of her ordeal, began to mend. The weight of despair was replaced with a profound sense of hope and inner peace.

As she remained in the pond, Lady Seraphina closed her eyes and let the healing energies envelop her entirely. She could feel the ancient wisdom of the forest working its magic, drawing out the darkness that had clung to her and filling the void with a renewed sense of vitality and purpose.

Time seemed to lose its meaning as Lady Seraphina bathed in the pond's waters. The healing process was a gradual one, a gentle transformation of body and soul. With each passing moment, she felt lighter, stronger, and more whole than she had in a long time.

After several weeks of bathing in the pond, Lady Seraphina underwent a profound transformation. Her physical ailments had gradually vanished, and the bruises and scars that once marred her body were now mere traces of her past struggles. But the changes extended beyond the physical; her spirit had been revitalized, and she felt as though she had been reborn. Emerging from the waters each time, she carried with her a newfound sense of strength and purpose, each bath deepening her connection to the pond's healing magic.

Sir Sterling, who had watched over her during her times in the pond, greeted her with a gentle nicker as if acknowledging the transformation that had taken place. Together, they stood by the luminous pond, surrounded by the enchanting beauty of the forest, and knew that they had found a sanctuary—

a place where healing and renewal were not just legends, but a tangible reality.

It was as if this place held a message, a testament to their enduring bond and the magic that surrounded them. The glittering orbs of enchantment that had accompanied them throughout their journey now danced above the pond, reflecting in its luminous waters.

Lady Seraphina and Sir Sterling stood together; their souls intertwined with the enchanting beauty of their newfound sanctuary. Here, in the heart of the enchanted forest, they felt a profound sense of peace and belonging. The trials and hardships they had endured had brought them to this moment, reinforcing the unbreakable bond between human and steed.

The soft melodies of the forest's creatures filled the air, a harmonious celebration of their reunion. The glittering orbs continued to swirl around them, their radiance reflecting in the luminous pond's waters. These manifestations of magic pulsed with the very essence of the forest, rejoicing in the enduring love and connection that Lady Seraphina and Sir Sterling shared.

As Lady Seraphina gazed at the luminous flowers and listened to the enchanting melodies of the forest, she knew that she had found a sanctuary—a place where their bond would flourish and where they would heal from the scars of their past. In this enchanted forest, amidst the magic and wonder that surrounded them, they were ready to face the challenges ahead, united in their unwavering love and the enchantment of their newfound home.

As Lady Seraphina and Sir Sterling made their way back to the cottage nestled deep within the enchanted forest, a sense of tranquility and renewal accompanied them. The luminous flowers and the enchanting melodies of the forest whispered promises of a future filled with magic and wonder. It was a sanctuary where their bond would flourish, and where they would find solace from the scars of their past. With hearts filled with newfound hope, they were ready to face the challenges that lay ahead, united in their unwavering love and the enchantment of their newfound home.

Upon their return to the cottage, Lady Seraphina was greeted by the elven warriors who had guided her to the enchanted forest. Their ethereal beauty and grace were a testament to their connection with the enchanted realm. Among them, a distinguished figure stood tall—a warrior with an aura of wisdom and authority. His name was General Elowen, a revered leader among the elves.

General Elowen approached Lady Seraphina with a nod of respect and greeted her with a warm smile. His eyes, like sapphire pools, held a depth of knowledge that spoke of centuries spent in the heart of the enchanted forest. His voice was gentle yet carried the weight of authority as he addressed her.

"Lady Seraphina," General Elowen began, "we are grateful that you have found solace in the healing waters of our sacred pond. However, there are matters of great importance that we must discuss. If you would be willing, we request your presence in the Elven Kingdom hidden behind the waterfall within this enchanted forest."

Lady Seraphina nodded in understanding. She had heard whispers of the Elven Kingdom and its mystical beauty during her research, but the opportunity to visit it was a privilege she had never imagined. With a sense of curiosity and anticipation, she agreed to accompany General Elowen and the elven warriors to their hidden realm.

Together, they embarked on the journey to the Elven Kingdom, with Lady Seraphina riding Sir Sterling and the elven warriors guiding the way. The path led deeper into the heart of the enchanted forest, where the trees seemed to part to reveal a magnificent sight—the waterfall.

The waterfall was unlike any Lady Seraphina had ever seen. It was a majestic cascade of crystalline water, its surface shimmering with the same ethereal light that graced the luminous pond. The sound of the rushing water was both soothing and invigorating, a harmonious symphony that echoed through the forest.

As they drew closer to the waterfall, Lady Seraphina realized that it concealed a hidden passage behind its veil of water and mist. A grotto, shrouded in the gentle roar of the falls, beckoned them forward. General Elowen, with a graceful gesture, indicated for Lady Seraphina and Sir Sterling to follow him through the grotto.

They entered the grotto, and the sensation of water droplets brushing against their skin added to the enchantment of the moment. Inside, the grotto was illuminated by bioluminescent crystals embedded in the walls, casting a soft, iridescent glow that danced across the rocky surfaces.

The journey through the grotto felt like a passage through time and space, a transition from the mundane world into one of mystical beauty. The sounds of the waterfall gradually faded, replaced by a sense of stillness and wonder. Lady Seraphina's heart quickened as they emerged from the grotto and into the heart of the Elven Kingdom.

The sight that greeted them was beyond imagination. The Elven Kingdom was a realm of breathtaking beauty, a harmonious blend of nature's wonders and elven craftsmanship. Towering trees with leaves of gold and silver formed natural canopies while cascading vines adorned with colourful blossoms hung like living tapestries.

Elven dwellings, crafted from the living wood of the forest, seemed to meld seamlessly with their surroundings. They were intricately furnished with intricate carvings and decorated with natural gems that shimmered in the soft light. Bridges woven from delicate vines spanned crystal-clear streams, leading to platforms where elves engaged in various activities.

The elves themselves were a sight to behold. Tall and graceful, with features that reflected the beauty of their forest home, they moved with an ethereal elegance that spoke of their deep connection to nature. Their attire was woven from leaves, flowers, and the silken threads of enchanted spiders, creating garments that seemed to shift and change with the light.

General Elowen led Lady Seraphina and Sir Sterling through the heart of the Elven Kingdom, explaining the history and significance of their hidden realm. The elves, he explained, were guardians of the enchanted forest, charged with protecting its magic and ensuring the balance between the natural world and the mystical realm.

As they walked, Lady Seraphina marveled at the harmony of the Elven Kingdom. The air was filled with the sweet fragrance of blooming flowers, and the soft melodies of the forest creatures created a symphony of enchantment. She could sense the presence of ancient spirits and mystical beings, all living in harmony within this hidden paradise.

General Elowen finally led Lady Seraphina to a magnificent palace at the heart of the Elven Kingdom. Its towering spires reached for the sky, and its walls were adorned with living vines that seemed to pulse with energy. This palace was where the elven council gathered, and it was here that Lady Seraphina would join them to discuss the way forward.

As they entered the palace, Lady Seraphina couldn't help but feel a profound sense of privilege and wonder. She had stepped into a world of magic and beauty that transcended the ordinary, a world where the bond between humans and the mystical wonders of nature was celebrated and revered.

In the presence of the elven council, Lady Seraphina was welcomed with grace and respect. The elves had recognized the significance of her journey and her connection to the enchanted forest. General Elowen, as their spokesperson, addressed her once more.

"Lady Seraphina, we are honoured by your presence in our realm," General Elowen said. "The enchanted forest has chosen you, and your bond with Sir Sterling is a testament to the enduring magic of this place. We have much to discuss, for the balance of our world and the challenges that lie ahead require our collective wisdom."

Amidst the serene beauty of the Elven Kingdom, Lady Seraphina took her place among the elven council, ready to engage in discussions that would shape the path forward. She felt a profound sense of purpose and anticipation as she sat among the wise and ethereal beings who had welcomed her into their realm. In the heart of the enchanted forest, surrounded by its unparalleled beauty and wonder, she realized that she had become an integral part of a profound and timeless story—a story where the bonds between humans, nature, and magic were celebrated, and where the destiny of the enchanted realm was intricately woven with her own.

The council, with General Elowen at its helm, gathered around a majestic stone table adorned with symbols of nature and magic. Their presence exuded a sense of ancient wisdom and reverence for the natural world. General Elowen began to speak, his voice carrying the weight of the important matters to be discussed.

"Lady Seraphina," General Elowen began, "we have brought you here not only to welcome you into our realm but also to share with you a matter of grave concern that affects both our world and yours. Count Malachi, the one who held you captive, has crossed a threshold that should never have been breached."

Lady Seraphina listened intently, her heart sinking as she anticipated the dire news.

General Elowen continued, "Count Malachi has delved deeper into dark and forbidden forces, shifting from his human state to something far more malevolent and demonic. This transformation has granted him unprecedented power, and it threatens not only mankind but the very heart of the enchanted forest itself."

Lady Seraphina's brow furrowed with worry. The implications of Count Malachi's transformation were deeply troubling.

"The dark and malevolent forces he now commands are in direct opposition to the magic that sustains our enchanted forest," General Elowen explained.

"Our protective spells and natural enchantments are no match for his newfound power. The balance that has existed for centuries is in jeopardy."

A heavy silence settled over the council chamber as the gravity of the situation weighed on everyone present.

General Elowen continued, "We have sought to restore the balance and protect both our realms. To do so, we must call upon the Crusade Army, a force blessed by the divine power of God. Their strength and righteousness are needed to combat the darkness that Count Malachi has unleashed."

Lady Seraphina understood the magnitude of the decision. The Crusade Army was a formidable force, known for its unwavering commitment to righteousness and the protection of innocent lives. Their involvement signified the gravity of the situation.

As the council discussed the details of their plan and the alliance they sought with the Crusade Army, Lady Seraphina couldn't help but reflect on her own journey. She had endured captivity, betrayal, and suffering at the hands of Count Malachi. Now, she found herself at the center of a battle between light and darkness, with the fate of two worlds hanging in the balance.

In the midst of their deliberations, General Elowen shared another troubling revelation. The elves, in their efforts to aid Lady Seraphina, had reached out to one of the highborn families in her kingdom, the Veridales who lived nearest to the North edge of the enchanted forest. They were close family friends of Lady Seraphina's family, and their support would have been invaluable in her rescue and protection.

General Elowen explained that the elves had informed the Veridales of Lady Seraphina's escape from Count Malachi's realm and offered to return her to them so they may aid in her reuniting with her family. However, the response they received was far from what they had expected. The Veridales, driven by self-preservation and a desire to protect their own interests, had shown no compassion or concern for Lady Seraphina's well-being.

In a heart-wrenching twist, the Veridales had written a response to the elves, expressing their intent to abandon Lady Seraphina to her fate. They saw her as nothing more than a sacrificial offering to Count Malachi, a means to ensure their own safety and the continued protection of their highborn status. In a cruel and selfish act, they had not only refused to help but had also burnt the letter from the elves to conceal their treacherous decision.

Lady Seraphina's heart ached at the betrayal of the Veridales, a family she had considered close and trusted. The realization that they had never even informed her own family of her whereabouts added another layer of pain to her already burdened heart.

As she absorbed this revelation, Lady Seraphina couldn't help but feel a deep sense of isolation and betrayal. The world she had known had crumbled around her, and the only allies she had were the elves and the divine power of the Crusade Army if they accepted the invitation to fight for this cause.

Amidst the council's discussions and the revelation of the Veridales' betrayal, Lady Seraphina resolved to do everything in her power to stand against the darkness that Count Malachi had become. She knew that the fate of both her world and the enchanted forest hung in the balance, and she would not rest until justice was served, and the balance was restored. In the heart of the Elven Kingdom, surrounded by the beauty and wonder of the enchanted forest, Lady Seraphina had found her purpose—a purpose intertwined with the destiny of two realms and the enduring bonds between humans, nature, and magic.

After the council meeting concluded, it was customary for the elves to partake in a grand feast, a tradition that signified goodwill and the absence of ill intent following important discussions and decisions. General Elowen, leading Lady Seraphina, guided her through the majestic palace of the Elven Kingdom to a large balcony that overlooked their enchanting realm.

The balcony was a breathtaking sight to behold. It extended outward from the palace, providing an unobstructed view of the Elven Kingdom below.

Trees with leaves of gold and silver swayed in the gentle breeze, and bioluminescent flowers cast a soft, ever-changing glow upon the landscape. Crystal-clear streams meandered through the kingdom, their waters reflecting the ethereal light of the surroundings.

The dining hall on the balcony was adorned with intricate carvings and decorations that celebrated the natural beauty of the enchanted forest. A long, elegant table was set with fine elven craftsmanship—a feast fit for both royalty and honoured guests. Lady Seraphina's eyes widened in wonder as she beheld the magnificent spread.

The feast was a symphony of colours and flavours, a testament to the elves' connection to the natural world. Plates were filled with dishes crafted from the bounties of the forest—exquisite fruits, succulent herbs, and vegetables that seemed to shimmer with their own inner light. Crystal goblets brimmed with an assortment of wines, each one a unique creation from the enchanted vines that adorned the kingdom.

As Lady Seraphina took her seat at the table, she was filled with a sense of gratitude for the elves' hospitality and kindness. It was a stark contrast to the treachery she had experienced at the hands of Count Malachi and the indifference of her own highborn family friends, the Veridales.

Throughout the feast, the council members engaged Lady Seraphina in conversation, sharing stories of their realm, their connection to the enchanted forest, and the ancient traditions that had been upheld for centuries. Lady Seraphina listened with rapt attention, eager to learn more about the magical world she had become a part of.

As the feast continued, General Elowen approached Lady Seraphina with a warm smile, holding a delicate, shimmering garment in his hands. The fabric was unlike anything Lady Seraphina had ever seen, light as a feather, yet strong and resilient, it changed colour with the shifting light like mother of pearl.

"Lady Seraphina," General Elowen said, "we have prepared a gift for you—a wardrobe crafted with the finest elven materials. It is not only breathtakingly beautiful but also designed to aid in your movements and provide protection. This garment has been created for your Lady statue, allowing you to partake in combat should the need arise."

Lady Seraphina's eyes sparkled with astonishment and gratitude as she accepted the gift. She marveled at the craftsmanship of the elven wardrobe, its ethereal beauty a testament to the artistry of the elves. She thanked General Elowen and the council for their generosity, feeling a deep sense of appreciation for their unwavering support.

The elven garment gifted to Lady Seraphina was a masterpiece of both elegance and functionality, designed to seamlessly blend the grace of a lady with the practicality required for battle. Crafted with the finest elven materials and enchanted with magic, it was a true work of art.

The fabric of the garment was a marvel. It felt incredibly soft and light to the touch, like the finest silk, yet it possessed a remarkable durability that made it perfect for combat. Woven with threads that seemed to shimmer with their own inner light, the fabric had an ethereal quality, reflecting the changing colours of the surrounding environment. It would adapt to the lighting conditions, ensuring Lady Seraphina always appeared radiant and elegant.

The gown had a flattering silhouette that accentuated Lady Seraphina's natural grace. It featured a high neckline adorned with delicate lace and intricate embroidery, creating a regal and ladylike appearance. The bodice was fitted to her form, offering both comfort and flexibility, while the long, flowing skirts allowed for freedom of movement. The gown was a harmonious blend of style and functionality as the gown was split in the middle from the waist, seamlessly transitioning into matching trousers. This innovative split allowed for even greater freedom of movement, making it a harmonious fusion of style and practicality.

For protection, the elven garment was equipped with hidden layers of enchanted padding, strategically placed to safeguard Lady Seraphina from harm. These protective layers were discreetly integrated into the design, ensuring that the gown remained elegant and unobtrusive.

The sleeves of the gown were designed to be easily rolled up, revealing forearm protectors that could be quickly fastened into place during combat. The forearm protectors were made from a combination of lightweight but durable materials that offered both defense and flexibility.

At Lady Seraphina's waist, a sash of elven design served as both a decorative element and a functional utility. It could be tightened to secure any weapons or tools she might need during battle. The sash was adorned with elven symbols, each imbued with protective magic to ward off harm.

To complete the ensemble, Lady Seraphina was provided with a pair of supple, knee-high boots made from the same enchanted material as the gown. These boots were designed for agility and comfort, allowing her to move swiftly and silently through various terrains.

The elven garment was not only a symbol of her alliance with the elves but also a testament to their craftsmanship and their understanding of both beauty and practicality. With this attire, Lady Seraphina was prepared to face the challenges that lay ahead, whether they be in the realm of politics or on the battlefield. It was a reminder that she was a lady of strength and grace, ready to protect and defend her newfound home and the enchanting forest that had welcomed her with open arms.

As the feast continued, Lady Seraphina's thoughts turned to the discussion of her training. She had long been a scholar, with knowledge of ancient texts and a deep appreciation for history and lore. However, the world she now found herself in required more than just knowledge; it demanded strength and skill in the face of darkness.

Lady Seraphina approached General Elowen and the council with a request. "I wish to learn the ways of combat," she said, her voice resolute. "I want to be prepared to face the darkness that threatens our realms. Will you teach me?"

The council members exchanged knowing glances and nodded in agreement. General Elowen spoke on behalf of the council, "Lady Seraphina, your determination and bravery are evident. We shall provide you with training in the use of the sword and bow and arrow. It is a task that will require dedication and discipline, but we have faith in your abilities."

Lady Seraphina accepted their offer with gratitude and a sense of purpose. She knew that her journey had led her to this moment, where she would not only seek justice for herself but also play a crucial role in protecting the enchanted forest and her own world from the darkness that threatened them.

Lady Seraphina felt a profound sense of belonging and hope. Surrounded by the beauty of the Elven Kingdom, the enchantment of the forest, and the support of her new allies, she was ready to embrace her destiny—a destiny intertwined with the bonds between humans, nature, and magic, and a destiny that would shape the future of three realms.

As the feast continued, Lady Seraphina turned to General Elowen with a gleam of determination in her eyes. "General," she began, her voice steady yet brimming with urgency, "We must discuss how we will approach the Crusade army, how we will extend our hand to them and convince them to stand with us in our battle against Count Malachi. Do you have a plan in mind?"

General Elowen met Lady Seraphina's gaze with a resolute expression. "My Lady," he replied, his voice carrying a tone of confidence, "We should send a messenger to the Crusade army's leader, bearing a letter that details the dire threat Count Malachi poses not only to our realm but to the very ideals the Crusade army upholds. With our plea for unity and justice, I am confident that they will be swayed to join our fight."

Seraphina's Training

The training with the elves was a rigorous process that pushed Lady Seraphina to her limits. The first aspect of her training focused on the use of the sword, a weapon that required both skill and finesse. The elves gifted her a sword made of a special type of steel known as "Luminaforge Steel." This remarkable material was not only exceptionally strong but also imbued with the ability to catch and refract light, giving the blade an ethereal shimmer.

Luminaforge Steel was a rare and extraordinary material forged within the heart of the enchanted forest, a place where the boundaries between the natural world and the mystical realm were blurred. Its origins were deeply intertwined with the magic that permeated the forest, and it was this unique blend of natural and supernatural elements that made it exceptionally strong and extraordinary.

The source of Luminaforge Steel could be traced to a hidden forge known only to the most skilled elven blacksmiths and artisans. Located in a secluded glade, this forge was a sacred place, protected by powerful enchantments and guarded by ancient spirits. It was said that the forge's existence dated back to the earliest days of the enchanted forest, forged by the first elves who sought to harness the magical energies of their realm.

What made Luminaforge Steel truly exceptional was the blend of elemental forces used in its creation. The elven blacksmiths would gather rare ores and minerals from the depths of the forest, each imbued with its own unique magical properties. These materials included moonstone dust, which enhanced the blade's connection to the user's intuition; sapphire shards, known for their ability to instill mental clarity and focus; and amethyst fragments, which promoted spiritual balance and inner strength.

To create Luminaforge Steel, these magical materials were carefully combined with the finest steel obtained from the enchanted forest's ancient trees. The blacksmiths would heat the steel over mystical flames that danced with the colours of the aurora borealis, infusing it with the latent magic of the forest. As the steel absorbed the magical energies, it would undergo a transformation, becoming both stronger and more resonant with the enchantment of the forest.

The final step in the forging process involved a secret ritual performed by the elven blacksmiths. This ritual was a closely guarded tradition, handed down through generations, and it involved channeling the energies of the enchanted forest itself. With the guidance of the forest's spirits, the blacksmiths would imbue the steel with the essence of the natural world, creating a blade that was in perfect harmony with its surroundings.

The result of this intricate process was Luminaforge Steel—a material that not only possessed extraordinary strength but also a unique connection to the mystical energies of the enchanted forest. Its name, "Luminaforge," reflected its ability to catch and refract light, giving the blade an ethereal shimmer. It was said that when wielded under the light of the forest's bioluminescent flora, the blade would appear to dance with its own inner radiance.

Beyond its physical attributes, Luminaforge Steel held a deeper significance for the elves. It was a symbol of their bond with the enchanted forest, a testament to their understanding of the natural world's magic, and a representation of their commitment to protect their realm from darkness. The elves believed that the blade's resonance with the forest's energies would guide the hand of its wielder, ensuring that it was used in the service of light and justice.

It was with great reverence that the elves gifted Lady Seraphina a sword made of Luminaforge Steel, recognizing her as a champion of their cause and a defender of the enchanted forest. The sword's presence in her hands served as a powerful reminder of the intertwined destinies of humans, nature, and magic, and the vital role she would play in their shared future. With this sword in her possession, Lady Seraphina was prepared to face the darkness that loomed on the horizon, armed with a blade forged from the very heart of the enchanted forest.

The sword's hilt, a masterpiece of craftsmanship, bore an intricate design that concealed its mystic nature. It was intricately decorated with precious stones, each chosen with meticulous care for its unique magical properties. Moonstones graced the pommel, their ethereal glow enhancing Lady Seraphina's intuition and empathy, guiding her decisions in the heat of battle. Sapphires, set into the guard, bestowed upon her mental clarity and unwavering focus, ensuring her mind remained sharp even amidst chaos. However, it was the amethyst that held a secret of its own. Initially, the large amethyst decorating the hilt gleamed with its usual regal purple hue, promoting spiritual balance and inner strength. But when Lady Seraphina's spirit wavered and darkness clouded her intent, the amethyst would transform, its once vibrant shade fading to an ominous and foreboding black.

It was customary among the elves for a sword to bear a name, a reflection of the bond between the wielder and their weapon. The council allowed Lady Seraphina the honour of naming her sword. After much contemplation, she chose the name "Astrafyre," a combination of "Astra," meaning star, and "Fyre," representing the inner fire of determination and purpose. The name embodied her journey and her resolve to bring light to the darkness.

Training with the sword began under the guidance of elven masters who were both patient and demanding. Lady Seraphina found herself struggling at first, her movements clumsy and uncoordinated. It was a humbling experience, and she faced frustration at her initial failures.

During one of their training sessions, General Elowen, with his perceptive wisdom, noticed Lady Seraphina's struggles. He observed her wielding her sword with intensity fueled by anger and resentment. Approaching her with a gentle yet firm tone, he shared his insights, "Lady Seraphina, I sense your anger, and it is a natural response to the injustices you've endured. But remember, anger can be a powerful force, yet it can also cloud your judgment and darken your thoughts. Look at the amethyst, how it has changed colour."

Seraphina listened intently as General Elowen continued, "You have every right to feel anger, but you also have the power to decide how you will channel it. Instead of letting it consume you, use it as fuel, as determination. Let it disperse through your body with each swing of your blade, freeing your mind to focus on the task at hand."

General Elowen's wisdom didn't end there, he imparted invaluable wisdom to Lady Seraphina. He stressed the sword's significance as more than just a weapon—it was a reflection of her inner self, a mirror to her intentions. "Moreover, Lady Seraphina," he had solemnly added, "remember that the sword you wield is more than just a weapon. It is a reflection of your inner self. If it senses that you are fighting from a place of darkness, it may resist your control and fight against you. To harness its full power, you must align your spirit with the light of your purpose. It is the essence of the sword to be an instrument of justice, and it will serve you faithfully if you wield it with a heart focused on righteousness." These words echoed in her mind as she understood the true significance of the amethyst's transformation—an unmistakable warning that her inner darkness threatened to corrupt the very weapon meant to uphold justice.

General Elowen continued his tutelage, emphasizing the significance of the Luminaforge Steel, the precious material from which Seraphina's sword was crafted. "You must understand, Lady Seraphina, that the Elves have safeguarded the use of Luminaforge Steel for generations. It is not merely a matter of its physical properties but also a testament to our commitment to the cause of light and justice. The steel itself resists being turned into a weapon of darkness. It is a symbol of purity and a force that counters malevolence. The Elves have entrusted you with this blade because they believe in your dedication to the light and your resolve to wield it for a just cause. Remember, it is not just your skill with the sword, but the purity of your heart that will make you a formidable champion against Count Malachi's darkness."

Lady Seraphina absorbed the general's words, recognizing the depth of his guidance not only in honing her physical skills but in forging the harmony between her inner self and the weapon that would be instrumental in their battle against Count Malachi's tyranny.

With those words, Lady Seraphina decided to take the general's advice to heart. She adjusted her mindset, channeling her anger differently. As she practiced, the anger that had once been a hindrance began to transform into a driving force behind her every move. It fueled her determination and resolve to master the art of the sword and the amethyst return to purple.

Day by day, she improved, her movements becoming more fluid and precise. The elves continued to instruct her, their guidance and support invaluable in her progress. Lady Seraphina trained tirelessly, dedicating herself to the path of the warrior.

Once she had achieved a certain level of proficiency with the sword, the training moved on to archery. She learned to wield the bow and arrow with skill and precision, honing her accuracy and agility. Initially, her aim was far from true, and her arrows often missed their marks.

The Elven bow and arrows were works of ethereal craftsmanship, designed to blend seamlessly with the enchanting beauty of the Elven Kingdom. The bow itself was a masterpiece of slender elegance, carved from the sacred wood of the ancient Lumina Trees. Its surface bore intricate engravings that seemed to dance with eldritch light, reflecting the innate magic of the forest. The string, made from the finest strands of moonlit spider silk, sang with a haunting melody when drawn. But there was a secret woven into the heart of the bow as well. A small amethyst gem, concealed within the bow's core, mirrored the one on Lady Seraphina's sword.

The arrows were no less remarkable. Each shaft was fashioned from the same Lumina Wood, adorned with delicate etchings that glowed softly in the moonlight. The arrowheads, forged from Luminaforge Steel, gleamed with an otherworldly radiance, granting them unparalleled piercing power. As Seraphina learned to wield these mystical tools, she discovered their harmonious connection with her spirit, as though the bow and arrows themselves were alive and attuned to her quest for justice.

Sir Sterling, her stalwart companion, seemed to sense Lady Seraphina's moments of frustration during her archery training. Whenever she missed her marks with a bow and arrow, he would let out soft, reassuring nays that carried a playful, almost whimsical tone. It was as though he understood that laughter, even in the face of setbacks, could be a beacon of light in the darkness. His gentle encouragement helped Lady Seraphina find solace in those moments, reminding her not to be too hard on herself and to embrace the joy that could be found even in the challenges of her training. It was a bond of understanding and support that deepened their connection, forging an unbreakable link between warrior and steed.

The elves instructed her in the art of archery, teaching her to feel the bow as an extension of herself and to let her intuition guide her aim. She practiced relentlessly, first on foot and later from the back of Sir Sterling, who had been equipped with elven-made armour for protection. As her proficiency with the bow grew, Seraphina soon discovered another mystical aspect of these elven-crafted weapons. Just as with the Luminaforge Steel sword, the arrows seemed to possess a sentient quality. If her intentions were not aligned with the light, if her heart wavered towards darkness, the arrows would purposefully miss their mark and the amethyst would turn black, a subtle yet powerful reminder of the Elves' dedication to keeping their weapons only in the hands of those who fought for righteousness. It was a lesson in both skill and character that Seraphina embraced with unwavering determination.

Sir Sterling's armour was a marvel in itself. Crafted from enchanted materials, it was lightweight yet impenetrable, providing him with the necessary protection without impeding his agility. The armour bore intricate elven designs and symbols, further enhancing the enchantment that surrounded the enchanted forest.

Lady Seraphina's horse armour was equally impressive. It was adorned with luminous stones that emitted a soft, ambient light, casting a gentle glow around them as they moved through the forest. The armour was designed to safeguard Sir Sterling in the event of battle, ensuring that he remained a stalwart companion on the battlefield.

As Lady Seraphina continued her training, she experienced moments of frustration and doubt. The journey from scholar to warrior was fraught with challenges, but she was determined to persevere. The memory of her captivity and the darkness she had witnessed fueled her resolve.

She remembered the words of General Elowen and how she had chosen to channel her anger differently. It became her driving force, the fire that burned within her as she practiced tirelessly. With each day that passed, she grew stronger and more skillful, her movements becoming fluid and graceful.

As her training progressed, Lady Seraphina began to embody the qualities of a true warrior—strength, discipline, and unwavering resolve. She transformed into a skilled and formidable force, ready to face the darkness that threatened both her world and the enchanted forest.

In the heart of the Elven Kingdom, amidst the magic and wonder that surrounded her, Lady Seraphina's journey continued. She had embarked on a path of transformation, one that would see her evolve from a scholar into a warrior, a beacon of light against the encroaching darkness.

After each grueling day of training with the elves, Lady Seraphina's body would ache from head to toe. Her muscles, unaccustomed to the rigorous physical demands of combat training, throbbed with the effort she had exerted. Blisters formed on her hands from the repeated grips on her sword and bow, a testament to her relentless dedication to mastering the skills required of a warrior.

But as the sun dipped below the horizon, signaling the end of another day's training, Lady Seraphina and Sir Sterling would embark on a ritual of healing and recovery. They would make their way to the secluded and enchanted pond just outside the Elven Kingdom, to alleviate physical and emotional ailments.

The pond's waters shimmered with an otherworldly light, casting a serene and inviting aura. Luminous flowers bloomed on its banks, casting a soft, ever-changing glow that bathed the area in a gentle, ethereal light. It was a place where the magic of the forest and the mystical properties of the water converged, creating a sanctuary for those in need of restoration.

Lady Seraphina and Sir Sterling would approach the pond, the water's surface cool and inviting against their weary bodies. With great care, Lady Seraphina would disrobe and wade into the soothing waters, her muscles relaxing as the enchantment of the pond worked its magic. Sir Sterling, ever watchful and protective, would stand nearby, occasionally dipping his own hooves into the water as if to share in the rejuvenation.

As Lady Seraphina bathed in the magical pond, she could feel the aches and pains of the day gradually melt away. The water seemed to possess an innate ability to soothe her sore muscles and heal her blisters. It was as if the pond's waters held the wisdom of centuries, knowing exactly how to mend the wear and tear of a warrior's body.

But the healing didn't stop at the physical. The pond's enchantment reached into the depths of her being, offering solace to her spirit as well. It was a place of reflection and release, where Lady Seraphina could let go of the day's frustrations and doubts, allowing the waters to cleanse her of the emotional burdens she carried.

As they bathed in the luminous pond, the bond between Lady Seraphina and Sir Sterling grew stronger. It was a moment of connection and renewal, a silent understanding that transcended words. In the serene ambiance of the enchanted forest, they found a profound sense of peace and unity, as though the magic of the waters flowed through their very souls.

After their bath, Lady Seraphina and Sir Sterling would return to the Elven Kingdom, where the elves ensured they were well taken care of. A hearty meal awaited them, filled with nourishing foods that aided in their recovery. Lady Seraphina's blisters would be tended to by skilled elven healers, who applied soothing salves and enchantments to speed up the healing process.

The elves understood the importance of rest as well, providing Lady Seraphina with a comfortable place to sleep within the heart of the Elven Kingdom. It was a peaceful haven, where the gentle rustling of leaves and the soothing melodies of the forest's inhabitants lulled her into a deep and restorative slumber.

One evening Lady Seraphina bathed in the enchanted pond, the ethereal ambiance of the forest came alive around her. The luminous waters caressed her skin, their soothing embrace working its magic on her weary body. But it was not just the healing properties of the pond that captured her attention; it was the enchanting dance of the fairies above her head that truly made the experience magical.

The fairies, delicate and ethereal beings of the enchanted forest, were drawn to the pond like moths to a flame. They came in a myriad of colours, each one representing a different facet of nature's beauty. Some were the soft hues of morning dew, while others shone with the brilliance of the setting sun. Their wings glistened with iridescent patterns, and their laughter was like the tinkling of wind chimes.

As Lady Seraphina reclined in the shimmering waters, she looked up to see the fairies flitting about in graceful choreography. They moved with a fluidity and grace that seemed to defy the laws of physics, creating intricate and ever-changing patterns in the sky above her. It was as though they were weaving a tapestry of light and colour, a living masterpiece that unfolded in the canvas of the forest's canopy.

The fairies' dance was a symphony of beauty and grace, a manifestation of the forest's magic in its purest form. They moved in perfect harmony with one another, their movements synchronized like a well-practiced ballet. Their tiny forms left streaks of colour in their wake, painting the sky with vibrant hues that mirrored the luminescent flowers that surrounded the pond.

Lady Seraphina watched in awe as the fairies' dance continued, each twirl and pirouette leaving a trail of sparkling light. Their tinkling bell laughter was a melodic accompaniment to their aerial ballet. It was a performance unlike anything she had ever witnessed, a reminder that the enchanted forest was a realm where magic and wonder knew no bounds.

The fairies' presence added a sense of enchantment to Lady Seraphina's bath, making her feel as though she had been transported to a realm of dreams and fantasy. Their playful antics and joyful laughter lifted her spirits, dispelling the weariness that had clung to her after a day of intensive training.

As Lady Seraphina closed her eyes and leaned back in the water, she felt the fairies' delicate touch on her skin. They would flit around her, occasionally brushing her cheeks with their tiny fingers or playfully tugging at a strand of her hair. It was a sensation that sent shivers of delight through her, as though the very essence of the enchanted forest was embracing her in its embrace.

The fairies' dance continued well into the evening, their luminescent display casting a soft, enchanting glow over the entire area. Lady Seraphina felt as though she was bathed in starlight, surrounded by the magic of the forest and the playful presence of these otherworldly creatures.

As she eventually emerged from the pond, refreshed, and rejuvenated, Lady Seraphina couldn't help but feel a deep sense of gratitude for the fairies and their enchanting dance. Their presence had transformed a simple bath into a magical experience, a reminder of the boundless wonders that the enchanted forest held.

With a smile on her face, Lady Seraphina knew that she carried not only the strength of her training but also the enchantment of the fairies with her. It was a combination that made her feel invincible, ready to face whatever challenges lay ahead in her quest to protect the enchanted forest and all the magic it held.

All these efforts were part of a comprehensive regime designed to prepare Lady Seraphina and Sir Sterling for the battles that lay ahead. Each day of training pushed them to their limits, but the healing powers of the enchanted pond and the care of the elves ensured that they emerged stronger, both physically and spiritually.

In the heart of the Elven Kingdom, amidst the magic and wonder that surrounded them, Lady Seraphina's journey continued. She was being forged not only as a warrior but as a symbol of resilience and hope. With each passing day, she grew closer to her destiny, a beacon of light ready to face the darkness that threatened both her world and the enchanted forest.

Amidst the enchanting beauty of the Elven Kingdom, Lady Seraphina's transformation into a formidable warrior was well underway. The daily regime, under General Elowen's watchful eye, pushed her and Sir Sterling to their physical limits. The Elven archery lessons, swordplay, and rigorous exercises were a testament to their commitment to prepare for the impending battles. But amid all the training and physical preparations, there was one aspect that Lady Seraphina struggled with – her mental health.

Despite her growing proficiency in combat and her strengthening physical form, there were moments when the weight of her past burdens seemed insurmountable. The memories of Count Malachi's cruelty, the loss of loved ones, and the lingering trauma weighed heavily on her mind. In the quiet hours of the night, she would often find herself battling inner demons, her sleep disrupted by haunting nightmares.

The elves, ever attentive to her well-being, noticed the toll it was taking on her spirit. They tried to offer solace through their enchanting songs, soothing tales, and even shared the healing waters of their enchanted pond. Yet, the darkness within Seraphina persisted, a relentless storm in her heart that she could not calm.

General Elowen, with his perceptive wisdom, recognized the turmoil in her eyes. He knew that her journey was not just about physical prowess but also about inner strength. One evening, after a particularly grueling training session, he approached her with a solemn expression.

"Lady Seraphina," he began, his voice filled with empathy, "I see the struggle that rages within you. The battles of the heart and mind are as significant as those on the battlefield. You've faced unimaginable horrors, and they have left scars that may never fully heal. But remember, it's okay to seek help and guidance, even in the midst of war."

Seraphina, her guard momentarily lowered, nodded in acknowledgment. She knew he was right, but the burden of her past seemed inescapable.

General Elowen continued, "You carry the weight of not just your own destiny but the destiny of our realms. It's a heavy burden, and it's natural to feel overwhelmed. But your strength lies not only in your skill with a sword or bow but also in your resilience. Seek counsel, lean on your allies, and know that you are not alone in this journey."

As the days passed, Seraphina took his words to heart. She began to open up to the elves, sharing her fears and insecurities. They offered their support, teaching her ancient meditation techniques and guiding her in finding inner peace amidst the chaos.

As Lady Seraphina's mental health faltered under the weight of her past traumas, an unexpected consequence began to manifest in her once-familiar weapons. The sword forged from Luminaforge Steel, which had once felt like an extension of her very being, now seemed heavy in her grasp. The bow, a masterpiece of Elven craftsmanship, suddenly became unwieldy, its elegant curves and delicate etchings feeling burdensome.

These shifts were not due to any physical deterioration, but rather a reflection of the delicate balance that had been disrupted. The inner turmoil she carried impacted not only her spirit but also her physical abilities. The weight of her past seemed to have found its way into her weapons, a tangible reminder that her mental and emotional well-being were inextricably linked to her prowess as a warrior.

General Elowen, perceptive as ever, noticed these subtle changes and recognized that the equilibrium of physical, spiritual, and mental well-being was now more crucial than ever. Seraphina's journey was not just about mastering combat techniques but also about nurturing her inner strength and resilience. It was a profound lesson in the interconnectedness of her being, a reminder that true strength arose from the harmony of all aspects of herself.

Lady Seraphina's nights were plagued by unsettling dreams that felt like memories she couldn't quite grasp. In these troubling reveries, she would often find herself in situations that challenged her commitment to goodness and harmony. It was as if Count Malachi had found a way to infiltrate her thoughts and plant seeds of doubt within her mind. These dreams left her feeling shaken, questioning her own integrity, and fearing that the darkness was encroaching upon her very soul.

Lady Seraphina couldn't help but wonder if the malevolent spirits and dark forces channeled through the sword were responsible for these unsettling visions. As she struggled to decipher the truth from the illusions Count Malachi had woven around her, she knew that confronting both the physical and spiritual challenges imperative if she was to break free.

The Darkness Within

Lady Seraphina had embraced the path of a warrior with a fierce determination that burned as brightly as the finest forge. She had channeled her anger, fear, and pain into every strike of her blade, every grueling training session. Her spirit was unyielding, her skill unmatched, and her resolve unbreakable. She had transformed from a noble lady into a formidable warrior, a testament to her unwavering determination.

But beneath the armour and the sword, beneath the facade of strength and courage she displayed to the world, there lay a deep and festering wound—the haunting memories of the abuse she had endured at the hands of Count Malachi. It was a wound that refused to heal, a black stone embedded deep within her soul, a constant reminder of the horrors she had faced.

In the dead of night, when the elven castle was shrouded in silence, Lady Seraphina would often find herself alone in her chamber, grappling with the ghosts of her past. The echoes of Count Malachi's cruel laughter, the searing pain of his touch, the helplessness that had consumed her—all would come rushing back with a vengeance, like a relentless storm that threatened to drown her.

Lady Seraphina's life as a warrior was a constant battle against her own demons, and when the haunting memories of her abuse by Count Malachi resurfaced, they hit her like a sudden storm in the midst of a calm sea.

In the midst of a seemingly ordinary day, an innocuous sight, sound, or scent could trigger a flashback—a vivid, unwelcome journey back to the horrors she had endured. The anxiety that gripped her in those moments was like a vice closing in on her chest, squeezing the air from her lungs.

As the memories flooded her mind, Lady Seraphina's heart would race, pounding against her ribs as if trying to escape the relentless onslaught of the past. Her breathing would become shallow and rapid, as though she were gasping for air in a suffocating darkness. It was as if the very air around her had turned thick and heavy, making each breath a struggle.

Her body would tremble uncontrollably, her muscles quivering with tension as the terror of those memories enveloped her. Cold sweat would bead on her forehead, and her skin would turn pale, drained of its natural colour. Her hands, once steady and skilled with a blade, would shake as if they had forgotten their strength.

Lady Seraphina's mind would become a chaotic whirlwind, a maelstrom of anguish and fear. She would lose touch with the present, transported back to the moments of her torment, reliving them with agonizing clarity. It was as though time itself had collapsed, and she was trapped in the past, a helpless witness to her own suffering.

The world around her would blur and distort, the sounds of the training yard or the castle's corridors fading into a distant, incomprehensible hum. She felt detached from her own body, as though she were watching herself from a great distance, unable to exert control over her own actions.

Each second that passed felt like an eternity, and Lady Seraphina would be consumed by a desperate longing to escape the relentless grip of the memories. Her thoughts would spiral into a vortex of despair, as she grappled with the overwhelming sense of helplessness and vulnerability that the flashbacks brought.

In those moments of torment, Lady Seraphina was trapped in a suffocating darkness, unable to see a way out. It was a battle not against external foes, but against the demons that resided within her own mind. And even as she emerged from the depths of a flashback, the physical and emotional toll of the experience would linger, a stark reminder of the scars that had been etched into her soul.

Her training had taught her to be resilient, to push through physical and mental challenges, but there was no preparation for the nightmares that haunted her sleep. Count Malachi's face would leer at her from the depths of her dreams, his malevolent presence casting a shadow over her every thought.

As the days turned into weeks, and the weeks into months, Lady Seraphina's outward strength grew, but the turmoil within her festered. She found herself plagued by a growing resentment, not only towards Count Malachi, for he was a creature of darkness and cruelty, but toward her own kingdom and the highbred families who had chosen her for this role.

Why had they selected her? Why had they condemned her to a life marred by unspeakable horrors? These questions gnawed at her soul, like a relentless hunger that could not be sated. She had once been a lady of grace and privilege, but those days felt like distant memories now, overshadowed by the relentless torment she had endured.

In the training yard, she sparred with fellow elven warriors, honing her skills and proving herself time and again. When aligned with the light she fought with an intensity that left her opponents in awe, her movements a mesmerizing dance of precision and strength. But as the sweat trickled down her brow and the adrenaline coursed through her veins, she couldn't escape the gnawing bitterness that had taken root within her.

During these training sessions, her weapons, the Luminaforge Steel sword and the Elven bow, began to display a disconcerting trait. They seemed to sense the darkness that sometimes clouded her heart and fought back, resisting her control. The sword's strikes lacked their usual grace and precision, and the arrows from her bow veered off course, as if guided by an unseen force.

This inner battle, both against her own darkness and the defiance of her weapons, was a constant struggle. Lady Seraphina found herself expending precious energy realigning herself to the light, to the unwavering sense of purpose that had brought her here. It was a task that left her physically and mentally drained, as if the weight of her past sins bore down on her with each swing of her blade and each nocking of an arrow.

General Elowen, witnessing these battles on the training field, understood the toll it was taking on her. He offered guidance, reminding her that her weapons were forged to be instruments of light and justice and that they would only obey her when her heart was in harmony with those principles. The constant struggle to maintain that alignment was an exhausting endeavor, but it was also a testament to her determination to overcome the darkness that had plagued her.

Seraphina's journey was not just about mastering combat techniques; it was about confronting her inner demons, finding the light within herself, and proving that even in the face of her own darkness, she could emerge as a beacon of hope and resilience. The battles she faced within herself were the most challenging, but they were also the ones that would ultimately define her.

The kingdom that had once been her home now felt like a prison. The people who had once revered her now seemed like distant strangers. Lady Seraphina had become a symbol of hope, a beacon of strength, but she couldn't help but wonder if the price she had paid was too steep. Was her sacrifice worth the salvation of the kingdom?

In the quiet moments, when she was alone with her thoughts, she would often gaze out of her chamber window, her thoughts fixed on her kingdom beyond. The rolling hills, the flourishing fields, the bustling villages—they were all part of a world that had moved on without her, a world that seemed oblivious to the torment she had endured.

As she learnt how the kingdom thrived since she left, Lady Seraphina's resentment grew. She had given up everything, sacrificed her innocence, and endured unspeakable horrors, and for what? To protect a realm that had cast her aside like a broken doll, to serve a kingdom that seemed ungrateful for her sacrifices.

The slither of darkness that had once resided within Count Malachi had found a new home within her heart, a growing shadow that threatened to consume her from within. She longed for a way to escape the memories that haunted her, to break free from the shackles of her past. But there was no escape, no respite, only the relentless march of time and the weight of her duty.

She had become a warrior, a symbol of strength and resilience, but beneath the armour and the sword, she was still the haunted girl who had been chosen to be sacrificed to the darkness. Lady Seraphina knew that she could never erase the scars of her past, but she couldn't help but resent the kingdom that had chosen her to bear them.

Lady Seraphina had initially harboured little resentment toward Count Malachi; she had seen him as nothing more than a cruel and malevolent force, a creature of darkness whose actions were driven by a thirst for power and control. But over time, as she endured the relentless torment and abuse at his hands, a transformation occurred within her—a metamorphosis from a victim to a warrior, and from a quiet loathing to an all-consuming hatred.

This newfound loathing was unlike any other emotion Lady Seraphina had ever experienced. It burned within her with an intensity that felt as if it could melt her very skin off her bones. It was a hatred that seemed to have been forged in the darkest depths of her soul, a hate so treacherous that it could only be born from the slither of darkness that had taken root within her.

The fire of her hatred for Count Malachi raged within her, a relentless inferno that threatened to consume her from the inside out. It was a hate that eclipsed all reason, all sense of restraint. Every cruel word, every tormenting touch, every nightmare inflicted upon her fueled the flames of her hatred, stoking the fires until they burned hotter and brighter with each passing day.

As Lady Seraphina continued her training and embraced her role as a warrior, she channeled her hatred into every swing of her sword, every clash of steel against steel whilst trying to remain aligned within the light. It was a powerful motivator, a driving force that pushed her to excel, to become a formidable force to be reckoned with. She used her newfound strength to fight back against the darkness that had once consumed her, to stand tall in defiance of Count Malachi's malevolence.

But even as she honed her skills and grew stronger, her hatred for Count Malachi remained a constant, an ever-present companion. It was a hate that coloured her every thought and action, a hate that seemed to seep into every corner of her being. It was a reminder of the horrors she had endured, a reminder that she could never truly escape the shadow of her past, the shadow of the serpent!

The mere thought of Count Malachi sent a surge of rage coursing through her veins. She longed for the day when she could confront him, when she could finally exact her revenge for the unspeakable atrocities he had committed. Her hatred fueled her determination, her unwavering commitment to bring him to justice.

Yet, as time passed, Lady Seraphina began to realize that her hatred for Count Malachi was a double-edged sword. It was a powerful weapon, yes, but it also threatened to consume her from within. It was a darkness that had taken root in her heart, and she could feel it gnawing at her sanity, threatening to turn her into something she did not want to become.

She saw the effects of her hatred in the eyes of those around her—her fellow elven warriors who looked upon her with a mixture of admiration and concern, the loyal elven servants who saw the torment in her eyes, and even in the way she viewed her own kingdom, with a growing resentment that seemed to taint her love for her people.

The fire of her hatred had grown so hot that it threatened to consume everything in its path, including Lady Seraphina herself. She knew that she needed to find a way to harness that hatred, to use it as a tool for justice rather than allowing it to consume her entirely.

But the journey to master her own hatred would prove to be a challenge unlike any she had faced before. It was a battle not against external foes, but against the darkness that had taken root within her own soul. Lady Seraphina knew that she could not let her hatred define her, that she had to find a way to rise above it and become the warrior—and the person—she was meant to be.

Not even bathing in the Healing Waters, the tranquil pond nestled deep within the enchanted forest, could remove the darkness that had taken root within Lady Seraphina. It was something that ran deeper than any physical ailment, something no magic could remove. As she submerged herself in the soothing waters, she had hoped to find solace, to cleanse herself of the fire of hatred and resentment that consumed her. But the pond's mystical properties, while potent in their ability to mend the body, proved powerless against certain festering wound in her soul.

The pond, with its crystal-clear waters shimmering in the dappled sunlight filtering through the ancient trees, had beckoned her with its promise of rejuvenation. Lady Seraphina had removed her armour and dipped her bare feet into the cool waters, seeking relief from the relentless turmoil within her. For a fleeting moment, as the water caressed her skin, she had felt a glimmer of peace.

But as she waded deeper into the pond, the water's soothing embrace turned frigid, as if recoiling from an invisible force. It was as though the Healing Waters themselves sensed the darkness that had taken root within her and refused to cleanse it.

Lady Seraphina's heart sank as she realized the futility of her efforts. The darkness she carried within her was not a simple malaise; it was a profound and festering hatred, a fire that consumed her from within. It was a part of her, deeply embedded in her soul, a darkness that no magic, no matter how powerful, could wash away.

With a heavy heart, she emerged from the waters, the weight of her despair settling upon her like an unshakable burden. As she wrapped herself in a robe, she wondered if there was any hope left for her, any way to free herself from the consuming hatred that threatened to devour her spirit.

As Lady Seraphina stood on the edge of the pond, her thoughts lost in the depths of her own despair, a soft voice broke the stillness of the forest. A fairy, no taller than a blade of grass, fluttered down from the branches above, her delicate wings shimmering with an otherworldly light.

The fairy's tiny sapphire-like eyes gazed at Lady Seraphina with a mixture of curiosity and compassion. She had sensed the change within the noble warrior, the fire of hatred that consumed her from within.

"Brave warrior," the fairy began, her voice as soft as a whisper, "the Healing Waters are a gift to those who seek physical healing, but the wounds of your soul run deeper than any pond can reach. Your darkness, embedded within you, defies even the most powerful magic."

Lady Seraphina's shoulders slumped as the weight of her despair settled upon her. "Then how can I ever hope to find peace? How can I free myself from this consuming hatred?"

The fairy's tiny wings fluttered as she floated closer to Lady Seraphina. In her delicate hand, she held a necklace adorned with a stone of the deepest, richest blue—a stone that seemed to capture the essence of a starry night sky.

"This stone," the fairy explained, "is called 'Starheart.' It cannot remove the darkness within you, for that is a journey only you can undertake. But it can help you find your way back to the light when the fire of hate threatens to consume you."

Lady Seraphina accepted the necklace, feeling the weight of its significance in her palm. The Starheart stone was unlike anything she had ever seen. Its surface bore a mosaic of tiny, shimmering stars, each one a glimmering reminder of the vastness of the universe.

The fairy continued, "When the darkness surges within you, when the flames of anger and hatred threaten to overwhelm, hold this necklace close to your heart. Let the Starheart remind you that there is light even in the darkest of nights. It will ground you, anchor you to the present, and guide you through the storm within."

With the necklace clasped around her neck, Lady Seraphina felt a newfound sense of hope. It was not a magic that would erase her pain or her hatred, but it was a lifeline—a reminder that even in her darkest moments, she could find a way back to herself.

Over the days and nights that followed, Lady Seraphina began to wear the Starheart necklace always, its presence a comforting weight against her skin. When the fire of hatred threatened to consume her, when panic attacks came to haunt her in the stillness of the night, when her fighting began to align more with the darkness, she would hold the necklace close, its cool surface a lifeline to sanity.

The Starheart stone had a calming effect on her, like a beacon of serenity in the midst of a tempest. It helped her ground herself, find her center, and navigate the treacherous waters of her own emotions. It did not remove the darkness within her, but it gave her the strength to confront it and to align to the light.

Lady Seraphina continued her training as a warrior, her resolve stronger than ever, but now tempered by the knowledge that she held the power to control her own destiny. The fire of her hatred for Count Malachi still raged within her, but with the guidance of the Starheart, she had found a way to harness it, to use it as a tool for justice rather than allowing it to consume her entirely.

In the midst of her battles and her quest for vengeance, Lady Seraphina would often find herself gazing at the Starheart stone, its tiny stars glittering like beacons of hope. It was a reminder that even in the darkest of nights, there was a glimmer of light, a path back to herself, a way to heal the wounds of her soul.

The journey to confront Count Malachi and bring him to justice was far from over, but Lady Seraphina faced it with a newfound strength and determination. The darkness within her remained, but it no longer held her captive. She was the master of her own fate, guided by the light of the Starheart, and ready to confront the demons of her past with unwavering resolve.

In the heart of the ancient Elven Kingdom, a land of towering trees and shimmering cascades, there resided a wise and revered ruler, King Thaladir. He was known throughout the mystical realm as a guardian of the delicate balance that held the worlds of magic, spirits, and humans in harmony. It was said that his keen eyes could perceive even the subtlest shifts in the mystical tapestry that bound their existence together.

One day, as King Thaladir walked through the enchanted forest that cradled his kingdom, his senses pricked with a subtle disturbance in the magical currents that flowed around him. It was a change so slight that most would not have noticed, but to the Elven King, it was a whisper of discord in the symphony of nature.

He paused in a glade bathed in the ethereal light of the setting sun, and as he closed his eyes to attune himself to the balance, he saw it—a ripple in the fabric of their world. It was a small but undeniable disturbance, like a stone dropped into a still pond, sending ripples outward.

King Thaladir's eyes opened, concern etching lines on his ageless face. He knew that such disturbances, no matter how minor, could have far-reaching consequences. With a graceful step, he summoned his most trusted advisor, Lady Elowen, a wise and revered elf who possessed knowledge of the deepest mystical arts.

"Lady Elowen," King Thaladir began, his voice as soft as a whispering breeze, "I have sensed a change in the balance, a disturbance that threatens the harmony of our realms. I fear that it may be tied to Lady Seraphina, the noble warrior training for the impending war."

Lady Elowen nodded, her silver hair cascading like a waterfall over her shoulders. She was well aware of Lady Seraphina's presence in the kingdom, for the echo of her struggles had reached even the tranquil depths of the elven woods. "Your wisdom rarely falters, my liege. What have you perceived?"

King Thaladir explained the subtle shift he had sensed in the magical currents. "It is as though a shadow has begun to spread within her, a darkness that threatens to eclipse her inner light. She walks a dangerous path, and the consequences could be dire."

Lady Elowen's brow furrowed in concern. "But what of the impending war, my liege? Lady Seraphina's skills as a warrior are unmatched. Without her, we may not stand a chance against our adversaries."

King Thaladir regarded her with a solemn gaze. "It is precisely because of her unparalleled skills that I fear the consequences. The balance of our worlds is delicate, and her inner turmoil threatens to tip the scales in ways we cannot predict. If she does not learn to control the darkness within her, the war may be won at a cost too great to bear."

In the days that followed, a summons was sent to Lady Seraphina, requesting her presence in the heart of the elven kingdom. She arrived with humility and a sense of remorse, for she knew that her actions had not gone unnoticed by the wise King Thaladir.

The meeting took place in a glade bathed in the soft light of the moon, where ancient trees stood as silent witnesses to their conversation. King Thaladir, seated upon a stone carved with elven runes, regarded Lady Seraphina with a gaze that seemed to pierce her very soul.

"Lady Seraphina," he began, his voice carrying the weight of centuries of wisdom, "I have called upon you because I have sensed a change within you, a darkness that threatens the delicate balance of our realms."

Lady Seraphina bowed her head, her auburn hair catching the moonlight like a cascade of fire. "Your Majesty, I am deeply sorry for any disturbance I may have caused. I am training to become a warrior to protect our lands, but I understand that my inner turmoil may pose a threat."

King Thaladir nodded, his eyes reflecting both understanding and concern. "Your intentions are noble, Lady Seraphina, but the path you walk is fraught with peril. The balance of our worlds is intricate, and any disruption can have far-reaching consequences."

He then shared with Lady Seraphina the vision he had seen—the subtle ripple in the mystical currents that surrounded her. It was an example of the imbalance she had inadvertently caused, a testament to the growing darkness within her.

"As you train for the impending war," King Thaladir continued, "you must also train to control the darkness that threatens to consume you. The fate of our realms hangs in the balance, and your actions could tip it one way or the other."

Lady Seraphina's heart weighed heavily with the gravity of the situation. She had never intended to endanger the realms she held dear, and yet her hatred and darkness had brought her perilously close to doing just that.

"Your Majesty, I promise you," she said, her voice resolute, "I will find a way to heal the darkness within me. I will not allow it to jeopardize our world."

King Thaladir regarded her with a measured expression. "You are a noble soul, Lady Seraphina, and your courage is unquestionable. But remember that healing the darkness within you will be a journey fraught with challenges. You must confront the demons of your past and find a way to harness the light within."

With those words of wisdom, King Thaladir dismissed Lady Seraphina, knowing that the fate of their realms hung in the balance. Lady Seraphina left the elven kingdom with a newfound determination, vowing to confront the darkness within her and find a way to ensure that the mystical balance remained intact.

Her training as a warrior continued, but now it was intertwined with a deeper quest—to heal the wounds of her soul and learn to control the darkness that threatened to consume her. She sought guidance from the wise elders of the elven kingdom, delving into ancient texts and mystical rituals in her pursuit of balance.

Throughout Lady Seraphina's training while she tried to confront the darkness within her, there was one steadfast companion who never wavered—an unwavering source of comfort and solace. It was her loyal and noble steed, Sir Sterling, who stood by her side through every trial and tribulation. His strong presence and deep bond with Lady Seraphina served as a constant reminder that there was goodness and purity in the world, even when darkness threatened to consume her.

Sir Sterling's velvety coat bore the emblem of their family—a gallant horse galloping fearlessly across a majestic field, symbolizing strength, determination, and courage. He had been with Lady Seraphina since she was a child, and their connection ran deeper than words could express. In times of despair, she would seek refuge in the quiet moments spent with her beloved stallion, their hearts intertwined in a silent understanding that transcended the trials of their world. Sir Sterling's unwavering presence was a beacon of hope, a reminder that there was a light worth fighting for, and that together, they could overcome the darkness that threatened to engulf them both.

Desperation fueled Lady Seraphina's resolve to reclaim the peace in her mind and heart. In her quest to break free she turned to her steadfast companion, Sir Sterling. The gallant stallion, with his velvety coat and the family emblem emblazoned upon it, had been her unwavering companion since her childhood. Their bond ran deep, rooted in a silent understanding that transcended the trials and tribulations of their world. In the quiet moments spent with Sir Sterling, she found solace, strength, and a flicker of hope that there was a light worth fighting for. Together, they were determined to overcome the encroaching darkness that threatened to engulf Seraphina.

Secrets Unveiled

In the heart of their ancestral home, the Veridales family held a secret that threatened to shatter the already fragile peace within the kingdom. It was a secret entrusted to them by the wise elves concerning Lady Seraphina's whereabouts. Upon receiving the letter from the elves, it was swiftly and deliberately consigned to the flames, its contents forever concealed from the prying eyes of the council and even King Alaric himself.

As the sun dipped below the horizon, casting long shadows across the castle's ancient walls, Lady Veridales, a formidable matriarch, and her husband, Lord Veridales, gathered in their dimly lit chamber. There, they composed a scroll destined for Count Malachi, a close ally in secret. The message was concise, conveying the elves' revelation about Lady Seraphina's location. It was a dangerous secret to guard, but one that the Veridales believed Count Malachi had the right to know.

The intricate alliance between the Veridales and Count Malachi had its roots deeply entwined in the complex tapestry of their shared interests and mutual ambitions within the kingdom.

It began in a time when both parties found themselves facing a common enemy, a shadowy force that threatened the very fabric of their existence. This external threat, be it marauding invaders or a dark sorcerer, was a formidable adversary that neither the Veridales family nor Count Malachi could vanquish alone. Faced with the prospect of their lands and legacies being consumed by this menace, they saw the wisdom in forging an alliance.

The Veridales, a highbred family known for their political acumen and cunning strategies, recognized that joining forces with Count Malachi could provide them with the military might and dark magic necessary to repel the encroaching darkness. Count Malachi, on the other hand, saw in the

Veridales a source of political leverage and influence within the kingdom's court, a position he could exploit to further his dark ambitions.

Shared interests also played a pivotal role in cementing their alliance. Both the Veridales and Count Malachi harboured desires for power, wealth, and control over specific territories within both kingdoms. Their alliance allowed them to pool their resources and pursue these ambitions with a unified front.

Historical ties further solidified their partnership. Over generations, the Veridales and Count Malachi's lineage had been intertwined through familial bonds and past interactions, creating a sense of trust and kinship that made the alliance a natural progression.

However, it wasn't a partnership without its darker aspects. Count Malachi held certain secrets and leverage over the Veridales, using this knowledge to ensure their compliance. His mastery of dark magic and the fear he instilled in those who opposed him made him a formidable figure who could not be easily defied.

Strategically, the alliance brought many advantages. Count Malachi's dark powers and resources could tip the scales in their favour in times of conflict or turmoil. The Veridales, with their political savvy, could manipulate the Kingdom Alaric's court to their advantage, ensuring that Count Malachi's interests were protected.

Opportunism played a significant role in their partnership as well. Both parties recognized the potential benefits of an alliance and seized the opportunity to strengthen their positions. As their relationship evolved, it became clear that their destinies were intertwined, for better or worse.

In a world where alliances could be as treacherous as the enemies they faced, the Veridales and Count Malachi's partnership was a reflection of their shared interests, ambitions, and the delicate dance of power that defined their tumultuous kingdoms.

With the scroll sealed, it was time to send word to Count Malachi. The Veridales had a unique method of delivering their message—a raven of the deepest black, a creature not bound by the ordinary laws of nature but rather an emissary of shadow and intrigue. The raven's eyes gleamed with an otherworldly intelligence as it took flight, descending from the sky to land gracefully on the windowsill of Count Malachi's fortress.

With an ominous presence, the raven dropped the sealed scroll at Count Malachi's feet and then departed into the night, vanishing into the inky darkness like a phantom. Count Malachi had been preoccupied with his dark incantations when the raven arrived, but this interruption was more than welcome. The news of Lady Seraphina's location filled him with a malevolent satisfaction that sent shivers down his spine.

Without hesitation, Count Malachi gathered his dark disciples and servants, readying them for a journey to retrieve Lady Seraphina from the elven kingdom. He knew that the time was ripe, and he would stop at nothing to reclaim her.

Unbeknownst to Count Malachi, Lady Seraphina had embarked on a divergent journey within the heart of the elven kingdom. She was on a quest for knowledge, the kind that could unveil a path to a celestial city and a sacred spring—a path that held the promise of liberating her from the darkness that loomed ominously over her soul.

As their respective forces stirred, the stage was subtly being prepared for a confrontation that would soon ensnare them all. Within the looming shadows of secrets and mysteries, destiny was poised to forge a collision that would test courage and resilience, ultimately charting the destiny of the realms themselves.

Lady Seraphina found herself irresistibly drawn to a place of profound enchantment—the grand library. It was a sanctuary of boundless wisdom and ancient knowledge, where the very essence of time seemed to stand still. Here, amidst the hallowed halls, the whispers of countless ages echoed from the pages of age-old tomes, creating an atmosphere that transcended the mortal realm.

The library itself was a masterpiece of elven craftsmanship. Its towering shelves, intricately carved from the heart of ancient trees, stretched high above, furnished with delicate filigree and enchanted glyphs that shimmered in the soft, ethereal light. Crystalline windows allowed the gentle rays of the sun to filter through, casting a luminous glow upon the countless volumes that lined the shelves. The air was heavy with the scent of parchment and the faint fragrance of blooming moonflowers, making it a place of both intellectual pursuit and tranquil reflection.

As Lady Seraphina wandered through the library's labyrinthine corridors, her fingertips brushed against the spines of countless books, each bearing the weight of centuries of elven wisdom. It was in this sacred space that she chanced upon an ancient volume, a relic of forgotten times. Its once-ivory pages had aged into a golden hue, and its leather cover bore intricate designs that seemed to pulse with eldritch energy. The book was a testament to the craftsmanship of a bygone era, a portal to a world of forgotten lore.

With delicate reverence, Lady Seraphina opened the book, its pages whispering secrets long held in obscurity. The tales contained within were like fragments of a celestial dream, recounting the legend of a city of angels perched atop a mountain, so close to the heavens that the very air shimmered with ethereal light.

According to the text, this celestial city was a realm of unparalleled beauty and serenity, a bastion of divine tranquility amidst a turbulent world. But it was not the city's splendor that captured Lady Seraphina's heart; it was the revelation of a sacred spring hidden within its hallowed confines. The spring was said to be a font of purest essence, touched by the divine, and it held a power beyond mortal comprehension.

The ancient text proclaimed that those who dared to drink from this mystical spring and sought solace in the presence of the angels would be granted a profound kind of soul healing. The celestial beings themselves would extend their benevolent hands, aiding in the purification of a soul tainted by darkness, a soul burdened by the weight of iniquity.

As Lady Seraphina delved deeper into the book's pages, her heart quickened with a newfound hope. Could this celestial city and its healing spring be the key to her salvation, a beacon of light that could pierce the darkness threatening to engulf her soul? A sense of purpose surged within her, igniting a determination that had long lain dormant.

With the ancient tome clutched in her hand, Lady Seraphina left the library, her mind ablaze with the boundless possibilities that lay ahead. She understood that her journey was far from over, that the path she must tread would be fraught with trials and tribulations. Yet, she bore a secret weapon—an ancient knowledge that held the promise of liberation from the shadows that sought to consume her.

Unbeknownst to Lady Seraphina, a malevolent force was already in motion, as Count Malachi and his dark acolytes set their sinister plans into action, closing in on the elven kingdom.

Lady Seraphina's discovery of the ancient tome had ignited a spark of hope within her heart—a hope that she believed could lead her to a celestial city of angels and a healing spring that might purge the darkness threatening her soul. With newfound purpose, she sought an audience with the Elven King, the wise and enigmatic ruler named King Thaladir, to share this newfound knowledge.

The Elven King's court was a place of ethereal beauty and timeless elegance. Elven nobles in resplendent robes moved gracefully through halls adorned with intricate silver filigree, while ancient trees with silver leaves whispered secrets in the courtyard. It was here, amidst the grace and wisdom of the elven people, that Lady Seraphina approached King Thaladir's throne.

Bowing gracefully, Lady Seraphina addressed the Elven King with reverence. "Your Majesty, I come before you with a revelation of great importance, one that may hold the key to my salvation and the well-being of our realms."

King Thaladir regarded her with an inscrutable gaze, his ageless eyes filled with a depth of wisdom that transcended the mortal world. "Speak, Lady Seraphina. I am eager to hear of this revelation that has stirred your heart."

With measured words, Lady Seraphina recounted her discovery in the library—the ancient tome, the tales of the celestial city, and the sacred spring. She shared her belief that this city could offer her the means to rid herself of the encroaching darkness, the darkness that Count Malachi had sown within her.

As she spoke, King Thaladir's countenance remained composed, though his eyes betrayed a glimmer of intrigue. When she concluded her account, he leaned forward, his voice a soft murmur that held the weight of centuries. "Your discovery is not without merit, Lady Seraphina. Indeed, the celestial city you speak of is real, and the spring it guards possesses a healing power beyond measure."

Lady Seraphina's heart soared with hope, but King Thaladir's next words tempered her expectations. "However, you must understand that the City of Angels, known as Aeloria, is a place of unparalleled spiritual purity. It exists on the cusp of the heavens, and no elf may set foot within its hallowed ·confines."

A sense of solemnity washed over Lady Seraphina as she absorbed the gravity of the Elven King's words. "Then, Your Majesty, how am I to seek this city and the healing spring it houses?"

King Thaladir's gaze remained steady; his voice filled with ancient wisdom. "You may embark on this journey alone, Lady Seraphina, for the magic that courses through your veins will not be repelled by Aeloria's purity. However, know that it is a path fraught with peril, and you must be prepared to face the trials that await."

He continued, his voice lowering to a whisper that carried the weight of generations. "You may ride with an elven warrior as far as the city's edge, but there will come a point where they must wait, for no creature of magic may enter Aeloria's sacred domain. The journey beyond that point will be yours and yours alone."

Lady Seraphina nodded, understanding the gravity of her undertaking. "I am prepared, Your Majesty. The darkness within me must be vanquished, and I will do whatever it takes to see it done."

King Thaladir's eyes softened with a mixture of empathy and admiration. "Your resolve is commendable, Lady Seraphina. Seek out the wisdom of the ancient city and let its healing waters wash away the shadows that haunt you. Remember, the fate of our realms may rest upon your shoulders, and the light you bring back from Aeloria may be our last hope."

With the Elven King's blessing and the weight of her mission heavy in her heart, Lady Seraphina embarked on a journey that would test her courage, resilience, and the very limits of her spirit. The knowledge she carried, the mysteries of Aeloria, and the looming confrontation with Count Malachi would all converge in a fateful collision that would determine the destiny of all realms.

The weight of destiny rested heavily on Lady Seraphina's shoulders as she embarked on a journey to the celestial city of Aeloria, in search of a sacred spring that could cleanse her soul of the encroaching darkness. With the wisdom of King Thaladir's guidance, it was time to select the elven warrior who would accompany her on her perilous quest.

Among the skilled and honourable elven warriors, one stood out—Elyndra, a formidable and graceful warrior known throughout the kingdom for her courage and unwavering loyalty. Lady Elyndra possessed an aura of quiet strength, her brown hair cascading like a waterfall down her back, and her keen eyes, a shade of ethereal blue, held a wisdom beyond her years.

Lady Seraphina and Lady Elyndra, accompanied by their trusted steeds, made their way to the enchanted forest where the healing pond awaited. As they approached the mystical grove, the air seemed to shimmer with an otherworldly radiance, and the soft rustling of leaves carried an enchanting melody to welcome them.

Beside the pond, fairies with iridescent wings flitted about, their laughter like tinkling bells. Lady Seraphina wore the necklace gifted to her by one of these fairies—a necklace adorned with a shimmering stone that held the power to ground her in times of darkness. This necklace, her only magical companion on this quest, seemed to resonate with the enchantment of the forest.

As they dismounted from their horses and approached the pond, the fairies gathered around Seraphina. Their tiny voices chimed together in a harmonious greeting, their words delicate and ethereal.

"Welcome, Lady Seraphina," they sang, their wings creating a kaleidoscope of colours. "We have watched over you, and we see the light within you seeking to overcome the shadows."

Lady Seraphina smiled at their words, grateful for their presence. "Thank you, dear fairies. Your guidance and protection have been a comfort on this journey."

The fairies nodded in unison, their gazes filled with a mixture of fondness and concern. "We shall accompany you to the edge of Aeloria's realm, but we cannot enter with you," they explained, confirming King Thaladir's earlier words. "For mystical creatures, like ourselves, are not of the human realm and are not pure enough to step within its sacred borders."

Seraphina furrowed her brow in confusion. "But if one's heart is pure and intentions are good, why should the realm of angels be closed to them?"

One fairy, older and wiser than the others, stepped forward. Her name was Elara, and her wings bore the hues of a setting sun. She spoke with the authority of age and wisdom, her voice carrying a reassuring warmth.

"You see, Lady Seraphina," Elara began, "the realm of Aeloria is a place of spiritual purity. It exists on the cusp of the heavens, where the boundary between the human realm and the spiritual realm is at its thinnest. Humans, unlike mystical creatures, possess both a body, spirit and soul, and it is their connection to the spiritual realm that allows them to enter such a sacred place."

Lady Seraphina listened intently, her confusion slowly giving way to understanding. "So, it is the presence of a soul within us that grants us access to Aeloria?"

Elara nodded with a gentle smile. "Precisely. Humans are a unique blend of the physical, mental and spiritual, and only those whose souls are pure and good may enter. Mystical creatures, though magical and wondrous, do not possess souls, possess spirit only, and thus, they remain separate from this realm."

Seraphina absorbed this revelation, the weight of its significance settling upon her. Her soul was her key to Aeloria, a realm of healing and purity. She knew that her intentions were noble, her heart steadfast in its desire to vanquish the darkness that threatened her soul.

With newfound clarity, Lady Seraphina turned to Lady Elyndra, her chosen companion on this quest. "Elyndra, we shall continue our journey to Aeloria, where I must seek the wisdom of the angels and the healing spring. You will accompany me as far as the city's edge, and from there, I must go alone."

Elyndra nodded, her eyes reflecting unwavering loyalty and determination. "I will stand by your side, Lady Seraphina, until the very threshold of Aeloria. Together, we shall face the trials that await, and I shall await your return from Aeloria."

With the blessings of the fairies and the resolve of kindred spirits, Lady Seraphina, accompanied by Elyndra, embarked on their mystical journey into the heart of the enchanted forest. Two ethereal fairies, Tilly and Tally, joined them as their guides and guardians. Tilly was a petite and graceful fairy, her delicate wings shimmering with an iridescent, silvery glow. Her hair, the colour of moonlight, cascaded in elegant waves, and her eyes held a mischievous sparkle. Tally, on the other hand, was slightly taller, radiating an aura of quiet wisdom. Her wings were adorned with intricate patterns resembling the constellations, and her eyes bore a serene, ancient knowledge that seemed to pierce through time itself. Together, they were a harmonious duo, embodying the magic and wisdom of the enchanted forest.

With their radiant wings aglow, Tilly and Tally led the way, their ethereal presence illuminating the path toward the celestial city of Aeloria. As they ventured deeper into the heart of the enchanted forest, the mysteries of the city, the sacred healing spring, and the looming confrontation with Count Malachi converged in a fateful collision. The destiny of all realms hung in the balance, and the journey ahead promised to be a tapestry of wonder, danger, and profound revelations that would forever alter the course of their lives.

Sir Sterling seemed to welcome the addition of another horse to their party. The newcomer, a spirited and sleek stallion named Aelion, was a magnificent creature with a coat as dark as midnight, adorned with a single star–shaped marking on his forehead. Aelion's presence brought a sense of camaraderie to their journey, and he quickly formed a bond with Sir Sterling.

As they rode through the enchanted forest, Sir Sterling and Aelion moved in harmony, their hooves creating a rhythmic cadence that echoed through the ancient trees. The two horses seemed to communicate in their own silent language, sharing a camaraderie born of the shared trials of their riders.

Occasionally, they would nuzzle each other playfully, their equine affection a testament to the unspoken connection between them. When they paused to rest by a babbling brook, the horses grazed side by side, their companionship a source of solace in the mystical realm they traversed. It was as though the spirits of the forest had bestowed their blessing upon this unlikely alliance, recognizing the importance of their united journey.

The Count's Web

Count Malachi was a man driven by an insatiable thirst for power. His kingdom sat in the shadows, concealed by the dense canopy of the evil forest. Count Malachi ruled with an iron fist over the sinister realm of Shadowmoor. This malevolent wood was home to twisted trees, where darkness reigned. Yet, even darker was the heart of the evil witch who dwelled there – Morgana. Morgana's dilapidated cottage was nestled deep within the heart of the evil forest, a place where the trees seemed to lean menacingly towards it, as if protecting their sinister inhabitant.

Morgana was a figure of both fascination and fear in the kingdom of Shadowmoor. She dwelled within a decaying cottage nestled deep within the heart of the evil forest. Her name was whispered in hushed tones by those who dared to speak of her, and her reputation cast a shadow over the surrounding lands.

Her appearance was as unsettling as her reputation. Morgana possessed long, tangled black hair that cascaded like a waterfall of midnight down her bony shoulders. Her skin was deathly pale, almost translucent, and her eyes were a striking shade of emerald green that seemed to pierce the very soul of anyone who met her gaze. Those eyes held secrets that no one dared to uncover, and they seemed to glimmer with an otherworldly wisdom.

Morgana's attire was equally enigmatic. She often wore a tattered, ebony robe that billowed around her like a shroud, adding to her eerie presence. Her fingers were adorned with twisted silver rings, each one engraved with ancient symbols that hinted at her mastery of dark arts. Her nails were long and sharpened, like claws, a reflection of the darkness that had consumed her soul.

The interior of Morgana's cottage was a reflection of her unsettling nature. The walls were adorned with grotesque paintings and eerie tapestries depicting scenes of torment and suffering. Shelves were filled with jars containing various herbs, roots, and creatures preserved in eerie, glowing liquids. The air was thick with the scent of herbs and incense, creating an atmosphere of mysticism and dread.

In the center of the cottage stood a gnarled wooden table, upon which Morgana conducted her dark rituals. It was cluttered with an array of spell books, scrolls, and potions. Candles flickered with an unnatural light, casting eerie shadows that danced upon the walls. A crystal ball, cloudy and foreboding, rested at the center of the table, a tool through which Morgana communed with forces beyond the mortal realm.

Morgana's power was undeniable. She possessed an extensive knowledge of ancient incantations, curses, and hexes that she had gathered over centuries of study. The evil forest itself seemed to bow to her will, its sinister inhabitants answering her call. She could summon storms that blotted out the sun, and her laughter echoed through the trees like a haunting melody.

Count Malachi had approached Morgana with a proposition that intrigued her dark heart. He promised her even greater power, access to forbidden knowledge, and dominion over the evil forest itself. Morgana, driven by her insatiable thirst for power, had agreed to become one of Count Malachi's most formidable allies.

Under his influence, Morgana had unleashed her malevolence upon his kingdom, casting dark enchantments and curses that spread fear and despair among its inhabitants. She brewed potions of terror and concocted elixirs that ensnared the minds of those who dared cross her path. Her alliance with Count Malachi had only deepened her mastery of the dark arts, making her a force to be reckoned with.

As Morgana continued to serve Count Malachi's bidding, her reputation as the malevolent witch of Shadowmoor grew. Tales of her wickedness were told in hushed voices, and mothers warned their children not to venture too deep into the evil forest, lest they incur her wrath. She reveled in the fear she inspired, knowing that it only solidified her power and control over the kingdom.

Morgana's cottage remained a place of dread and mystery, a beacon of darkness within the heart of the evil forest. It was a testament to her unwavering allegiance to Count Malachi and her relentless pursuit of ever greater power. As long as she continued to serve her dark master, the kingdom of Shadowmoor would remain ensnared in her malevolent web of magic and terror.

Count Malachi had grown increasingly desperate to tighten his grip on the kingdom of Ravenshadow. He knew that to achieve ultimate dominion, he needed powers beyond his own considerable abilities. His ally, the malevolent witch Morgana, held the key to finding Lady Seraphina who was critical in the counts plan for ultimate power!

On a moonless night, Count Malachi set out on a treacherous journey through the twisting labyrinth of the evil forest on foot. Shadows loomed like sentient beings, and the very trees seemed to whisper ominous secrets. His destination was clear – Morgana's decaying cottage, the heart of darkness within Shadowmoor.

As he arrived at the witch's eerie abode, he rapped a twisted, silver knocker on her heavy wooden door. The sound echoed through the forest, and a moment later, Morgana appeared, her eyes gleaming with curiosity. She ushered him inside, the door creaking ominously behind him.

"What brings you here, Count Malachi?" Morgana's voice was a chilling melody as she studied him with those piercing emerald eyes.

Count Malachi wasted no time in revealing his purpose. "I seek your darkest magic, Morgana," he said, his voice low and urgent. "I need a potion, a dust that, when sprinkled over someone, will allow me to control their mind."

Morgana's lips curled into a sinister smile, revealing her sharp teeth. "Ah, the allure of manipulation," she purred. "Very well, Count Malachi, I have just the potion you seek. It's a concoction of rare herbs, venom from the deadliest serpents, and the essence of fear itself. But it comes at a price."

Count Malachi nodded, understanding that Morgana's aid would not come freely. "Name your price," he replied, his determination unwavering.

Morgana's price was as chilling as her reputation, driven not only by her insatiable desire for power but also by her keen insight into the demonic shift that had overtaken Count Malachi. She demanded a lock of his hair, a vial of his blood, and a binding promise that he would return to her whenever she called upon him, regardless of the task. Count Malachi, aware of the darkness that had consumed him and the potency of the magic he sought, agreed without hesitation. The sinister alliance forged between them would bind their fates together, intertwining their destinies in their relentless pursuit of ever-greater power.

Morgana swiftly prepared the sinister potion. The potion glowed with an eerie, greenish light, and its mere presence sent shivers down Count Malachi's spine. She poured it into a small, ornate vial, sealed it with dark wax, and handed it to him with a wicked grin.

"Now, use it wisely, Count Malachi," she cautioned. "Once the dust touches their skin, their minds will be yours to command."

With the potion in his possession, Count Malachi departed from Morgana's cottage, leaving behind the shadows and the haunting laughter of the witch.

But his quest for power was far from over. He needed to find the path that Lady Seraphina and the Elven warriors had taken to reach the enchanted forest. Morgana's powers of divination were legendary, and he had come to her with that purpose in mind.

Returning to the following night, Count Malachi sought Morgana's guidance once more. She prepared a ritual, a complex dance of incantations and runes. As the candles flickered and the crystal ball at the center of her table seemed to come alive, Count Malachi watched with bated breath.

Morgana's voice grew low and haunting, and the crystal ball filled with images. He saw Lady Seraphina and the Elven warriors embarking on their journey to the enchanted forest. Morgana's magic revealed the winding path, the hidden traps, and the secrets of the ancient forest that lay between the enchanted forest and the malevolent woods. It was a path that only those pure of heart could tread, and Count Malachi knew that he would need to employ every dark art at his disposal to follow in their footsteps. However, the true challenge lay beyond the entrance to the enchanted forest, for her vision could not pierce the veil further. The Elves possessed an ancient magic, driven by the crystals that surrounded their kingdom and lay beneath it, concealing themselves within the enchanted forest, making them nearly invisible to the dark forces. Morgana's assistance was thus invaluable, as she had shown him the point of entry, leaving him to navigate the treacherous and enchanted forest with nothing but darkness and determination as his guides.

With the knowledge Morgana had provided, Count Malachi had the means to pursue Lady Seraphina and the Elven warriors into the enchanted forest, where he hoped to fulfill his darkest ambitions and seize Lady Seraphina for himself once more. Morgana had proven herself to be an invaluable ally in his quest for power, and he knew that he would continue to rely on her malevolent talents as he ventured deeper into the heart of darkness.

On the other side of the kingdom lay the enchanted forest, a realm of enchantment and beauty. Within its boundaries lay the Elven Kingdom, ruled by the wise King Thaladir. The forest was bathed in the gentle glow of crystals that emitted an ethereal light, protecting the elves from the forces of darkness. Count Malachi's influence had extended even here, but not without limitations.

Beneath the forest floor lived the goblins, led by the cunning and ruthless Grizzletooth. Grizzletooth was a grotesque figure with matted hair, sharp teeth, and eyes that gleamed with malice. The goblins' underground town was a nightmarish place, filled with treacherous traps and secret tunnels. Their hatred for the crystals that lay beneath the Elven Kingdom was visceral; they could not abide the light they emitted. Count Malachi had manipulated them, using their aversion to the crystals to further his nefarious goals.

Grizzletooth, the cunning and ruthless goblin leader who ruled beneath the enchanted forest, was a nightmarish figure that struck fear into the hearts of all who encountered him. His appearance was a reflection of the treacherous and brutal world in which he thrived.

Standing at a mere three feet in height, Grizzletooth was surprisingly formidable. His gnarled and hunched frame was wrapped in tattered, filthy rags that bore the marks of countless battles and close encounters with danger. The goblin's skin, a sickly shade of gray–green, was covered in scars, testament to the numerous conflicts he had endured and emerged victorious from.

Grizzletooth's most distinctive feature was his head, which bore an array of grotesque deformities. His ears, stretched and pointed, resembled those of a bat, allowing him to hear even the faintest of sounds in the darkest corners of the underground goblin town. His nose, long and crooked, was equipped with an uncanny sense of smell, enabling him to detect intruders or threats long before they drew near. But it was his mouth, from which his name was derived, that struck the most terror into the hearts of his subjects and enemies alike.

Grizzletooth's mouth was a gruesome spectacle, filled with jagged, razor–sharp teeth that jutted out at all angles. Some of these teeth were stained with the blood of his foes, and they glistened with malevolence as he grinned with a sinister pleasure. His bite was as deadly as any weapon, capable of tearing through flesh and bone with ease. It was said that Grizzletooth had earned his name by gnashing his teeth together in a gruesome display of dominance during a particularly brutal power struggle among the goblins.

His eyes were small, beady orbs that glowed with a malevolent intelligence. They radiated a sinister gleam, revealing a cunning mind that constantly plotted and schemed to maintain his control over the goblin horde. Grizzletooth's gaze could freeze even the bravest of goblins in their tracks, for they knew that disobedience or betrayal would be met with swift and merciless punishment.

Grizzletooth's attire, if it could be called that, consisted of a tattered loincloth made from the rotting remains of some long-forgotten fabric. It was adorned with gruesome trophies of his victories – the teeth and bones of his fallen adversaries, strung together like grisly jewelry. A crude belt, fashioned from the sinewy vines that grew underground, held the loincloth in place and carried a wickedly curved dagger that was never far from his grasp.

Around his neck, Grizzletooth wore a necklace of assorted trinkets and charms, each one imbued with its own dark magic. These charms were said to grant him protection from the crystals that lay beneath the Elven Kingdom, allowing him to venture closer to the enchanted forest than any other goblin dared. They also enhanced his senses, enabling him to track intruders or potential threats with uncanny precision.

On his gnarled fingers, Grizzletooth wore crude, twisted rings fashioned from stolen gemstones and the bones of fallen foes. Each ring represented a victory, a testament to his dominance over the goblin horde and the fear he instilled in their hearts.

But perhaps the most chilling aspect of Grizzletooth's appearance was the mantle of authority he bore. Draped across his hunched shoulders was a cloak made from the tattered remains of a once-majestic Elven warrior's cape. It was a gruesome symbol of his power and a constant reminder to his subjects that even the mightiest of foes could be brought low by his cunning and brutality.

Grizzletooth ruled the underground goblin town with an iron fist, his terrifying appearance and ruthless demeanor serving as a constant source of inspiration and fear. Under his leadership, the goblins carried out Count Malachi's bidding, spreading chaos and fear throughout the enchanted forest, while always avoiding the crystals that protected the Elven Kingdom above. Grizzletooth was a living nightmare, a force of darkness that thrived in the shadowy depths of the enchanted forest, and his reign of terror showed no signs of ending anytime soon.

The underground goblin town, concealed beneath the enchanted forest, was ominously named "Netherholm." It stood as a stark contrast to the beauty of the world above, existing in perpetual darkness.

Netherholm's entrance was hidden deep within the labyrinthine depths of the enchanted forest, accessible only to those who possessed knowledge of its secret pathways and concealed passages. As one descended into the subterranean world, the immediate transition from daylight to darkness was palpable. The rough-hewn stone walls were sporadically lit by dim torches, casting eerie, flickering shadows that seemed to take on a sinister life of their own.

The labyrinthine tunnels of Netherholm twisted and wound like a maze, confounding and disorienting any intruders who dared venture into its depths. These goblins had an intimate familiarity with the tunnels, navigating them effortlessly, while outsiders would often become hopelessly lost in the inky blackness. Along the tunnel walls, strange markings and symbols, some rendered in blood, served as guides and warnings to those who dared to penetrate this subterranean realm.

Netherholm's architecture was a manifestation of the goblins' dark and twisted sensibilities. Caverns, hewn from the living rock, served as their dwellings. Gruesome trophies and sinister totems adorned these chambers, and the walls bore grotesque carvings that depicted scenes of violence and domination, all designed to reinforce Grizzletooth's unyielding rule.

One of the most eerie aspects of Netherholm was the pervasive feeling of isolation. The goblins seldom ventured to the surface world, and their underground town was compartmentalized into separate districts, often isolated from one another. Grizzletooth had intentionally designed this segregation, adhering to the principle of division to maintain his subjects' isolation and prevent them from uniting against his rule.

At the heart of Netherholm lay the central chamber, a vast cavern where Grizzletooth held his grim court. The cavern was dominated by a jagged, obsidian throne upon which Grizzletooth presided like a malevolent king. The throne was adorned with gruesome decorations, including the skulls of vanquished foes and the bones of those who had challenged his authority.

Around the throne, braziers cast a dim, reddish glow, creating an oppressive and malevolent atmosphere. Grizzletooth's loyal subjects, the goblins who had pledged their unwavering allegiance to him, congregated in the chamber to receive his commands and to pay homage to their brutal leader. Goblin guards, armed with wickedly sharp weapons and clad in crude armour, stood watch with fierce loyalty.

Netherholm was a place of ceaseless activity. Goblins toiled diligently, fulfilling various tasks that served Grizzletooth's dark purposes. Some crafted crude weapons and armour, while others brewed noxious potions and concocted sinister spells. New tunnels and chambers were excavated with relentless determination to expand their underground dominion.

Perhaps the most disturbing aspect of Netherholm was the lower levels, housing a network of grim prison cells. These cells imprisoned those who had dared to defy Grizzletooth or cross his path. Within those cells, prisoners endured unspeakable torment, their anguished cries echoing through the dark tunnels as a haunting reminder of the consequences of disobedience.

Despite the grim and oppressive nature of Netherholm, its inhabitants regarded Grizzletooth with awe and reverence. They believed him to be the embodiment of power and saw his rule as their source of dominance over the kingdom above. In the shadowy depths of this subterranean goblin town, their dark society thrived, bound by loyalty to their brutal leader and an unwavering commitment to execute Count Malachi's bidding while maintaining their grip on the enchanted forest.

Within the grim depths of Netherholm, Grizzletooth, the formidable goblin leader, presided over his malevolent kingdom. The underground town, shrouded in perpetual darkness, was his domain, and his ruthless rule had instilled terror in the hearts of the goblin horde.

One sinister night, as Grizzletooth contemplated his next nefarious move, a peculiar disturbance stirred within the shadowy depths of Netherholm. Unearthly whispers echoed through the caverns, causing the goblins to exchange nervous glances. It wasn't long before the source of the disturbance became evident.

Demonic worms, ghastly creatures with slick, writhing bodies, began to emerge from the crevices and cracks in the cavern walls. These abhorrent creatures were known for their ability to traverse the darkest recesses of the underworld, serving as messengers for entities of unspeakable darkness.

The goblins watched in eerie fascination as the worms slithered toward Grizzletooth's throne, their eyes gleaming with malevolence. These grotesque messengers bore the unmistakable mark of Count Malachi, and Grizzletooth knew that their arrival heralded an ominous summons from his dark master.

The demonic worms that emerged from the crevices and cracks in the cavern walls were grotesque and nightmarish creatures to behold. Their slick, writhing bodies were coated in a noxious, oily substance that seemed to glisten in the dim light of the cavern. These abhorrent creatures moved with an eerie grace, their sinuous forms undulating as they slithered across the cold, damp ground.

Their skin was a sickly shade of grayish black, marred with pulsating, vein-like patterns that seemed to writhe beneath the surface. These patterns emitted an eerie, faint luminescence, casting a haunting glow around them. Rows of sharp, jagged spines adorned their backs, each one seemingly designed to inflict pain and terror upon any who dared approach.

The worms had no discernible eyes, but their presence was unnerving nonetheless. Instead, their malevolence was evident in the way they moved, with a sinister, deliberate intent. As they slithered toward Grizzletooth's throne, the air seemed to grow heavy with their malevolent aura, and a sense of dread settled upon all who witnessed their approach.

These grotesque messengers, bearing Count Malachi's unmistakable mark—a twisted, crimson sigil that resembled a coiled serpent with wicked, piercing eyes—were harbingers of unspeakable darkness, and their very presence sent shivers down the spines of those in the cavern. Grizzletooth, the goblin king, knew all too well that their arrival signaled an ominous summons from his dark master, a summons that would undoubtedly lead to further malevolent deeds in the shadowy depths of their world.

With an unnerving grace, the worms converged before Grizzletooth, writhing and twisting in unsettling patterns. They formed a grotesque sigil on the cavern floor, an unholy symbol that pulsed with a sinister energy. Grizzletooth, ever the cunning leader, recognized the sign, and his eyes narrowed with grim anticipation.

The worms, pulsating with malevolent intent, coiled and wriggled to form a macabre message. Their movements were hypnotic and unnerving, as they spelled out the dark words of Count Malachi's command. Grizzletooth's eyes darted across the floor as the message took shape.

"Grizzletooth, Lord of Netherholm," the message began, "I, Count Malachi, summon you and your goblin horde to the surface world. Lady Seraphina, a key to my dominion, roams the enchanted forest. I task you with tracking her every move, but harm her not. Capture, ensnare, but do not inflict harm. Report her whereabouts to me."

Grizzletooth's grim visage darkened as he absorbed the message. Count Malachi's orders were clear, and he knew that defiance was not an option. Lady Seraphina had become an integral part of Count Malachi's plans, and her capture was paramount.

The goblin leader summoned his trusted advisors and warriors, relaying the dire message from Count Malachi. The goblins, though apprehensive, recognized the significance of the command and began to prepare for their ascent to the surface world.

The preparations were meticulous and swift. Grizzletooth ensured that his goblin army was armed with the darkest of weapons and ensorcelled traps designed to ensnare rather than maim. They crafted crude armour from the shadows of Netherholm and armed themselves with wickedly sharp blades. Their goal was to subdue, to capture, and to report Lady Seraphina's whereabouts, as Count Malachi had decreed.

As dawn broke above the enchanted forest, Grizzletooth and his goblin horde emerged from the hidden entrance to Netherholm. The goblins were an eerie sight, their twisted forms and malevolent weaponry a stark contrast to the enchanting beauty of the forest above.

They moved with stealth and cunning, tracking Lady Seraphina's path through the enchanted woods. Grizzletooth knew that she possessed an innate connection to the enchanted forest, and he could sense the challenge that lay ahead. The forest itself seemed to resist his presence, its ancient magic working against the intruders from below.

Days turned into nights as Grizzletooth and his goblin army combed the enchanted forest, setting traps and laying snares to capture Lady Seraphina without causing her harm. The goblins' knowledge of the forest's treacherous terrain gave them an edge, but the task was far from simple.

With Count Malachi's commands echoing in his mind, Grizzletooth was determined to fulfill his dark master's wishes. His ruthless cunning, combined with the goblins' relentless pursuit, closed the net around Lady Seraphina. It was only a matter of time before the elusive prey would be ensnared, and her whereabouts reported to Count Malachi.

As the goblin horde continued their relentless pursuit, Grizzletooth couldn't help but wonder about the significance of Lady Seraphina and the dark plans Count Malachi had in store. The enchanted forest held its secrets close, but with the goblin town's ominous presence lurking below, the balance of power in the kingdom hung in a precarious balance, ready to tip into the abyss of darkness.

In King Alaric's Kingdom, Ravenshadow, the Veridales family, a once-respected noble lineage, had become entangled in a clandestine alliance with Count Malachi. Unbeknownst to the kingdom's inhabitants, they had become instruments in his sinister schemes, lured by the promises of power he whispered to them.

The Veridales were a noble family that lived on the outskirts of the kingdom, far from the intrigues of the court. They were known for their loyalty and discretion, and Count Malachi had long been an ally of the family.

On a dark and stormy night, Count Malachi summoned his most trusted servant, a wizened old man named Thorne, and gave him a message to deliver to the Veridales. The message was to be carried by a raven, a bird that could fly swiftly and silently, unseen by prying eyes.

The message was simple but carried with it the weight of life and death. It read: "To the Veridales family, I beseech you to keep what I am about to reveal a secret known only to you. Lady Seraphina has still not returned to Shadowmoor, and no one in King Alaric's kingdom must know of her whereabouts. If you come across her or learn of her location, you must inform me immediately."

Thorne carefully attached the message to the leg of the raven, a majestic black creature with feathers as dark as night. With a whispered command, he released the bird into the stormy sky, watching as it disappeared into the distance. The raven's wings beat against the wind as it carried Count Malachi's urgent plea to the Veridales family.

Count Malachi would journey to the Veridales family, seeking the aid of his trusted allies. His mode of transportation was a nightmarish carriage, a terrifying vehicle that struck fear into the hearts of all who gazed upon it. This carriage was a colossal, iron-clad abomination, adorned with eerie symbols and menacing, sharp spikes. It appeared almost sentient, as though it had been crafted from the very essence of the shadows themselves. Instead of being drawn by horses, it was propelled forward by six gigantic black wolves, their malevolent red eyes gleaming ominously in the darkness. Their breath created spectral plumes in the frigid night air as they glided forward with an unnatural, silent grace. The carriage itself, with its iron frame and sinister embellishments, boasted six foreboding doors and six imposing wheels, each one adding to the overall sense of dread that surrounded it.

Count Malachi's journey to the Veridale family was fraught with anticipation and dread. The night was shrouded in darkness, and a bone-chilling wind whispered through the trees as his nightmarish carriage, drawn by the six enormous black wolves, approached the Veridales estate. The carriage, a grotesque and intimidating sight, seemed out of place amidst the tranquility of the countryside.

As the carriage pulled into the Veridales estate, it sent shivers down the spines of the family members who had gathered to meet Count Malachi. The eerie symbols and sharp spikes that adorned the iron-clad monstrosity caught the dim moonlight, casting eerie shadows across the faces of the onlookers. The wolves, with their red eyes glowing like embers of hellfire, moved with an uncanny, almost ghostly silence.

The Veridales, known for their unwavering loyalty and steadfastness, had never seen Count Malachi arrive in such a sinister manner. They exchanged bewildered glances, their eyes wide with shock and disbelief. The children clung to their parents, sensing the unnatural presence that had descended upon their home.

Count Malachi, cloaked in a dark and billowing robe that seemed to absorb the very light around him, stepped out of the carriage with an air of foreboding. His presence alone was enough to send a chill through the air, and the family members could not help but feel a sense of unease wash over them.

As he approached the Veridales, Count Malachi's normally composed and refined demeanor had undergone a sinister transformation. His eyes, once filled with warmth and familiarity, now gleamed with an otherworldly intensity. His voice, when he spoke, carried an eerie resonance, as if it were not entirely his own.

"Loyal friends of old," he intoned, his words dripping with an unsettling charm, "I have come to you in this dire hour, seeking your aid and discretion in a matter of utmost secrecy."

Lady Veridales, a woman of grace and composure, stepped forward, her eyes fixed on Count Malachi. She could sense a demonic shift in him, a darkness that had not been there before. Her voice quivered slightly as she responded, "Count Malachi, what has happened to you? You arrive in such an ominous fashion, and you bear an aura of darkness that chills our very souls."

Count Malachi's lips curled into a chilling smile, revealing teeth that seemed sharper and more menacing than before. "My dear Lady Veridales," he murmured, "you must understand that desperate times call for desperate measures. The kingdom is in turmoil, and I have been entrusted with a grave responsibility—one that requires me to embrace the shadows."

The Veridales family exchanged worried glances, their concern for their friend and the kingdom growing. They had always known Count Malachi as a man of cunning and wit, but the transformation they witnessed was beyond anything they could have imagined.

With a wave of his hand, Count Malachi dismissed his eerie carriage and the six black wolves. The monstrous contraption vanished into the night, leaving only a lingering sense of dread in its wake. It was then that he revealed the true reason for his visit—a message of dire importance regarding Lady Seraphina.

The Veridales listened in rapt attention as Count Malachi recounted the escape of Lady Seraphina. He implored them to keep this knowledge a secret, to guard it with their lives.

As Count Malachi spoke, the family members could not help but feel a growing sense of unease. His words carried a weight and a darkness that hung in the air like a foreboding storm. They knew that they had been drawn into a web of intrigue and danger that extended far beyond their peaceful estate.

With heavy hearts, the Veridales pledged their loyalty to Count Malachi and his cause. They would do whatever it took to locate Lady Seraphina and help bring about the change that their kingdom so desperately needed. Little did they know that their allegiance would lead them down a treacherous path, one filled with secrets, lies, and the ever-present darkness that seemed to surround Count Malachi.

As Count Malachi's influence grew, the kingdom was ensnared in his dark web. Morgana brewed potions and cast spells in the evil forest, Grizzletooth and his goblins spread fear and chaos beneath and within the enchanted forest outside the Elven realm, and the Veridales family did Count Malachi's bidding in King Alaric's Kingdom.

Count Malachi's lust for power was insatiable, and his network of influence grew stronger with each passing day. Both kingdoms trembled under his shadow, and the people lived in fear of the malevolent force that had ensnared their land. Little did they know that a web had been spun, one that stretched far and wide, ensnaring not only Lady Seraphina but all who dared to challenge Count Malachi's dominion. In the darkness of the night, as the Veridales family pledged their loyalty, they unwittingly became another thread in this intricate tapestry of deception and intrigue, bound by a destiny that had been set into motion by Count Malachi's unholy ambitions.

Count Malachi, shrouded in the cloak of his insatiable lust for power, stood amidst the eerie silence of the Veridales darkened estate grounds. The moon hung low in the night sky, casting an eerie pallor over the twisted trees and the cobblestone path that led to his foreboding fortress in the distance. His network of influence had indeed grown stronger with each passing day, and his malevolent force had ensnared not only the two trembling kingdoms but all who dared challenge his dominion.

Tonight was a night of unholy ambitions, a night when Count Malachi would once again forge a sinister alliance with the devil himself. As he stood there, his eyes gleaming with a wicked intensity, he beckoned with a subtle gesture. In response, a haunting, otherworldly howl pierced the night, echoing through the forest that surrounded the Veridales Estate.

From the depths of darkness emerged the mysterious and sinister creatures that Count Malachi had forged an unholy bond with— creatures that bore the unmistakable mark of the devil. The wolf carriage, a grotesque and fearsome creation, stood before him. Its shadowy form seemed to meld seamlessly with the darkness, obscuring the horrors that lurked within.

Without a word, Count Malachi stepped into the wolf carriage, his black cloak billowing around him. The moment his foot touched the carriage's interior, an eerie transformation occurred. The carriage itself seemed to come alive, its demonic essence pulsating with malevolence. The very air within grew heavy with an oppressive darkness, and a cold, unnatural chill settled in.

The journey back to Count Malachi's castle commenced, the wheels of the wolf carriage turning silently, as if guided by some unholy force. The path before them was bathed in an eerie, dim light, casting twisted, elongated shadows that danced grotesquely along the way. As they moved deeper into the night, the carriage seemed to devour the very essence of the surroundings, leaving nothing but an abyss in its wake.

Within the confines of the carriage, Count Malachi's thoughts were consumed by the devilish plans that he had hatched. His ambitions knew no bounds, and he was willing to strike any unholy bargain to achieve his desires. He knew the risks, the price that would be demanded by his infernal ally, but he cared not for the consequences. Power, dominion, and unending control over the kingdoms were his only obsessions.

The journey felt surreal, as if time itself had warped in the presence of such malevolent power. Count Malachi could hear the whispers of the devil, a sinister voice that echoed in his mind, tempting him with promises of unmatched power and unending dominion. The allure was intoxicating, and he felt himself drawn deeper into the abyss of his own dark desires.

Finally, the wolf carriage arrived at Count Malachi's castle—a looming, imposing fortress that stood as a testament to his unquenchable thirst for power. The castle's walls seemed to absorb the very darkness of the night, and its turrets reached towards the heavens like the spires of a malevolent cathedral.

As Count Malachi stepped out of the wolf carriage, the atmosphere around him crackled with an eerie energy. He knew that he was now bound by a destiny of his own making, one that had been set into motion by his unholy ambitions. The devil's deeds awaited him within the castle's shadowy halls, where secrets, treachery, and dark magic swirled like a malevolent storm.

With each step he took toward his castle, Count Malachi's heartbeat faster, his anticipation growing. He was ready to make more unholy deeds with the devil, ready to pay any price for the power and dominion he craved. The night was his ally, the darkness his cloak, and the devil his sinister accomplice in a world where the boundaries between the mortal and the infernal had blurred into a nightmarish reality.

Forbidden Alliance

The first rays of dawn filtered through the dense canopy of the enchanted forest, casting a gentle, ethereal glow over the serene landscape. Lady Seraphina and her faithful steed, Sir Sterling, stood amidst the tranquil clearing, the air crisp and filled with the soft hum of nature's magic. Elyndra, an Elven warrior known for her unparalleled skills, rode upon her majestic mount, Aelion. Tilly and Tally, two fairies with shimmering glows—Tally a radiant sapphire blue and the Tilly a vibrant ruby red—fluttered about, casting a delicate luminescence around the pair.

As the morning light bathed the forest, the companions enjoyed a hearty breakfast gathered from the bountiful offerings of the enchanted woods. Fruits, nuts, and sweet nectar from the flora provided sustenance, and the gentle sounds of the forest creatures served as a soothing backdrop.

With renewed energy and purpose, Lady Seraphina and Elyndra prepared to continue their journey westward, toward the fabled Angel city of Aeloria. Their resolve was unshaken, for they knew that the fate of their lands rested on their shoulders, and the whispers of hope carried on the forest winds fueled their determination.

It was then that the forest itself seemed to respond to their presence. A subtle rustling of leaves, a harmonious murmuring of the ancient trees, and the mystical aura of the woods converged to offer them a means of transportation. From the heart of the forest emerged two ethereal beings, their forms resembling great stags with antlers adorned in radiant autumnal leaves. These magnificent creatures radiated an aura of serenity, and their eyes held ancient wisdom.

Lady Seraphina, filled with awe and gratitude, approached the larger of the two forest spirits, a regal being named Lysandor. With a sense of reverence, she extended her hand, and Lysandor bowed its antlered head, allowing her to mount. Elyndra, equally moved by the presence of the forest, did the same with the other spirit, named Thalindra.

Their journey continued on these majestic forest steeds, moving with an otherworldly grace and swiftness. The fairies, Tilly and Tally, perched delicately on the antlers of their respective mounts, their radiant glows guiding the way through the ever-shifting paths of the enchanted forest.

With Lady Seraphina and Elyndra gracefully mounted on the enchanted forest spirits, Lysandor and Thalindra, the burden of weight was lifted from Sir Sterling and Aelion. The noble horses now moved with an unburdened grace, their powerful strides matching the pace of their riders as they trotted alongside. This respite allowed the horses to conserve their strength and navigate the enchanted forest with a newfound vitality, while Lady Seraphina and Elyndra remained vigilant, their swords ready and their spirits unwavering, ready to face any challenge that lay ahead.

Yet, as the day wore on and the companions ventured deeper into the forest, a sense of unease settled upon them. The once serene woods seemed to grow restless, and an unsettling stillness hung in the air. It was as if the very heart of the forest held its breath, anticipating an impending threat.

Suddenly, the tranquility shattered. Goblins, vile creatures with grotesque features, swung down from the trees on crude vine ropes, while others burst forth from the underbrush with savage yells. Some even emerged from hidden tunnels in the ground, clawing their way up to the surface with malicious intent.

The goblins, led by the cunning and malevolent Grizzletooth, had ambushed Lady Seraphina and Elyndra. Weapons raised, the goblins encircled their prey, their eyes filled with a hunger for violence and conquest. In a moment of swift decision, Lady Seraphina and Elyndra gracefully dismounted from their majestic steeds, Lysandor and Thalindra. With a swift turn, the majestic steeds sprinted toward the shadows and almost seemed to vanish into thin air, relying on their majestic agility to evade capture.

Meanwhile, Sir Sterling and Aelion, their loyalty unwavering, stood firm beside their masters. With a fierce determination, they fought alongside Lady Seraphina and Elyndra. Kicking and biting at the encroaching goblins, they sent the vile creatures sprawling, their powerful hooves and jaws becoming formidable weapons in the battle. The loyal steeds' presence was a testament to the unbreakable bond between them and their riders, as they defended their companions with unwavering devotion.

Tilly and Tally, the fairies, took to the air, their shimmering glows casting an enchanting light across the battlefield. They darted around the goblins, causing momentary confusion and distraction with their bewitching presence.

The sounds of Lady Seraphina's sword clashing against the goblins' weapons rang like a battle hymn through the heart of the enchanted forest. Her movements were a dance of grace and precision, as if she and her sword were one entity in perfect harmony. With every strike, her blade cut through the air with an otherworldly swiftness, leaving trails of sparkling light in its wake. Her unwavering determination shone through, a beacon of hope amidst the chaos of the goblin onslaught.

As Lady Seraphina clashed with her foes, she remained steadfast in the light, her resolve unwavering. The amethyst at the hilt of her sword glowed with a radiant purple hue, a testament to her unwavering commitment to righteousness. Her every movement was bathed in the gentle luminescence of her purpose, and it seemed as though the sword and its wielder were inextricably linked, moving as one to defend against the encroaching darkness. Her actions inspired awe and fear in equal measure, as the goblins witnessed a force of light that refused to be extinguished.

Elyndra's fighting style was a testament to the graceful and fluid ways of the Elves. With her sword in hand, she moved with an ethereal elegance that seemed to defy gravity itself. Each of her movements was a mesmerizing display of precision and agility as she weaved through the chaotic battlefield, her blade a silvery streak of deadly grace.

Her strikes were a mesmerizing blend of offense and defense, a delicate balance between parrying the goblins' attacks and delivering her own swift counters. Elyndra's footwork was as light as a leaf carried by the wind, enabling her to swiftly reposition herself and evade danger effortlessly. Her keen Elven senses allowed her to anticipate her foes' moves, and she countered with finesse and dexterity, disarming her opponents with elegant swipes and thrusts.

Elyndra's combat style was a symphony of deadly artistry, each clash of steel a mesmerizing dance that left goblins bewildered and awestruck. Her movements seemed to flow seamlessly from one form to another, a testament to the age-old Elven martial traditions passed down through the generations. In the midst of battle, she embodied the timeless beauty and lethal precision of her people, a living testament to the enduring grace and strength of the Elves.

For every goblin that Lady Seraphina and Elyndra managed to defeat with their skill and valor, it seemed as though ten more emerged from the shadowy depths of the forest like an unending tide. It was a relentless onslaught, akin to trying to stem the flow of an unyielding river. The goblins came forth in such numbers that the companions felt as if they were locked in a nightmarish struggle against an inexhaustible horde.

The forest echoed with the cacophonous battle cries of the goblins, their malevolent presence like an infestation that threatened to overwhelm all reason and hope. The companions fought valiantly, but the odds were stacking impossibly against them. With each passing moment, the goblin ranks swelled, and the sense of being besieged by an unending swarm grew more oppressive.

Amidst the chaos of the goblin onslaught, Tilly and Tally, the two fairies with their shimmering glows, began to whistle a high-pitched, haunting tune that pierced through the clamor of battle. The melody carried an enchanting quality, weaving through the air like a spell. As the ethereal notes filled the forest, some of the goblins found themselves momentarily entranced, their weapons lowering as they were lulled by the enchanting music. It was as if the fairies' song had momentarily disarmed their aggression, creating a surreal moment of respite amidst the relentless battle.

But just as the battle seemed to reach a precarious equilibrium, a mighty roar pierced the chaos. From above, a massive creature descended with the grace of a hunting hawk and the power of a thunderstorm. It was a Griffin, a magnificent fusion of eagle and lion, its plumage a striking combination of fiery red and golden bronze.

The Griffin landed amidst the goblins, its wings unfurling to their full span, casting a shadow that sent shivers down the goblins' spines. With a swipe of its powerful claws, it dispatched several of the creatures, sending them fleeing in terror. Its eagle-like beak snapped with precision, and its roar echoed with an intensity that could strike fear into even the bravest of hearts.

The tide of battle shifted dramatically in favour of Lady Seraphina and Elyndra. With the Griffin by their side, they became a formidable trio, a force of nature that the goblins could scarcely contend with.

In a desperate bid to regain control of the spiraling battle, Grizzletooth, the cunning goblin leader, raised a horn to his twisted lips. The horn itself was a grotesque and sinister artifact, carved from the bone of a long-forgotten beast. It bore eerie, dark etchings that seemed to writhe and squirm as if cursed with malevolence. When Grizzletooth blew into the horn, the sound that emanated from it was a cacophonous wail, a shrill, unearthly cry that echoed through the forest like a banshee's lament.

The eerie sound of the horn sent shivers down the spines of both friend and foe. It was a signal of retreat, a harsh acknowledgment that the goblins were losing too many numbers in the face of Lady Seraphina, Elyndra, and their newfound ally, the Griffin. Grizzletooth's face contorted in anger and frustration as he realized that victory was slipping through his clawed fingers like grains of sand.

With a resentful glare, Grizzletooth issued a guttural command to his remaining goblins, and they scurried back toward the hidden tunnels from which they had emerged. The goblin leader's rage was palpable as he watched his forces retreat, defeated and humiliated. The tunnels swallowed the retreating horde, and the forest seemed to sigh in relief as the malevolent presence of the goblins receded, leaving behind a battle-scarred landscape and a lingering sense of foreboding.

As the goblins retreated in disarray, Lady Seraphina and Elyndra turned toward the Griffin, their swords at their sides but not raised in hostility. The majestic creature had answered the fairies' call for help, their haunting whistle reaching its ears like a distant cry. Elyndra, however, bore a conflicted expression, her distrust of Griffins evident in her wary stance.

Lady Seraphina raised her hand, urging restraint. "Hold, Elyndra. Let us hear why this Griffin chose to aid us."

The Griffin regarded them with eyes that held both intelligence and ancient wisdom. With a voice that rumbled like distant thunder, it spoke, "I am Raelthor, Guardian of this part of the Enchanted Forest. My kind and yours have not always been allies, but I sensed the purity of your intent and the desperate need for your quest. I cannot stand idly by when the balance of these woods is threatened. The goblins are agents of darkness, and their presence here is an affront to the very essence of the forest."

Elyndra cast a wary glance toward Lady Seraphina, her voice a cautious whisper. "Lady Seraphina, we must tread carefully with this Griffin. It is not a mere chance that Elves do not trust their kind. Griffins, while they possess their own majestic qualities, have often been enigmatic and unpredictable in their alliances. Our ancestors have shared tales of their treacherous ways, their motives as elusive as the wind that carries them."

She paused, her gaze locked on Raelthor, the Guardian of these parts of the Enchanted Forest, who stood nearby. "It is true that this creature aided us against the goblins, but we must not forget the ancient stories that speak of Griffins using their cunning for their own agendas. We cannot be certain of its true intentions, Lady Seraphina, and in these uncertain times, we must exercise caution before placing our trust in one who dwells on the fringes of our ancient alliances."

Raelthor, the Griffin, regarded Elyndra with a sense of ancient wisdom and grace. His voice, as he responded, carried the weight of centuries of knowledge. "Elyndra, wise and graceful Elf, you speak of tales passed down through the generations. It is true that history, like the shifting leaves of the forest, can be distorted and altered with each retelling. Our kind has its own stories of betrayal by the Elves, just as you have yours of treacherous Griffins."

He continued, his gaze steady. "But remember, there are always three sides to the truth—the Elves' version, the Griffins' version, and what truly transpired, known only to the Oracles of Time. The roots of our distrust may be lost in the mists of history, and it is not for me to lay blame on either side. I am here now as a Guardian of this forest, to protect it from the encroaching darkness. Let our actions in this moment speak of our intentions, and may we find common ground in the face of a shared enemy."

Elyndra, her gaze unwavering, sought to sway Lady Seraphina from trusting the Griffin. "Lady Seraphina, you must tread cautiously with this creature. The alliance between Elves and Griffins has long been forbidden, for their motives can be as elusive as the wind. We should not forget the ancient tales that speak of their treacherous ways."

Lady Seraphina, torn between her trust in her fellow Elf and her gratitude for the Griffin's aid, hesitated. She knew that Elyndra's words held wisdom, but in this dire moment, she could not ignore the undeniable help the Griffin had provided. She turned her gaze back to Raelthor, her decision weighing heavily on her heart.

Elyndra hesitated but nodded in reluctant acceptance of Raelthor's explanation. Lady Seraphina extended her hand to the Griffin, a gesture of gratitude and understanding. "Thank you, Raelthor, Guardian of the Enchanted Forest. We are honoured by your aid and humbled by your wisdom. Together, we shall face the darkness that threatens not only our lands but this sacred realm."

With newfound unity and purpose, the trio—Lady Seraphina, Elyndra, and Raelthor the Griffin—set forth once more on their journey through the enchanted forest. The fairies, Tilly and Tally, danced around them, their glows shining brighter with renewed hope. They knew that their path was treacherous, but with the Guardian of the Forest at their side, they were determined to confront whatever challenges lay ahead and continue their quest to reach the Angel city of Aeloria.

As they ventured deeper into the forest, Raelthor, the Griffin, maintained a vigilant presence, his majestic form soaring above the treetops, keeping a watchful eye on their surroundings. The companions traveled through the enchanting woods, the dappled sunlight filtering through the ancient branches, casting a mosaic of light and shadow on their path while traveling via horseback on their noble steeds.

However, as they journeyed further westward, Raelthor addressed Lady Seraphina and Elyndra with a solemn tone. "My companions, I have vowed to protect this part of the Enchanted Forest, and my duty as its Guardian calls me to remain within its boundaries. I will be with you until we reach the western edge of this realm, but beyond that point, I must let you continue your journey alone."

Lady Seraphina nodded in understanding, a sense of gratitude and respect for the Griffin filling her heart. "Raelthor, Guardian of the Enchanted Forest, we are thankful for your aid and guidance thus far. We will honour your duty to this realm and journey on with the strength and wisdom you have bestowed upon us. May the light of your forest guide us safely."

Elyndra, though still harbouring some distrust, acknowledged the Griffin's role with a nod. "Indeed, Raelthor, your presence has been invaluable. We shall respect your boundaries and carry your wisdom forward on our quest. But first, let us make the most of the time we have together in these enchanted woods."

With renewed determination, the trio continued their trek, each step bringing them closer to the western edge of the Enchanted Forest. Along the way, Raelthor shared tales of the forest's ancient magic and the creatures that dwelled within, imparting knowledge that would serve Lady Seraphina and Elyndra well on their journey.

One of the first lessons Raelthor offered was the importance of balance in nature. He explained how the forest's delicate equilibrium relied on every creature, no matter how small or seemingly insignificant. He taught them to respect and coexist with the creatures of the forest, for their actions could have far-reaching consequences on the forest's well-being. This lesson reminded Lady Seraphina and Elyndra of the interconnectedness of all life and the responsibility they carried as guardians of the natural world.

Raelthor also shared insights into the power of patience and observation. He encouraged them to listen to the whispers of the forest, to watch for subtle signs and hidden truths. Under his guidance, they learned to decipher the forest's language, recognizing when to step lightly and when to stand firm. This knowledge would serve them well in deciphering the challenges and mysteries that lay ahead.

Another invaluable lesson Raelthor imparted was the need for adaptability. He explained that the Enchanted Forest was ever-changing, and those who sought to navigate its depths must be willing to adjust their course and embrace the unexpected. Lady Seraphina and Elyndra learned to trust their instincts and adapt to the shifting tides of their quest, knowing that rigidity could lead to stagnation.

As the days passed, the companions faced myriad challenges, from treacherous terrain to encounters with mystical creatures. Yet, with Raelthor's guidance and the unity forged through their shared trials, they overcame each obstacle. The Griffin's presence served as a reminder that even in a land as enchanted and perilous as this, there were allies to be found, and alliances to be forged.

Finally, as the western edge of the Enchanted Forest came into view, Raelthor landed gracefully before the trio. His powerful wings folded with a regal grace, and he addressed Lady Seraphina and Elyndra once more. "Our journey together has come to its appointed end. Beyond this point, the forest's magic shifts, and my duty as Guardian calls me to remain. Know that my spirit will watch over you from afar, and my hope is that you find success in your quest to reach Aeloria."

Lady Seraphina offered a warm smile, a bond of trust and respect having grown between them. "Raelthor, Guardian and friend, we shall carry your wisdom and protection with us on our journey. Your guidance has been a beacon of hope in these enchanted woods."

Elyndra, her initial distrust now replaced with a measure of respect, added, "Indeed, Raelthor, your aid has not gone unnoticed. We will journey on with the strength you've helped us find within ourselves."

With their farewells exchanged, Lady Seraphina, Elyndra, and the two fairies, Tilly and Tally, continued their quest westward, leaving the Guardian of the Enchanted Forest behind. Raelthor watched them go, his majestic form fading into the depths of the forest, his heart filled with hope that the light of their purpose would guide them safely on their path to Aeloria.

King Thaladir, ruler of the Elves, gazed upon the parchment before him with a sense of gravitas that weighed heavily on his regal shoulders. The fate of their realm hung in the balance, and he knew that a desperate plea for aid was their only hope against the malevolent ambitions of Count Malachi. With a deep breath, he dipped his quill into the inkwell and began to compose the letter that would be their beacon of hope.

"To the Noble and Honourable General of the Crusade Army,

I, Thaladir, King of the Elves, send this missive with a heart heavy with concern and a plea for aid in our time of dire need. Our once-peaceful realm, nestled within the embrace of the Enchanted Forest, has fallen under the shadow of Count Malachi, a being whose lust for power knows no bounds. His network of influence grows stronger with each passing day, and his malevolent force ensnares our land, casting it into despair.

Our people live in fear, their lives marred by the malevolence that Count Malachi has wrought upon us. Our ancient realm, known for its serenity and magic, now trembles under his dominion. It is a dominion that threatens not only us but the very balance of the natural world we have long cherished.

We beseech you, noble General, to lend us the strength of the Crusade Army. Your mighty forces, known throughout the lands for their valor and unwavering resolve, are our last hope against Count Malachi's dark ambitions. Our enchanted forest, once a sanctuary of light and wonder, now faces the encroaching darkness, and we cannot defend it alone.

We humbly request your aid in driving back Count Malachi's forces and restoring the peace and harmony that our realm once knew. Our plea carries with it the solemn promise of alliance and gratitude, for we understand the weight of the debt we would owe to the Crusade Army.

May this letter find you in good health and your heart filled with noble purpose. We eagerly await your response, and with hope in our hearts, we stand ready to unite against the malevolent force that threatens our realm.

With utmost sincerity,

Thaladir, King of the Elves"

With the letter penned and sealed with the royal insignia, King Thaladir dispatched a trusted envoy to deliver it to the Crusade Army, which was known to be encamped in the distant western lands. This army, renowned for its valor and unwavering commitment to justice, had earned a formidable reputation as defenders of the realm.

The Crusade Army, based in the fortified city of Valorian, was a formidable force known throughout the realm for its unwavering dedication to maintaining peace and order. Situated in the western reaches of the realm, Valorian was a bastion of strength, its towering walls and gleaming spires a testament to the army's prowess and the city's strategic importance.

The soldiers of the Crusade Army were a sight to behold, clad in gleaming armour that reflected the sunlight with a radiant brilliance. Their armour was masterfully crafted, each piece a work of art adorned with intricate engravings and symbols of their righteous cause. Polished to a mirror–like sheen, their armour was a symbol of their unwavering commitment to justice and honour.

At the helm of the Crusade Army stood General Eldric Ironheart, a man of unmatched valor and wisdom. His reputation as a fearless leader and a strategist of unparalleled skill had earned him the respect and admiration of his troops. With a commanding presence and golden eyes that bore the weight of countless battles, General Ironheart had a deep well of experience to draw from.

General Ironheart was a man of unwavering dedication to his troops and his people. His leadership extended beyond the battlefield, as he was known for his compassion and sense of justice. His silver hair, streaked with the wisdom of years, flowed down to his shoulders, framing a face that bore the scars of countless battles. Yet, his eyes sparkled with a fire that had not dimmed with time, and his voice carried a gravitas that commanded respect from all who heard it.

As the envoy bearing King Thaladir's letter arrived at the gates of Valorian, it was General Ironheart himself who received the royal missive. With a solemn nod, he broke the royal seal and read the contents, his expression grave and contemplative. The fate of their realm now rested in his hands, and he knew that the decision he would make would shape the destiny of their land and its people.

General Eldric Ironheart wasted no time in summoning a meeting with his army's highest-ranking leaders, five individuals whose wisdom and counsel he valued above all else. They were the pillars of the Crusade Army, each one carrying the weight of their own experiences and perspectives.

The first among them was Lady Titania Stormbringer, a formidable warrior with a fierce dedication to justice. Her silver hair, a striking contrast to her sapphire blue eyes, framed a face marked by the trials of countless battles. Lady Isolde had earned her place as a leader through her unwavering commitment to protecting the realm, and her voice was one of authority and strength.

The second was Sir Alden Frostbane, a seasoned tactician and strategist known for his icy composure even in the heat of battle. His piercing blue eyes seemed to see through any challenge, and his strategic brilliance was a valuable asset to the army. Sir Alden's analytical mind often brought a pragmatic approach to their decisions.

The third leader was Captain Elara Swiftwind, a skilled archer and scout whose connection to the natural world was unparalleled. With his fiery red hair and forest-green eyes, he embodied the spirit of the wildlands they sought to protect. His insights into the terrain and the subtleties of the enchanted forest had been invaluable.

The fourth was Lord Cellok Stoneforge, a master of the art of siege warfare and fortifications. His rugged appearance, adorned with a salt-and-pepper beard and scarred hands, spoke of his years spent in the crafting of defenses. Lord Cellok was the guardian of Valorian's walls and an unwavering protector of the city.

The final leader was Lady Serabella, a mage of great power and wisdom. With long, flowing hair the colour of moonlight and black eyes that held the secrets of arcane knowledge, she brought a mystical element to their ranks. Lady Serabella's connection to the unseen world and her ability to harness magic made her an enigmatic presence among the leaders.

As they gathered in the war room of Valorian's citadel, General Ironheart addressed them with a sense of urgency. "My esteemed comrades, we face a grave decision that will shape the fate of our realm. We have received a plea for aid from King Thaladir of the Elves, who faces a dire threat in the form of Count Malachi's dark ambitions."

Lady Stormbringer, her voice filled with determination, spoke first. "General, we have sworn to protect the realm from all threats. If the Elves are in peril, it is our duty to aid them, regardless of their mystical nature. Justice knows no boundaries."

Sir Frostbane, ever the pragmatist, countered, "While I agree that our duty is to protect the realm, we must consider the implications of such an alliance. The Elves, as mystical creatures, are not of the human realm. We tread into uncertain territory, and we must weigh the risks."

Captain Swiftwind, his connection to the natural world evident, voiced his support for aiding the Elves. "General, the enchanted forest is a part of the natural world we hold dear. Its balance affects us all. We should protect it, even if the Elves are our allies in this endeavor."

Lord Stoneforge, ever mindful of defenses, added, "I understand the importance of fortifying our borders. But if we turn our backs on the Elves in their hour of need, what message does that send? Our unity and strength in the face of darkness are our greatest defenses." Lady Serabella, the mage, brought her mystical perspective to the discussion. "General, the arcane forces within the enchanted forest hold great power. We should harness that power against Count Malachi's malevolence. Together, we can achieve what none could alone."

General Ironheart listened to their arguments, each voice carrying weight and wisdom. With a heavy heart, he realized that the decision was not unanimous. Turning to the five leaders, he spoke with a solemn tone. "I respect each of your perspectives, and I value your counsel. But this decision weighs heavily on our shoulders, and we cannot afford to be divided. I propose that we put it to a vote."

Lady Stormbringer and Captain Swiftwind nodded in agreement, firmly in favor of aiding the Elves. Sir Frostbane and Lord Stoneforge exchanged a thoughtful glance before nodding as well, agreeing to the vote. Lady Serabella, her mystical gaze fixed on the unseen, remained silent, her perspective known to all.

With the vote cast, General Ironheart knew that the fate of their realm now rested in the hands of the Crusade Army's leaders. The decision would determine not only their course of action but also the strength of their unity in the face of Count Malachi's ominous threat.

General Eldric Ironheart took a moment to collect his thoughts as he watched the parchment bearing the Crusade Army's decision take flight, carried by a graceful dove. The fate of their realm now hung on the wings of that bird, and he couldn't help but feel the weight of their choice. With a firm resolve, he released the dove, watching it soar into the sky toward the distant Elven realm.

The letter, inscribed with words of alliance and hope, carried the promise that the Crusade Army would aid the Elves in their dire struggle against Count Malachi. It bore the general's signature, a symbol of their commitment to the cause. As the dove disappeared into the horizon, General Ironheart couldn't help but wonder how this alliance would shape their future.

Before he could dwell too long on his thoughts, a soft voice interrupted his reverie. "General Ironheart, I sense a change in the winds of fate."

Turning to face Lady Serabella, the mage of their ranks, he couldn't help but be struck once again by her ethereal beauty. With long, flowing hair the colour of moonlight and eyes that seemed to hold the mysteries of the arcane, she was a vision of enchantment. Her slender fingers, adorned with delicate rings, reached out to gently touch his broad, strong, and muscular shoulders.

General Ironheart met her gaze, his own eyes a deep shade of hazel that reflected the weight of his responsibilities. "Lady Serabella, your insights are always valued. What do you sense?"

Her touch lingered on his shoulders as she spoke, her voice carrying a sense of foreboding. "This quest, General, holds the potential for great change, not only for the safety of our realms but for something more profound. I sense that it will shape the very core of who you are. You, who have always been a steadfast guardian of our lands, may find yourself facing not only external threats but the depths of your own soul."

General Ironheart absorbed her words, his gaze unwavering. "I have always known that our duty comes with sacrifice. If this quest changes me, so be it. I will face it with the same resolve that has guided me thus far."

Lady Serabella smiled softly, her fingers leaving his shoulders as she took a step back. "Your strength is unwavering, General, and your resolve is admirable. Whatever lies ahead, know that we stand with you, united in purpose."

The general nodded, gratitude shining in his hazel eyes. "Thank you, Lady Serabella. Your wisdom and support mean more than words can express."

As they turned to leave the war room, their hearts filled with the weight of their decision and the uncertainty of the future, General Ironheart couldn't help but reflect on the profound changes that lay ahead. The alliance with the Elves was but the beginning of a journey that would test not only their valor but the very essence of who they were as guardians of the realm.

As they made their way out of the war room, the subtle shift in the atmosphere didn't escape General Ironheart's notice. He felt a gaze upon him, an intense longing that seemed to emanate from Lady Serabella. As he turned to look back at her, their eyes met, and in that fleeting moment, the unspoken connection between them deepened. It was as if the weight of their shared responsibilities and the uncertainty of the future had brought them closer, forging an unbreakable bond that transcended their roles as guardians of the realm. In her eyes, he saw a vulnerability and longing that mirrored his own, and it was in that moment that where they found meaning in one another's longings for love.

The intensity of that shared gaze lingered in the air, a silent invitation that spoke volumes. Lady Serabella's heart raced as she held General Ironheart's gaze, and in that heartbeat, she made a decision that would change the course of their lives. With a subtle, almost imperceptible nod, she conveyed her desire, and he understood.

That evening, as the castle settled into a quiet stillness after the day's training and council meetings, Lady Serabella sent a discreet message to General Ironheart. She had arranged for a flickering candle to be placed on the windowsill of her chambers, casting a warm, inviting glow into the darkness of the night. With a soft knock on her door, he arrived, his presence both commanding and reassuring.

As General Ironheart stepped into her chambers, the flickering candlelight revealed a room bathed in shadows, creating an intimate atmosphere that matched the depths of their unspoken emotions. The tension between them was palpable, a combination of longing, desire, and the weight of their responsibilities.

Without a word, Lady Serabella approached him, her eyes locked onto his. Her hand reached out, trembling slightly, and touched his chest, where his heart beat strong and steady. Their lips met in a kiss that spoke of longing and forbidden passion, igniting a fire that had smoldered beneath the surface for far too long.

In the hushed moments that followed, they found solace in each other's arms, but it was not love that had brought them together. Unbeknownst to General Ironheart, Lady Serabella had cast a gentle enchantment, kindling an irresistible attraction within him. As their bodies entwined, their connection deepened, driven by the magical influence that bound them. In that night, they shared a passion born of enchantment, a secret that would forever alter the course of their destiny.

In the soft, flickering candlelight that bathed Lady Serabella's chambers, General Ironheart's touch was gentle as he traced her body with his fingertips. His hands moved with reverence, exploring the curves of her form as she lay naked before him. His fingers glided over the arch of her neck, down the gentle slope of her collarbone, and along the curve of her waist, where her skin felt as soft as silk. Every contour and curve were an invitation, an invitation he accepted with a mixture of desire and admiration.

As he sat on the edge of the bed, the dim light cast tantalizing shadows across her body, accentuating the graceful curves that defined her femininity. Her skin, kissed by the soft glow of the candle, seemed to shimmer like moonlight on water. General Ironheart's eyes moved slowly, taking in every nuance of her beauty, from the gentle swell of her breasts to the inviting curve of her hips. Each touch of his fingertips elicited a soft, barely audible sigh of pleasure from Lady Serabella, and the intensity of their connection deepened with every passing moment.

In that intimate space, their desires and passions intertwined, guided not only by the enchantment that had brought them together but also by the undeniable chemistry that had always simmered beneath the surface. The candlelight played its part, casting a seductive allure over Lady Serabella's body, inviting General Ironheart to explore every inch of her soft curves, as they surrendered to the magnetic pull that had drawn them into this clandestine embrace.

Shadows of Fear

Grizzletooth, the cunning goblin leader, had a message to deliver to Count Malachi, the relentless pursuer of Lady Seraphina. Despite his failure to capture her, Grizzletooth's resourcefulness had borne fruit, for he had a spy in the form of a mystical creature known as a "mysti-monk." The mysti-monk, named Fizzlewick, was a small, agile being resembling a monkey, but with shimmering emerald fur and luminous azure eyes. It possessed the ability to blend seamlessly into its surroundings, making it an ideal scout.

As Grizzletooth prepared the message, Fizzlewick chattered softly, relaying the details of Lady Seraphina's whereabouts. She had traveled to the Western edge of the enchanted forest embarking on a journey to the Aeloria.

Grizzletooth tied the scroll to the leg of a raven, and with a flap of wings, the bird took off, embarking on its perilous journey to Count Malachi's fortress.

Count Malachi awaited news of Lady Seraphina with bated breath. He was a master of dark magic and a formidable warrior, and his obsession with capturing the elusive Lady Seraphina had consumed him for months. Her presence was a threat to his dominion, and he had pursued her relentlessly, always narrowly missing her trail.

When the raven landed with the scroll bearing the news of Seraphina's location, Count Malachi was thrilled beyond measure. He unfurled the message and read it with a wicked grin. Finally, he had her location, and it was within the Enchanted Forest, a place where even his dark powers struggled to penetrate.

Malachi's next move was swift and decisive. He summoned his army of loyal soldiers and, most notably, his fearsome steed, a monstrous creature known as "Dracohound." Dracohound was a terrifying amalgamation of a dog and dragon, with scales as dark as night and fiery breath that could incinerate anything in its path. What set Dracohound apart was its wings, which, although smaller than a true dragon's, served a unique purpose. They allowed Dracohound to glide gracefully between gallops, providing an uncanny advantage in traversing challenging terrain. Its piercing red eyes glowed with malevolent intelligence, and as Count Malachi mounted this formidable beast, he knew that they possessed the perfect blend of power and agility to confront their elusive quarry within the Enchanted Forest.

Count Malachi mounted Dracohound, and together they led his army out of the fortress, the ground trembling beneath their feet as they rode towards the Enchanted Forest. The anticipation of finally capturing Lady Seraphina fueled Malachi's dark resolve.

As they reached the borders of the Enchanted Forest, the atmosphere grew eerie and foreboding. The tall trees seemed to whisper secrets, and the air was thick with enchantments that defied intrusion. Count Malachi, undeterred, urged Dracohound forward, and with a thunderous roar, they entered the mystical realm.

Deep within the forest, Grizzletooth and his goblin warriors awaited Count Malachi's arrival. The goblin leader, though small in stature, exuded a fierce determination as he stepped forward to greet the Count. "Count Malachi," he began, bowing low, "we have tracked Lady Seraphina to this very place. She is near the West edge!"

Count Malachi's eyes gleamed with anticipation as he dismounted from Dracohound. "You have done well, Grizzletooth," he hissed, his dark cloak billowing ominously. "This time, she will not escape me."

Together, the goblins and the dark army advanced deeper into the Enchanted Forest, guided by the information Fizzlewick had provided. The dense foliage and eerie illusions of the forest presented formidable obstacles but Count Malachi's dark magic and Dracohound's fearsome presence cleared their path.

The arrival of Count Malachi and his dark army, accompanied by the fearsome Dracohound, sent ripples of fear throughout the Enchanted Forest.

Sensing the impending danger, the mystical creatures that called this mystical realm their home began to retreat deeper into the heart of the forest, seeking refuge in hidden groves and secret glades. Elves, fairies, and magical beasts alike withdrew into the shadows, their presence concealed by ancient enchantments. It was as if the very essence of the forest had come alive, cloaking its inhabitants in an impenetrable veil of secrecy, leaving only whispers of their existence behind. The once vibrant and bustling realm now stood silent, as the creatures bided their time, waiting for the outcome of the impending clash between Count Malachi and the enigmatic Lady Seraphina.

In the heart of the Elven Kingdom, nestled among ancient trees and shimmering glades, news of Count Malachi's ominous arrival in the Enchanted Forest sent shockwaves through the land. General Elowen, a wise and formidable leader of the Elves, immediately recognized the gravity of the situation. Lady Seraphina, a cherished ally and protector of the realm, was in grave danger. It was imperative that the Elven Kingdom be brought into the highest form of protection to ensure the safety of the elves.

General Elowen, the wise and revered leader of the Elven Kingdom, understood that their sanctuary needed protection beyond the magic of the invisible veils. As the evil within the enchanted forest escalated, he summoned the council of elders, and together they invoked ancient enchantments that would safeguard their kingdom. Along the entrance to their realm, the trees grew thicker, their branches intertwining like vigilant sentinels. The very ground seemed to respond to their call, rising and forming a natural barrier that concealed the city from prying eyes. The mist from the majestic waterfall, which cascaded down from the towering cliffs above, thickened as if to hide the Elven Kingdom entrance from view, veiling their home in a shroud of enchantment.

Amidst the crystalline beauty that adorned their realm, the precious gems beneath and around the city began to shine even brighter. The crystals, long a source of wonder and power for the Elves, seemed to respond to the call of protection. Their luminous glow intensified, casting an ethereal light that danced upon the water's surface and shimmered through the thickening mist. It was as if the very essence of the forest had awakened to defend its guardians, infusing the barrier with an otherworldly strength that would deter any intrusion from hostile forces.

Elowen and his council of elders watched with determined resolve as the enchantments they had woven safeguarded their kingdom. The impenetrable shield, a harmonious blend of nature's magic and their ancient crystals, stood as a testament to their unwavering commitment to protect their realm from those who sought harm. In the midst of turmoil, the Elven Kingdom remained a hidden haven, its secrets hidden within the heart of the forest, and its beauty preserved for generations to come.

But General Elowen knew that mere barriers might not be enough to safeguard the Kingdom. In their time of need, the Elves turned to their ancient allies, the giant eagles. These majestic creatures, known as Skywardens, were truly colossal, with wingspans that spanned the width of a grand hall. Their feathers shimmered with an otherworldly iridescence, reflecting the colours of the forest canopy.

The Skywardens were bonded to the Elves through a sacred pact, and their loyalty ran deep. They possessed the strength to carry out a crucial mission that would tip the scales in the elves' favour. With the aid of Elven craftsmen, gigantic baskets were fashioned, woven from the finest vines and enchanted to be both sturdy and light. Each basket was vast enough to accommodate ten men and ten horses, providing a swift means of transportation through the skies.

As dawn broke over the Elven Kingdom, the Skywardens were summoned from their roosts high in the treetops. General Elowen, draped in robes of forest green, stood at the helm of this endeavor. With a series of ancient melodies and whispered incantations, the Skywardens descended from the heavens, their wings creating a spectacle of light and shadow. These magnificent beings possessed an air of regal grace, and their eyes radiated wisdom as they landed gracefully before the assembly of elves.

Elowen approached the lead Skywarden, a majestic creature named Lirion, with reverence. "Dear Lirion," he began, his voice carrying the weight of the kingdom's plea, "we beseech you and your kin to aid us in this dire hour. Count Malachi threatens the Enchanted Forest, and with him rides a monstrous hound of darkness. We must come to the aid of Lady Seraphina. Will you and your brethren carry our kin and allies to her side?"

Lirion dipped his massive head in agreement, his eyes conveying a solemn promise. With a series of resonant calls, the Skywardens summoned their kin, and soon, a squadron of these colossal eagles stood ready for the mission.

Meanwhile, in the heart of the Valorian, General Ironheart and his council were deep in discussion, strategizing the most efficient route for their ride to the Enchanted Forest. They were absorbed in the planning when, to their surprise, the majestic eagles arrived, their colossal wings casting shadows over the assembly.

The skies above suddenly darkened as the Skywardens, with their gigantic baskets, descended from the heavens like celestial messengers. Their wings beat with an otherworldly power, creating gusts of wind that rustled leaves and sent ripples across forest pools. The sight of these colossal eagles was awe-inspiring, their iridescent feathers catching the dappled sunlight.

General Ironheart, a stalwart figure in gleaming armour, approached the first of the giant baskets. "Men!" he called to his loyal soldiers. "Prepare to embark on these noble creatures, for we fly to the aid of the Elves!"

With practiced efficiency, the crusade army mounted the baskets, securing their horses and themselves for the journey ahead. Each basket was attached to two Skywardens, their powerful talons gripping the woven vines securely. The elves had ensured that the baskets were not only spacious but also enchanted to withstand the rigors of flight.

General Ironheart, astride his own majestic eagle, surveyed the assembled forces. "Onward, my comrades!" he declared, his voice filled with unwavering resolve. "We fly to protect the Enchanted Forest and aid the Elves. Together, we shall confront Count Malachi and his dark forces, and our alliance will be their undoing!"

With a resounding chorus of war cries and the beat of colossal wings, the Skywardens took flight, carrying the crusade army aloft into the azure sky. The Elven Kingdom's intervention had come just in time, and now, united by their common cause, they soared toward the heart of the Enchanted Forest, to meet the elves within their Kingdom.

Unbeknownst to the gathering armies, Lady Seraphina and Lady Elyndra had safely exited the western reaches of the Enchanted Forest and found themselves on a vast, flat ancient terrain. The landscape stretched endlessly in all directions, an open canvas with a sense of boundless potential. As they rode onward, their gaze fixed on the distant horizon, they beheld a towering mountain, its peak shrouded in the very clouds that kissed the sky. This was the mount that concealed the fabled Angel City, their ultimate destination, and they rode forth with unwavering determination towards its celestial heights.

The colossal eagles, with their grand baskets carrying the Crusade army of a hundred men, descended upon the heart of the Elven Kingdom with a graceful majesty that left the Elves in awe. As they touched down upon the forest floor, the elves could scarcely believe their eyes, for the arrival of such an unusual assembly of allies was an event of immense significance.

General Elowen, a figure of regal authority with flowing silver hair and a robe woven from shimmering leaves, emerged from the midst of the elven hosts. His presence was commanding, and his keen elven eyes assessed the situation with a mixture of curiosity and apprehension. With a gesture of greeting, he approached General Ironheart, who had dismounted the eagle's basket with the other members of his council.

"Welcome to the Elven Kingdom," General Elowen said with a courteous nod, his voice imbued with grace. "We have been eagerly awaiting your arrival, for the imminent threat of Count Malachi has reached our ears. Please, follow me. We shall escort you to the heart of our realm."

With that, the crusade army was led through the elven forest, their footsteps barely making a sound on the soft earth beneath the towering trees. They arrived at the grand palace of the Elves, a structure that seemed to have been woven from the very trees themselves, its intricate architecture a testament to the mastery of the elven craftsmen.

Inside the palace, a feast had been prepared in honour of their guests. Long tables were laden with fruits, wines, and dishes that seemed to glow with an otherworldly luminescence. Elven musicians played enchanting melodies that filled the air, and the atmosphere was one of celebration and camaraderie.

General Elowen led the crusade army to the high table at the head of the hall, where the most honoured guests were seated. Here, they would have the privilege of meeting King Thaladir, the wise and ancient ruler of the Elven Kingdom. The elven king, with his silvery hair and regal bearing, welcomed them warmly, acknowledging the significance of their alliance.

Amidst the festivities, the elves seemed to take an immediate liking to Lord Stoneforge, his charm and hearty laughter endearing him to their hosts. Captain Swiftwind and Lady Srormbringer, nimble and graceful fighters themselves, found camaraderie among the elven warriors, and Sir Frostbane, with his stoic demeanor, earned the respect of the elven elders.

However, as the evening wore on, the elves couldn't help but sense an underlying discord in the air when it came to Lady Isabella. The enchantress had a captivating beauty, yet her demeanor carried an air of self-importance that didn't sit well with the perceptive elves. Some whispered that her enchantments on General Ironheart were not merely for protection but might have been influenced by her own selfish desires.

Lady Stormbringer, with her wild and untamed spirit, found herself more accepted among the elves, who admired her fierce loyalty and connection to the natural world. Yet, the air of suspicion around Lady Isabella cast a shadow over the evening's festivities.

As the feast continued, songs were sung and stories exchanged, and the crusade army and their elven hosts began to find common ground. King Thaladir addressed General Ironheart, expressing his gratitude for their alliance and emphasizing the importance of their united front against Count Malachi.

"The threat that Count Malachi poses is dire, and the protection of the Enchanted Forest is paramount," King Thaladir spoke with an air of ancient wisdom. "Let us work together, as allies, to ensure the safety of this realm and all who call it home."

General Ironheart nodded in agreement, pledging the unwavering support of his crusade army. The evening wore on, and despite the initial tensions, the celebration continued into the night, fostering a sense of camaraderie between the crusade army and their elven hosts.

However, the elves remained vigilant, and their doubts about Lady Isabella lingered in the shadows, a subtle undercurrent that would require further scrutiny as they prepared for the impending confrontation with Count Malachi and his dark forces.

The early morning sun painted the treetops of the Elven Kingdom with hues of gold and amber, and the forest was alive with the songs of birds welcoming the day. In their chambers within the grand palace, General Ironheart and his council, still in the midst of peaceful slumber, were suddenly roused by the delicate tinkling of tiny bells that seemed to dance upon the morning breeze. The enchanting sound of these bells was accompanied by the gentle hum of wings, and as the council members groggily opened their eyes, they were met with a sight both magical and surreal.

Hovering before them were hummingbirds, their iridescent feathers shimmering with an ethereal light. These hummingbirds were unlike any others, for they bore tiny rings of delicate bells that adorned their wings. As the birds flitted about the chamber, the soft music of the bells filled the air, gradually coaxing Ironheart and his council from their sleep.

With a sense of wonder, they followed the hummingbirds as they led the way out of their chambers and through the grand halls of the Elven palace. The tiny birds flitted gracefully through open windows, guiding them towards the lush, vibrant heart of the forest.

At the riverbank, beneath the shade of towering trees, General Elowen awaited their arrival, his robes of silver and green blending seamlessly with the natural surroundings. Beside him stood his wife, Lady Elowen, her presence as ethereal and graceful as a morning mist.

With a warm smile, General Elowen greeted General Ironheart and his council. "I apologize for the early awakening," he said, his voice carrying the serenity of the forest. "But there are matters of great import that require your attention."

General Ironheart, ever the stoic leader, nodded in understanding, and his council members gathered around, their curiosity piqued. Lady Isabella, however, bore an expression of thinly veiled irritation.

General Elowen began to speak, his words carrying the weight of ancient knowledge and profound wisdom. "I wish to share with you the story of Lady Seraphina," he said, and at the mention of her name, the birds in the trees seemed to fall silent in reverence.

He continued, recounting the tale of Lady Seraphina's origins, how she had been a sacrifice from the kingdom of King Alaric to Count Malachi, a dark and sinister figure who had subjected her to unspeakable torment. The elves had found her, broken and battered, and had taken her under their wing, both literally and figuratively.

Lady Elowen interjected, her voice soft as a summer breeze. "We nurtured her back to health, body and spirit," she said, her eyes filled with a compassionate light. "Lady Seraphina possessed a deep well of inner strength, and we helped her harness it, molding her into the formidable warrior she has become."

The tale unfolded, revealing Lady Seraphina's remarkable journey of healing, resilience, and training. Under the guidance of the elves, she had developed her mindset, honed her combat skills, and become a beacon of hope in the ongoing battle against Count Malachi's darkness.

General Ironheart listened intently, his interest in Lady Seraphina piqued. Her strength and resilience in the face of adversity were qualities he admired deeply. He recognized that her presence in the ongoing struggle against Count Malachi could be a game-changer, a symbol of resistance that could tip the scales in their favour.

However, as the council members exchanged glances and thoughts, Lady Isabella's disapproval of the entire situation was palpable. Her enchantments on General Ironheart had not only created a bond but had also nurtured a possessive streak, and the idea of another powerful woman entering the fray seemed to unsettle her.

Despite the undercurrent of tension, the significance of Lady Seraphina's role in the ongoing war was undeniable. The elves and the crusade army would need to unite, harness their combined strengths, and stand together in the face of the looming threat posed by Count Malachi. The balance of this war hung in the balance, and Lady Seraphina held the key to its outcome.

As the council members continued to absorb the weight of Lady Seraphina's story, the elves looked to General Ironheart with a silent plea for unity and cooperation. It was a pivotal moment, one that would shape the course of their struggle against the forces of darkness, and General Ironheart understood that their alliance would be tested in ways they could not yet foresee.

Amidst the serene backdrop of the Elven forest, Lady Isabella's simmering jealousy could no longer be contained. With a tone laced with frustration, she scolded the elves for their deliberate omission in the letter and demanded to know why they had kept the knowledge of Lady Seraphina's whereabouts hidden.

"Why, in the name of all that is just, did you not disclose this critical information in the letter you sent us?" Isabella's voice quivered with a mixture of anger and anxiety. "This knowledge could have altered our entire approach to the situation."

Lady Elowen, her grace undisturbed by Isabella's outburst, replied with a calm demeanor. "The secrecy surrounding Lady Seraphina's location is not without reason," she explained. "Count Malachi's web of minions is far-reaching, and they are relentless in their pursuit of her. We needed to ensure that your crusade army was not only willing to be our allies but could arrive within the confines of our kingdom, where we could trust that the information would be handled discreetly."

General Ironheart, sensing the tension in the air, interjected with a firm tone. "Where is Lady Seraphina now? I wish to meet her and understand her role in this conflict."

General Elowen, his gaze unwavering, nodded in agreement. "I shall share her whereabouts with you, but I believe our conversation is best kept private. Lady Elowen, if you would be so kind as to lead the rest of our council and Lady Isabella to breakfast."

With a gentle gesture, Lady Elowen led the remaining council members and Isabella towards a quaint, sunlit courtyard where breakfast awaited them. The setting was nothing short of enchanting, with a table carved from a massive tree trunk, surrounded by lush greenery and the soft hum of the forest. Elven dishes, infused with flavours and colours found only in their mystical realm, adorned the table, inviting the council members to partake in a feast of both sustenance and camaraderie.

Lady Isabella, however, kept glancing back toward the secluded conversation between General Ironheart and General Elowen. Lady Elowen, perceptive as ever, gently nudged her toward the breakfast table, a subtle reminder that their alliance rested on trust and cooperation.

As the council members engaged in lively discussions, the breakfast scene was filled with the delicate clinking of silverware against fine porcelain plates and the laughter of allies bonding over a shared purpose. The enchanting melodies of elven musicians, hidden among the foliage, added an ethereal layer to the ambiance, as birds perched on nearby branches, harmonizing with the music.

Meanwhile, General Ironheart and General Elowen had ventured to a secluded glade, far from prying eyes. The canopy above filtered the morning sunlight, casting dappled patterns of light and shadow upon the forest floor. It was here that General Elowen began to reveal the true nature of Lady Seraphina's circumstances. "Count Malachi had requested a sacrifice from the kingdom of King Alaric," General Elowen began, his voice carrying the weight of sorrow for the plight of Lady Seraphina. "Her life was one of torment, subjected to the darkest of abuses at the hands of that malevolent sorcerer. When we found her, she was broken in body and spirit, but she possessed an inner strength that astounded us all."

General Elowen continued, recounting Lady Seraphina's transformation under the elves' care, how she had become a fierce warrior and a beacon of hope. "She has blossomed into a formidable guardian of this realm," General Elowen emphasized, "but the darkness still lingers within her, threatening to take hold once more. We fear that Count Malachi's cruel influence has left scars that even our magic cannot fully mend, that is why Lady Seraphina is on a journey to Aeloria to help her rid the darkness."

As General Ironheart absorbed this revelation, General Elowen produced a necklace with a pendant of a gleaming green stone. The stone was unlike any other, possessing an otherworldly luminescence that seemed to capture the very essence of the forest.

"This pendant is a welcoming gift," General Elowen explained, offering it to General Ironheart. "But it carries a special enchantment. It will shield you from any external magical influences that might seek to sway your judgment or actions."

General Ironheart, appreciating the gesture, accepted the pendant and clasped it around his neck, unaware of its hidden purpose. "Thank you, General Elowen," he said with genuine gratitude. "I am honoured by your gift and the trust you have shown in us."

Unknown to General Ironheart, the pendant was not just a welcoming gift; it was a safeguard against the enchantments of Lady Isabella, who had been growing increasingly possessive and manipulative due to her growing infatuation with him.

As the morning sun bathed the Elven Kingdom in its golden light, the alliance between the crusade army and the elves deepened. Unbeknownst to all, Lady Isabella's jealousy and the looming threat of Count Malachi's darkness would test the bonds of this newfound partnership, as they prepared to confront the shadows that lay ahead and protect the fragile balance of their enchanted realm.

With the pendant gifted by General Elowen securely around his neck, General Ironheart returned to the breakfast table where his council and Lady Isabella awaited him. The enchanting melodies of elven musicians continued to fill the air, lending an air of serenity to the scene.

As General Ironheart settled into his seat, Lady Isabella, unable to contain her curiosity and growing frustration, leaned closer to him. "What did General Elowen want to discuss with you?" she inquired; her voice laced with a thinly veiled impatience.

General Ironheart, aware of Lady Isabella's persistent prying, offered a polite yet dismissive response. "Our discussion was of strategic matters, my lady," he replied with a calm tone. "Nothing that concerns you at this moment."

Lady Isabella, her desire for information unfulfilled and her ego stung by Ironheart's dismissiveness, could hardly contain her displeasure. Her irritation grew into an indignant rage, and she abruptly rose from her seat, causing her chair to scrape across the ground.

"Excuse me," she muttered tersely before storming off from the breakfast table, her enigmatic demeanor leaving the council members bewildered.

The council, left to ponder Isabella's sudden departure, redirected their attention to General Ironheart. "Where is Lady Seraphina?" one of the council members inquired, their curiosity mirrored by the rest of the group.

General Ironheart, fully aware of the importance of their alliance with the elves, decided to offer a measured response. "Lady Seraphina is currently on a journey," he explained, choosing his words carefully. "We expect her return in due time, but until then, we must focus on preparing our crusade army for the challenges ahead."

The council members exchanged knowing glances, their understanding clear. The fate of their alliance with the elves and the success of their mission rested on Lady Seraphina's role in the conflict. Her return would undoubtedly hold great significance.

As the discussion continued, the council recognized the need for their crusade army to train alongside the elven warriors. The combined strength of their forces would be their greatest asset against Count Malachi's dark forces, and the training needed to commence without delay.

General Ironheart nodded in agreement, his resolve unwavering. "We shall begin our training with the elven warriors at once," he declared. "It is only through unity and cooperation that we can hope to thwart Count Malachi's sinister plans and protect this enchanted realm."

The council members concurred, and the morning's discussions turned toward the practicalities of their training regimen, their focus unwavering as they prepared to face the looming threat that awaited them.

The training commenced in the heart of the Elven Kingdom, where the lush forest provided an ideal backdrop for honing their skills. Elven warriors, renowned for their agility and precision, guided the crusade army through rigorous exercises. Archery and swordplay sessions were interwoven with lessons in the subtleties of forest warfare, teaching the crusaders how to navigate the enchanted terrain to their advantage. As the days passed, the camaraderie between the two forces grew, and a mutual respect began to blossom.

Amidst the training, Lady Isabella, a mage of considerable power, found herself grappling with her role in this unique alliance. Her magic, while potent, required careful consideration in the context of both the crusade army and the elves. She struggled to find her place, torn between the desire to support her allies and her personal ambitions. It became apparent that her arcane abilities needed to be harnessed strategically, a puzzle she was determined to solve as she sought to prove her worth in the unfolding training.

Little did anyone know that the necklace would play a pivotal role in the unfolding drama. The stone, a rare and enchanting gem, possessed properties not entirely understood by the mortals. Its origins were shrouded in mystery, a testament to the Elves' ancient wisdom.

In the beginning, Lady Isabella's enchantments held a captivating allure over General Ironheart. Her mastery of magic was mesmerizing, her charm irresistible. However, as the days turned into weeks, the necklace with the green stone began to exert its subtle influence. The gem seemed to emit a calming energy, one that shielded General Ironheart from the enchantments that had once ensnared his senses.

General Ironheart, once entangled in Lady Isabella's web of desire, found himself increasingly immune to her charms. It was as though a veil had been lifted from his eyes, revealing the true nature of their relationship. He realized that his fascination with the mage had been artificially induced, a product of her magic rather than genuine attraction.

The General's newfound clarity was a double-edged sword. While he was no longer ensnared by Lady Isabella's allure, their relationship had undergone a profound transformation. The passion that had once burned between them had extinguished, replaced by a sense of camaraderie born out of their shared mission. Their once-intimate encounters had become a distant memory, a reflection of a time when they were both ensnared by a potent enchantment.

Lady Isabella, however, could not ignore the change in General Ironheart's demeanor. She felt his distance keenly, a rejection that cut deep into her heart. As a mage of considerable power, she was not accustomed to being denied anything she desired. The General's newfound indifference was a bitter pill to swallow, and it stoked the fires of anger within her.

In the quiet moments when the campfire crackled and the soldiers rested, Lady Isabella's thoughts turned to her failed attempts at seduction. She had used her magic to captivate many before, bending their wills to her desires. But General Ironheart was different. The green stone's protective aura had rendered him immune to her spells, and it wounded her pride.

She watched as he conferred with his fellow commanders, his attention focused on strategy and the well-being of his troops. Gone were the stolen glances and secret rendezvous they had once shared. Instead, they stood side by side as allies, their connection severed by the very gem gifted by the General Elf.

Lady Isabella's anger festered, and she began to view the necklace as an object of resentment. It represented not only her failure to enchant the General but also a barrier between them. The green stone, with its mysterious power, had become a symbol of rejection, a constant reminder of her thwarted desires.

As the training with the Elves intensified, Lady Isabella's frustration grew. She had sought to prove her worth through her magical prowess, but the green stone continued to shield General Ironheart from her charms. Her inner turmoil manifested in her spells, which became increasingly erratic and unpredictable.

General Ironheart, aware of Lady Isabella's struggles, tried to offer guidance and support. He recognized her potential as a valuable ally in their quest, but the romantic connection they had once shared was irreparably broken. It was a bitter irony that the very necklace gifted by the Elves to protect him had also severed the bond between them.

One evening, amidst the lush forests and ancient trees, Lady Isabella's anger and rejection reached their zenith. She confronted General Ironheart, her voice trembling with a mixture of fury and vulnerability. "You have rejected me," she accused him, her eyes blazing with unbridled emotion. "Your precious necklace has made you immune to my charms, and now you stand as nothing more than an ally, a comrade in this war."

General Ironheart met her gaze, his expression filled with regret. "It was never my intention to hurt you, Lady Isabella. The necklace's power is beyond my control. I value your skills and your loyalty, but our romantic entanglement was an enchantment, not true affection."

Lady Isabella's heart ached as she heard his words, a painful realization washing over her. She had used her magic to create a false connection, and now she reaped the bitter harvest of her own spells. The green stone had exposed the illusion, leaving her with a sense of emptiness she had never experienced before.

In the midst of their confrontation, the training commenced, and they were forced to put aside their personal turmoil to face the greater threat. Lady Isabella channeled her anger and frustration into her magic, becoming a formidable force on the training-field. General Ironheart, protected by the green stone, led his troops with unwavering determination.

The necklace adorned with the mesmerizing green stone had wrought a profound transformation upon General Ironheart and Lady Isabella. Its mystical aura had shielded the valiant leader from the enchantments that once ensnared his senses, unmasking the truth behind their connection. The passionate allure that had once burned between them had dimmed, replaced by a sense of camaraderie that had blossomed from their shared mission. Intimate encounters had become distant memories, fading into obscurity like a forgotten melody.

In the depths of Lady Isabella's heart, however, a shadow of doubt loomed. She couldn't shake the feeling of rejection that now haunted her. The necklace, while protecting the General from her charms, had also severed the bonds of romance that had once bound them. As the training with the Elves reached its climax, she found herself questioning her place in General Ironheart's council. The painful realization of her failed attempts to seduce him gnawed at her, and she wondered if she could truly be an ally to him in this dire conflict. The temptation to leave his council and seek a different path began to whisper in her ear, a siren's call that threatened to lure her away from the crusade and the man who had once held her heart captive.

The unity of the Crusade army and the Elven warriors was of paramount importance in the looming battle against Count Malachi's dark forces. General Elowen understood that any division among their ranks could provide Count Malachi with a vulnerable point to exploit. As the forces of light and harmony, they needed to stand together in unwavering solidarity, their strength magnified when they fought as one cohesive unit. It was only through this unity that they could hope to overcome the malevolent powers that Count Malachi had harnessed and protect the enchanted realm from its impending doom.

To achieve this unity, General Ironheart, and the Elven leaders held numerous council meetings, fostering open communication and understanding among their troops. They emphasized the common purpose that bound them—a commitment to preserving Ravenshadow and the enchanted realm and all that was good within it. Together, they forged strategies that leveraged their unique strengths and talents, recognizing that the harmony of their alliance was the key to Lady Seraphina's success.

Unforgivable Crimes

The mountain stood as an imposing sentinel at the edge of the flat terrain, its name whispered only in the most reverent of tones – Mount Eldurith. It was a colossal monolith, its towering peak hidden amidst the clouds, its rocky terrain unforgiving and treacherous. Lady Seraphina and her steadfast companion, Lady Elyndra, had embarked on a perilous journey to the heart of this ancient land, with the noble steeds, Sir Sterling and Aelion, by their side, and the two mischievous fairies, Tilly and Tally, flitting about in playful anticipation. As they ventured further into the vast expanse of the plateau, the true grandeur of Eldurith unfolded before them, a sight that would leave an indelible mark on their souls.

As the sun dipped low on the horizon, casting long, golden rays across the vast, ancient terrain, a surreal landscape stretched out before the eyes of any fortunate enough to witness it. This was a place where time seemed to stand still, where the past and present coexisted in a harmonious dance of nature and geology. The flat expanse of land extended endlessly in all directions, like a great, weathered canvas upon which the story of ages had been painted.

In the heart of this timeless terrain, a colossal mountain rose with a majestic grandeur that defied the imagination. Its towering form dominated the landscape, a monolithic behemoth that commanded attention from every corner of the vast plain. This mountain, known as "Eldurith," was not merely a geological wonder; it was a symbol of enduring strength and resilience.

The terrain itself was flat, an expansive plateau that stretched for miles in every direction. It was as if the land had been meticulously smoothed by some ancient, divine hand, leaving a perfectly level canvas for the grandeur of Eldurith. The ground beneath one's feet was a mixture of fine, powdery sand and small, smooth pebbles, worn smooth by countless millennia of wind and water erosion.

As the sun continued its descent, the sky transformed into a breathtaking display of colours. Shades of crimson and fiery orange painted the heavens, casting a warm and ethereal glow upon the flat terrain below. The distant horizon seemed to blur and meld with the sky, creating an illusion of infinite space that stretched on forever.

At the base of Eldurith, a forest of gnarled, ancient trees thrived. These trees, with their twisted branches and weathered bark, were a testament to the unyielding power of nature. They had stood for centuries, their roots intertwined with the very essence of the mountain itself, drawing sustenance from its depths.

The mountain's surface was a patchwork of textures and colours. Massive boulders, some as large as houses, littered its slopes, while hardy shrubs and wildflowers clung tenaciously to any crevice they could find. The rock itself bore the scars of eons, with deep gouges and weathered crags etched into its surface by the relentless forces of wind and rain.

Eldurith's peak, a distant and elusive crown, seemed to touch the very heavens. Its snowy cap gleamed in the dying light, a stark contrast to the warm tones of the plateau below. Only the most intrepid of explorers dared to venture to its summit, where the air was thin and the elements unforgiving.

The vastness of the terrain was humbling, a reminder of the insignificance of humanity in the face of the natural world. It was a place where one could contemplate the mysteries of time and existence, where the weight of history and the promise of the future converged.

As twilight descended upon the land, the mountain and the plateau faded into shadows, becoming silhouettes against the darkening sky. Stars began to twinkle overhead, their light piercing the veil of night. The ancient terrain, with its colossal mountain at its heart, stood as a testament to the enduring beauty and power of the natural world, a place where time itself seemed to pause, allowing the wonders of the past to coexist with the promise of the future.

As they reached the base of Mount Edurith, the enormity of the task ahead became all too apparent. The mountain's rocky slopes stretched upward as far as the eye could see, disappearing into the heavens themselves. It was a place where the air grew thin, where the winds whispered secrets carried from the distant skies.

Lady Elyndra, Tilly, and Tally exchanged solemn glances, their expressions mirroring the formidable nature of the mountain they now faced. They had accompanied Lady Seraphina on her journey, offering guidance, companionship, and support, but this was where their path diverged. The rocky terrain ahead was treacherous and unforgiving, and they could go no further.

"We'll set up camp here," Lady Elyndra declared, her voice steady and unwavering. "We shall await your return, Lady Seraphina."

As Lady Seraphina and her loyal companions prepared to make camp at the base of the mighty mountain, they noticed a remarkable sight nearby. A colossal tree, ancient beyond reckoning, stood proudly amidst the rocky landscape. Its massive trunk soared into the sky, and as they approached, they discovered an astonishing secret—it was hollowed out, creating a natural shelter of immense proportions.

The interior of the tree was awe-inspiring, with a spacious, hollow chamber that could easily accommodate their needs. The walls were smooth and worn from the passage of countless years, revealing the tree's age and resilience. Sunlight filtered through gaps in the gnarled branches, casting a warm, dappled glow within the tree's cavernous interior.

Seraphina and her companions exchanged amazed glances, realizing that they had stumbled upon a perfect sanctuary amidst the rugged terrain. It was a stroke of good fortune, a haven provided by nature itself. Without hesitation, they decided to make camp within the ancient tree, finding solace in its protective embrace.

With the assistance of Sir Sterling and Aelion, they brought their supplies and provisions into the hollowed-out sanctuary. Elyndra kindled a gentle fire at the center of the chamber, its dancing flames casting a soft, comforting light throughout their newfound home. Tilly and Tally, the playful fairies, flitted about, adding their magical touch to the surroundings, making it feel like a cozy haven.

As night descended upon the land, the companions huddled together within the colossal tree, the wind rustling through its branches providing a soothing lullaby. It was a night of shared stories and laughter, a moment of respite before the formidable ascent that awaited Lady Seraphina on Mount Edurith's treacherous slopes. The ancient tree, with its hollowed heart, had become both a symbol of nature's strength and a sanctuary for their weary souls, a testament to the enduring power of the natural world in this ancient, timeless terrain.

Seraphina, her eyes filled with determination. "Thank you, my friends," she said, patting Sir Sterling and Aelion affectionately. "I must journey to the peak alone, but I carry your strength with me."

Sir Sterling, the noble steed whose loyalty to Lady Seraphina knew no bounds, neighed in distress, sensing the impending separation. His deep, soulful eyes searched Seraphina's face, silently pleading for her not to leave him behind.

Seraphina approached her beloved steed, her gentle hand stroking his mane soothingly. "Fear not, my dear Sterling," she whispered. "I shall return to you. Until then, you have Lady Elyndra, Tilly, and Tally."

The fairies, understanding the gravity of the moment, fluttered around Sir Sterling, offering their whimsical reassurances and promising to keep him entertained with their playful antics. Gradually, the distressed steed began to calm, finding solace in the presence of his newfound friends.

With one final, lingering look at her companions, Lady Seraphina steeled herself for the ascent. Her determination was unwavering, her purpose clear. She knew that the destiny of the enchanted realm rested upon her shoulders, and she was prepared to face the challenges that awaited her on the towering peak of Mount Edurith.

As the night passed and the early morning sun began to cast its gentle light upon the ancient landscape, the companions awoke to a soft, melodic sound. It was the delicate tinkling of dewdrops falling from the leaves of the colossal tree that sheltered them. Each droplet sparkled in the morning light, like tiny diamonds adorning the tree's branches.

Seraphina and her companions emerged from their slumber, their spirits refreshed by the serene beauty of the moment. The air was crisp and invigorating, and the world seemed to come alive with the promise of a new day. It was a reminder that nature, in all its grandeur, was their constant companion on this arduous journey.

With renewed determination, Seraphina prepared to continue her ascent of Mount Edurith, knowing that the mountain held both challenges and secrets waiting to be discovered. As she bid farewell to her companions and set out on her path, the soft sounds of dewdrops continued to serenade her, a gentle reminder that even in the face of the formidable mountain, nature's beauty and resilience would accompany her every step of the way.

As she began her arduous climb, the terrain proved as unforgiving as it appeared from a distance. Jagged rocks jutted out from the mountainside like the teeth of a sleeping giant, and narrow ledges demanded precision and balance. The air grew thinner with each step, and the cold winds tugged at her cloak, as if urging her to turn back.

Yet, Lady Seraphina pressed on, her spirit unwavering. She drew strength from the memories of her trials and tribulations, from the teachings of the elves, and from the enduring bond with her steeds and the mischievous fairies who had accompanied her on this journey.

As she climbed higher, the world below seemed to shrink into insignificance. The forest and its ancient beauty lay far below, a realm untouched by the turmoil that had befallen her kingdom. She could hear the distant song of the fairies and the gentle nicker of Sir Sterling and Aelion, offering her encouragement even from afar.

Hours turned into days as Lady Seraphina ascended the treacherous slopes of Mount Edurith. Her determination was her constant companion, her will unwavering. She faced challenges that tested her physical strength and her mental fortitude, scaling sheer cliffs, navigating narrow crevices, and enduring the biting cold of the high altitudes.

As Lady Seraphina continued her arduous climb up Mount Edurith , the relentless wind howled around her with an eerie, mournful wail. The sound of the wind magnified her feelings of solitude and loneliness, its haunting echoes seeming to underscore the immense challenges of her journey. The mountain had grown even more treacherous as she ascended, with sheer cliffs and precarious ledges testing her every step.

With each gust of wind, the mountain seemed to mock her determination, as if daring her to turn back. The isolation and harsh conditions wore on her, and a sense of desolation began to creep into her heart. Doubt and uncertainty gnawed at her resolve, and she felt a profound loneliness that threatened to engulf her.

In those moments, Seraphina knew that her greatest adversary was not the unforgiving terrain or the biting cold; it was the battle within her own mind. She had to navigate the labyrinth of her thoughts and emotions, forging ahead despite the overwhelming sense of solitude that surrounded her.

As she climbed higher, she clung to the memories of her past victories and the strength she had drawn from her companions. She recalled the camaraderie with Lady Elyndra, the playful antics of Tilly and Tally, and the unwavering loyalty of Sir Sterling and Aelion. These memories became her lifeline, a tether to the world she had left behind.

Seraphina's breaths came in ragged gasps as she continued her ascent, the thin air adding to the physical strain. But she knew that it was not just her body that was being tested; it was her spirit, her will to persevere despite the overwhelming solitude that threatened to pull her into despair.

She focused on each step, each foothold, and the rhythmic beat of her heart. She chanted words of encouragement to herself, a mantra of determination that reverberated within her soul. She reminded herself of the purpose that had driven her to embark on this perilous journey, the fate of her kingdom and the balance of the enchanted realm hanging in the balance.

As she climbed, Seraphina also found solace in the natural beauty that surrounded her. The rugged grandeur of the mountain, the crystal-clear streams that flowed down its slopes, and the hardy flora that clung to life in this harsh environment all spoke of the resilience of nature. She saw herself mirrored in the mountain's determination to rise above adversity, and it gave her the strength to press on.

With each passing hour, the loneliness that had threatened to overwhelm her began to ebb away. She felt a connection to the world around her, to the mountain itself, and to the countless generations of climbers who had faced these challenges before her. She knew that she was not truly alone, that the spirits of those who had tread these paths whispered encouragement in the rustling leaves and the rustling of the wind.

On the third day of her ascent, as the sun bathed the mountainside in a golden glow, Lady Seraphina finally reached the summit. The air was thin, and her breaths came in ragged gasps, but she stood triumphant, her heart filled with a sense of accomplishment and purpose.

As she gazed out over the barren expanse of the rocky summit, her heart sank like a stone. There was no celestial city of Aeloria, no radiant spires reaching into the heavens, only a desolate and unforgiving landscape.

However, what struck her more profoundly than the stark desolation was the bone-chilling cold that gnawed at her very core. The summit of Mount

Edurith was not a place of warmth and welcome; it was an ice-capped realm where the frigid winds pierced through her clothing, seeping into her very bones. Every breath she took felt like inhaling shards of ice, and her skin grew numb with each passing moment.

The tears welled up in Seraphina's eyes, not only from the weight of her disappointment but also from the physical pain of the biting cold. She collapsed to her knees on the unforgiving ice, the harsh reality of her situation washing over her like a relentless blizzard. She cried out to the sky, her voice carrying the anguish of her shattered dreams, but it was quickly swallowed by the relentless howling of the freezing winds.

"Lord, why have you forsaken me?" she cried, her words becoming frozen puffs of air in the frigid atmosphere. The wind seemed to howl around her as if in answer, its mournful cry a haunting backdrop to her despair.

As the sobs wracked her body, Seraphina felt as though the cold had become an embodiment of her isolation, a cruel reminder of her solitude on this desolate, icy mountaintop. The darkness that had plagued her kingdom, the suffering of her people, and the burden of her quest had all led her to this frozen wasteland, where there was nothing but emptiness and an all-encompassing cold that seemed to sear her very soul.

She clutched at the icy ground beneath her, her fingers scraping against the unforgiving surface. The tears froze on her cheeks, her cries of anguish muffled by the unrelenting chill. In that moment, she felt as though the cold had invaded her heart, that it would forever be a part of her, an inescapable, icy grip that would haunt her for all eternity.

The weight of her disappointment and the biting cold pressed down upon her like a suffocating blanket, making her feel even more alone and isolated in this desolate, frozen realm. She wondered if she had been a fool to believe in the promise of Aeloria, if the cold and emptiness around her were the only companions she would have on this desolate mountaintop.

Descending from the heavens like a divine apparition, a magnificent angel appeared before her. His presence was ethereal, bathed in a soft, radiant light that cast a warm and comforting glow over the desolation of the mountaintop.

The angel was tall and regal, his countenance radiating an aura of grace and benevolence. His hair cascaded in golden waves around his shoulders, and his eyes, the colour of the clearest sapphires, held a depth of wisdom that seemed beyond mortal comprehension. His wings, expansive and resplendent, shimmered with iridescent hues that shifted with every beat.

He was adorned in robes of celestial splendor, woven from the purest threads of moonlight and stardust. A diadem adorned his brow, encrusted with precious gems that glittered like a thousand stars. His presence was a testament to the divine beauty of the heavens, and Seraphina felt as though she beheld a being of incomprehensible majesty.

The angel regarded her with gentle compassion, his voice like the sweetest of melodies as he spoke. "Dear lady, why do you weep?" he inquired, his eyes filled with empathy.

Seraphina, her voice trembling with emotion, wiped away her tears and spoke with a quivering voice. "I climbed this mountain to find Aeloria, the Angel City, but all I found was emptiness and despair. My heart is heavy with disappointment."

The angel's smile was like the dawn breaking through the darkest of nights. "Fear not, Lady Seraphina," he said in a voice that radiated comfort and assurance. "Sometimes, the most wondrous treasures are hidden behind veils of enchantment. Allow me to show you the truth."

With a graceful sweep of his hand, the angel drew forth a fiery sword, its blade shimmering with divine light. He raised it high into the air and, with a single, precise stroke, cut through the invisible barrier that had concealed the celestial city of Aeloria.

As the fiery sword cleaved through the air, it sent ripples of magic cascading outward. Seraphina watched in astonishment as an enchanting veil, like an ethereal curtain, slowly descended to reveal the true splendor that had been hidden from her sight.

And there it was, unveiled in all its breathtaking glory – Aeloria, the Angel City. It was a place of unparalleled beauty, a realm that seemed to exist at the intersection of heaven and earth. The city's spires reached skyward, adorned with crystalline towers that shimmered like the morning dew. Streets of pure alabaster stretched out below, their cobblestones glistening with an otherworldly radiance.

The city was bathed in a soft, golden light that seemed to emanate from every corner, casting a warm and welcoming glow over its ethereal architecture. Seraphina's eyes brimmed with tears, not of sorrow, but of overwhelming joy and wonder.

She felt as though she had stepped into a realm of pure enchantment, a place where dreams and reality merged into one. The air was filled with the sweet strains of celestial music, and the inhabitants of Aeloria, radiant and graceful angels, greeted her with smiles of pure serenity.

As Lady Seraphina beheld the beauty and majesty of Aeloria, a profound sense of awe and gratitude washed over her. The disappointment that had weighed so heavily on her heart was replaced by a feeling of profound fulfillment and purpose. She had found not only the Angel City but also the strength to confront the darkness that threatened her kingdom.

The angel who had guided her, with a gentle smile, extended his hand toward the city and said, "Welcome to Aeloria, Lady Seraphina. Your journey has only just begun, and the destiny of your realm awaits. You are the light that will dispel the shadows, and the heavens have watched over you with great hope."

With a heart overflowing with gratitude and determination, Seraphina stepped forward, ready to embrace the challenges and wonders that awaited her in the celestial city of Aeloria.

As Lady Seraphina walked beside the angel, her heart filled with wonder and gratitude, she felt compelled to ask the celestial being his name. She turned to him, her eyes filled with curiosity and reverence, and spoke with a voice filled with awe, "May I know your name, noble angel?"

The angel turned his sapphire gaze upon her, his expression filled with warmth and kindness. "I am called Archangel Sariel," he replied, his voice like a gentle breeze that carried the secrets of the heavens.

Seraphina smiled, grateful for the opportunity to address her celestial guide by name. "Thank you, Archangel Sariel," she said, her words filled with reverence. "Your presence has been a beacon of hope in my darkest hour."

Archangel Sariel nodded in acknowledgment, his radiant wings shimmering with ethereal light. "It has been my honour to guide you, Lady Seraphina," he replied. "I have watched over you with great care, for I knew of the darkness that plagues your heart."

Seraphina's heart skipped a beat at his words, and she regarded him with a mixture of surprise and curiosity. "You know of the darkness within me?" she inquired, her voice barely above a whisper.

Archangel Sariel nodded, his expression filled with understanding. "Yes, dear lady," he replied. "The heavens have borne witness to your struggles and your quest to rid your kingdom of the darkness that threatens it. Your journey here was not only physical but also a test of your inner strength and resolve."

Seraphina's eyes brimmed with a mixture of emotions—vulnerability, determination, and a profound sense of purpose. She had climbed the treacherous slopes of Mount Celestia not only to find the Angel City but also to confront the darkness that had taken root within her. And now, with Archangel Sariel's guidance, she felt that her path was clearer than ever.

With renewed determination, she walked alongside Archangel Sariel, ready to face the challenges and revelations that lay ahead. She knew that the destiny of her realm rested on her shoulders, and she was prepared to confront the darkness within her with unwavering resolve and the guidance of her celestial companion.

As Archangel Sariel led Lady Seraphina through the ethereal beauty of Aeloria, they came upon a place of extraordinary wonder. Nestled amidst the radiant splendor of the celestial city, there lay a spring of remarkable significance. It was a spring that bubbled forth from a golden rock, its crystal-clear waters forming a pristine pool at the base.

Seraphina's eyes widened in awe as she beheld the shimmering waters, the pool reflecting the golden hues of its source. She felt drawn to the spring, a deep resonance echoing within her as if the very essence of her being recognized its significance.

With reverence, Seraphina spoke to Archangel Sariel, her voice filled with awe and wonder. "This spring," she began, "it is said to possess healing properties, a source of restoration and renewal. I have read of it in the ancient books of the Elven Kingdom's library."

Archangel Sariel nodded, his azure eyes holding a knowing gleam. "Your knowledge is correct, Lady Seraphina," he replied. "This spring is indeed a source of healing, a gift from the heavens to those who seek its solace."

But then Archangel Sariel added a condition, his voice carrying the weight of profound wisdom. "However," he continued, "the true healing this spring offers requires more than its waters alone. It calls for an act of surrender, a letting go of all that burdens your heart."

Seraphina's brow furrowed in contemplation as she pondered the angel's words. She knew that the darkness within her, the burden she carried, was not something that could be easily shed. But the prospect of true healing, of being free from the shadow that had clung to her soul, was a temptation she could not resist.

With a determined nod, she turned to Archangel Sariel and said, "I am willing to do whatever it takes to be free of this darkness. Please, guide me in this act of surrender."

Before she surrendered all to God and the healing waters of the spring, Lady Seraphina couldn't help but voice her deepest anguish. Her voice trembled as she spoke of the unforgettable crimes done to her, the scars that marred her soul, and the overwhelming feeling of being forever tainted and dirty. It was a confession of her darkest fears, the wounds that had festered within her for far too long.

Archangel Sariel listened with compassion; his eyes filled with empathy. When Seraphina had poured out her heart, he gently replied, "Dear lady, the darkness that haunts your soul is not a reflection of your worth, but a seed of doubt planted by the forces of evil. God's love for you is unconditional and unwavering, regardless of the trials and tribulations you have endured. You are not defined by the actions of others but by the purity and goodness that reside within your heart."

Archangel Sariel smiled with gentle reassurance. "Now, dear lady, let us kneel together by the spring and offer a prayer to the heavens, laying all your burdens at the feet of God."

They knelt beside the spring, and Seraphina closed her eyes, her heart filled with a mixture of hope and trepidation. Archangel Sariel's voice rose in a melodious prayer, a supplication to the divine for guidance and healing.

Seraphina's own words followed, her voice quivering with sincerity as she poured out her heart. "Lord," she began, "I surrender to you all that is dark within me, all the burdens I carry. I place them at your feet, for I am ready to be free."

As the prayer echoed through the celestial realm, a profound sense of peace settled over Seraphina. She felt as though a weight had been lifted from her shoulders, a release of the darkness that had long held her in its grip.

With the prayer concluded, Archangel Sariel nodded approvingly. "Now, dear lady," he said, "you are ready to drink from the spring and receive healing grace."

Seraphina dipped her hands into the spring, cupping the cool, clear water in her palms. She brought the water to her lips, drinking deeply as the spring's essence flowed through her being. With each sip, she felt a warmth spreading from within, a soothing balm that seemed to reach the deepest recesses of her soul.

And then, something miraculous happened. As she continued to drink, she felt the darkness that had felt like a heavy stone within her begin to diminish. It was as if the spring's waters were washing away the shadows, leaving behind a newfound sense of lightness and purity.

Archangel Sariel watched with a serene smile as the transformation unfolded before him. "The healing has begun, Lady Seraphina," he said. "But healing takes time. I offer you this flask, filled with the spring's water. Continue to drink from it over the coming week, and you shall find the darkness receding further."

Seraphina accepted the flask with gratitude, her heart filled with profound joy and relief. She knew that she had taken the first step on a journey of healing and redemption, and she was filled with hope for the future.

With a final blessing, Archangel Sariel summoned a cloud, and Seraphina was gently carried down from the summit of Mount Celestia. As she descended, she knew that her path was clearer than ever, and she was determined to confront the darkness that threatened her kingdom with renewed strength and faith.

As Lady Seraphina descended from the celestial heights of Mount Eldurith, cradled on a cloud summoned by Archangel Sariel, she was met with the eager anticipation of her noble companions who had patiently waited below. Lady Elyndra, Tilly, Tally, Sir Sterling, and Aelion stood on the ground of the flat terrain, their eyes filled with a mixture of relief and concern.

Lady Elyndra, her loyal and steadfast friend, rushed forward to embrace Seraphina as she stepped off the cloud. "Seraphina," she exclaimed, her voice filled with both joy and worry. "We feared for your safety. Are you alright?"

Lady Seraphina returned Lady Elyndra's embrace, her heart touched by the genuine concern of her dear friend. "I am well, Elyndra," she replied with a reassuring smile. "The journey was arduous, but I have found what I sought."

Tilly and Tally, the two devoted fairies who had accompanied Seraphina on her quest, fluttered around her in excitement. "We were so worried," Tilly chirped, her tiny wings a blur of iridescent colours.

Tally nodded in agreement, her eyes shimmering with relief. "Yes, we were," she chimed in. "But now that you're back, we can't wait to hear all about it!"

Sir Sterling, Seraphina's noble steed and trusted companion, whinnied with a mixture of joy and concern as he nuzzled her gently. His large, expressive eyes held a depth of emotion that only a faithful steed could convey. It was as if he had been waiting anxiously for her return.

Seraphina stroked Sir Sterling's mane, her heart filled with gratitude for his unwavering loyalty. "I missed you too, my noble friend," she whispered, her voice filled with affection.

Aelion, Elyndra's loyal steed, nickered in greeting and nuzzled her as well. His presence was a source of comfort, a reminder that she was never truly alone on her journey.

But it was Sir Sterling's reaction that stood out the most. As Seraphina looked into his deep, soulful eyes, she could sense the depths of his emotions. It was as if he had sensed the darkness that had clung to her and had been waiting anxiously for her return, a silent guardian who would stand by her side through thick and thin.

Tears welled up in Seraphina's eyes as she gazed at Sir Sterling. "You have been my steadfast companion," she whispered to him. "And I will forever be grateful for your unwavering loyalty."

Elyndra, Tilly, Tally, Aelion, and Sir Sterling gathered around Seraphina, eager to hear of her journey to Mount Eldurith and the revelations she had discovered. They knew that she had embarked on a quest of great importance, one that held the destiny of their kingdom in the balance.

With a deep breath, Seraphina began to recount her experiences, the presence of Archangel Sariel, and the healing spring she had encountered at the summit of the mountain. She described the act of surrendering all to God and the transformative power within the spring's waters.

As she spoke, her companions listened with rapt attention, their faces reflecting a mixture of awe and wonder. Elyndra's eyes shone with pride, Tilly and Tally fluttered with excitement, and Aelion and Sir Sterling stood with unwavering support.

When Seraphina had finished her tale, there was a moment of reverent silence as her companions absorbed the profound significance of her journey. It was clear that they understood the gravity of her mission and the importance of the healing she had undergone.

Elyndra was the first to break the silence, her voice filled with admiration. "You are truly remarkable, Seraphina," she said. "To have faced such trials and emerged with newfound strength and purpose is a testament to your courage and resilience."

Tilly and Tally nodded vigorously in agreement, their tiny wings buzzing with excitement. "Yes, yes!" Tilly exclaimed. "You're like a hero from one of our fairy tales!"

Seraphina smiled at their enthusiasm, grateful for their unwavering support. "I could not have done it without all of you by my side," she replied.

Aelion and Sir Sterling exchanged a knowing look, their noble steed bond evident in their silent communication. Sir Sterling then stepped forward, his large head lowered to nuzzle Seraphina once more. It was as if he was offering his silent approval and affirmation of her journey.

With her companions by her side, Lady Seraphina knew that she was not alone in her quest to rid their kingdom of the darkness that threatened it. Their unwavering loyalty and support were a source of strength and inspiration, a reminder that they would face the challenges ahead together, as a united and determined force for good.

As Lady Seraphina reached for her sword, the hilt adorned with a resplendent purple amethyst, she could feel the familiar weight of the weapon in her hand. But something was different this time. As her fingers closed around the hilt, the amethyst gem glowed with an intensity she had never seen before. Its purple light shimmered and pulsed, radiating a brilliant hue that seemed to mirror the strength of her resolve.

Seraphina's heart swelled with hope and determination as she beheld the glowing amethyst. It was as if the gem itself was confirming that the darkness within her was indeed beginning to recede, like a vanquished foe retreating in the face of her newfound inner light. With the radiant sword in hand, she knew that she was ready to face the challenges that lay ahead, armed not only with her physical prowess but with the renewed strength of her spirit and healing of her soul.

With the brilliant glow of the amethyst sword still fresh in their minds, Tilly and Tally chimed in with their characteristic enthusiasm. "It's time to head back to the enchanted forest and give Count Malachi a taste of his own medicine!" they exclaimed in unison. Their determination and eagerness to confront the looming threat resonated with Lady Seraphina and her noble companions, fueling their resolve to return to the enchanted forest and face whatever challenges awaited them. The path ahead was clear, and with unwavering unity, they would take a stand against the darkness that threatened their realm.

As they retraced their steps through the ancient terrain, they arrived once more at the colossal hollow tree that had sheltered them before. It stood as a silent sentinel, its massive trunk reaching skyward, a symbol of nature's enduring strength.

"We shall make camp here once more," Elyndra announced, her voice filled with authority. The hollow tree offered the perfect shelter from the biting cold that had plagued the summit of Mount Edurith.

Seraphina, Sir Sterling, Aelion, Tilly, Tally, and Elyndra worked together to prepare their makeshift camp within the colossal tree. They gathered firewood, and with the aid of flint and steel, Elyndra kindled a warm, crackling fire at the center of the chamber. The flames danced and flickered, casting a comforting, golden light that banished the darkness.

Their supplies were carefully arranged, and they shared a simple meal, breaking bread together and sipping from leather flasks filled with wine. The camaraderie of the group and the shared sense of purpose renewed their strength and determination.

As the night fell and the temperature dropped, they huddled together within the massive hollow chamber. The echoes of their laughter and conversation filled the space, creating a warm and inviting atmosphere. Tilly and Tally, with their playful antics and mischievous pranks, added a sense of lightheartedness to their mission.

The night passed, and as the first light of dawn crept through the gaps in the colossal tree's branches, the companions awoke to a soft, melodious sound. It was not the haunting tinkling of dewdrops this time, but rather the gentle chorus of birdsong. The enchanted forest, their ultimate destination, was not far now.

With renewed determination and a sense of anticipation, the companions broke camp within the hollow tree. They extinguished the fire, leaving no trace of their presence, and prepared to set off on the final leg of their journey. The enchanting melodies of the forest beckoned, promising both challenges and wonders that awaited them.

Seraphina took one last look at the sheltering embrace of the ancient tree, grateful for the respite it had provided. With the memory of the amethyst sword's glow and the camaraderie of her companions, she stepped out into the early morning light, ready to face the enchanted forest and confront the darkness that threatened their realm.

As they ventured deeper into the heart of the enchanted forest, the air grew thick with enchantment and mystery. The towering trees seemed to whisper secrets, and the dappled sunlight played tricks on their senses. The companions were united in purpose, their spirits high, and their determination unwavering.

The path ahead was fraught with uncertainty, but they were guided by the promise of the amethyst sword's light and the knowledge that they were bound by a bond stronger than any magic. The enchanted forest held both peril and possibility, and Lady Seraphina and her companions were prepared to face whatever lay ahead in their quest to restore light and hope to their beloved realm.

After their journey through the enchanted forest, where they encountered mystical creatures and overcame magical trials, Lady Seraphina and her companions finally emerged from the ancient woods. The transition from the enchanted forest to the ancient flat terrain at the base of the mountain marked a significant shift in their surroundings.

The air, once thick with enchantment, now felt open and expansive as they stepped onto the vast, flat expanse that stretched westward. The towering trees of the forest gave way to a seemingly endless horizon of gently rolling terrain. The path they now followed was a departure from the whimsical twists and turns of the enchanted forest, replaced by the straightforward simplicity of the ancient landscape.

The companions paused for a moment to take in the change in scenery. The enchanted forest, with its mysterious allure, had been both a sanctuary and a place of trials. Now, they faced the open terrain of the flat expanse, where the elements and the elements alone dictated the landscape.

The wind brushed against their faces, carrying with it the whispers of the ancient terrain. The ground beneath their feet was a mixture of fine sand and smooth pebbles, a stark contrast to the enchanted forest's lush undergrowth and magical creatures. As they began their journey across the flat terrain, they felt a sense of both anticipation and resolve.

The enchanted forest lay behind them, its mysteries and challenges conquered. Ahead, on the west side of the ancient flat terrain, awaited the enchanted forest's counterpart—a place of equal wonder and danger, where they hoped to find the answers they sought. The amethyst sword, its radiant light still etched in their memories, was their beacon of hope, guiding them forward as they continued their quest to bring light and hope back to their beloved realm.

With each step they took across the ancient flat terrain, Lady Seraphina and her companions left behind the enchantment of the forest and embraced the vastness of the open expanse. Their journey was far from over, and the challenges that lay ahead were unknown, but their determination remained unwavering. In the distance, the west side of the enchanted forest beckoned, a place where they would continue to forge their path and confront the darkness that threatened their realm.

Somehow, amidst the uncertainty, Lady Seraphina felt a holy blessing embracing her quest, a reminder that she was not alone in her mission to protect the realms and preserve the light and harmony that defined it.

The Road to Redemption

Lady Seraphina, accompanied by her loyal companions Lady Elyndra, Tilly, and Tally, had embarked on a perilous journey through the ancient flat terrain, hoping to reach the elusive west side of the enchanted forest. Their quest was fraught with danger, for the forest's magic was unpredictable and its inhabitants enigmatic.

As they ventured deeper into the heart of the forest, the air seemed to thicken with enchantment. A subtle change in the atmosphere caught their attention – the absence of birdsong. It was an eerie silence that descended upon the woods, as if the forest itself were trying to hide from unseen hunters. The absence of the usual symphony of chirping and singing birds left a void that sent shivers down their spines.

Undeterred by the eerie silence, Lady Seraphina and her companions continued their journey, riding their noble steeds through the winding trails of the Enchanted Forest. Their keen eyes scanned the surroundings, taking note of the shifting shadows and the whispering leaves. The forest had always been unpredictable, but this time, it felt as though it held its breath, as if secrets were lurking in every shadow.

As Lady Seraphina and Lady Elyndra continued their perilous journey through the Enchanted Forest, they remained vigilant, aware that danger could lurk around any corner. Unbeknownst to them, their presence had not gone unnoticed by the forest's mystical inhabitants. Among the enchanted creatures that called the forest home, there was one peculiar scout named Fizzlewick.

Fizzlewick was a creature that resembled a monkey but possessed an otherworldly, magical quality. His fur was a vibrant shade of emerald, green, perfectly blending with the foliage of the forest. His eyes, however, were the most striking feature—piercing golden orbs that seemed to hold an uncanny intelligence.

Hidden amongst the dense canopy, Fizzlewick spotted Lady Seraphina and Lady Elyndra riding through the forest. With a sudden burst of energy, he began emitting a series of howling monkey sounds, a cacophony that echoed through the trees. It was a sound like nothing Lady Seraphina and Lady Elyndra had ever heard, a strange, haunting chorus that sent shivers down their spines.

Startled by the eerie and unfamiliar sounds, Sterling and Aelion, their noble steeds, reared up in fright. Their powerful hooves churned the forest floor as they whinnied nervously. Lady Seraphina and Lady Elyndra struggled to calm their steeds, realizing that something extraordinary and potentially perilous was afoot.

Then, as suddenly as the cacophony had begun, it went deathly silent. The silence that descended upon the forest was heavy, laden with an unspoken tension. Both Lady Seraphina and Elyndra remained on high alert, their senses keen and their hearts racing. They exchanged a knowing glance, their expressions reflecting their unease.

Sterling and Aelion, still skittish from the sudden fright, stomped their hooves and snorted nervously, their ears swiveling to catch any hint of danger. The forest seemed to hold its breath, as if it were watching and waiting. Lady Seraphina and Elyndra knew that they needed to press on, for their mission to reach the Elven Kingdom was of utmost importance.

With a shared resolve, they urged their steeds forward, slowly but surely continuing their journey through the Enchanted Forest. Their senses remained sharp, and their eyes scanned the shadows, knowing that the strange encounter with Fizzlewick had left an indelible mark on their quest. The eerie silence and the unsettling encounter with the enchanted monkey-like creature served as a stark reminder that the Enchanted Forest held many secrets, both wondrous and perilous, waiting to be discovered.

Their lingering unease transformed into stark dread as they ventured deeper along the forest path, for it was here that an insidious ambush awaited. Suddenly and without warning, the menacing figure of Grizzletooth, the ruthless goblin leader, emerged from the shadows with his vile army in tow. The goblins, their eyes gleaming with malice, brandished crude weapons and wicked grins, springing forth from the underbrush like malevolent specters, swiftly surrounding Lady Seraphina, Elyndra, and their loyal steeds.

A sinister hush enveloped the forest as Grizzletooth's wicked laughter echoed through the ancient trees, each chilling note punctuating the looming danger. "Thought you could slip through our grasp, did ya?" Grizzletooth jeered, his voice dripping with malevolence. "Not so fast, little lady," he hissed, his words laced with a promise of peril and impending chaos.

Lady Seraphina exchanged a grim look with Elyndra, her trusted friend and confidante. They knew they had to stand their ground, for they were on a quest of great importance. With determination, they dismounted their noble steeds, Sterling and Aelion, and drew their gleaming swords, ready to face the goblin horde on foot.

Yet, what truly froze Lady Seraphina's blood was not merely the menacing presence of Grizzletooth and his horde of goblins; it was the sudden, ominous emergence of Count Malachi himself, who had tirelessly pursued them to sabotage their mission. Count Malachi materialized like a sinister apparition from the shrouded depths of the forest. He perched regally atop his fearsome Dracohound, a nightmarish beast whose scales bore the darkness of midnight and whose eyes blazed with a sinister malevolence.

But the dread did not stop there. In Count Malachi's wake, a legion of warriors, clad in obsidian armour adorned with serpentine accents, materialized with an eerie, silent precision. These ominous soldiers rode lizard–like horses, their sinewy forms resembling serpents poised for a strike. Their steely gazes were unyielding, locked onto Lady Seraphina and her loyal companions as if fate itself had aligned them for this perilous confrontation. The forest seemed to hold its breath in the face of such a malevolent assembly, leaving Lady Seraphina and her allies to grapple with the overwhelming gravity of the situation.

The lizard-like horses ridden by Count Malachi's serpent-armoured soldiers were a fantastical and otherworldly sight to behold. These creatures, known as "Serpentsteeds," were a unique blend of reptilian and equine features, perfectly suited for navigating the mystical terrain of the Enchanted Forest.

Serpentsteeds possessed sleek, scaled bodies that shimmered with an iridescent, obsidian-like sheen. Their scales were arranged in overlapping patterns, providing both protection and an elegant aesthetic. These creatures had long, sinuous tails that ended in a sharp, barbed tip, reminiscent of a serpent's tail. The tails served both as a defense mechanism and a means of balance while navigating the forest's treacherous paths.

Their heads were a striking combination of horse-like features with elongated, reptilian snouts. These snouts were equipped with rows of sharp teeth, perfect for tearing through foliage or deterring any would-be attackers. Their eyes were piercing and predatory, with slitted pupils that allowed them to see clearly in the dim light of the Enchanted Forest.

Serpentsteeds moved with a graceful and sinuous gait, their muscular bodies undulating in a serpentine manner as they traversed the forest floor. Despite their intimidating appearance, they were incredibly agile and sure-footed, capable of navigating even the most treacherous terrain with ease.

These mythical Serpentsteeds were well-suited to Count Malachi's army, providing both mobility and an air of mystique as they moved in unison through the enchanted woods, adding to the aura of darkness and foreboding that surrounded their formidable leader.

The realization of their dire predicament gripped Lady Seraphina's heart with icy fingers. Count Malachi was a formidable foe, and his presence, combined with Grizzletooth's goblin horde, created a dire situation. Her voice trembling, she whispered to Elyndra, "We must fight, for there is no other choice. Our quest depends on it."

As the battle began in earnest, Lady Seraphina and Elyndra fought valiantly, their swords flashing through the air, cutting down goblins with precision and determination. Sterling and Aelion, their noble steeds, joined the fray, using their powerful hooves and sharp instincts to fend off the goblin attackers.

Tilly and Tally, the two fairies who had accompanied Lady Seraphina and her companions on their journey, realized the danger of the situation. With swift and graceful movements, they fluttered into the trees, hidden from view. Their tiny forms blended with the leaves and branches, making them nearly invisible as they watched the battle unfold.

The clash of steel and the cries of goblins filled the air, but Lady Seraphina couldn't shake her fear of Count Malachi and his ominous presence. She knew that facing him and his Dracohound would be a formidable challenge.

Count Malachi, atop his fearsome Dracohound, barked orders to his serpent-armoured soldiers, and they surged forward, their lizard-like steeds hissing and snapping at the goblins. The forest seemed to come alive with chaos and conflict as the two opposing forces clashed.

As Lady Seraphina locked eyes with Count Malachi, a sudden and overwhelming wave of panic surged through her. Her heart raced, and her breath grew shallow as anxiety gripped her like a vice. The world around her began to warp and distort, as if time itself were slowing to a crawl. The sounds of battle and the chaos of the forest muffled in her ears, distant echoes in a surreal dreamscape.

Elyndra, perceptive to the profound change in Seraphina, witnessed her companion's distress. Desperation surged within her as she realized that Seraphina had become frozen in her movements, lost in the grip of an incapacitating trance. Struggling to maintain her own defense against the encroaching goblins, Elyndra called out to Seraphina, her voice a desperate plea for her friend to snap back to reality.

"Seraphina!" Elyndra cried, her voice cutting through the haze of Seraphina's panic-stricken mind. "Snap out of it! We need you!" Her words were a lifeline, a plea for Seraphina to rejoin the battle, but the panic was unyielding, refusing to release its grip.

As the goblins closed in, Elyndra fought valiantly to fend them off, trying to protect them both from the encroaching threat. But Seraphina, lost in the throes of her panic attack, collapsed to her knees, her vision blurred and her strength sapped by the overwhelming anxiety that had taken hold. The world continued to move in eerie slow motion around her, and all she could do was struggle to regain her composure, as the battle raged on, a desperate and uncertain ordeal.

The forest, a realm steeped in ancient magic and timeless wisdom, had long been a silent observer of the unfolding chaos. As the battle raged on between Lady Seraphina, Elyndra, and their companions against Grizzletooth's goblin horde, and Count Malachi's sinister forces, the very essence of the forest stirred with a profound and ancient power.

The rumbling sound that emerged from beneath the forest's floor was unlike anything anyone present had ever heard. It was as if the very earth itself was awakening, responding to the imminent threat that encroached upon its sacred realm. The vibrations beneath their feet resonated through the hearts of all who stood there, commanding their attention with an eerie, primal force.

The combatants, both goblins and the serpent-armoured soldiers, as well as Lady Seraphina's party, paused in a momentary truce. All eyes turned to the source of the disturbance, an unearthly sound that seemed to herald the awakening of something ancient and formidable.

As the rumbling intensified, the forest floor seemed to tremble, and the towering trees lining the battlefield swayed in harmony with the earth's awakening. It was then that the true marvel of the Enchanted Forest unfolded, for from the very ground itself, roots unearthing themselves like slumbering giants began to make their presence known.

Massive, gnarled roots, as thick as a man's waist, burst forth from the earth with a sound akin to thunder. They reached out with an eerie grace, snaking through the air like serpents seeking their prey. The goblins and Count Malachi's soldiers watched in awe and terror as the very ground they stood upon came to life, a manifestation of the forest's latent power.

But the awakening of the forest's guardians did not end there. Among the trees that had stood sentinel for centuries, ancient treants stirred from their deep slumber. These colossal, sentient beings, known as treants, resembled immense humanoid forms crafted from bark, moss, and living wood.

Their eyes, like pools of wisdom, gleamed with an age-old knowledge, and their limbs stretched and creaked as they rose from their rooted resting places. With an undeniable presence, the treants lumbered forward, their massive forms casting shadows over the battlefield.

As they advanced, the treants unleashed the latent magic of the forest, wielding it like a weapon. Long, sinuous vines, as thick as ropes, sprouted from their massive bodies. These vines lashed out with uncanny speed and precision, ensnaring goblins and serpent-armoured soldiers alike. With a single flick of their branch-like hands, the Treants swatted their foes away like bothersome insects.

The goblins' crude weapons and the serpent-armoured soldiers' advanced armour were no match for the ancient might of the treants. They were flung through the air, their cries of fear and agony drowned out by the eerie symphony of the forest's vengeance.

As the treants closed the distance, their colossal forms casting a shadow of hope upon Lady Seraphina and her companions, the goblins and Count Malachi's soldiers began to scatter, their ranks in disarray. The forest had awakened, and its protectors had arisen to defend their sacred realm.

With every step the treants took, the earth quivered in response, and the very air seemed charged with the potent energy of nature's fury. Lady Seraphina and Elyndra, who had been battling fiercely to defend their mission, watched in awe and gratitude as the forest itself came to their aid.

The Treants moved with an otherworldly grace, their mighty forms a testament to the enduring power of the Enchanted Forest. Their branch-like arms and vines continued to whip and lash at the retreating goblins and serpent-armoured soldiers, clearing a path of safety for Lady Seraphina and her companions.

With each strike and each bellowing roar that echoed through the forest, it became clear that the ancient guardians of the Enchanted Forest would not allow their realm to be desecrated.

The ancient guardians of the Enchanted Forest, known as treants, continued their relentless advance, their colossal forms casting shadows over the battlefield. As they drew closer, their massive bodies moved with an otherworldly grace, their branch-like arms and sinuous vines lashing out with uncanny speed and precision. The goblins and Count Malachi's serpent-armoured soldiers were in disarray, their crude weapons and advanced armour proving no match for the ancient might of the treants.

But then, amidst the chaos, a sudden turn of events occurred. Out of fury, Count Malachi led Dracohound forward, a fearsome creature with the ability to breathe fire. With a deafening roar, Dracohound unleashed a torrent of flames, engulfing the treants in a blaze of fire.

The treants, ancient guardians of the forest, emitted a deep, mournful groan as the flames licked at their bark and moss-covered bodies. The groan echoed through the battlefield, a sound that seemed to resonate with the very heart of the Enchanted Forest.

In response to the treants' plight, the forest itself reacted once more, this time from the river that ran beside the battle spot. The river's waters began to churn and froth, and towers of water rose into the air. These towering columns of water were inhabited by freshwater mermaids known as eamaids.

These eamaids were ethereal beings, with luminous, aquatic features. Their hair flowed like the current of the river itself, and their eyes shimmered like the depths of the clearest waters. They were protectors of the river and had a deep connection to the Enchanted Forest.

With graceful movements, the eamaids emerged from the towers of water. They had long, sinuous tails that allowed them to move effortlessly through the river's depths. With a melodious song that echoed through the forest, they approached the treants.

The eamaids used their powers over water to help the treants extinguish the flames. They splashed water onto the burning bark and moss, creating a soothing cascade of liquid that quenched the fire. The treants groaned once more, but this time it was a sigh of relief as the flames were gradually extinguished, leaving behind charred patches on their ancient forms.

As the eamaids assisted the treants, they also turned their attention to the goblins who had been driven close to the river's edge. With a flick of their tails, they conjured waves that crashed onto the goblins, washing them away in a torrent of water. The goblins struggled and cried out, but the eamaids were relentless in their pursuit of protecting the forest's sanctity.

Meanwhile, Count Malachi and his remaining soldiers watched in horror as the forest itself seemed to rise against them. They saw the treants, once engulfed in flames, now being aided by the eamaids. The goblins that had survived the battle were scattered and disoriented, their morale shattered by the overwhelming forces of nature.

Realizing that they were no match for the combined might of the treants, the eamaids, and the Enchanted Forest itself, Count Malachi ordered a retreat. The remaining serpent–armoured soldiers and goblins turned and fled; their once–sinister intentions now replaced by sheer terror.

Lady Seraphina and Elyndra, deeply grateful for the intervention of the forest and its mystical allies, watched as the invaders retreated. They understood that their mission to protect the Enchanted Forest had been successful, thanks to the ancient magic and profound bond between the natural world and those who sought to defend it.

The ancient guardians of the Enchanted Forest, known as treants, continued their relentless advance, their colossal forms casting shadows over the battlefield. As they drew closer, their massive bodies moved with an otherworldly grace, their branch-like arms and sinuous vines lashing out with uncanny speed and precision. The goblins and Count Malachi's serpent-armoured soldiers were in disarray, their crude weapons and advanced armour proving no match for the ancient might of the treants.

After Count Malachi's hasty retreat, Lady Seraphina and Elyndra stood in awe, gazing at the treants and eamaids with deep gratitude. The ancient guardians and mystical river protectors regarded them with a curious and knowing gaze. Seraphina stepped forward, her voice filled with reverence, and addressed them, "We are eternally grateful for your aid in our time of need." In response, the treants and eamaids nodded with a solemn acknowledgment, their age-old wisdom and benevolence shining through their ancient eyes.

The eamaids were ethereal beings with luminous, aquatic features. Their hair flowed like the current of the river itself, and their eyes shimmered like the depths of the clearest waters. They were protectors of the river and had a deep connection to the Enchanted Forest.

The leader of the eamaids, known as Liriana, approached Lady Seraphina and Elyndra with a gentle and melodious voice. "Noble guardians of the forest," she began, "it is no longer safe for you to travel through the forest's depths. The malevolent forces that sought to desecrate our realm may return. Instead, we shall guide you along the river, a path less known to those who would harm this sacred land."

Understanding the wisdom of Liriana's words, Lady Seraphina and Elyndra nodded in agreement. "Thank you for your guidance," Lady Seraphina replied with gratitude.

Liriana and the other eamaids used their mystical abilities and webbed hands to help the treants build a sturdy raft for Lady Seraphina, Elyndra, and their two loyal steeds, Sterling and Aelion. The raft was a marvel of natural craftsmanship, constructed from massive, gnarled roots intertwined with vines that seemed to shimmer with an inner light. Soft moss cushions decorated the seating area, providing a comfortable space for the travelers.

As Lady Seraphina and Elyndra prepared to embark on their river journey, Tilly and Tally, who had been hiding during the battle, emerged from their secret spot among the leaves. They fluttered before the treants and eamaids, their tiny wings aglow with gratitude.

"Thank you, ancient and benevolent beings," Tilly exclaimed, her voice tinkling like a bell. "Your aid in our time of need is greatly appreciated."

Tally added, "We promise to protect the Enchanted Forest with all our might and to keep it safe from harm."

With gracious smiles, the treants and eamaids acknowledged the fairies' words. As Lady Seraphina, Elyndra, Sterling, and Aelion boarded the raft, Liriana, with her radiant presence, spoke once more. "We shall guide you through the river's secret channels, leading you to the hidden entrance of the Elven Kingdom at the base of the waterfall."

The eamaids, their tails shimmering, gracefully entered the water and swam alongside the raft. With each stroke of their powerful tails, they guided the raft through the winding river, revealing the hidden beauty of the Enchanted Forest from a new perspective.

The river journey was serene and enchanting, as the travelers marveled at the lush foliage and vibrant wildlife that thrived along the water's edge. The eamaids' voices harmonized with the rustling leaves, creating a tranquil melody that enveloped the raft.

As they glided down the river on the beautifully crafted raft, Elyndra turned to Lady Seraphina with a concerned expression. "Seraphina," she began gently, "I couldn't help but notice during the battle, there was a moment when you seemed frozen, as if lost in your thoughts. Can you tell me what happened?"

Lady Seraphina took a deep breath, her eyes distant for a moment as she recalled the harrowing memories. "It was when I saw Count Malachi," she confessed in a hushed tone, her voice trembling. "For a brief moment, it felt like I was back in his castle, enduring his abuse. I felt entrapped by my own thoughts, unable to move."

As Lady Seraphina shared her painful experience, the eamaids, who were gracefully pushing the raft downstream, listened attentively. Liriana, their leader, spoke gently to Seraphina, "Dear guardian of the forest, what you experienced was a relapse, a reminder of past trauma. It's a normal response to such a threatening encounter. But please know that we see a brightness within you, a resilience that will carry you forward."

Seraphina's eyes welled with tears as she nodded, her heart touched by Liriana's words. "I sought healing at the Angel City," she admitted. "I sipped from the Spring of Healing, and it gave me strength to face my past."

Liriana smiled warmly, her luminous presence radiating compassion. "Time will allow you to bloom into who you are meant to be," she assured Seraphina. "The Enchanted Forest recognizes your courage, and we will support you on your journey."

With renewed hope and a sense of camaraderie, Lady Seraphina, Elyndra, and their loyal steeds continued their river journey, knowing that the wisdom and guidance of the eamaids, along with their own inner strength, would lead them to the secrets of the Elven Kingdom and beyond.

Finally, the journey led them to the base of a magnificent waterfall, its cascading waters sparkling like liquid crystal. Liriana guided the raft to a hidden alcove behind the waterfall, revealing the secret entrance to the Elven Kingdom.

With profound gratitude, Lady Seraphina and Elyndra bid farewell to the eamaids, who promised to keep watch over the forest's waters. As they stepped into the hidden passage, they knew that their quest to protect the Enchanted Forest was far from over, but with the mystical guidance of the eamaids and the blessings of the ancient guardians, they were ready to face the challenges that lay ahead.

As Lady Seraphina, Elyndra, and their companions entered the Elven Kingdom through the hidden passage behind the sparkling waterfall, they were met with a heartwarming sight. The first Elves who caught sight of them were filled with overwhelming joy at their return. These Elves, held magnificent horns crafted from iridescent seashells. When they saw Seraphina and Elyndra, they raised these extraordinary instruments to their lips.

The horns, made from the shells of ancient sea creatures, had spiraled patterns that shimmered with colours of the ocean. As the Elves blew into them, the sound that emanated was nothing short of magical. It was a harmonious blend of nature's melody, echoing through the Elven Kingdom like a gentle breeze, carrying a sense of peace and unity.

General Ironheart, who had been overseeing the crusade armies training, turned around in curiosity upon hearing the enchanting sound of the horn. His eyes widened in awe as he laid eyes on Lady Seraphina for the first time. Her presence seemed to radiate a unique brilliance, and he couldn't help but feel a deep sense of respect and admiration for the guardian of the Enchanted Forest who had returned to their realm.

General Elowen, the guardian of the Elven Kingdom, stood at the entrance to the grand hall, his elven features radiant with warmth and anticipation. His long, silver hair cascaded down his back. As Lady Seraphina and her companions entered, Elowen's crystal eyes sparkled with recognition and joy.

"Seraphina, welcome back to the heart of our kingdom," he greeted with a graceful curtsy. His melodic voice echoed through the hall. "We have long awaited your return and the wisdom you bring from the Enchanted Forest."

Lady Seraphina bowed in return, her emerald-green cloak billowing behind her. "It is an honour to be here, General Elowen. The forest's guardians and mystical allies have guided me safely back."

Elowen led Seraphina further into the grand hall, where a council of leaders awaited. Among them was General Ironheart, waiting patiently for his turn to address Lady Seraphina. As Seraphina was introduced to the council, she couldn't help but notice the stern gaze of Lady Isabella.

During the council meeting, Lady Isabella made no effort to hide her skepticism and unfriendliness towards Lady Seraphina. She questioned the guardian's motives and the forest's decision to align with outsiders. General Ironheart, however, remained silent, his gaze fixed on Seraphina with a deep curiosity that seemed to grow with each passing moment.

That evening, the Elven Kingdom celebrated Seraphina's safe return with a grand feast. The hall was furnished with ethereal lights, and the air was filled with the enchanting melodies of Elven musicians. Seraphina was seated at the head of the table, flanked by General Elowen and General Ironheart. Lady Isabella sat at a distant end; her disapproval evident in her every gesture.

As the night unfolded, Lady Seraphina noticed the longing glances from General Ironheart, whose eyes seemed to be drawn irresistibly towards her.

She could sense an unspoken connection, a curiosity that went beyond mere diplomacy. It was as though the forest's magic had woven a unique thread between their souls.

The following morning, as the first rays of sunlight filtered into General Ironheart's bedchamber, he was awakened by the rhythmic sounds of clashing swords and the soft, melodic hum of Seraphina's voice. Curiosity piqued, he rose from his bed and made his way to the window, where he was met with a breathtaking sight.

There, on the training grounds below, Lady Seraphina moved with a graceful fluidity that seemed almost ethereal. Her sword danced through the air, each movement precise and deliberate. Her emerald eyes sparkled with determination as she practiced her martial skills with unmatched dedication. It was a mesmerizing display of strength and agility that left Ironheart in awe.

Unable to resist the urge to learn more about this enigmatic guardian, General Ironheart descended from his chamber and made his way to the training grounds. As he approached, Seraphina's emerald eyes met his, and a warm smile graced her lips.

"General Ironheart," she greeted with a nod, her sword at rest. "I hope the morning finds you well."

Ironheart returned the greeting, his molten gold eyes fixed on. "You are a formidable warrior, Lady Seraphina," he admitted. "Your skills are impressive."

Seraphina inclined her head in acknowledgment. "I have trained diligently to protect the Enchanted Forest and those who dwell within it."

Their conversation flowed effortlessly as they spoke of their respective roles and responsibilities. It was during this candid exchange that Seraphina chose to reveal the painful chapter of her past, the abuse she had endured in Count Malachi's castle, and her quest for healing in the Angel City.

General Ironheart listened with a mixture of empathy and respect, his admiration for her resilience deepening with each word she spoke. He could sense the weight of her past and the strength it had taken to overcome it. Seraphina's vulnerability only served to strengthen the bond that had begun to form between them.

As the morning sunbathed them in its golden light, Seraphina and General Ironheart found themselves not as adversaries, but as kindred spirits united by a shared purpose—the protection of their realms and the pursuit of a brighter future. Their connection would prove to be a powerful force in the challenges that lay ahead, forging a path of unity and strength in the face of adversity.

Lady Isabella, the mage, watched with burning jealousy from afar as General Ironheart and Lady Seraphina shared a deepening connection. The warmth in her heart turned to a seething rage as she witnessed their camaraderie and mutual respect. It was a sight that gnawed at her, for her own feelings towards Ironheart were clouded by unrequited love, and seeing him grow closer to another ignited a consuming envy within her.

Unable to bear the torment of her emotions any longer, Lady Isabella stormed from the grand hall, her silver hair swirling behind her in a frenzy of emotions. She mounted her horse and rode with unchecked fury, her heart heavy with resentment. She rode further and further from the Elven Kingdom, her anger propelling her into the depths of the surrounding forest.

As she ventured deeper into the woods, the enchantment of the Elven Kingdom began to fade, replaced by a more sinister and ancient atmosphere. Isabella, lost in her turmoil, failed to notice the gradual transformation of the once-vibrant forest into a foreboding wilderness.

It was only when the trees grew gnarled and the shadows darker that Isabella finally realized how far she had ridden. Panic welled up within her as she glanced around, the unfamiliar surroundings sending a shiver down her spine. She had ventured into a realm that was alien and hostile.

A malevolent cackle pierced the silence, and Isabella's heart raced. Out of nowhere, a figure materialized before her—the Witch Morgana, a being of dark and twisted magic. Morgana's eyes gleamed with an eerie light as she regarded Isabella with a sly grin.

"I sense your turmoil, dear Lady Isabella," Morgana purred, her voice dripping with venom. "Jealousy can be such a potent emotion, can it not? But I offer you a way to quench that burning rage."

Taken aback by Morgana's appearance and her knowledge of Isabella's inner turmoil, the mage hesitated. "How do you know of my feelings?" Isabella demanded, her voice wavering.

Morgana's laughter echoed through the eerie forest. "Once you cross a certain threshold in pacts with the devil, my dear, there are powers and knowledge far beyond your understanding. I can grant you unimaginable abilities, control over others, and the power to make General Ironheart yours. All you have to do is sell your soul to the devil."

Isabella was tempted by Morgana's words, the desire for power and control burning within her. She was on the verge of agreeing when, ever so faintly, a whisper reached her ears. It was a regal voice, one she recognized as Lady Elowen's, urging her not to give in to the darkness.

"Isabella," the voice whispered, "there is always hope for a better future, even if the present is not what you expected. Do not let jealousy lead you down a path you will regret."

The whisper was like a lifeline, pulling Isabella back from the precipice of darkness. She hesitated, her gaze shifting between Morgana and the unseen presence of Lady Elowen's voice. Finally, her resolve strengthened, and she turned her horse away from Morgana.

"No," Isabella declared, her voice filled with newfound determination. "I will not surrender my soul to darkness. There is hope for a better path."

Morgana's eyes blazed with fury, and she hissed, "You will regret this, Isabella."

With that, Lady Isabella rode away from the malevolent presence of Morgana, the forest gradually returning to its enchanted state as she neared the Elven Kingdom. Her heart remained heavy, but she clung to the hope that Lady Elowen's whispered wisdom had offered her—the hope of a better future, where love and light might still find their way into her heart, even in the face of jealousy and turmoil.

As Lady Isabella rode back toward the enchanted waterfall that concealed the entrance to the Elven Kingdom, her heart heavy with the weight of her recent temptation, she was startled by a melodious voice calling out to her. "Lady Isabella," the voice beckoned from the crystal-clear waters.

Isabella reined in her horse and dismounted, her eyes widening in awe as a breathtaking sight unfolded before her. Emerging from the sparkling waterfall was a creature unlike anything she had ever seen—a freshwater mermaid, known as an Eamaid.

The Eamaid's beauty was ethereal, with luminous, aquamarine skin that shimmered like the gentle ripples of a tranquil river. Her long, flowing hair cascaded like liquid silver, glinting with a faint iridescence. The Eamaid's eyes were a mesmerizing shade of emerald green, reflecting the lush colours of the forest. Her slender form was detailed with intricate patterns of river-inspired tattoos, further enhancing her enchanting appearance.

The most captivating feature of the Eamaid, however, was her tail. It was long and sinuous, covered in iridescent scales that shifted in colour as she moved, resembling the colours of a flowing river. At the end of her tail, she had a pair of gracefully shaped fins that resembled the delicate wings of a butterfly. These fins, decorated with patterns that resembled intricate lace, fluttered gently as she treaded the water.

Isabella could only stare in wonder at the Eamaid's breathtaking beauty. "I have heard of your kind, but I never imagined I would see one," she whispered in awe.

The Eamaid smiled warmly, her voice like the gentle flow of a river. "I am Liriana, guardian of the river and a protector of the Enchanted Forest. I have watched your struggles and temptations, Lady Isabella."

Isabella's heart skipped a beat, realizing that Liriana had witnessed her moments of weakness. "You know of my inner turmoil?"

Liriana nodded, her emerald eyes filled with compassion. "I do. And I believe it would be unwise to let jealousy and anger guide your path. Your heart and your talents could be better used in service to a greater cause."

Isabella's brow furrowed as she considered Liriana's words. "What do you suggest I do, then?"

Liriana's gaze held a wisdom that transcended her years. "Go to Ravenshadow, the kingdom of humans beyond the enchanted forest. Seek an audience with King Alaric. He is a wise and just ruler. Offer your skills and abilities to serve the kingdom there, rather than allowing your jealousy toward Lady Seraphina and General Ironheart to consume you. Such resentment will only serve as a risk to our cause."

Isabella's heart felt heavy with the weight of her choices and the realization that her jealousy had led her astray. "You speak the truth, Liriana," she admitted, her voice filled with remorse. "I will seek King Alaric and offer my service to Ravenshadow."

Liriana's smile brightened, and she nodded in approval. "Your decision is wise, Lady Isabella. May your journey be one of redemption and growth and may the Enchanted Forest's blessings be with you."

With Liriana's wise counsel still resonating in her heart, Lady Isabella turned her horse away from the enchanting waterfall and embarked on her journey toward Ravenshadow. Her hope was to discover a new purpose and heal the wounds that had plagued her soul. Liriana, the enchanting Eamaid of the river, had provided her with guidance that illuminated a path toward a brighter, more promising future—a path free from the dark shadows of jealousy and resentment that had once clouded her spirit.

As Lady Isabella walked through the grotto b whine the waterfall to enter the Elven Kingdom, her thoughts were filled with determination and anticipation. She knew her destination was Ravenshadow, the kingdom beyond the enchanted woods. She was resolved to offer her skills and service to King Alaric, hoping to find redemption and a greater cause to devote herself to.

Upon reaching the elven palace, Lady Isabella sought an audience with General Ironheart. She needed to inform him of her decision and gain his blessing for her journey to Ravenshadow. General Ironheart, with his molten gold eyes and imposing presence, received her with a mixture of curiosity and concern.

"Isabella," he began, "I understand your desire to seek a new purpose, but I had hoped you would stay and continue to contribute to our cause."

Isabella met his gaze with a solemn expression. "General, my presence here has been marred by jealousy, and it could jeopardize everything we strive for. I believe it's best for all that I seek my path elsewhere."

General Ironheart's stern facade softened as he considered her words. "Very well," he conceded. "If you believe this is the right course of action, I will not stand in your way. May your journey be fruitful, and may you find the peace and purpose you seek."

General Elowen, the guardian of the Elven Kingdom, overheard their conversation and approached them with a regal presence. "Isabella's decision is a wise one," he affirmed. "To heal one's heart is a noble pursuit. I believe it is in the best interest of our kingdom that we support her."

With a gracious nod, he instructed three skilled Elven warriors to accompany Lady Isabella on her journey to Ravenshadow. "They will guide you safely to your destination and provide protection along the way. May the blessings of the forest be with you, Isabella, and may your path lead you to the brighter future you seek."

Lady Isabella felt a profound sense of gratitude and determination as she set out once more, this time with the company of her Elven companions. The shadows of her past would soon give way to the promise of a new beginning, and she rode toward Ravenshadow with hope in her heart and a commitment to find her place in a world free from the clutches of jealousy and resentment.

General Ironheart couldn't shake the feeling of guilt that lingered within him after Lady Isabella's departure. He couldn't help but wonder if he had somehow failed her, if there was something he could have done differently to make her stay. The weight of her decision weighed heavily on his heart, and he found himself grappling with a sense of responsibility for her departure.

In the solitude of his chambers, Ironheart reflected on their interactions and the moments that had led to her decision. He recalled the times they had fought side by side, the shared battles and triumphs, and the subtle bond that had formed between them. He couldn't help but feel that he had let her down in some way, that he had betrayed her trust, even if unintentionally.

Seeking counsel, General Ironheart gathered his trusted advisors—the Council of Elders. Captain Elara Swiftwind, Lady Titania Stormbringer, Sir Alden Frostbane, and Lord Cellok Stoneforge assembled in the grand chamber, their expressions marked by a mix of puzzlement and understanding as they discussed Lady Isabella's departure.

Captain Swiftwind, known for his keen insights and unwavering loyalty, spoke first. "General, Lady Isabella's decision is a personal one. It reflects her own journey and choices, and we must respect that."

Lady Stormbringer, the master of diplomacy, added, "Sometimes, one must embark on a path of self-discovery and healing. It is not a betrayal, but rather an act of courage."

Sir Frostbane, the voice of reason among them, nodded in agreement. "General, you have always led with honour and integrity. Lady Isabella's decision is not a reflection of your leadership."

Lord Stoneforge, the keeper of tradition and wisdom, spoke solemnly. "The Enchanted Forest has a way of guiding each of us on our unique journeys. We must trust that Lady Isabella's path will lead her to where she needs to be."

General Ironheart listened to his council's wise words, finding solace in their support. He realized that Lady Isabella's departure, though tinged with sorrow and uncertainty, was ultimately a testament to her own strength and resilience. He could not blame himself for her choice, nor could he hold onto feelings of guilt.

With newfound clarity, General Ironheart made a silent vow to honour Lady Isabella's decision and continue to lead his army with unwavering dedication. The Enchanted Forest was a realm of boundless possibilities, and he knew that their paths might cross again in the future, each on their own journey of self-discovery and growth.

General Ironheart was a man of unyielding honour, his steadfast commitment to his principles as unshakeable as the mountains that surrounded the enchanted realm. However, his unwavering kindness often proved to be his vulnerability. He couldn't help but extend his benevolence even to those who did not reciprocate it, a trait that had occasionally been exploited by those with less noble intentions. Yet, it was precisely this kindness that endeared him to his troops and to Lady Isabella herself, for they saw in him not just a formidable leader but a compassionate and understanding friend.

A Fragile Trust

As Lady Seraphina and General Ironheart continued to train together in the enchanting realm of the Elven Kingdom, their bond deepened with each passing day. The more time they spent together, the stronger the connection between them seemed to grow. Ironheart was captivated not only by Seraphina's grace and skill in combat but also by the inner strength and resilience that radiated from her.

They trained with swords, their blades flashing through the air in a mesmerizing dance of skill and precision. General Ironheart couldn't help but be impressed by Seraphina's swordsmanship. Her movements were fluid and effortless, a testament to months of dedicated training. She wielded her weapon with a blend of elegance and fierceness that left him in awe.

They also practiced archery, with Seraphina displaying an uncanny accuracy that few could match. Her arrows found their mark with unerring precision, striking true and hitting bullseyes repeatedly. It was as if her connection to the forest itself imbued her with an otherworldly aim.

General Ironheart, ever the patient and observant leader, admired her abilities but also sensed that there was more to Seraphina's story than met the eye. He could see the shadows in her eyes, the remnants of past pain and trauma. It was clear that she carried scars not only on her body but deep within her heart.

One day, as they finished their training, General Ironheart noticed Seraphina heading towards the stables. Her destination was clear—Sir Sterling, her loyal white stallion, who stood regally among the other horses. Ironheart followed her, his curiosity piqued.

He marveled at the sight of Sir Sterling, a magnificent white stallion with a coat that gleamed like freshly fallen snow. The stallion exuded an air of nobility and strength, his eyes filled with intelligence and a deep loyalty to his mistress.

As Ironheart approached, he couldn't help but notice a delicate scar on Sir Sterling's shoulder, decorated with mother-of-pearl inlays. The scar seemed to tell a story of hardship and resilience, and Ironheart couldn't ignore the desire to know more. He turned to Seraphina with a gentle expression.

"What happened to Sir Sterling's shoulder?" he inquired softly, his molten gold eyes filled with a quiet understanding.

Seraphina's gaze shifted to the scar, and for a moment, her expression darkened with the weight of painful memories. She hesitated, then sighed, deciding to share her truth with Ironheart. "It's a reminder of an abusive incident, a time when I was under the cruel grasp of Count Malachi."

Ironheart's heart ached for Seraphina as he listened to her confession. He longed to reach out to her, to offer comfort and solace, but he knew that trust had to be earned, especially for someone who had suffered as she had.

Ever so patient, he extended his hand toward her, his touch gentle as a whisper of wind. Seraphina, still working through the trauma of her past, flinched instinctively, pulling her hand away. She offered a shaky apology, her eyes filled with a mixture of vulnerability and determination.

"I'm still learning to trust," she admitted, her voice barely above a whisper. "But I appreciate your patience, General Ironheart."

He nodded, understanding the significance of her words. "I'll earn your trust, Seraphina, slowly and patiently. I promise you, I would never harm you, and I will be here whenever you're ready."

As if in agreement with Ironheart's vow, Sir Sterling, the loyal stallion, stepped closer to the general, nuzzling his hand with a show of affection. It was as if the majestic horse recognized the kindness and sincerity in Ironheart's heart and welcomed him into their world.

With Sir Sterling's silent approval, Seraphina allowed herself a small smile, a glimmer of hope shining in her emerald-green eyes. She knew that healing would take time, but she also sensed the possibility of a brighter future, one where the scars of the past could be transformed into the strength and resilience of the present.

And as they stood together in the stables, a sense of unity and understanding filled the air, binding their hearts and souls in a promise of trust, patience, and the blossoming of a love that had the power to heal even the deepest wounds.

High in the treetop canopy of the Elven Kingdom, King Thaladir, the venerable ruler of the Elves, stood alongside General Elowen, the guardian of the realm, and his beloved wife, Lady Elowen. They watched from a discreet distance as the kindling of love between Lady Seraphina and General Ironheart slowly unfolded below.

King Thaladir, with his ageless wisdom and measured gaze, observed the budding affection between the two with a sense of wariness. He understood the power of love, a force that could both build and destroy, and he knew that it had the potential to tip the delicate scales of fate in unpredictable ways.

General Elowen, on the other hand, viewed the situation with a more hopeful perspective. He believed that Lady Seraphina and General Ironheart were two souls who had finally crossed paths in the vast tapestry of destiny. In his eyes, they were kindred spirits, and if they learned to love each other in the right way, they could become a formidable force that the realms might need to defeat the sinister Count Malachi.

Lady Elowen, standing beside her husband, echoed his sentiments, her voice soft and filled with conviction. "Love, my lord, can be a powerful catalyst for change. When nurtured and guided with wisdom, it has the potential to bring forth great strength and unity."

As they watched, a magical phenomenon began to manifest around Lady Seraphina and General Ironheart. Tiny, luminescent wisps of light, resembling fireflies but with an ethereal glow, appeared around them. These wisps were known as Whisks, delicate creatures that were drawn to the energies of love and connection.

The Whisks emitted a soft, melodic hum, a sound akin to the tinkling of wind chimes on a gentle breeze. Their tiny wings fluttered in a synchronized dance, creating a mesmerizing display of light and sound. It was as if they were celebrating the potential love between Seraphina and Ironheart, their presence a silent blessing.

As the Whisks encircled the pair, Lady Seraphina and General Ironheart exchanged glances, their hearts warmed by the enchanting spectacle. Seraphina reached out to touch one of the Whisks, and it responded by gently brushing against her fingertips, leaving a trail of shimmering stardust in its wake.

Just as the magical display began to reach its peak, Elyndra, the elven warrior, and the two mischievous fairies, Tilly and Tally, entered the stables. They couldn't help but be drawn to the enchanting scene unfolding before them.

Elyndra, with her deep connection to the mystical energies of the forest, smiled in delight as she witnessed the Whisks' dance. She spoke with a gentle tone, "It seems that the spirits of the forest have recognized a special connection between you two."

Tilly and Tally, the playful fairies, giggled and fluttered around Lady Seraphina and General Ironheart, their tiny wings creating an intricate ballet with the Whisks. They sang songs of joy and love, filling the air with their whimsical melodies.

Lady Seraphina and General Ironheart exchanged knowing glances, their hearts filled with a newfound warmth and hope. The presence of the Whisks, Elyndra, and the fairies seemed to symbolize the magic and potential of their budding love—a love that had the power to bring about positive change and unite their strengths against the looming threat of Count Malachi.

As the enchanting dance of light and sound continued around them, Lady Seraphina and General Ironheart took a step closer to each other, their hands brushing against one another's, and in that fleeting touch, they found a promise of love and courage to face the challenges ahead, together.

Lady Seraphina noticed the delicate touch of General Ironheart's hand on her own, she felt a newfound sense of comfort and security. It was the first time she hadn't instinctively retracted or tried to hide from a man's touch. Ironheart's hand was warm, and it seemed to radiate an unspoken reassurance.

Encouraged by this unspoken connection, Seraphina found herself reaching out for a stronger touch, wanting to feel the warmth of Ironheart's hand against her own. However, in her eagerness, she accidentally grazed a small cut on his hand. Ironheart's reaction was immediate, a slow withdrawal of his hand, his brow furrowing in pain.

"I'm sorry," Seraphina quickly apologized, her voice filled with genuine concern. "I didn't mean to hurt you."

Ironheart, though still wincing slightly, shook his head with a reassuring smile. "It's alright, Seraphina. It's just a minor cut, nothing to worry about."

Elyndra, who had been observing the exchange with a knowing twinkle in her eyes, decided to playfully intervene. With a cheeky smile and a wink, she suggested, "Perhaps it's time to visit the healing pond, Seraphina. It has wondrous properties, you know."

Seraphina blushed at the suggestion and glanced down shyly. Ironheart, curious about the healing pond, asked, "A healing pond, you say?"

Seraphina nodded, her embarrassment fading as she mustered the courage to speak. "Yes, it's not far from here. It's better if I show you."

With a shared understanding, Seraphina mounted her loyal steed, Sir Sterling, a majestic white stallion with a coat as pure as snow, and a presence that exuded regality. Ironheart, on the other hand, mounted his own horse, a noble steed named Orion, known for its strength and resilience.

General Ironheart's horse, a noble and magnificent steed, was named Orion. Orion was a testament to strength, resilience, and unwavering loyalty. His coat was a deep, rich chestnut brown, with a sleek and well-groomed mane and tail that flowed gracefully with every stride.

Orion possessed a regal presence, standing tall and proud with a well-muscled physique that reflected his robust health and vitality. His molten gold eyes held an intelligence and depth that hinted at a deep bond with his rider, Ironheart. His powerful legs and graceful movements made him a formidable companion in battle and a trusted ally in their adventures.

Despite his strength, Orion was known for his gentle disposition and a calming presence that complemented Ironheart's commanding presence. Together, they formed a formidable duo, forging a connection that transcended words and spoke of a shared history and understanding. Orion was not just a horse to Ironheart but a trusted friend and companion on their journeys through the enchanting realm of the Elven Kingdom.

The ride to the healing pond was a beautiful journey through the enchanting forest. The very heart of the forest seemed to sense the budding connection between Seraphina and Ironheart, and it responded in kind. The birds serenaded them with a melodic chorus, their songs filled with the promise of love and the magic of the moment.

As they approached the healing pond, the forest seemed to hold its breath in anticipation. The pond was a hidden gem, nestled in a tranquil glade surrounded by ancient trees and vibrant flora. The air was filled with the soothing scent of wildflowers, and the gentle babbling of the clear, crystalline water beckoned them closer.

But it wasn't just the sight of the pond that took Ironheart's breath away. It was Seraphina herself, standing in the midst of this enchanting setting. The soft, dappled sunlight filtering through the leaves above cast a warm glow upon her, accentuating her beauty and grace. Her emerald-green eyes shimmered with a hint of mischief and a touch of vulnerability, making her all the more captivating.

The pond itself was adorned with luminous water lilies that glowed a soft, ethereal red, their petals reflecting the colours of the setting sun. The water was pristine and inviting, radiating a sense of healing and renewal.

Ironheart couldn't help but feel a deep sense of wonder and gratitude as he took in the beauty of the healing pond and the woman who had brought him here. It was as if the forest itself had conspired to create the perfect backdrop for a moment that felt like the beginning of something magical—a love that had the potential to heal both their hearts and create a future filled with promise and hope.

Seraphina and General Ironheart stood at the edge of the tranquil healing pond, the soft, ethereal glow of the luminous water lilies casting a serene ambiance around them. The pond seemed to hold a certain mystique, as if it held the answers to both their past and future.

As they gazed upon the serene waters, a soft, melodious tune filled the air. The fairies, with Tilly and Tally, had taken to the sky, their delicate wings creating colourful streaks of light against the canvas of the evening sky as they danced a joyful dance of being reunited. Their dance was a spectacle of vibrant hues and graceful movements, and the streaks of colour they left behind added to the enchantment of the moment.

General Ironheart, his curiosity piqued, couldn't help but ask, "How does this healing pond work, Seraphina?"

Seraphina, her emerald-green eyes reflecting the shifting colours of the fairies' dance, turned to him with a warm smile. "It's quite simple, really," she explained. "After rigorous training sessions or when I first arrived here after escaping Count Malachi, I would bathe in these waters. The pond has remarkable healing properties, both for the body and the mind."

Ironheart listened attentively, his molten gold eyes fixed on Seraphina as she spoke. The image of her bathing in the pond after training sessions played in his mind, and he had to make a conscious effort to keep his thoughts from wandering into more tantalizing territory.

As the possibility of using the healing pond presented itself, Ironheart couldn't help but feel a mixture of intrigue and vulnerability. He looked at Seraphina and asked softly, "Should we both...?"

Seraphina, understanding his unspoken question, nodded and turned away, her gaze focused on the forest beyond to give him the privacy he needed. "Yes, I'll look away."

With Seraphina's consent, Ironheart began to undress, his movements deliberate and respectful of the moment. He removed his armour, revealing a physique that was a testament to his years of training and battles. His body was sculpted and strong, every muscle finely honed, and he indeed possessed the body of a warrior.

As Seraphina turned her attention away, the fairies couldn't resist having a bit of playful mischief. One of them, a mischievous sprite with twinkling wings, flew up to Seraphina and whispered in her ear, "You know, Lady Seraphina, General Ironheart has quite a nice bum."

Seraphina couldn't help but giggle at the unexpected comment, her cheeks flushed with amusement. She replied softly, "Thank you, silly. I appreciate your... observation."

Ironheart, from the pond, overheard the exchange and couldn't help but chuckle. He knew the fairies were known for their playful antics. "What was that about, Seraphina?" he called out, a hint of amusement in his voice.

Seraphina turned back toward the pond, her cheeks still tinged with a rosy hue. "The fairies were just being funny," she explained with a smile.

Ironheart, feeling at ease with Seraphina's response, decided it was safe to turn around. When Seraphina finally faced him, she found him standing hip-deep in the clear waters of the healing pond. The soft, shimmering light from the luminous water lilies reflected on his skin, accentuating his strong and powerful form.

For a moment, Seraphina was captivated by the sight of Ironheart in the tranquil pond. His presence exuded strength and vulnerability, a combination that stirred a complex array of emotions within her. She felt a desire, a longing that went beyond mere physical attraction. It was a connection that spoke to her heart and soul, a yearning to be closer to this man who had entered her life like a beacon of hope.

As Ironheart gazed at Seraphina, he, too, felt a surge of desire, an undeniable pull toward this remarkable woman who had captured his heart. The pond's healing waters seemed to amplify the intensity of their connection, creating an atmosphere charged with unspoken promises and the potential for a love that could heal even the deepest wounds.

In the midst of the enchanting surroundings, with the fairies' playful spirits dancing above, Seraphina and Ironheart stood on the precipice of a moment that held the promise of something beautiful and profound—a love that had the power to mend not only their bodies but also their souls.

As Seraphina watched Ironheart submerge himself in the healing pond, she couldn't help but feel a sense of anticipation. The waters held a unique magic, one that seemed to work differently for each individual. She knew that the pond had the potential to bring about remarkable transformations.

Ironheart swam out deeper, immersing himself entirely in the luminous waters of the pond. As he did, a profound change began to wash over him. An old ache in his hip, a lingering injury from a past war against giants, started to fade away. It was as if the healing pond was breathing new life into his body, rejuvenating his very core. The cut on his hand, a reminder of their earlier encounter, vanished before his eyes.

When he swam back to the bank, the expression on his face was one of awe and wonder. Seraphina, who had been observing his transformation, couldn't help but smile in response. "I know, it's amazing, right?" she replied.

Ironheart, still amazed, turned to her and asked, "Would you like to bathe, Lady Seraphina?"

Seraphina considered the offer for a moment before responding, "Yes, but I'm not quite ready to bathe together."

Ironheart chuckled, his eyes dancing with playful mischief. He cheekily used his finger to make a twirling motion in the air as he said, "May I, my lady?"

Seraphina giggled at his charming gesture and turned around, facing away from the pond, granting him the privacy to exit the water, dry himself off, and dress once more. Orion, the ever-loyal companion, observed the entire transformation with a sense of awe. He seemed to understand the significance of Ironheart's newfound vitality, and there was a proud glint in his eye as he looked at his rider.

On the other hand, Sir Sterling, Seraphina's faithful steed, had a knowing look in his eyes. It was as if he could sense the subtle shifts in the relationship between his beloved mistress and General Ironheart. With a subtle snort, he seemed to say, "I know what's happening here."

Ironheart, now dressed and feeling invigorated, walked over to Seraphina and said, "Your turn, my lady." He extended his arm in a polite gesture, turning away so that she could undress in privacy.

Sir Sterling, ever the protective companion, positioned himself between Seraphina and Ironheart, as if to ensure that there would be no inadvertent glances at her as she disrobed. With a graceful and protective demeanor, he walked alongside Seraphina as she approached the water, ensuring her safety.

Seraphina, once in the pond, allowed the water to cover her, rising until it gently enveloped her breasts. She turned to face away from Ironheart, granting him the same respect and privacy that he had offered her. After a moment, when she felt comfortable, she softly spoke, "It's safe to turn around."

When Ironheart turned back to face her, what he saw took his breath away. The ethereal glow of the pond reflected off her skin, accentuating her natural beauty. Her emerald-green eyes seemed to sparkle with the magic of the moment, and the water clung to her form in a way that was both alluring and enchanting.

Seraphina, in that moment, was a vision of breathtaking beauty, and Ironheart couldn't help but feel a rush of desire and admiration. The healing pond had transformed not only his body but also the dynamics between them, deepening the connection that had been growing ever since their paths had crossed.

As Seraphina bathed in the rejuvenating waters of the healing pond, she couldn't help but relish the sensation of renewal that washed over her. The soothing embrace of the pond seemed to wash away any residual weariness or tension from their recent battles. It was a moment of respite, a sanctuary amidst the chaos of their world.

As they bathed, Seraphina and Ironheart exchanged stories of their respective kingdoms and experiences. They spoke of the lush forests and grandeur of the Elven Kingdom, the valor and honour of the Crusade Army, Ravenshadow and the challenges they had faced in their roles as leaders.

Each story shared brought them closer, bridging the gap between their different backgrounds.

It was then that Sir Sterling, ever intuitive, gave a soft, affectionate nay to Seraphina as if to say, "Bath time is now done." Both Seraphina and Ironheart chuckled at the unspoken communication. With a nod to her loyal steed, Seraphina understood the message.

Ironheart, in a show of respect and courtesy, turned around to give Seraphina privacy as she dried off and dressed. Sir Sterling, ever the protector, positioned himself between them to ensure that Seraphina's modesty was preserved.

After she was dressed, Seraphina called out, "It's safe to turn around, General Ironheart."

With that assurance, Ironheart turned back to face her. The fairies, Tilly and Tally, reappeared briefly, hovering in the air before them. Seraphina thanked the fairies for their guidance during their journey to the Angel City, and the fairies replied with heartfelt gratitude.

"It was an honour," they chimed in unison before vanishing, their vibrant wings leaving a trail of sparkles in their wake.

With Seraphina and Ironheart now dressed and ready to depart, they mounted their steeds—Sir Sterling and Orion—and began their ride back to the Elven Kingdom. The bond between them had deepened during their time at the healing pond, and as they rode side by side, they felt a sense of unity and understanding that extended beyond words.

The enchanting forest seemed to echo their connection with the gentle rustling of leaves and the melodic birdsong. The journey back was filled with a comfortable silence, as if the world itself recognized the burgeoning connection between Lady Seraphina and General Ironheart, a connection that held the promise of something beautiful and profound in the days to come. Upon their return to the stables, Seraphina and Ironheart ensured that their loyal steeds, Sir Sterling and Orion, were comfortable for the restful night. They groomed them, fed them, and exchanged gentle words of gratitude and affection with their equine companions. Both horses, in their own way, seemed to understand the unspoken connection between their riders.

As they ascended the steps that led to the Elven Palace, the night had cast a different enchantment over the Elven Kingdom. The flora that adorned the landscape seemed to come alive, emitting a soft, ethereal glow that bathed the surroundings in a gentle, mystical light. It was as if stars themselves had descended from the night sky and nestled among the vibrant foliage, casting a serene and otherworldly ambiance.

They reached the stairs that led to their respective chambers, Seraphina to the right and Ironheart to the left. There, beneath the canopy of enchanted trees and illuminated flora, their paths diverged for the night. Ironheart turned to Seraphina with a charming, romantic smile and said, "Goodnight, Lady Seraphina."

Seraphina, her heart aflutter, returned his smile and replied in kind, "Goodnight, General Ironheart."

But as they stood there, the magnetic pull between them seemed to override any formality or decorum. Their hearts, almost as if they had a will of their own, drew them closer together until their lips met in a soft, tender kiss. It was a kiss filled with the promise of a connection that transcended words, a kiss that spoke of budding affection and the beginning of something beautiful.

Their lips brushed against each other's with a gentle and unhurried grace. There was no urgency or lust in the kiss; instead, it carried a sense of purity and warmth that enveloped them both. As their lips parted, they lingered close for a moment, their eyes locked in a silent exchange of feelings and emotions. When they finally stepped back, their cheeks tinged with a delicate blush, both Seraphina and Ironheart could feel a sense of delight and anticipation coursing through them. It was a moment they would carry with them into their separate chambers, a promise of the connection that had grown between them and the potential for a love that could change their lives forever.

With hearts aflutter and a shared, secret smile, they bid each other goodnight once more and continued their separate journeys to their chambers. The enchanted night of the Elven Kingdom was a beautiful setting for their first kiss, and as they drifted into slumber, they knew that the coming days held the promise of something beautiful and profound.

As Ironheart lay in his chamber that night, he couldn't help but reflect on the profound difference between his past encounters with Lady Isabella and the growing intimacy he shared with Lady Seraphina. With Isabella, their interactions had always been marked by a fiery and passionate desire, driven primarily by the physical. It had been a connection fueled by lust and the relentless pursuit of bodily pleasure. However, with Seraphina, he felt a profound shift—a connection that seemed to emanate from the depths of their souls. It was a connection that transcended the physical realm, a merging of hearts and minds that felt both tender and genuine. Ironheart realized that with Seraphina, it was not just about desire; it was about a deep and meaningful connection that went beyond the superficial.

In her own chamber, Seraphina lay in quiet contemplation, her thoughts drifting to her past experiences with Count Malachi. In her darkest moments, he had been like a vampire, feeding on her in every sense—using her body as sustenance without a hint of care for her well-being. It had been a relationship steeped in manipulation, control, and abuse, leaving her scarred and broken. But now, in the presence of Ironheart, she felt a stark contrast. His approach was one of utmost care and gentleness, as if he were handling something precious and fragile. Seraphina recognized that Ironheart was not driven by selfish desires, but rather by a genuine concern for her happiness and healing. It was a revelation that brought both comfort and hope, as she realized that she was finally experiencing the kind of love and intimacy she had always deserved.

The Serpent's Lair

The Veridales Estate stood as a magnificent testament to the opulence and grandeur of Ravenshadow Kingdom. The sprawling mansion, with its architectural blend of ancient and marble aesthetics, exuded an air of regal sophistication. As Lady Isabella and the three elven warriors approached the estate, they couldn't help but be captivated by its sheer beauty and the lush gardens that surrounded it. Tall, ancient trees stood sentinel along the winding path that led to the entrance, their leaves whispering secrets of centuries gone by.

The sun was beginning to dip below the horizon, casting long shadows that stretched across the estate's manicured lawns. The sky was painted in hues of crimson and gold, as if the very heavens were celebrating the arrival of their distinguished guest. For Lady Isabella, this was a world far removed from her usual haunts as a mage and a council of General Ironheart. Here, on the edge of Ravenshadow, she was surrounded by an aura of elegance and refinement that seemed at odds with her past affiliations.

The three elven warriors, their graceful forms clad in ethereal elven armour, led Lady Isabella to the imposing entrance of the Veridales Estate. The large wooden doors swung open with a creak, revealing a grand foyer decorated with tapestries that told the tales of Ravenshadow's history. The echoes of their footsteps reverberated through the marble floors as they were welcomed by their hosts.

The Veridales were a noble family of Ravenshadow, known for their influence and their commitment to maintaining the balance between the human and elven realms. Lord Veridales, a distinguished figure with salt-and-pepper hair and an air of authority, greeted Lady Isabella with a warm smile. Lady Veridales, a vision of elegance with dark-coloured hair and dark, mysterious eyes, extended her hand in welcome. The warriors then returned to their Elven Kingdom.

The dining hall of the Veridales Estate was a sight to behold. The room was adorned with intricate woodwork, the walls furnished with rich tapestries that depicted scenes of Ravenshadow's natural beauty. Tall, arched windows allowed the evening light to filter in, casting a soft, golden glow over the room. A crystal chandelier hung from the ceiling, its myriad of facets catching the light and scattering it in a dance of brilliance.

The long dining table, made from dark, polished wood, was set with fine silverware and crystal goblets. Elaborate floral arrangements graced the center of the table, their fragrance filling the room with a delicate perfume. Candles in ornate holders were strategically placed, their flames flickering softly, adding a warm and inviting ambiance to the scene.

Lady Isabella, her attire carefully chosen for the occasion, wore a gown of midnight blue silk that seemed to shimmer with every step. The dress was furnished with intricate silver embroidery that traced delicate patterns along the bodice and sleeves. Her moonlight-coloured hair cascaded down her back, partially concealed beneath a veil that added an air of mystique to her appearance. Dark eyes, filled with curiosity and a hint of apprehension, scanned her surroundings as she took her seat at the table.

Lady Veridales, her own attire a reflection of her refined taste, wore a gown of pale silver silk that seemed to catch the moonlight and reflect it back in a soft glow. The dress was detailed with delicate lace, and a tiara of moonstones decorated her dark-coloured hair. Her eyes, like polished onyx, held a warmth and grace that put Lady Isabella at ease.

As the dinner progressed, the Veridales' skilled chefs presented a sumptuous feast. The first course consisted of a velvety mushroom soup, rich and flavorful, accompanied by freshly baked bread still warm from the oven. The main course featured succulent roasted meats, seasoned to perfection, and an array of seasonal vegetables drizzled with fragrant herbs and olive oil. The dessert, a masterpiece in its own right, was a decadent chocolate torte furnished with edible flowers, a sweet conclusion to the exquisite meal.

Throughout the dinner, Lady Isabella engaged in conversation with her hosts. Lord Veridales spoke of the history and traditions of Ravenshadow, while Lady Veridales regaled her with tales of the kingdom's natural wonders and its unique blend of culture. The evening was filled with laughter and camaraderie, and Lady Isabella found herself drawn into the enchanting world of Ravenshadow.

As the elegant dinner progressed in the grand dining hall of the Veridales Estate, Lady Isabella found herself engrossed in the conversation with her hosts. The delectable dishes were savored with every bite, but Lady Isabella's curiosity extended beyond the culinary delights. At one point during the meal, as the candlelight cast a warm and inviting glow, she couldn't resist the urge to inquire about King Alaric, the ruler of Ravenshadow.

With an air of genuine interest, Lady Isabella turned her attention to Lady Veridales, her moonlight-coloured hair cascading gracefully over her shoulders, and asked, "Lady Veridales, would you be so kind as to share your impressions of King Alaric? I am quite eager to learn more about the esteemed ruler of Ravenshadow."

Lady Veridales, her own moonstone tiara gently catching the light, offered a warm and welcoming smile as she began to describe the king. Her dark, mysterious eyes held a glimmer of admiration and respect as she spoke of the monarch who held sway over the kingdom.

"King Alaric," Lady Veridales began, her voice a melodious cadence that filled the room, "is a figure of great stature and dignity. He possesses a regal bearing that commands respect from all who have the privilege of being in his presence. His rule is marked by fairness and wisdom, and he has a deep commitment to the well-being of Ravenshadow and its people."

As Lady Veridales continued to speak, she painted a vivid picture of King Alaric—a charismatic ruler known for his ability to bridge the gap between the human and elven realms. His fair and just rule had earned him the loyalty and admiration of his subjects, and his wisdom was sought after not only within his kingdom but also among neighboring realms. Lady Isabella listened intently, her curiosity satisfied as she gained insight into the esteemed monarch she was soon to meet.

Throughout Lady Veridale's description, the dining hall was filled with the soft, melodic tones of her voice, and Lady Isabella couldn't help but feel a sense of anticipation. She had embarked on this journey with a purpose, and the prospect of meeting King Alaric was both an honour and a source of intrigue. As the evening unfolded, it became evident that Ravenshadow held not only beauty but also a rich tapestry of history and culture, and Lady Isabella was eager to immerse herself in this captivating realm.

As dessert was being served, and the warm candlelight flickered, a haunting sound echoed through the night air, causing everyone in the dining hall to pause. The eerie resonance sent shivers down their spines, even the composed Veridales showing signs of unease. They exchanged concerned glances, and the atmosphere in the room grew tense.

The Veridales hurried to the windows, their expressions etched with worry, and Lady Isabella followed suit. She couldn't help but feel a sense of foreboding as she gazed out into the moonlit night. In the distance, they witnessed a chilling sight—Count Malachi, mounted atop the fearsome Dracohound, was approaching the estate.

The sight of the formidable creature, with its fiery eyes and imposing presence, sent a shiver down Lady Isabella's spine. The Veridales, who had been gracious hosts just moments ago, now appeared apprehensive as they watched Count Malachi draw nearer. It was clear that something sinister was afoot, and the peaceful atmosphere of the Veridales Estate had been shattered by an unexpected and unwelcome visitor.

Count Malachi's malevolent presence loomed over the Veridales Estate as he dismounted his fearsome Dracohound. His sinister grin sent shivers down the spines of all who beheld him, his eyes ablaze with an unsettling intensity. The dining hall, once a bastion of warmth and camaraderie, fell into an eerie silence as he uttered the name "Lady Isabella" with a tone that sent a chill through the air.

Lady Isabella, dressed in her midnight-blue gown that shimmered like the night sky, met Count Malachi's cold gaze with defiance. She had longed for freedom within Ravenshadow, and her spirit rebelled against the idea of assisting him in any way. Her moonlight-coloured hair cascaded elegantly over her shoulders as she stood her ground.

"I will have nothing to do with your bidding, Count Malachi," she declared, her voice carrying a note of determination.

Count Malachi, however, had a twisted offer to make—one that would weigh heavily on Lady Isabella's heart. With a wicked smile, he leaned in closer, lowering his voice to a dangerous whisper. "Think, Lady Isabella," he hissed. "Think of the one you care for, the one named Ironheart. I can promise his safety if you comply. Refuse, and his fate shall be sealed."

The mention of Ironheart, the gallant general who had touched Lady Isabella's heart with his kindness, was a dagger to her soul. She couldn't bear the thought of him coming to harm, and Count Malachi knew it. Reluctantly, she nodded her agreement, and Count Malachi's grin widened as he revealed a serpent brooch—ornate and sinister in design.

"This shall be your link to me," Count Malachi explained as he handed her the brooch. "Wear it always, and you shall hear my voice in your mind, ready to command."

With a heavy heart, Lady Isabella fastened the serpent brooch to her gown. Its coiled form seemed to writhe with dark energy, and she couldn't shake the feeling that it held her in an unbreakable bond with Count Malachi. This unsettling connection would prove to be her conduit to his malevolent will.

The next day, under the shadow of Count Malachi's threat and her loyalty to Ironheart, Lady Isabella was escorted to the court of King Alaric. She entered the grand chamber, her gown now finished with the sinister brooch, and approached the throne where King Alaric, a figure of regal stature and grace, sat in all his majesty.

Lady Isabella, her dark eyes shimmering with an air of mystery, curtsied gracefully before the king. Her moonlight-coloured hair, partially concealed beneath a veil, added to her enigmatic aura. As she spoke, her voice held a soft, enchanting quality that seemed to captivate all who heard it.

"Your Majesty," she began, her words flowing like a gentle spell, "I am Lady Isabella, a mage. I have come to serve you and your kingdom in any way I can."

King Alaric, his noble bearing softened by a glimmer of fascination, regarded Lady Isabella with a sense of intrigue. His eyes, like pools of wisdom, studied her as he considered her offer. Though his advisers had warned against accepting the services of a mage, he felt a pull towards this mysterious woman who had entered his court.

"Welcome to Ravenshadow, Lady Isabella," King Alaric replied with a gracious nod. "Your presence is an unexpected but not unwelcome one. If you are indeed here to serve, then I shall accept your offer."

With those words, Lady Isabella began to weave her enchantments. Count Malachi's dark influence flowed through the serpent brooch, guiding her as she worked her magic. Slowly but surely, Ravenshadow became entangled in the web of deception, as King Alaric's will was ensnared by the malevolent force that sought to manipulate the fate of the kingdom.

The enchantment, subtle and insidious, would gradually erode the kingdom's resolve to join the impending war. King Alaric's decisions would be swayed by the serpentine whispers in Lady Isabella's mind, all in service to Count Malachi's sinister designs. As the days passed, the darkness of deception settled over Ravenshadow, and Lady Isabella found herself entangled in a web of intrigue and deceit that threatened to unravel the very fabric of the realm.

Deep within the shadowy chambers of Count Malachi's forbidding castle, a sinister plan was unfurling, one that would unleash an unimaginable tide of malevolence upon the realm. Count Malachi, his eyes ablaze with a demonic fervor, had delved into dark and forbidden rituals, seeking to open a portal to the very abyss itself. The ritual chamber, shrouded in ominous runes and pulsating with an eerie, crimson light, served as the crucible for this unholy endeavor.

With every incantation and sacrifice, the portal's dark energies surged and writhed, like a ravenous serpent hungry for souls. As Count Malachi chanted, the very walls of his castle seemed to quiver in dread, for the foul miasma that permeated the chamber was beyond human comprehension. The air grew thick with malevolence, and a suffocating sense of foreboding hung heavy in the atmosphere.

Then, as the culmination of Count Malachi's dark incantations approached, the portal tore open with an otherworldly roar that shook the castle to its very foundations. A swirling vortex of torment and despair now gaped wide, a gateway to the abyss that threatened to consume all in its path. With a sinister grin, Count Malachi stepped through the portal, beckoning his loyal minions to follow.

The transformation that overcame Count Malachi's once-human army was nothing short of nightmarish. As they passed through the portal, their forms twisted and contorted, their flesh warping into grotesque, demonic semblances. Their eyes, once filled with humanity, now glowed with an unnatural, malevolent fire, and their very essence was tainted by the abyss.

Their armour, once polished and regal, became an amalgamation of jagged spikes and seething chains, adorned with macabre symbols of their infernal allegiance. Their weapons, once noble and gleaming, were now imbued with dark enchantments, dripping with the ichor of demons. Their voices, once human and filled with hope, now emitted guttural, otherworldly howls that sent shivers down the spine of any who dared to listen.

Among this legion of damned souls, the most grotesque transformation was reserved for Count Malachi's loyal mount, Dracohound. Once a formidable and fearsome creature, it now bore three hideous heads, each snarling with a malevolence that defied description. Its scales, once shimmering in noble splendor, had taken on a sickly, mottled hue, and its wings bore grotesque, leathery membranes adorned with serrated edges.

The countenance of Dracohound was a nightmarish fusion of dragon and hound, with rows of razor-sharp teeth and eyes that burned with an insatiable hunger for suffering. Its once-mighty roar had transformed into a cacophony of torment, a discordant symphony of wails and shrieks that echoed through the castle's cursed halls.

Count Malachi's castle, once a bastion of dark power, had now become a veritable lair for evil. The walls oozed with ichor, and the corridors were filled with the agonized moans of souls trapped in eternal torment. The very stones of the castle seemed to pulse with a malevolent life of their own, bearing witness to the atrocities that transpired within.

In the heart of the castle, Count Malachi presided over his newfound dominion, his throne now a twisted monstrosity furnished with the skulls of his enemies. From this seat of dark power, he commanded his demon-possessed army with an iron will, sending them forth to wreak havoc and sow chaos throughout the realm.

The sky above Count Malachi's castle turned a sickly shade of crimson, and a perpetual storm raged, casting an eerie, blood-red hue upon the cursed land. The very earth quaked with dread as the forces of darkness marched forth, their demonic war cries piercing the night like a symphony of despair.

As Count Malachi's malevolent army advanced, the realm itself seemed to recoil in terror. Villages were razed to the ground, and forests withered and died in the wake of their demonic onslaught. The very rivers ran black with corruption, and the air was choked with the acrid stench of burning despair.

The horrors unleashed by Count Malachi's malevolence were beyond comprehension, and the realm stood on the precipice of annihilation. The forces of good trembled before the onslaught of darkness, for Count Malachi's castle had become a nexus of evil, a blight upon the land, and the abyss from which it drew its power threatened to swallow the realm whole.

In the shadowy depths of Count Malachi's accursed castle, where darkness held sway and malevolence thrived, a wicked alliance was forged. Witch Morgana, envious of Count Malachi's unholy transformation and the dark power that had consumed him, sought to ascend to greater heights of malevolence. Her insatiable thirst for power led her to Count Malachi's doorstep, where a sinister conversation unfolded.

Count Malachi, his eyes gleaming with the malevolent knowledge of his newfound might, shared his sinister plans with Morgana. He spoke of his intention to lure the enchanted armies and the valiant elven warriors into his realm, where the very fabric of reality had been twisted and contorted by the abyss. In this cursed domain, his forces were at their zenith of power, bolstered by the proximity to the portal he had unleashed.

As Morgana listened, her desire for power burned like a searing flame within her, and her own dark magic seemed to pulsate in response to the malevolence that emanated from Count Malachi. It was then that Count Malachi, ever perceptive to the desires of others, sensed the very essence of Morgana's ambitions, her yearning to rise to his level of maleficence.

However, what Morgana did not anticipate was the treacherous nature of her unholy ally. Count Malachi, unwilling to share the pedestal of power with another, saw an opportunity to rid himself of a potential rival. With cunning deception, he lured Morgana into a chamber within his castle, leading her to believe it was a gateway to even greater dark power.

To her shock and horror, when Morgana entered the chamber, it was not the portal she had envisioned, but the lair of the monstrous Dracohound, Count Malachi's fearsome and grotesque mount. With a blood-curdling roar that shook the very foundations of the castle, Dracohound descended upon Morgana, his three heads snapping with ravenous hunger.

Morgana's anguished cries pierced the air as Dracohound tore her apart, his teeth and claws rending her body asunder. Dark magic clashed with dark magic, but in the end, it was the unholy beast who emerged victorious, leaving behind only a gruesome tableau of shattered ambition and a chilling warning to any who dared to covet Count Malachi's dominion of darkness.

In the depths of Count Malachi's treacherous castle, a malevolent plan began to take shape. Seeking to lure the enchanted armies and the valiant elven warriors into his dark realm, Count Malachi devised a cunning and sinister scheme. With a sly smile, he composed a message on a scroll, each word dripping with deceit and temptation.

The scroll bore an enchantment that would compel the reader to heed its message, and it read: "To the Noble Elves of the Enchanted Kingdom, we offer a truce and a chance for parley. Meet us at the threshold of our realm, where the darkness converges with the light. There, we shall negotiate terms that may spare the realm from further turmoil."

To deliver this beguiling message, Count Malachi employed a most unexpected and insidious method. He enlisted the aid of a swarm of flies, their tiny bodies each carrying a portion of the scroll's dark enchantment. These flies, imbued with a malevolent purpose, set forth on their flight toward the Elven kingdom.

As they reached the realm of the Elves, the swarm of flies descended upon the elven sentinels, who were taken aback by the unusual spectacle. The flies buzzed in a peculiar formation, and as the enchanted message was read aloud, its words found their way into the minds of those who listened, compelling them to consider the proposition it contained.

The sentinels, their thoughts now clouded by the scroll's enchantment, could not resist the temptation of a potential truce. They carried the message to the Elven council, who were swayed by the promise of negotiation and the hope of an end to the conflict. Unbeknownst to them, Count Malachi's sinister trap had been set, and the stage was now prepared for a confrontation that would determine the fate of the realm.

Count Malachi, the malevolent serpent lord, was a master of manipulation and cunning. As he set his dark plan into motion to draw the enchanted armies and valiant elven warriors into his realm, he knew that his strategy had to be flawless. Part of his sinister scheme involved ensuring the presence of Grizzletooth, the goblin chieftain, and his horde within the shadowy confines of his realm.

To accomplish this, Count Malachi dispatched a group of his most loyal serpent-armoured soldiers to seek out Grizzletooth and his goblin army. These soldiers, draped in their menacing armour, ventured deep into the labyrinthine tunnels and treacherous caverns that served as the goblins' domain. Their mission was twofold: to extend Count Malachi's invitation and to make certain that Grizzletooth could not resist the lure of war in the serpent lord's realm.

As the serpent-armoured soldiers descended into the goblin lairs, they brought with them a sealed message bearing Count Malachi's unmistakable seal—a serpent coiled around a dark orb. The message was written in a language understood by both serpent and goblin, and it conveyed an invitation that hinted at the promise of power, riches, and domination.

The message read: "To Grizzletooth, Chieftain of the Goblins, your prowess in battle is renowned throughout the realm. We, the servants of the Serpent Lord, invite you and your mighty horde to join us in the dark convergence. Great spoils and dominion await those who dare to heed this call."

The serpent-armoured soldiers presented the sealed message to Grizzletooth with an air of reverence, acknowledging the goblin chieftain's fearsome reputation. Grizzletooth, his eyes gleaming with avarice and the thrill of potential conquest, unsealed the message and read the invitation with a twisted grin.

"Count Malachi," he growled to his assembled goblin horde, "has called upon us to join his cause. The spoils of war, the taste of victory, and the chance to prove our might await us in his realm. We shall march to the dark convergence, and none shall stand in our way!"

The goblins, known for their love of chaos and plunder, erupted into raucous cheers, pounding their crude weapons against shields and rocks. Grizzletooth reveled in the anticipation of battle, imagining the treasures they would claim and the fear they would instill in their enemies.

With Grizzletooth and his goblin horde now committed to Count Malachi's dark cause, the serpent lord's plan was complete. The enchanted armies, the valiant elven warriors, and the goblin horde were all unwittingly drawn into his shadowy realm, where the very fabric of reality had been warped by the abyss. Count Malachi's malevolent forces were poised for a confrontation that would determine the fate of the realm and the balance between light and darkness. The stage was set for a cataclysmic clash that would reverberate through the annals of history.

As news of Grizzletooth and his goblin horde aligning themselves with Count Malachi's malevolent forces spread through the underworld, there was an eerie sense of jubilation among the denizens of the abyss. In the dark recesses of the netherworld, where malevolence and chaos thrived, the goblins' decision was seen as a triumph for Count Malachi's shadowy cause. The very fabric of reality itself seemed to warp and shift, as the underworld celebrated the alliance that had tipped the scales further toward darkness.

With Grizzletooth and his goblin horde now committed to Count Malachi's dark cause, the serpent lord's plan was complete. The enchanted armies, the valiant elven warriors, and the goblin horde were all unwittingly drawn into his shadowy realm, where the very fabric of reality had been warped by the abyss. Count Malachi's malevolent forces were poised for a confrontation that would determine the fate of the realm and the balance between light and darkness.

Allies and Adversaries

Deep within the heart of the Enchanted Forest, an isolated glade lay hidden from the prying eyes of mortal beings. This sacred gathering place was known solely to the mystical creatures who called the forest home, and it was here that a crucial council convened. The glade was a haven of natural wonder, its lush carpet of emerald moss providing a soft, verdant floor beneath the ancient trees. Shafts of dappled sunlight pierced the canopy, casting a gentle, ethereal glow upon the assembly. Flowers of every hue dotted the perimeter, their fragrance weaving a fragrant tapestry in the air. The murmurs of crystal-clear streams danced nearby, adding a soothing melody to the council's deliberations. It was within this enchanted haven that the mystical creatures, both light and shadow, gathered, for they knew that the fate of their beloved realm hung in the balance, and the signs of an impending war loomed ominously.

A palpable tension hung in the air, for the signs where clear war was on the horizon, threatening to engulf their realm. It was a time for the denizens of the forest to decide where their loyalties would lie.

High above the Enchanted Forest, the Iridescent Phoenix, Lysandra, had been in a deep slumber for a thousand years, her luminous feathers cloaked in the gentle embrace of the ancient canopy. She had nestled herself amidst the verdant branches of a towering tree, cradled by the wisdom of the forest itself. The tree was an elder sentinel, its roots anchored in the very heart of the Enchanted Forest, and its wood was imbued with the secrets of ages past.

It was not the passage of time that awakened Lysandra, but the sound of a horn carved from the sacred wood of the treants. This horn, when sounded with a pure heart and intent, possessed the power to rouse even the deepest slumbers. In the heart of the Enchanted Forest, one of the forest elves, distinguishable from their kin by their affinity for nature's camouflage and their deep connection to the forest's secrets, had fashioned this horn from the treant wood.

These forest elves, whose features were intertwined with the very flora and fauna they protected, were masters of blending into their surroundings. Their hair cascaded like cascading waterfalls, adorned with leaves and petals, and their eyes mirrored the colours of the forest's vibrant blooms. Their skin bore patterns that mimicked the tree bark, allowing them to vanish into the woodland at will. When the forest elf blew the treant horn, its echoing notes sang of harmony with nature itself, awakening Lysandra from her timeless slumber.

With a majestic sweep of her iridescent wings, Lysandra, the Iridescent Phoenix, took to the air in a breathtaking display of grace and power. As she ascended, the very air around her seemed to shimmer with the colours of a thousand gemstones, casting a spell of enchantment upon the forest. Her feathers, each a vibrant hue of blues, greens, and purples, caught the dappled sunlight filtering through the canopy, transforming it into a kaleidoscope of dancing rainbows that painted the leaves and branches below. The harmonious sound of her flight was like a symphony of wind chimes, a melody that whispered through the trees and stirred the hearts of all who heard it. Lysandra's presence was a living testament to the beauty and magic of the Enchanted Forest, and her arrival at the council was met with awe and reverence by the assembled creatures, who knew that her radiant presence symbolized hope and renewal in their realm.

Amidst the council's gathering beneath the ancient tree canopy, representatives of the opposing factions stood at its center. There, the Iridescent Phoenix, known as "Lysandra," graced the assembly as Lady Seraphina's noble emissary. With wings spanning the breadth of the glade, Lysandra's plumage formed a mesmerizing kaleidoscope of ethereal blues, luminescent greens, and silvery purples. Each feather held a fragment of starlight, casting a gentle, enchanting glow upon the assembled creatures. Lysandra's eyes, deep pools of wisdom and compassion, mirrored the very essence of Lady Seraphina herself. Her regal presence and majestic aura conveyed the hope and grace that Lady Seraphina represented, inspiring those in the council to choose the path of light and harmony for the Enchanted Forest.

Ascending to a luminous perch, the Iridescent Phoenix, Lysandra, cast prismatic reflections across the glade with her wings. Her regal bearing and serene demeanor heralded the moment as she began to speak. "Mystical beings of the Enchanted Forest," her voice resonated like the harmonious chime of crystal bells, "I stand before you as the emissary of Lady Seraphina, the guardian of our realm's beauty and light. In these uncertain times, when the shadows of darkness threaten our sanctuary, let us remember the sacred balance we have long upheld. Our strength lies in unity, in the delicate harmony of our diverse talents and gifts. Lady Seraphina's essence is woven into the very fabric of this forest, and her wisdom teaches us that it is through cooperation and the preservation of our natural wonders that we shall prevail."

Lysandra's eyes radiated with an inner fire as she continued, "We are the stewards of this enchanted realm, tasked with the sacred duty of preserving its wonders for generations to come. The Great War approaches, but with Lady Seraphina's guidance, we need not falter. Choose the path of light and beauty, for it is the essence of our forest home. Together, we shall stand as a beacon of hope, protecting the Enchanted Forest from the encroaching darkness, and ensuring that its enchantment continues to thrive, casting its radiant magic upon all who dwell within." Her words resonated deep within the hearts of those gathered, renewing their resolve to protect their beloved home.

The Forest Elves, known as the scouts of the Elven Kingdom, bore a distinct appearance that set them apart from their kin. Tall and graceful, their forms blended seamlessly with the enchanting woodland that surrounded them. Clad in iridescent gowns woven from the forest's own fabrics, they embodied the spirit of the Enchanted Forest itself. These elves were unwavering in their loyalty to Lady Seraphina, for she symbolized the very essence of their realm. Guided by her radiant light, their arrows always found their mark, and their songs echoed with the resilience of the forest, which they had vowed to protect as representatives of all elves dwelling within the Enchanted Forest.

The fairies, tiny and delicate with iridescent wings that shimmered like opal, flitted about the glade like living stars. Their allegiance to Lady Seraphina was steadfast, as they drew their power from the heart of the forest itself. Her protection ensured the vitality of their enchanted blooms.

Next to the fairies, nestled amidst the delicate petals of enchanted blooms, were the whimsical creatures known as the Whisks. These miniature beings shared the ethereal beauty of their fairy counterparts, but they were distinct in their own right. Fairies possessed iridescent wings that shimmered like opal, while the Whisks had wings fashioned from delicate, translucent leaves that glistened with an inner glow. The fairies' voices were like the tinkling of silver bells, while the Whisks' melodies were soft and lilting, reminiscent of a forest stream's gentle babble.

The fairies, each bearing a vial of shimmering fairy dust in a different hue, lent their magical gifts to the assembly. Their dust, a reflection of their individual powers, ranged from vibrant blues, lush greens and bright yellows and reds, and when sprinkled upon the gathered creatures, it bestowed them with blessings of protection and resilience. Meanwhile, the Whisks, resembling graceful orbs of azure light, glided with an otherworldly grace, weaving through the council with a serenity that mirrored the tranquil forest streams. Their shared blue glow, like fragments of the clearest sky, emanated an aura of calm and unity, infusing the council's atmosphere with an ethereal sense of purpose. Together, the fairies and the Whisks, united in their allegiance to Lady Seraphina, forged a harmonious alliance that would shine as a beacon of hope in the darkening shadows of the Enchanted Forest.

In this momentous gathering, both the fairies and the Whisks had chosen to align themselves with Lady Seraphina's radiant grace. Their decision marked the unity of the woodland's most delicate and enchanting denizens, all standing as one in defense of the Enchanted Forest's purity and magic. Together, their combined magic and unwavering commitment formed a powerful force of light against the encroaching darkness that threatened their realm.

As the eamaids, with their glistening scales and webbed hands, emerged from the crystal-clear streams of the forest, a hush fell over the council. They gathered in a circle, their ethereal voices rising in a mesmerizing, harmonious melody. Their song, a hauntingly beautiful ode to Lady Seraphina's grace, resonated through the glade like a gentle breeze.

"Beneath the moon's enchanting glow,

In Lady Seraphina's grace, we bask and know,

Her light guides our hearts, her love's embrace,

In this enchanted forest, our sacred space.

Oh, Lady of the woods, with your radiant light,

We pledge our voices to your endless flight,

In crystal streams, your beauty we adorn,

In your name, Enchanted Forest, we're reborn.

Through whispered tales and ancient lore,

We've guarded waters from every shore,

With webbed hands and hearts so true,

For Lady Seraphina, we'll always renew.

Oh, Lady of the woods, with your radiant light,

We pledge our voices to your endless flight,

In crystal streams, your beauty we adorn,

In your name, Enchanted Forest, we're reborn."

The treants, ancient sentient trees with gnarled bark and wise eyes, rumbled in approval as their branches swayed in unison. Their roots delved deep into the forest's heart, and they vowed to protect their home against any desecration, guided by Lady Seraphina's benevolence.

The leader of the treants, an ancient and venerable oak tree known as "Eldertree," stood at the forefront of his towering kin. Eldertree's bark was etched with the wisdom of millennia, its gnarled surface adorned with symbols of nature's harmony. His branches reached high into the heavens, casting dappled shadows upon the council, and his wise eyes shone with an inner light that seemed to encompass the very soul of the Enchanted Forest.

Eldertree's voice rumbled like the deep resonance of a thousand whispers of the wind through leaves as he addressed the council. "We, the treants, have slumbered for thousands of years, our roots intertwined with the very essence of this enchanted realm," he declared. "But now, we have awakened, for the ancient whispers of malevolence have reached even our dreams. We sense the impending darkness that threatens our home, and we stand united with Lady Seraphina, the embodiment of all that is good and pure in our beloved forest."

The treants, their colossal forms swaying in resolute agreement, extended their massive limbs as a gesture of loyalty. Eldertree's words carried the weight of millennia of wisdom, and they vowed to protect their realm, guided by Lady Seraphina's benevolence. With the treants on her side, the council knew that the Enchanted Forest's ancient guardians would once again rise to defend their realm against the encroaching shadows.

On the opposing side were those who had aligned themselves with Count Malachi, a malevolent sorcerer of shadow and darkness. He was not physically present at the council, but his ominous influence was felt through his representatives.

Fizzlewick, a mysti-monk whose chants and incantations had a sinister edge, stood forth as a dark beacon amidst the council's gathering. His robe, as dark as midnight, seemed to absorb the surrounding light, and his eyes gleamed with a malevolent spark. With an air of persuasive charisma, he raised his gnarled staff finished with dark runes and began to speak. His voice carried a hypnotic quality, luring the curious and the wavering into his web of persuasion.

"Mystical beings of the Enchanted Forest," Fizzlewick's words oozed like venom, "Consider the promise of Count Malachi, a master of the arcane arts, whose power knows no bounds. Together, we can grasp the very fabric of reality and shape it to our will. The allure of dominion over this realm, of unmatched power and wealth, awaits those who dare to embrace the shadows. Lady Seraphina's light may be comforting, but it is power that truly shapes destiny. Join us, and together we shall wield forces that even the forest itself shall tremble before."

His chants took on a hypnotic cadence, echoing through the glade, seeking to sway those who were susceptible to his corruptive words. The council members felt a shiver run down their spines as Fizzlewick's promises of dark power and dominion hung in the air, a stark contrast to the purity and harmony that Lady Seraphina and her allies embodied. The fate of the Enchanted Forest hung in the balance as the mystical creatures faced their ultimate choice.

Amidst the haunting cadence of Fizzlewick's persuasive incantations, two goblins stepped forth from the shadows. Known as Snik and Slag, they bore the distinct mark of Grizzletooth, a cunning and ambitious goblin warlord who had cast his lot with Count Malachi. Snik and Slag, their wiry forms clad in tattered, darkened garments, had been sent as emissaries to represent their malevolent leader. Their eyes gleamed with avarice as they glanced around the glade, the allure of power and riches promised by Count Malachi luring them like moths to a treacherous flame. With a subtle nod to Fizzlewick, they made their allegiance clear, aligning themselves with the sorcerer of darkness in the face of the looming Great War. Their choice marked a division within the council, for the allure of the shadows had claimed its first converts.

Raelthor, the majestic griffon, had long been a revered guardian of the Enchanted Forest, known for his golden plumage that shimmered like sunlight. He had soared the skies and patrolled the forest's borders, keeping watch over its tranquility and safeguarding its magic. However, when Count Malachi's promises of dominion and untold power reached his ears, a profound conflict stirred within him.

Torn between his loyalty to the forest and the allure of Count Malachi's dark offers, Raelthor wrestled with a profound inner struggle. The very essence of the forest whispered to him through the rustling leaves and the murmurs of the woodland streams, reminding him of his true purpose as a protector of the Enchanted Forest. It was a calling that resonated deep within his being, and he knew that the preservation of the forest's beauty and light was a duty he could not abandon.

As Raelthor contemplated his decision, the memories of all the enchanting moments he had shared with the mystical creatures of the forest flooded his mind—the laughter of the fairies, the serenity of the treants, and the soothing songs of the eamaids. These memories served as a testament to the irreplaceable bond he shared with the Enchanted Forest. At first, doubt had clouded his judgment, torn between the allure of power and his innate loyalty to this realm. However, as the recollections of his cherished moments intertwined with the spirit of the forest, clarity dawned on him. He understood that the true magic and harmony resided within the heart of the forest, and the promise of power paled in comparison. With a doubtful heart, Raelthor chose to stand by Lady Seraphina's side, determined to protect the Enchanted Forest against the encroaching darkness, his decision now unshakable and resolute.

As Raelthor wrestled with his inner conflict, one of the forest elves, known as Thalindris, possessed a unique sensitivity to the emotions of the mystical creatures in the Enchanted Forest. She had observed the griffon's inner turmoil and the profound struggle that had gripped his majestic heart. As Raelthor made his unwavering choice to stand by Lady Seraphina's side, Thalindris approached him with a gentle grace rarely seen among the mystical beings of the forest.

With a soft and knowing smile, Thalindris extended her hand, her fingers brushing against Raelthor's golden feathers. It was an act of tenderness that held profound significance, for Raelthor, despite his awe-inspiring appearance, had often been misunderstood and misjudged by the forest's denizens. His fearsome visage had cast him as a solitary figure, and few had ventured close to him.

For Raelthor, this was an extraordinary moment, the first time another enchanted creature had shown him such affection and understanding. Thalindris' touch conveyed not only her empathy but also the forest's gratitude for his steadfast loyalty. It was a silent affirmation that he was not alone in his devotion to the Enchanted Forest, and that, despite his imposing exterior, he was cherished for the purity of his heart.

As Thalindris hand rested on Raelthor's golden feathers, a profound sense of peace washed over the griffon. In that tender moment, he felt an unbreakable bond not only with the forest but with the entire assembly of mystical creatures gathered around him. The doubts that had clouded his mind evaporated, and he knew, without a shadow of a doubt, that he had made the right choice in standing by Lady Seraphina's side.

With newfound resolve, Raelthor spread his magnificent wings, their golden plumage gleaming even brighter in the dappled forest light. His heart swelled with a sense of purpose, and he vowed to protect the Enchanted Forest with unwavering dedication, for he understood that the truest power lay not in dominion, but in the unity and harmony of all who called this mystical realm their home. The council witnessed this transformation, and the collective strength of their unity grew stronger as they faced the impending Great War with renewed determination and hope.

Lirion, a Skywarden with wings of silver that glistened like the moon's gentle glow and eyes that mirrored the endless expanse of the sky, had been a vigilant guardian of the Enchanted Forest for centuries. As one of the ancients of this mystical realm, he had borne witness to its countless seasons, each more wondrous than the last. Yet, never in all his years had he seen a threat to their beloved Enchanted Forest as formidable as the looming shadow of Count Malachi.

With a voice as clear as the wind's whisper, Lirion addressed the council, his words carrying the weight of timeless wisdom. "Mystical beings of this ancient woodland," he began, his wings arching in a graceful gesture, "we, the guardians of the Enchanted Forest, have seen the passage of countless ages, and our realm has flourished in unparalleled harmony. But now, a storm of malevolence brews on our horizon, the likes of which we have never known. Count Malachi threatens the very essence of this enchanted realm, a darkness that seeks to snuff out the brilliance of our world."

Lirion's eyes, pools of boundless knowledge, scanned the assembly. "Our loyalty to Lady Seraphina, the embodiment of all that is good and pure, is our compass in these trying times. For the survival of this forest, we must unite, drawing strength from the unity that has defined us for eons. Let our resolve shine as bright as the midday sun, for together, we shall defy this encroaching darkness and protect the Enchanted Forest from the gravest peril it has ever faced." His words resonated with an ancient wisdom that stirred the hearts of those gathered, reaffirming their commitment to the forest's preservation.

As the council convened beneath the ancient tree canopy, the mystical creatures deliberated the fate of their realm. Other enigmatic beings came forward, their allegiances uncertain. The Nighthollow, shadowy beings of twilight who thrived in the forest's darkest corners, watched with eerie anticipation. Would they align with Count Malachi's promise of darkness, or would they heed the call of Lady Seraphina's light?

In the depths of the Enchanted Forest, concealed from the sun's rays and shrouded in perpetual twilight, lay the realm of the Nighthollow. This enigmatic place was a labyrinth of intertwining vines and gnarled trees, their twisted branches casting eerie, elongated shadows upon the ground. Flickering bioluminescent mushrooms and phosphorescent mosses illuminated the winding paths, their faint, ghostly glow revealing glimpses of the shadowy creatures that called this place home.

The Nighthollow themselves were enigmatic beings, their forms melding seamlessly with the perpetual dusk. They had an ethereal quality, their features concealed beneath cloaks of shadow and darkness. Eyes that gleamed like twin crescent moons watched the council from the hidden recesses of the Nighthollow's domain.

As the deliberations continued, Fizzlewick, the mysti-monk who had stood as Count Malachi's advocate, found himself taken aback by the Nighthollow's decision. He had presumed that these shadowy beings would be drawn to the promise of darkness that Count Malachi offered. However, to his surprise, the Nighthollow stepped forth, their voices echoing with an otherworldly resonance as they pledged their allegiance to Lady Seraphina's light. It was a pivotal moment that left the mysti-monk baffled, as the Nighthollow's choice defied his expectations and reinforced the growing unity among the mystical creatures of the forest in their stand against the encroaching darkness.

The Nighthollow, their voices like the whispered secrets of the forest, stepped forward to explain their unexpected choice. With a wisdom born of their intimate connection to the twilight, they revealed, "In the depths of darkness, there can be no shadows, for shadows only take form when kissed by the light. We are creatures of both realms, existing in the delicate balance between the day and night. Without the radiance of Lady Seraphina's light, our shadows would cease to dance and our existence would fade into obscurity. It is her brilliance that allows us to thrive, and it is in her light that our shadows find their meaning." Their words resonated through the council, revealing the profound symbiosis between light and shadow within the enchanted realm.

Amidst the deliberations, another group of mystical creatures known as the Lumisprites floated gracefully around the glade. These tiny orbs of pure light radiated an ethereal glow, their luminous presence captivating the attention of all. Their loyalty, like the gentle breeze that rustled the leaves, seemed to sway in uncertainty, a testament to their impartial nature. Whichever side the Lumisprites ultimately chose would undoubtedly tip the balance of power in the Enchanted Forest.

As the Lumisprites fluttered, their twinkling radiance illuminated the faces of the assembled creatures, revealing expressions of hopeful anticipation. They hovered near Lady Seraphina's emissary, the Iridescent Phoenix Lysandra, and with a collective, gentle shimmer, they made their choice known. Their decision was clear, aligning with Lady Seraphina's radiant grace, and their luminous presence added a radiant flourish to the assembly. The Lumisprites' choice further solidified the resolve of those gathered, who understood the significance of their allegiance in the impending battle against Count Malachi's encroaching darkness.

In the hushed stillness of the Enchanted Forest's sacred glade, where the council of mystical creatures had convened to determine their allegiances, a palpable tension hung heavy in the air. The Lumisprites' choice to align with Lady Seraphina's radiant light had sent a resounding message, and the unity among the mystical beings had grown stronger. But for Fizzlewick, the mysti-monk who had sought to persuade others to embrace Count Malachi's promises of darkness, and the two goblins, Snik and Slag, the council's decision bore a bitter sting.

Lysandra, the Iridescent Phoenix and Lady Seraphina's noble representative, turned her luminous gaze toward Fizzlewick and the two goblins. Her eyes, pools of wisdom and compassion, bore a sorrowful weight as she spoke with a voice that resonated like the sweetest melody of a crystal chime. "Mystical beings of the Enchanted Forest," she began, "our council has borne witness to the choices made by our kindred spirits. The Lumisprites have embraced Lady Seraphina's light, reaffirming our commitment to the harmony and purity of our realm."

Fizzlewick, his sinister chants silenced, exchanged a wary glance with Snik and Slag. The forest's enchantment was undeniable, and it had swayed the hearts of those assembled in favour of Lady Seraphina. Their dark agenda had failed to find resonance among the mystical creatures of the forest. The mysti-monk swallowed hard, realizing the gravity of their situation.

Lysandra continued, her radiant presence casting an aura of grace and determination. "But darkness, too, has its place within the grand tapestry of our world. Fizzlewick, Snik, and Slag, your allegiance lies with Count Malachi, and his path is not one we share. For the sake of the Enchanted Forest, and in the spirit of our unity, it is with a heavy heart that I must bid you farewell from this council and the sanctuary of our realm."

Fizzlewick's eyes flared with a hint of resentment, but he understood the council's decision. He nodded solemnly, and Snik and Slag followed suit, their expressions a mixture of resignation and determination.

With a graceful motion of her iridescent wings, Lysandra summoned a rift in the fabric of the enchanted glade. It was a portal that would lead Fizzlewick, Snik, and Slag out of the Enchanted Forest and into the realm where Count Malachi's shadowy ambitions held sway. The mystical creatures watched in silence as the three departed, their silhouettes fading into the portal's shimmering depths.

As the rift closed behind them, a heavy silence settled over the council. Lady Seraphina's emissary, Lysandra, turned her radiant gaze to the assembled beings, her voice resonating once more through the glade. "Mystical beings of the Enchanted Forest, the choices made here today have reaffirmed our unity and commitment to the protection of our realm's beauty and light. The looming Great War will test our resolve, but together, we shall stand as a beacon of hope against the encroaching darkness."

The mystical creatures, touched by the Lumisprites' allegiance and inspired by Lady Seraphina's grace, renewed their resolve. The council continued, their discussions focused on strategies to defend the Enchanted Forest against Count Malachi's impending threat. The air was charged with determination and purpose as the denizens of the mystical realm prepared to face the greatest challenge their enchanted home had ever known.

And so, on the battlefield of destiny, where light would clash with darkness, the paths of those who had chosen Lady Seraphina and those who had embraced Count Malachi would inevitably converge once more. The Enchanted Forest, its ancient magic and timeless beauty at stake, awaited the outcome of the Great War, where the destiny of this mystical realm would be written by the choices made on that fateful day in the sacred glade.

In the heart of the mystical realm known as the Enchanted Forest, a battle of unprecedented magnitude loomed on the horizon. It was a conflict that would transcend the boundaries of the earthly realm and spill into the ethereal and spiritual domains, as the forces of light and darkness readied themselves for a cataclysmic clash.

Count Malachi, a dark sorcerer of formidable power, had assembled an unholy alliance that threatened the very essence of the enchanted realm. Among his malevolent allies stood Witch Morgana, a practitioner of dark arts with an insatiable thirst for power, and Grizzletooth, the cunning goblin warlord, and his goblin family. What set Count Malachi's army apart, however, was their sinister pact—a binding of their souls to the devil himself. Each member of his forces bore a demonic possession, and their strength was drawn from a legion of demons that answered Count Malachi's unholy summons.

On the opposing side, Lady Seraphina, the guardian of the Enchanted Forest and embodiment of all that was good and pure, rallied her allies. The creatures of the forest, both ancient and newly aligned, had pledged their unwavering allegiance to her side. Among them were the mystical beings who had stood before the council in the sacred glade, their unity symbolized by the Lumisprites' choice to embrace Lady Seraphina's radiant light. The forest's enchantment flowed through their veins, and their commitment to the realm's beauty and harmony knew no bounds.

The elves, also stood with Lady Seraphina. Their tall, elegant stature and expert archery skills made them formidable defenders of the enchanted realm. Together, they formed a powerful alliance, ready to protect their home against Count Malachi's impending threat.

But the battle transcended the earthly realm. Lady Seraphina's journey to the Angel City had forged a connection with the celestial realms. Her visit had aligned her not only with the forces of light but with the angels themselves. In the celestial realm, she had encountered the divine presence of God, and her unwavering commitment to goodness and harmony had earned her divine favour.

General Ironheart and his crusade army, renowned for their unwavering commitment to justice and righteousness, had become steadfast allies of Lady Seraphina. Their valor and dedication to preserving harmony within the Enchanted Forest mirrored her own ideals, and their union formed a formidable force for good. With their gleaming armour and unwavering resolve, General Ironheart's warriors were not only skilled in the arts of combat but also possessed hearts aflame with the desire to protect the realm's beauty and light. Together, they stood as a bulwark against the encroaching darkness, united in their pledge to safeguard the Enchanted Forest and all the mystical beings that called it home.

During a solemn prayer session in the heart of the Elven Kingdom, General Ironheart, leader of the crusade army, walked Lady Seraphina through a heartfelt prayer. They beseeched God to bless their battles and protect their realm from the encroaching darkness. It was a moment of profound spiritual significance, and their faith in divine intervention burned brightly.

As their prayer reached its zenith, a radiant figure descended from the heavens, his presence a beacon of celestial power. It was the archangel Michael, commander of God's heavenly armies, and his divine aura bathed the assembly in an ethereal light. He appeared clad in resplendent heavenly armour, each piece gleaming with divine radiance. His wings, majestic and vast, bore the iridescence of the morning sky.

Archangel Michael's eyes, deep pools of unwavering determination and wisdom, surveyed the gathering. With a voice that resonated like the celestial choir, he spoke, "Fear not, for God has heard your pleas. He has sent me with a message to reassure you. You shall not ride out alone to face Count Malachi and his dark alliance. The heavenly host and the armies of angels, with fire chariots ablaze, shall stand beside you in this momentous battle. Together, we shall wage both earthly and spiritual warfare to protect the realm of the Enchanted Forest and Ravenshadow."

The announcement sent waves of hope and determination through the assembly, and Lady Seraphina's heart swelled with gratitude and resolve. The battle ahead, already monumental in its earthly proportions, had now taken on a spiritual significance of profound magnitude. It would be a clash of realms, a testament to the unwavering commitment of those who stood for light, harmony, and the preservation of all that was good.

As the mystical creatures, the elves, and their celestial allies prepared for the impending conflict, the Enchanted Forest braced itself for a momentous battle—one that would test the very fabric of reality and shape the destiny of their mystical realm. Earthly and spiritual forces would unite in a harmonious symphony, and the outcome would determine the fate of the Enchanted Forest and the world beyond.

Uncovering the Truth

General Ironheart, with his silver hair and hazel golden eyes, found himself deeply moved by the profound words that had recently come to symbolize the connection between him and Lady Seraphina. It was a connection that had blossomed into something far more meaningful than he had ever known. Inspired by this revelation, he felt compelled to express his feelings to her, to share his thoughts and hopes for their shared future.

With quill in hand, he carefully composed a heartfelt letter, each word penned with sincerity and tenderness. "Dear Lady Seraphina," he began, "In the depths of our connections, we discover that desire alone is fleeting, but the union of souls, forged in tenderness and authenticity, transcends the physical realm, offering a love that is profound and enduring." His words flowed like a gentle stream, describing the depth of his feelings and the hope he held for their journey together. The letter spoke of their shared purpose and the strength they found in each other's presence, concluding with a promise to stand by her side through all challenges that lay ahead.

General Ironheart's intention was to deliver this heartfelt message to Lady Seraphina, and he knew of the enchanted swallows that dwelled within the enchanted forest, creatures imbued with magical qualities that made them ideal messengers. As he stepped out into the lush forest, he encountered one of these magnificent creatures—a swallow with iridescent feathers that shimmered like the morning sun. What made these swallows enchanting was their ability to convey not just words but also the emotions and intentions of the sender, allowing Lady Seraphina to feel the depth of his sentiments as she read the letter.

With a gentle touch, General Ironheart attached the scroll to the swallow's leg, ensuring it was secure. He whispered a message to the bird, instructing it to find Lady Seraphina and deliver his letter into her hands. The swallow, with its radiant plumage, took flight, soaring gracefully into the forest canopy as if guided by an unseen force.

Lady Seraphina, with her striking red hair and captivating green eyes, received the enchanted swallow with a sense of anticipation. She unrolled the scroll and read General Ironheart's words, feeling his emotions wash over her with each sentence. The profundity of his feelings resonated deeply within her, and she realized that they were bound not just by a common cause but by the unbreakable bond of their souls.

With a sense of purpose and determination, Lady Seraphina summoned the enchanted swallow that had delivered General Ironheart's heartfelt letter. The radiant bird descended gracefully, its iridescent plumage shimmering in the dappled sunlight of the enchanted forest. She whispered a message, asking the swallow to guide her to General Ironheart. With a melodious trill, the swallow signaled its understanding, and Lady Seraphina followed the graceful creature as it soared through the lush foliage.

The enchanting melody of the forest accompanied them as they journeyed through the ancient trees and verdant glades. The gentle babble of a nearby pond whispered secrets of ages past, and the azure waters reflected the brilliant emerald hues of the forest. General Ironheart stood beside the tranquil pond within the heart of the Elven kingdom, a serene oasis that seemed untouched by the turmoil of the outside world.

As Lady Seraphina approached, she was greeted by the sight of General Ironheart, standing amidst the natural beauty of the Elven realm. His silver hair gleamed like moonlight, and his hazel golden eyes held a warmth that mirrored the affection he felt for her. With an air of anticipation, she approached him, her heart filled with the connection they had forged through their shared experiences and the profound words that had brought them closer.

"General Ironheart," Lady Seraphina began, her voice carrying the sincerity of her feelings, "I hope you know that your words have moved me deeply. I believe that together, we have the potential to not only overcome the darkness that threatens our realm but also to grow together in love and understanding." Her eyes met his, filled with hope and a touch of vulnerability.

A soft smile tugged at the corners of General Ironheart's lips as he met Lady Seraphina's gaze. Her words resonated with him, reaffirming the depth of their connection and the shared purpose that bound them. He felt a warmth spread within him, a sense of fulfillment that transcended the challenges they faced. "Lady Seraphina," he replied, his voice filled with genuine affection, "Your presence has brought light and purpose to my life, and I cannot help but hope for a future where we face both the trials and joys together."

A delicate blush tinged General Ironheart's cheeks, a testament to the sincerity of his feelings. Their shared journey had forged a bond that extended beyond their shared cause, and he found himself embracing the prospect of a love that was as profound and enduring as the words they had exchanged.

In the tranquil beauty of the Elven kingdom, amidst the whispers of the forest and the melodies of nature, Lady Seraphina and General Ironheart stood as two souls drawn together by fate. They shared a connection that transcended the physical realm, one that promised not only to unravel the darkness woven by Count Malachi but also to illuminate their path with the light of love and understanding. As they ventured deeper into the enchanted forest and the challenges that lay ahead, they knew that their bond would serve as a beacon of hope, guiding them through the trials that awaited them in the quest to protect their realm and the profound love that had blossomed between them.

In the presence of this newfound connection, Lady Seraphina was struck by an idea—an idea that had the potential to unravel the dark web Count

Malachi had woven. She turned to General Ironheart and, with sincerity in her eyes, asked, "Will you accompany me to the Elven library? I believe there may be a way to uncover a weakness within Count Malachi's power." Her voice was filled with conviction as she explained her theory. Count Malachi had made deals with malevolent entities, and his power was derived from these unholy pacts. She believed that somewhere within those accords lay a vulnerability, a chink in his formidable armour.

General Ironheart, recognizing the wisdom in her words, agreed to accompany her. Together, they ventured into the heart of the enchanted elven forest, where the Elven library held ancient tomes filled with the secrets of their realm. Lady Seraphina's determination was unwavering as she sought answers, convinced that the key to Count Malachi's undoing lay hidden in the words of those who had come before them.

Hours turned into days as they delved deep into the texts, guided by the wisdom of the elves who had chronicled the history and magic of their realm. They learned of the malevolent entities Count Malachi had bargained with and the sources of his power. And then, amidst the faded pages of an ancient manuscript, they stumbled upon a revelation—a pendant, a dark and ominous relic that Count Malachi wore as a symbol of his allegiance to the malevolent forces.

Within the hallowed pages of the ancient manuscript, Lady Seraphina and General Ironheart discovered a revelation that sent shivers down their spines—a pendant, a dark and ominous relic that was inextricably linked to Count Malachi's malevolent alliance. Described in intricate detail within the text, the pendant was depicted as a sinister and ornate amulet, forged from obsidian and etched with ancient sigils of dark power. Its aura exuded an aura of dread, and it was said to be the key to Count Malachi's unholy pact with malevolent entities.

The pendant, they learned, was more than a mere adornment; it served as the linchpin that bound Count Malachi to the malevolent forces from which he drew his power. It was a conduit through which he channeled the abyssal energy that fueled his dark magic and dominion. Every sinister deal, every unholy alliance he had forged with malevolent beings, had woven a binding thread of malevolence into the pendant. As long as the amulet remained intact, Count Malachi's connection to the malevolent entities would persist, and his dark power would remain unchallenged.

The sigils etched upon the pendant were an intricate web of malevolent magic, interlocking and reinforcing each other. Their purpose was to maintain the unholy contract that Count Malachi had sealed with the malevolent forces of the abyss. These sigils, once deciphered, revealed the complexities of the dark pact and the means by which the pendant's power could be disrupted.

With newfound determination, Lady Seraphina and General Ironheart delved further into their research, seeking to understand the vulnerabilities of the pendant and how it might be severed from Count Malachi's malevolent grasp. The Elven library, with its wealth of knowledge, held the key to deciphering the sigils and the ritual required to break the pendant's malevolent bond. It was a formidable task, one that would require their combined expertise and a deep understanding of the enchantments woven into the amulet.

As they pored over ancient tomes and consulted with the wise elves, they began to piece together the intricate puzzle of the pendant's magic. It became clear that Count Malachi's malevolent power was directly tied to the amulet, and disrupting its connection to the abyss would weaken him significantly. The ritual required to sever this unholy bond was both intricate and perilous, as it involved the invocation of powerful protective spells and a deep understanding of dark magic.

With each passing day, their understanding of the pendant grew, and they devised a plan to confront Count Malachi and challenge his dominion. Armed with knowledge and determination, Lady Seraphina and General Ironheart prepared to embark on a perilous journey to confront the serpent lord, shatter the pendant, and free their realm from the malevolent forces that threatened its very existence. Their quest for the salvation of the enchanted forest and their love for one another propelled them forward, ready to face whatever challenges awaited them in the battle against Count Malachi and the darkness he embodied.

The pendant, they discovered, held the link between Count Malachi and the malevolence that fueled his dark powers. It was the linchpin that connected him to the abyss, and breaking it would sever his ties to the malevolent entities. The mere existence of this pendant offered hope—a weakness in the seemingly invincible Count Malachi. Lady Seraphina and General Ironheart knew that this pendant held the key to their realm's salvation, and with newfound determination, they began to strategize their plan to confront the serpent lord and shatter the source of his power.

Lady Isabella, a skilled mage with striking silver hair and dark, enigmatic eyes, had embarked on a treacherous path at the behest of Count Malachi. Her loyalty to the serpent lord had grown over time, fueled by the promises of power and dominion that he had whispered into her ear. But it was her enchantment of King Alaric, the monarch of Ravenshadow, that had become the cornerstone of her alliance with Count Malachi.

At first, Lady Isabella's influence over the king was subtle, like a whisper in the wind. She used her knowledge of ancient arcane arts to weave subtle spells and enchantments into her interactions with King Alaric. These enchantments clouded his judgment and made him increasingly susceptible to her suggestions. It began with small things, like swaying his decisions on court matters or influencing his choice of advisors.

As days turned into weeks, Lady Isabella's hold over King Alaric grew stronger. The more time she spent in his presence, the deeper her enchantments delved into his mind and heart. It was during their intimate moments that her influence over him was most potent. Their shared passion became a conduit through which she channeled her enchantments, entwining their souls in a dark, seductive dance.

With each passing day, King Alaric's willpower eroded, and he became more and more subservient to Lady Isabella's desires. He found himself unable to resist her commands, his thoughts and actions dictated by her every whim. It was as if he had become a puppet, dancing on her strings, his autonomy slipping away with each passing moment.

Lady Isabella reveled in the power she held over the king. She delighted in the way he obeyed her every command, his once strong and independent spirit now entirely at her mercy. Her heart, once touched by a glimmer of light, began to darken with each act of manipulation and domination. The allure of power, the taste of control, had consumed her, and she relished in her newfound authority over King Alaric.

As the days turned into months, Lady Isabella's enchantments over King Alaric became absolute. He was no longer the ruler of Ravenshadow; he was a pawn in her grand design, a tool to further Count Malachi's malevolent ambitions. She had pledged her allegiance to the serpent lord, and her loyalty was unwavering.

The more King Alaric fell under her sway, the further he strayed from the path of righteousness. His decisions as a ruler grew increasingly oppressive, and the people of Ravenshadow suffered under his tyrannical rule. Lady Isabella's dark influence extended beyond the court, infiltrating the very heart of the kingdom.

Rumors spread like wildfire through the shadowy alleys of Ravenshadow, whispers of the king's transformation into a puppet king, controlled by a mysterious mage with silver hair and dark eyes. The once-prosperous kingdom now languished under Lady Isabella's dark reign, and the people lived in fear of her and the king she manipulated.

In the depths of her chamber, Lady Isabella reveled in her newfound power. She had become Count Malachi's most potent weapon, and she relished the chaos and suffering she sowed in Ravenshadow. Her heart, once touched by the allure of darkness, had now fully succumbed to its malevolent embrace.

As the shadows deepened around her, Lady Isabella's descent into darkness continued, and her enchantment of King Alaric grew stronger with each passing day. The kingdom of Ravenshadow stood on the precipice of despair, its fate hanging in the balance as the puppet king danced to the sinister tune of the mage who had ensnared his very soul.

In the heart of Ravenshadow, the once-venerable council of King Alaric's advisors convened in a dimly lit chamber. Their faces bore the weight of concern, their brows furrowed with unease. The enchantment that Lady Isabella had woven around the king had not gone unnoticed by these astute counselors, and they had grown increasingly wary of her influence.

Lord Cedric, the aging chancellor with a wisened face and a lifetime of experience, cleared his throat and addressed the somber assembly. "My esteemed colleagues," he began, his voice trembling with apprehension, "it grieves me to say that our beloved king, Alaric, has fallen under the enchantment of Lady Isabella. It is evident that her hold on him has grown stronger with each passing day."

Lady Ella, the court mage known for her wisdom and insight into arcane matters, nodded gravely in agreement. "I have sensed the dark currents of magic at play within the palace walls," she added. "There can be no doubt that Lady Isabella wields powers beyond our comprehension. We must act swiftly to protect our king and our kingdom."

Sir Orlan, the stalwart captain of the royal guard, spoke with a hint of urgency in his voice. "I have seen the changes in the king's demeanor," he admitted. "He no longer resembles the just and benevolent ruler we once knew. Lady Isabella's influence over him is undeniable, and it threatens the stability of Ravenshadow."

The councilors knew that their duty was clear. The enchantment that Lady Isabella had placed upon King Alaric was not in the best interests of the kingdom. It was a dark magic that had clouded the king's judgment and threatened to lead Ravenshadow down a perilous path.

With heavy hearts, the councilors decided to seek the aid of the elves, the ancient guardians of the enchanted forest. They believed that the elves, with their deep connection to the realm's magic, could provide insights and assistance in breaking the enchantment and freeing the king from Lady Isabella's grasp.

Word of the council's decision reached General Ironheart, the crusader general who had long been a staunch ally of the elves. His heart ached as he heard of Lady Isabella's descent into darkness and the dire situation that had befallen King Alaric. He knew that they must act swiftly to protect Ravenshadow and restore Lady Isabella to the path of light.

General Ironheart, a formidable figure with a kind heart, summoned his elven allies to a secluded glade deep within the enchanted forest. The elven scouts, known for their keen senses and connection to nature, had already sensed the disturbances in Ravenshadow and were prepared to offer their assistance.

Deep within the heart of the enchanted forest, General Ironheart stood among the assembled elves, his gaze filled with determination and concern. The council of King Alaric's advisors had reached out to the elves for aid in breaking the enchantment that bound the king to Lady Isabella's will. The council believed that the elves, with their deep connection to the magic of the realm, held the key to unraveling the dark magic that had taken hold of Ravenshadow.

As the moonlight filtered through the ancient trees, General Ironheart addressed the gathered elves, his voice carrying the weight of their mission. "My dear friends," he began, "we face a grave threat to Ravenshadow. Lady Isabella has succumbed to dark forces, and King Alaric is ensnared in her enchantment. Our duty is clear: we must aid the council in breaking the enchantment and restoring Lady Isabella to the path of light."

The elves, with their ethereal beauty and timeless wisdom, nodded in agreement. They had long stood as protectors of the enchanted forest and its neighboring realms, and they understood the importance of preserving the balance between light and darkness.

General Elowen, a revered leader with silvery hair and piercing eyes, stepped forward. His voice, like a gentle breeze through the leaves, added depth to the discussion. "General Ironheart, I agree with your assessment. However, there is a matter we must address before we proceed. The council mentioned Lady Seraphina's involvement with Count Malachi, but it is crucial to clarify her current situation."

General Ironheart nodded in agreement, understanding the importance of clarifying Lady Seraphina's role in the unfolding events. "You are correct, General Elowen. Lady Seraphina's connection to Count Malachi is complex. She was indeed a sacrifice from Ravenshadow to Count Malachi, a desperate bid to prevent him from unleashing his malevolent forces upon their kingdom. However, Lady Seraphina managed to escape from Count Malachi's grasp, and since then, she has severed all ties with him."

General Elowen furrowed her brows in thought. "This information is crucial to our alliance with the council. Count Malachi views agreements as binding, and if he believes that Lady Seraphina's escape has broken the agreement, he may see it as an opportunity to unleash his evil onto Ravenshadow through Lady Isabella."

With a heavy heart, General Ironheart agreed. "You speak the truth, General Elowen. We must make it clear in our response to the council that Lady Seraphina is no longer affiliated with Count Malachi and that her escape may indeed have altered the terms of their agreement. Ravenshadow faces not only an enchantment crisis but also the looming threat of Count Malachi's darkness."

The elves and General Ironheart swiftly set to work, drafting a letter that would convey this critical information to the council of King Alaric. They explained Lady Seraphina's sacrifice, her escape, and the potential consequences of Count Malachi's twisted perception of their agreement. It was a message imbued with urgency, a plea for understanding and unity in the face of impending darkness.

Once the letter was sealed with elven magic and entrusted to a messenger swallow, the alliance between the elves and General Ironheart was fortified. Together, they would embark on their quest to break the enchantment that held King Alaric in its grip and confront the looming threat of Count Malachi's malevolent forces. The fate of Ravenshadow hung in the balance, and the bond between the realms would be tested as they ventured into the heart of darkness to protect their world.

The messenger swallow, imbued with the enchantment of the elves, soared through the night sky like a glimmering star, carrying the urgent message from the elves and General Ironheart to the council of Ravenshadow. As it approached the majestic city of Ravenshadow, the swallow's wings glowed with ethereal light, casting an enchanting radiance over the kingdom below.

The council of Ravenshadow, comprised of wise and experienced advisors, gathered within the grand chambers of the palace. They were known for their stern demeanor and commitment to the well-being of the kingdom. The arrival of the messenger swallow, however, brought a sudden and unexpected urgency to their usually measured proceedings.

The swallow gracefully descended into the council chamber, its arrival greeted by hushed murmurs and gasps of astonishment. The councilors, dressed in regal attire decorated with the emblem of Ravenshadow, looked upon the messenger swallow with wide eyes. It was a rare occurrence to receive a message through such mystical means.

The emblem of Ravenshadow is a symbol of power, unity, and protection, reflecting the essence and values of the kingdom. It consists of a majestic raven with outstretched wings, perched atop a sturdy oak tree. The raven is rendered in shades of deep ebony, its feathers glistening in the light. It is depicted with a watchful and vigilant eye, symbolizing the kingdom's constant vigilance against external threats.

The oak tree, sturdy and enduring, is depicted in rich, earthy tones, with gnarled roots that anchor it firmly to the ground. The branches of the oak tree stretch outward, providing shelter and refuge to all who seek it. This element of the emblem represents the kingdom's commitment to protecting its citizens and nurturing their growth and prosperity.

Together, the raven and the oak tree form a harmonious and powerful emblem. The raven's presence signifies the kingdom's watchfulness and readiness to defend itself, while the oak tree symbolizes the kingdom's strength, resilience, and the sense of community that binds its people together. The emblem of Ravenshadow serves as a unifying symbol, instilling a sense of pride and identity among its citizens, and a reminder of their commitment to safeguarding their realm.

With utmost care, the councilors retrieved the sealed scroll from the swallow's beak. As the parchment was unfurled and the words of the elven message were read aloud, a profound silence descended upon the chamber. Lady Seraphina's escape from Count Malachi had left the councilors in utter shock and disbelief.

Councillor Thaddeus, a man of stern countenance with a long, silver beard, broke the silence with a voice filled with incredulity. "This is impossible! Lady Seraphina, our sacred sacrifice, has escaped Count Malachi's clutches? How can this be?"

Councillor Elara, known for her sharp intellect and analytical mind, spoke next. "It seems she has severed all ties with Count Malachi. Her escape may have disrupted the terms of their agreement. But what concerns me more is her absence from Ravenshadow. Why has she not returned to her kingdom?"

A murmur of agreement rippled through the council chamber. The councilors were no longer solely preoccupied with aligning with Lady Seraphina to face

Count Malachi in the looming Great War. Instead, their primary concern shifted to their own safety and the repercussions of the broken agreement.

Councillor Malcolm, a man of practicality and pragmatism, voiced the collective fear that hung heavy in the chamber. "If Count Malachi views our agreement as broken, we are in grave danger. Lady Isabella's actions, while questionable, may have been an attempt to protect our kingdom from his wrath. Now, we are left to face his malevolent forces without Lady Seraphina's alliance."

Lady Seraphina's absence, coupled with Count Malachi's potential retaliation, left the councilors feeling vulnerable and exposed. The once unwavering determination to stand against Count Malachi now wavered in the face of the impending threat.

As the council deliberated their next steps, it became clear that they understood the gravity of the situation. Lady Isabella's actions, though dark and questionable, had been driven by a desire to shield Ravenshadow from the looming darkness of Count Malachi by appeasing him with her actions. The councilors wrestled with the realization that their safety now depended on navigating treacherous waters, where alliances could shift like shadows and the fate of their kingdom hung in the balance.

As the councilors of Ravenshadow grappled with the shocking revelation of Lady Seraphina's escape and the broken agreement with Count Malachi, the scroll containing the elven message held more secrets yet to be unveiled. With a sense of urgency, they continued to read aloud, their expressions shifting from astonishment to anger.

Councillor Thaddeus, who had initially expressed disbelief at Lady Seraphina's escape, furrowed his brows as the scroll was unfurled further. His voice trembled with frustration as he read the final portion of the message aloud. "And it is with great regret that we must inform you that Lady Seraphina's whereabouts were made known to the Veridales once she had escaped Count Malachi's clutches."

The council chamber erupted in a tumultuous mix of outrage and indignation. The councilors' eyes blazed with anger, and voices were raised in a cacophony of accusations and recriminations. It was clear that one of their own had failed in their duty to share critical information, an act that could have prevented the current crisis.

Councillor Elara, her usually composed demeanor shattered, slammed her hand on the council table. "This is an unforgivable betrayal! How could one among us withhold such vital information when the fate of Ravenshadow hangs in the balance?"

Councillor Malcolm, his face flushed with anger, pointed an accusatory finger. "We could have rectified this matter immediately had we known of Lady Seraphina's escape. Instead, we find ourselves in this perilous situation."

The councilors demanded answers, their voices resonating with anger and frustration. They were infuriated that the truth had been concealed from them, allowing the situation to escalate to its current dire state.

Amidst the chaos and anger that gripped the council chamber, there was a shared sense of urgency to understand who among them had kept this vital information hidden and why. The revelation of Lady Seraphina's escape and Count Malachi's impending threat had not only exposed their kingdom to danger but had also unveiled a disturbing betrayal from within their own council's ranks.

Lady Isabella stood alone in her dimly lit chamber, a heavy silence enveloping her. The flickering candles cast dancing shadows across the room, creating an eerie atmosphere. As she gazed into the ornate mirror that adorned her vanity, she felt an inexplicable sense of unease. Her reflection, usually a reflection of her own visage, began to waver and shift, as if the very glass itself held some hidden enchantment.

In a surreal twist of fate, her reflection transformed, and there, staring back at her from within the mirror, was not her own face but the sinister countenance of Count Malachi. His piercing, malevolent eyes bore into her, and a sardonic smile tugged at the corners of his lips.

"Isabella," his voice, filled with a chilling resonance, echoed from the mirror as he addressed her by name. "Do you still concern yourself with the well-being of General Ironheart?" he inquired, his tone laced with a hint of mockery.

For a fleeting moment, Lady Isabella's gaze faltered, torn between her own desires and the memory of the honourable general who had once held her heart. She hesitated, contemplating her response. "No," she finally replied, her voice laced with a newfound resolve. "I have found a deeper purpose and meaning in the power I hold over King Alaric. My desires have evolved."

Count Malachi's spectral reflection in the mirror seemed to grin wider, his dark amusement palpable. "Ah, Isabella," he murmured with a sinister satisfaction. "You have embraced the darkness that beckons you. Your hunger for power mirrors my own."

With those ominous words, Lady Isabella's reflection in the mirror shifted once more, returning to her own visage. However, a lingering sense of foreboding remained. The boundary between her world and the malevolent influence of Count Malachi had blurred, leaving her with an unsettling realization that their fates were irrevocably intertwined.

As Lady Isabella stood alone in her chamber, the shadows seemed to deepen, and the weight of her choices hung heavy in the air. She had made her decision, and the consequences of that choice now loomed ominously, casting a long and foreboding shadow over her future.

As Lady Isabella stood before her mirror, gazing upon her reflection with a newfound sense of power and allure, she heard a distinct knock at her chamber door. Startled by the unexpected interruption, she turned away from the mirror, her thoughts momentarily diverted.

With curiosity piqued, Lady Isabella crossed the room, her crimson gown swaying gracefully with each step. She reached for the ornate handle and pulled open the door to reveal a messenger, clad in the royal livery of Ravenshadow. His presence carried an air of urgency as he delivered a sealed message, bearing the unmistakable royal insignia—the mark of King Alaric himself.

The messenger's words were brief yet conveyed the gravity of the situation. The king had summoned Lady Isabella to his chambers, an unexpected command that stirred a whirlwind of thoughts and emotions within her. She accepted the message with a gracious nod, her dark eyes briefly meeting the messenger's before she closed the door.

With the missive in hand, Lady Isabella knew that this summons was more than a mere request for her presence; it was an opportunity to solidify her influence over King Alaric and further her ascent into the heart of Ravenshadow's power. As she turned back to the mirror, her thoughts raced, and she resolved to present herself in a manner that would leave an indelible impression on the king. Her transformation began anew, driven by a calculated intention to captivate and control the man who held the throne.

Her transformation began as she shed her previous attire, revealing a figure that exuded both confidence and seduction. Lady Isabella chose a gown of deepest crimson, a shade that seemed to ripple with hidden passions. The dress was an exquisite creation, crafted from the finest silk that clung to her every curve like a second skin. The bodice was finished with delicate black lace that traced an intricate pattern over her décolletage, hinting at mysteries hidden beneath.

The gown's neckline plunged daringly, a bold testament to her newfound audacity, and a cascade of raven-black curls framed her delicate features. Her hair, usually restrained, now tumbled in wild abandon, cascading down her back like a waterfall of midnight silk. In the dim candlelight, her emerald-green eyes sparkled with an enigmatic allure, their depths hinting at desires she had only recently embraced.

To complete her transformation, Lady Isabella selected a necklace furnished with a deep red pendant—a stark contrast to the pallor of her skin. The pendant, carved in the shape of a raven's wing, seemed to pulse with an otherworldly energy, a reflection of the darkness that now coursed through her veins.

With every detail meticulously attended to, Lady Isabella was ready to answer King Alaric's summons. She knew that this meeting would solidify her hold over him and further her ascent into the heart of Ravenshadow's power. As she made her way to the king's chambers, every step resonated with the seductive allure and newfound confidence that she had carefully cultivated.

With the message from King Alaric clutched firmly in her hand, Lady Isabella made her way through the dimly lit corridors of the palace, each step echoing with the anticipation of the impending encounter. The torches lining the passageway cast flickering shadows on the stone walls, creating an atmosphere of intrigue and suspense.

As she reached the door to King Alaric's chambers, Lady Isabella hesitated for a moment, her heart quickening in her chest. She knew that this meeting was of utmost importance, a pivotal moment in her intricate plan to cement her influence over the king.

Summoning her resolve, Lady Isabella pushed open the heavy wooden door, revealing the inner sanctum of the Ravenshadow monarch. The chamber was adorned with opulent furnishings, a testament to the kingdom's wealth and prestige. A grand tapestry depicting the kingdom's emblem, a raven in flight over a shadowy landscape, hung proudly on one wall.

Seated at a finely carved mahogany desk, bathed in the soft glow of candlelight, was King Alaric himself. He was a man of regal bearing, with a strong, chiseled jawline and piercing blue eyes that seemed to hold the weight of the kingdom's destiny. His silver hair, meticulously groomed, added an air of wisdom and authority to his visage.

The king's attire was both elegant and commanding. He wore a tailored doublet of deep royal blue, finished with intricate embroidery in gold thread that depicted scenes from Ravenshadow's storied history. A black velvet cape cascaded from his broad shoulders; its hem embroidered with the royal crest—a raven perched atop a scepter.

As Lady Isabella entered the chamber, she couldn't help but admire King Alaric's regal presence. His commanding stature and the rich tapestry of his attire spoke of a monarch who was firmly rooted in his role as the ruler of Ravenshadow.

"Enter," commanded King Alaric, his voice resonating with a blend of authority and curiosity. His eyes locked onto Lady Isabella as she crossed the threshold, her crimson gown casting a striking contrast to the chamber's decor.

With measured grace, Lady Isabella approached the king's desk, her dark eyes meeting his unwavering gaze. She knew that this moment would shape the course of her ambitions, and she was prepared to seize the opportunity that lay before her.

As Lady Isabella and King Alaric engaged in conversation, the atmosphere in the chamber became increasingly charged with tension. The king, eager to make a favorable impression, ordered a servant to bring forth a bottle of the finest Ravenshadow wine. Two ornate goblets were filled with the rich, crimson liquid, and he extended one toward Lady Isabella with a gallant gesture.

She accepted the goblet graciously, her fingers delicately tracing the intricate patterns etched into the silver. As they clinked their goblets together in a silent toast, their gazes locked in an unspoken agreement—an acknowledgment of the intricate dance they were about to partake in.

Sitting side by side on the edge of the grand bed, they continued to exchange flirtatious banter, each word laden with double meanings and hidden intentions. The wine, smooth and velvety, served as a catalyst, loosening their inhibitions and fueling the burgeoning chemistry between them.

However, as the minutes passed and the wine took its toll, Lady Isabella noticed a subtle change in King Alaric's demeanor. His words grew slower, his eyelids heavier. The potent wine had started to lull him into a gentle slumber, much to Lady Isabella's surprise.

As the king's breathing steadied and his head began to nod, Lady Isabella realized the opportunity that lay before her. She had successfully seduced the monarch of Ravenshadow, and he had unwittingly succumbed to her charms. It was a significant victory in her quest to maintain control and influence over him.

Just as she was contemplating her next move, a sudden disturbance in the chamber caught her attention. The torches lining the walls flickered, casting eerie shadows across the room. Lady Isabella's heart quickened as she turned toward the source of the disturbance, her eyes widening in disbelief.

Standing before her, his presence radiating malevolence, was Count Malachi. His dark silhouette seemed to materialize out of thin air, as if he had traversed the boundaries of reality to appear in King Alaric's chambers.

Count Malachi's eyes gleamed with a sinister light, and a cruel smile played upon his lips. It was clear that he possessed powers beyond mortal comprehension—powers that allowed him to traverse space and time with ease.

"Surprised to see me, Lady Isabella?" Count Malachi's voice dripped with malevolence as he advanced toward her. "It seems I've acquired a new skill— a talent for being in the right place at the right time."

Lady Isabella's thoughts raced as she grasped the implications of Count Malachi's newfound abilities. Her meticulously devised plans lay in ruins, leaving her stranded in the king's chambers with the very malevolent force she had aligned herself with. The absence of any means of escape heightened her anxiety.

"You look... delicious," Count Malachi growled, closing the distance between them and taking in the scent of her hair. A wicked grin curved on his lips. "It is time to seal our alliance with the binding of our flesh." His fingers trailed sensually down her arms, and Lady Isabella couldn't help but feel a shiver of both fear and curiosity.

"What will this gain me?" Lady Isabella inquired, her voice laced with uncertainty. Count Malachi's malevolent chuckle sent a chill down her spine as he replied, "Unimaginable power."

With that, Lady Isabella submitted to Count Malachi's desires, and their intimacy unfolded with a raw intensity. Their encounter was fierce, marked by deep, guttural sounds and passionate, entwined movements that resembled two serpents locked in a sensual dance. When Count Malachi had satisfied his desires, he rose from Lady Isabella, leaving her still on the floor, recovering from the intensity of their encounter. A sinister smile played on his lips as he declared, "It is done." And with that, Count Malachi vanished into the shadows.

Lady Isabella, still yearning for more, eventually rose from the ground. She awakened the king, igniting his desires, and throughout the night, they became entangled in each other's bodies in a passionate frenzy, therefore completing her plans she had earlier on.

Back in the Elven Kingdom King Thaladir, a ruler known for his wisdom and keen perception, had sensed a disturbing shift in Lady Isabella. Her once loyal demeanor had begun to waver, and the king's instincts told him that she had crossed a threshold from which there was no return. Troubled by his suspicions, he decided to consult General Ironheart, a trusted crusade general who had worked closely with Lady Isabella in the past.

In a private audience with the king, General Ironheart listened carefully as King Thaladir detailed his observations and apprehensions regarding Lady

Isabella's allegiance. The general had shared many strategic discussions with Lady Isabella in the past, and the thought of her straying down a dark path troubled him deeply. King Thaladir urged Ironheart that Lady Isabella could no longer be trusted.

Leaving the king's chambers with a heavy heart, General Ironheart knew that he had a difficult task ahead. He needed to inform his council that Lady Isabella had chosen to align herself with Count Malachi's malevolent cause. He decided to convene a meeting with his most trusted advisors, individuals who had served the crusade army faithfully and had their own experiences with Lady Isabella.

As General Ironheart gathered his council of advisors, each of them shared their own concerns and observations regarding Lady Isabella's recent decision.

The council was filled with a sense of melancholy as they realized that Lady Isabella had chosen a path that would lead to darkness and betrayal. They had hoped that she would find her way back to the light, but it seemed that her allegiance to Count Malachi had eroded her sense of duty and honour. The weight of her betrayal bore heavily on their hearts, and they mourned for the loss of a friend and ally.

In the midst of General Ironheart's grief and turmoil over the loss of his friend and trusted advisor, Lady Seraphina stood as a beacon of solace and support. With compassion in her eyes and a gentle presence, she offered him words of comfort, reminding him that they were not alone in their struggle against Count Malachi's darkness. Her unwavering support and empathy helped General Ironheart find solace in their shared mission and the allies who remained steadfast by their side, providing him with the strength to carry on in the face of adversity.

No matter how concealed or hidden it may be, the truth possesses an innate power to unveil itself in due time. Like a relentless force of nature, it emerges to illuminate what lies in obscurity.

Confronting the Darkness

As the sun dipped below the horizon, casting a soft, golden glow over the Elven Kingdom, a solitary bat emerged from the shadows, its wings slicing through the cool evening air. Clutched within its tiny claws was a scroll, sealed with dark, foreboding wax, bearing the unmistakable emblem of Count Malachi.

The bat navigated through the ancient trees of the enchanted forest, darting between branches and avoiding moonlit clearings, following a path known only to it. The forest seemed to hold its breath as the bat's journey continued, an eerie silence enveloping its passage.

In the heart of the Elven Kingdom, General Ironheart and his councilors gathered in somber anticipation. They watched as the bat approached, landing gracefully upon a moss-covered stone, the scroll clutched tightly in its grasp. The general's hazel eyes bore a mixture of wariness and curiosity as he extended his hand to receive the ominous missive.

As the wax seal was broken and the scroll unfurled, the words of Count Malachi's request were revealed. He summoned Lady Seraphina to a clandestine meeting in the ancient forest that lay between Shadowmoor and the enchanted forest—a place of dark secrets and shadows. The general and his councilors exchanged wary glances, their expressions a reflection of their unease.

General Ironheart, who had become Lady Seraphina's steadfast protector and confidant, was quick to voice his concerns. "My lady," he began, his voice tinged with worry, "this is a treacherous proposition. Count Malachi's intentions are seldom benign, and I fear for your safety."

The councilors nodded in agreement, their apprehension palpable. They had witnessed Count Malachi's malevolent influence firsthand, and they were not eager to see Lady Seraphina thrust into the heart of darkness.

General Elowen, standing among the gathered elven warriors, couldn't help but voice his own concerns as Lady Seraphina prepared to depart. His countenance, usually calm and composed, bore an unmistakable gravity.

"Lady Seraphina," he began, his voice resonating with a blend of respect and apprehension, "while your bravery and wisdom are unquestioned, the ancient forest is a place steeped in enigma and peril. It is said that the shadows there hold secrets older than time itself, and Count Malachi's invitation may conceal treacherous intent."

His blue eyes, usually reflecting the serenity of the forest, were now filled with worry for the safety of their beloved ally. "Should you choose to proceed, please know that the might of the elven warriors stands ready to shield you from harm. We are bound by our loyalty and duty to protect, but we also entreat you to tread cautiously in this shadowed realm."

General Elowen's words were a testament to the unity of their people, their shared concern for the warrior who had grown with grace and courage. As they embarked on this perilous journey into the heart of the ancient forest, it was clear that the entire elven realm held its breath, hoping for Seraphina's safe return and the chance to confront the looming darkness together.

However, Lady Seraphina, her emerald eyes resolute, stood her ground. "I understand your concerns, dear friends," she replied, her voice calm and measured. "But perhaps there is an opportunity here—an opportunity to confront Count Malachi directly, to seek a resolution that does not require the horrors of war. I must explore this path, for the sake of our realms and all that we hold dear."

Her words carried the weight of her determination, and the councilors exchanged another round of hesitant glances. They knew that Seraphina was not one to be swayed easily, and her innate wisdom often guided them through perilous times.

General Ironheart sighed, his hazel eyes filled with a mixture of affection and resignation. "Very well, my lady," he conceded, "but know that I will accompany you, as will our most skilled elven warriors. Your safety remains our utmost priority."

But Lady Seraphina gently shook her head, her resolve unwavering. "No, my dear General, I will go alone, as Count Malachi's scroll demands. I will not risk any more lives unnecessarily."

Her decision was met with reluctance from General Ironheart and the assembled warriors, their concern palpable. Yet, they respected her determination.

"Thank you, General," she continued, her gratitude shining through. "Though I walk this path alone, know that your unwavering support bolsters my spirit."

The following morning, beneath the verdant canopy of the enchanted forest, Lady Seraphina prepared to depart for her meeting with Count Malachi. Her steed, Sir Sterling, her majestic white stallion with a coat as pure as the driven snow, stood ready by her side. His velvety coat bore the emblem of their family—a gallant horse galloping fearlessly across a majestic field, symbolizing strength, determination, and courage.

General Ironheart, adorned in his resplendent armour, waited with the select group of elven warriors, their gazes holding a mixture of concern and determination as they prepared to see her off. Seraphina mounted her steed and gazed upon the assembly of loyal protectors, feeling a surge of gratitude.

"I appreciate your unwavering support," she said, her voice tinged with emotion. "Together, we shall face the shadows and bring light to our realm."

With a determined nod from General Ironheart, Seraphina set forth, venturing deeper into the enchanted forest, toward the ancient meeting place between realms—an encounter that held the promise of confrontation, revelation, and, perhaps, an end to the looming darkness.

As Lady Seraphina embarked on her solitary journey deeper into the heart of the enchanted forest, the world around her transformed. The dappled sunlight filtered through the dense canopy above, casting an enchanting play of shadows and light upon the lush undergrowth. The air was alive with the melodious symphony of the forest—birdsong, the gentle rustling of leaves, and the distant murmurs of woodland creatures. Every step she took felt like a communion with the ancient spirits that guarded this mystical realm.

The surroundings changed as she ventured further, and the vibrancy of the enchanted forest seemed to intensify. Vibrant ferns, resplendent in shades of emerald and jade, carpeted the forest floor, while towering trees with bark like aged leather reached skyward, their branches intertwined in a tapestry of life. Shafts of golden sunlight pierced through the foliage, illuminating pockets of wildflowers that danced in the breeze.

Amidst this enchanting landscape, Seraphina continued her journey on the back of her steed, Sir Sterling. The white stallion moved with an otherworldly grace, his hooves barely making a sound on the mossy path. Seraphina's auburn hair, a cascade of fiery waves, gleamed in the dappled sunlight as she rode on, her green eyes alight with determination.

As she drew closer to the designated meeting place within the ancient forest, a sense of foreboding hung in the air. The serenity that had permeated the enchanted forest began to wane, replaced by an unsettling stillness. Sir Sterling, her loyal companion, pricked his ears forward, his senses attuned to the changing atmosphere. His unease was palpable, and Seraphina's hand instinctively went to pat his sleek neck in a soothing gesture. Her fingers traced the scar on Sir Sterling's shoulder, a reminder of the painful incident when Count Malachi had harmed him. The mother of pearls that decorated the scar, a testament to elven craftsmanship, shimmered in the dappled forest light, and it made Seraphina's heart sink with a mix of sorrow and anger as she recollected that cruel moment. She knew that this encounter with Count Malachi held the potential for more pain, but she was determined to face it head-on, driven by her unwavering resolve to protect her realms and seek justice for those who had suffered.

They arrived at the designated spot—an eerie glade deep within the ancient forest, cloaked in shadows that seemed to linger even in the presence of sunlight. The glade was a patchwork of moonlight and shadow, with gnarled, ancient trees encircling a clearing of dew-kissed grass.

Seraphina dismounted and surveyed the area, her senses heightened. She could feel a palpable tension in the air, like the calm before a storm. Her heart raced as she realized that Count Malachi had not yet arrived, and a gnawing sense of dread settled in the pit of her stomach.

Sir Sterling pawed at the ground nervously, his ears flattened against his head. The unease that gripped him mirrored Seraphina's own apprehension. Something was amiss, and the soft, anxious sounds he made conveyed his deep discomfort with the situation.

Out of the shadows that clung to the outskirts of the glade emerged a sinister figure. Count Malachi, the harbinger of darkness, materialized like a wraith, flanked by his fearsome Dracohound—a grotesque abomination, a hybrid creature with the body of a massive dog and three serpent-like heads, their scales as black as the deepest abyss, and eyes aflame with malevolence.

Seraphina's heart quickened, and she knew that this meeting held more than just the promise of words. Count Malachi had an agenda, and it reeked of treachery. Her hand instinctively went to the hilt of her enchanted blade, its jewels gleaming with an ethereal light, as she shuddered at the sight of him, his visage now more demonic and malevolent than ever before.

Count Malachi's voice, smooth as silk but laced with malice, cut through the silence. "Ah, Lady Seraphina," he purred, his crimson eyes locking onto hers with an intensity that sent a shiver down her spine. "I see you've come alone. How... brave of you."

A flicker of movement caught her attention, and she realized that the Dracohound had begun to circle her, its predatory instincts keenly honed. Seraphina felt a bead of sweat form on her brow as she assessed her surroundings. She was indeed alone, and the odds were stacked against her.

With a cruel smile, Count Malachi continued, "You see, Lady Seraphina, I have no intention of engaging in idle conversation today. No, I've brought you here for a very specific purpose—one that will serve as a testament to my newfound power."

The air grew thick with tension, and the glade seemed to close in around her. Seraphina knew that this encounter would test her resolve, her strength, and her allegiance to the light. But she was determined to confront the darkness that loomed before her, even if it meant facing Count Malachi and his malevolent intentions head-on.

Count Malachi's command sent a shiver down Seraphina's spine as the three-headed Dracohound slunk back into the shadows, its predatory presence lingering. Sir Sterling, her loyal steed, stood steadfast behind her, his eyes filled with a mixture of protectiveness and wariness.

Count Malachi's chilling laughter filled the glade as he observed the tableau before him. "My, my," he mused, his crimson eyes glinting with dark amusement. "Is this not a sight I have seen before?" His words were a cruel reminder of a past encounter, one that still haunted Seraphina's memories.

It had been in the stables, a place of serenity and solace, where Seraphina had stood between Count Malachi and Sir Sterling. It was a moment etched in her memory when Count Malachi had drawn his blade, striking Sir Sterling and leaving a cruel gash upon the stallion's shoulder.

Summoning her courage, Seraphina shouted, "You will not harm him again, Count Malachi!" Her voice quivered with a mixture of defiance and anger, her gaze locked onto the malevolent figure before her.

Count Malachi chuckled, his laughter a twisted melody in the gloom of the ancient forest. "We shall see about that," he replied, his tone dripping with sinister intent.

With a swift, fluid motion, Count Malachi unsheathed his sword—a weapon decorated with the very jewels that once graced Seraphina's own wardrobe. The sight of her jewels, tainted and defiled, sent a surge of rage coursing through her veins. Without hesitation, Seraphina charged toward Count Malachi on foot, her sword raised in a battle stance.

Their swords clashed in a symphony of steel, the clash of metal ringing through the glade like a haunting melody. Count Malachi moved with unnatural grace, his strikes precise and deadly. Seraphina, fueled by her anger and determination, matched him blow for blow.

But something was amiss. As their battle raged on, Seraphina felt the purple amethyst at the hilt of her sword, a relic of her enchanted blade, begin to pulse and darken. It seemed to respond to the darkness that swelled within her, born of her loathing for Count Malachi and all he had wrought upon her loved ones and her realm.

The sword that had once been her ally now turned against her. It resisted her commands, as if seeking to subdue her with every swing. Count Malachi, ever observant, found this intriguing. He capitalized on her faltering strikes, dodging and parrying with malicious delight.

With a sinister grin, Count Malachi seized an opportunity, and his blade struck true. Seraphina's defenses crumbled under the relentless assault, and a searing pain lanced through her as she fell to the ground, her sword slipping from her grasp. Count Malachi's laughter echoed through the glade, triumphant and malevolent, as he looked down upon the fallen Lady Seraphina.

She lay on the forest floor, her chest heaving with exertion, her spirit battered but unbroken. Despite her defeat, her gaze remained defiant, locked onto Count Malachi. In that moment, even as she tasted the bitterness of failure, Seraphina swore that she would rise again, stronger and more resolute, to face the darkness that threatened her realm.

Count Malachi's voice oozed with sinister amusement as he looked down at Lady Seraphina, who knelt before him, her arm bleeding from the deep gash inflicted by his blade. "Now now, my dear," he cooed, his crimson eyes gleaming with dark mirth. "I am only having a little fun. The cut on your arm will heal—it is nearly a graze." His mocking tone only added to Seraphina's anger and determination to best him.

Though weakened, Seraphina's spirit remained unbroken. She attempted to stand, her body trembling with both pain and determination. Kneeling before the malevolent Count, she spoke with unwavering resolve, her voice trembling with fury. "I vow, Count Malachi, that I will take your life with my own sword, and I will bring justice to all those you have wronged."

Count Malachi's amusement vanished in an instant, replaced by a cold, calculated rage. With a swift, imperious gesture, he ordered his three-headed Dracohound to attack. The monstrous creature emerged from the shadows, its eyes gleaming with predatory hunger.

Sir Sterling, Seraphina's loyal steed, positioned himself between his mistress and the approaching Dracohound, his nostrils flaring with unease. The gallant white stallion was unwavering in his determination to shield his beloved rider, despite the formidable threat before them.

As the Dracohound lunged forward with a deafening roar, Sir Sterling reared on his hind legs, his hooves flashing with incredible speed as he attempted to ward off the monstrous beast. He bucked and whinnied, his muscles straining as he fought valiantly to defend himself and Lady Seraphina.

Desperation gripped Seraphina as she realized the dire situation. In her heart, she knew that she couldn't stand idly by while Sir Sterling fought for his life. Despite her own injuries and the treacherous terrain, she summoned every ounce of her strength and began to run toward her loyal companion.

Count Malachi, a malevolent grin on his face, observed the unfolding chaos with cruel delight. He had hoped to see the once-loyal steed fall to his monstrous creation.

Amidst the chaos of the battle, Count Malachi's three-headed Dracohound proved to be a relentless adversary. The monstrous creature, with its malevolent eyes and venomous fangs, continued its assault on Sir Sterling, Seraphina's loyal steed. Despite the gallant stallion's valiant efforts to defend himself and his beloved mistress, the Dracohound's ferocity was unmatched.

The Dracohound's relentless assault took various forms, each more gruesome than the last. It unleashed blighting breath that withered the lush foliage of the enchanted forest, leaving a trail of desolation in its wake. Its razor-sharp claws tore through the air, seeking to rend flesh and break bone. Each of its three heads snapped and lunged independently, biting at Sir Sterling's graceful form, attempting to subdue the valiant steed. Despite the dire circumstances, Sir Sterling displayed unwavering determination in the face of such relentless brutality.

The glade reverberated with the harrowing sounds of the fierce battle—a cacophony of savage roars from the Dracohound, the rhythmic pounding of hooves, and Seraphina's heart-wrenching screams. Her anguished gaze remained fixed on the relentless struggle, where her loyal companion, Sir Sterling, valiantly confronted the monstrous beast. His once-pristine white coat was now tainted with both the ichor seeping from the Dracohound's wounds and the blood that had spattered upon him in the ferocious skirmish.

Desperation and helplessness gripped Lady Seraphina's heart as she realized the dire situation. Her cries for Sir Sterling to stand strong were drowned out by the violent clash of the battle. In her heart, she knew she couldn't stand idly by while her beloved steed faced this monstrous adversary.

Summoning every ounce of her strength, Lady Seraphina charged toward the tumultuous fray. Her heart pounded with fear and determination as she approached the battleground, clutching her sword tightly in her trembling hand. She couldn't bear to watch Sir Sterling suffer any longer.

With tears streaming down her face and a resolute scream, Seraphina swung her sword at the Dracohound. The blade, once resistant and hostile, now seemed to respond to her heartfelt anguish and fury. It gleamed with renewed brilliance as it pierced the Dracohound's hide, causing it to howl in agony.

Amidst the tumultuous fray, the Dracohound, relentless in its pursuit of carnage, made a lightning-fast strike with one of its heads. The deadly bite found its mark on Sir Sterling's noble neck, causing the gallant steed to release a heart-rending cry of agony. Weakened by the brutal battle and now suffering from this fatal wound, Sir Sterling's life force rapidly dwindled away.

With tears blurring her vision, Lady Seraphina watched in sheer horror as her faithful companion fell to the forest floor. The heart-rending sound of his final cry pierced the air, a mournful symphony of anguish that echoed through the enchanted forest.

As the life faded from Sir Sterling's once-keen eyes, Lady Seraphina sank to her knees beside him, her anguished sobs echoing through the glade. Her cries were a painful lament, a sorrowful melody of loss that no one had ever heard before. In that moment, her world had shattered, and the bond she shared with her loyal steed had been irrevocably broken.

Count Malachi mounted his wounded Dracohound, his malevolent plan fulfilled, retreated into the shadows, leaving Lady Seraphina to grieve beside the fallen form of her beloved companion. The enchantment of the forest seemed to mourn with her, the leaves rustling in a melancholic breeze, as if sharing in her profound sorrow.

As Seraphina wept over Sir Sterling's lifeless body, the weight of her loss pressed upon her heart like a crushing darkness. Her journey had taken an unexpected and devastating turn, leaving her to confront a grief that threatened to consume her very soul.

Lady Seraphina, overwhelmed by grief, clung to her lifeless steed's body, her sobs wracking her frame. Tears streamed down her cheeks as she mourned the loss of her loyal companion, Sir Sterling, who had been with her since she was a child. Her heart felt as if it had been torn asunder, and the pain of his absence was a deep, unrelenting ache.

Amidst her sorrow, Lady Seraphina was politely interrupted by the arrival of four forest elves. Unbeknownst to her, they had been silently shadowing her journey, ever watchful in case she required assistance. The elves, like all creatures of the enchanted forest, held animals in the highest regard, understanding the unique bonds that existed between the forest's inhabitants.

With a gentle and empathetic demeanor, the forest elves approached Lady Seraphina. Their eyes mirrored her grief, and their presence was a testament to the unity and interconnectedness of the enchanted realm. They recognized the depth of her sorrow and offered their support in her time of need.

Together, they devised a plan to honour Sir Sterling's memory and lay him to rest in a place of tranquility and beauty befitting his noble spirit. The elves crafted a graceful, wooden sled from the enchanted forest's abundant resources, using delicate vines and branches intertwined with natural magic.

With great care and reverence, they lifted Sir Sterling's lifeless form onto the sled, ensuring that he lay in repose as if he were merely sleeping. Lady Seraphina, her tears still flowing, watched their actions with a heavy heart, grateful for their assistance.

The forest elves led the somber procession, with Lady Seraphina following closely behind, clutching a lock of Sir Sterling's mane as if it were a cherished relic. Together, they journeyed deeper into the heart of the enchanted forest, where the healing pond lay hidden beneath the lush canopy.

As they arrived at the tranquil pond, its surface shimmering with otherworldly light, the forest elves chose a pristine spot beneath ancient trees to lay Sir Sterling to rest. The area radiated with a sense of serene beauty, a sanctuary where the forest's magic was most potent.

With great reverence, they tenderly laid Sir Sterling's lifeless body on the forest floor. Lady Seraphina knelt beside him, her hand caressing his once-pristine white coat, now stained with the battle's toils. They began the solemn task of washing his body, cleansing away the remnants of the gruesome encounter, until his coat gleamed in its former purity once more.

The forest elves began the sacred burial ritual, their voices rising in a harmonious, mournful melody that resonated with the very essence of the enchanted forest. They sang songs of gratitude for Sir Sterling's unwavering loyalty, celebrating his spirit and the bond he had shared with Lady Seraphina.

"Amidst the ancient trees, our voices like a gentle breeze,

We gather here with hearts of sorrow, to bid farewell to one we'll borrow.

Sir Sterling, noble, pure, and true, beneath the sky so deep and blue,

In your presence, we found delight, now you journey into the eternal night.

Oh, gallant steed, with coat so white, your grace and strength were our guiding light,

Through the darkest woods, you led the way, by Seraphina's side, night and day.

Though tears may fall, we'll remember you, in our hearts, your spirit anew,

In the enchanted forest, where you'll rest, in nature's embrace, forever blessed.

Sir Sterling, our friend, now fare thee well, to fields of green where legends dwell,

Among the stars, your light shall gleam, forevermore in the elven dream.

With gratitude and love, we sing this song, as we bid you farewell, so strong,

In the enchanted forest, your memory lives on, forever in our hearts, where you've drawn."

As the last notes of their haunting melody faded into the forest's embrace, the earth beneath Sir Sterling's form began to shift and mold itself. Enchanted flora and delicate flowers emerged, weaving a natural shroud around him, adorned with the forest's most vibrant blooms.

Lady Seraphina, tears still glistening in her eyes, whispered her final farewells to her cherished steed, her voice a soft, heartfelt tribute to their enduring friendship. She thanked him for his unwavering companionship, for carrying her through countless adventures, and for being her steadfast guardian.

With gentle reverence, the forest elves completed the burial, covering Sir Sterling's resting place with earth and blossoms, leaving no trace of his presence except for the memory engraved in their hearts.

As the last rays of sunlight filtered through the forest canopy, bathing the tranquil grove in a soft, golden glow, a sense of serenity settled upon the enchanted realm. The whole forest seemed to mourn for Sir Sterling, whispering their condolences through rustling leaves and sighing breezes.

The magical creatures of the forest gathered, their eyes filled with sadness, as they paid their respects to the noble steed who had been an integral part of their world. The Lumisprites danced in solemn circles, their light dimmed in reverence, while the treants lowered their branches in a somber salute.

The enchanted pond itself seemed to respond to the loss, its waters shimmering with a gentle, mournful luminescence. The harmonious symphony of nature—the chirping of birds, the babbling of brooks, and the whisper of leaves—conveyed a deep sense of loss that resonated throughout the enchanted realm.

And so, beneath the ancient trees, amidst the tranquil pond, Sir Sterling, the valiant and noble steed, found his final rest, surrounded by the love and grief of those who cherished him. His memory would forever live on in the heart of the enchanted forest, a testament to the enduring bonds forged within its mystical embrace.

Lady Seraphina, accompanied by the forest elves, returned to the Elven Kingdom with a heavy heart. Her arrival was met with a mixture of joy and anticipation, as General Ironheart, the crusade army, and the elves eagerly awaited her return. However, the initial gladness quickly turned to somber concern when they realized that Sir Sterling was nowhere to be seen.

General Ironheart's expression shifted from relief to sorrow as he scanned the surroundings, his eyes finally resting on Lady Seraphina, who couldn't hold back her tears any longer. The realization hit them all like a heavy blow—Sir Sterling, the valiant and beloved steed who had been an inseparable part of Lady Seraphina's life, was no longer with them.

Without a word, General Ironheart rushed to Lady Seraphina's side, his arms open wide to offer her solace. She embraced him tightly, her mournful cries filling the air. The entire assembly of elves, warriors, and creatures of the enchanted forest looked on, their hearts heavy with sympathy for their beloved Lady Seraphina.

The forest elves, who had accompanied Lady Seraphina and had been witnesses to the loss of Sir Sterling, approached with solemn expressions. Their presence served as a silent reminder of the unity that existed between the enchanted forest and the Elven Kingdom.

As Lady Seraphina clung to General Ironheart, the elves extended their condolences and offered their unwavering support. They understood the depth of her grief, having witnessed the profound bond between her and Sir Sterling during their journey.

General Elowen, the leader of the elven warriors, stepped forward, his face etched with sympathy. "We share in your sorrow, Lady Seraphina," he spoke softly. "Sir Sterling was a noble companion, and his loss is felt by all who knew him."

Lady Seraphina, still overcome with emotion, managed a tearful nod of gratitude for their words of comfort. Her connection with Sir Sterling had been more than that of a mere rider and her steed—it had been a friendship and partnership built on trust and unwavering loyalty.

The enchanted forest creatures, too, paid their respects in their own unique ways. The Lumisprites, whose light had dimmed in mourning, danced a somber dance around Lady Seraphina, their twinkling movements expressing their sympathy. The treants, with their ancient and wise presence, lowered their branches in a solemn gesture of respect.

With a heavy heart, Lady Seraphina finally found the strength to speak. "Thank you, all of you, for your kindness and support," she said, her voice quivering with emotion. "Sir Sterling was more than a steed to me—he was a true friend. Your presence and condolences mean the world to me."

General Ironheart, who had been her pillar of support, squeezed her gently, understanding the depth of her grief. "We stand with you, Lady Seraphina," he affirmed. "Together, we shall honour the memory of Sir Sterling and continue our quest to bring light to our realms."

Lady Seraphina nodded, her eyes still filled with tears, but her resolve unbroken. She knew that she had a duty to fulfill, both for Sir Sterling and for the realm she loved. Their journey had taken an unexpected and heart-wrenching turn, but she was determined to confront the darkness that loomed and find a way to bring justice to all.

In the midst of their collective grief, the assembly stood together, united by a common purpose—to face the shadows, seek the truth, and bring light to their realm. Their bond, forged through trials and tribulations, remained unbreakable, a testament to the strength of their unity.

And so, beneath the sheltering boughs of the enchanted forest and amidst the mournful symphony of nature, they stood as one—a family of elves, creatures, and humans—ready to confront the challenges that lay ahead, their hearts forever touched by the memory of Sir Sterling and the enduring spirit of their beloved Lady Seraphina.

General Ironheart's keen eyes, accustomed to the details of battle and strategy, didn't miss the sight of the cut on Lady Seraphina's arm. He knew the importance of attending to such wounds promptly, as even the smallest injury could lead to complications if left untreated.

"Lady Seraphina," he began with gentle concern, "that cut on your arm should be tended to. We ought to make our way to the healing pond, where its waters can aid in your recovery."

Seraphina, her eyes still glistening with tears from the loss of Sir Sterling, nodded in agreement. "Yes, you're right, General Ironheart. But before we go, there's something I'd like to show you. It's where Sir Sterling rests."

The general understood the depth of the bond between Seraphina and her steed, and he willingly complied. With a gentle gesture, he offered his hand to help her mount Orion, his own noble steed. Seraphina graciously accepted, and together they rode toward the serene healing pond.

As they rode side by side, Seraphina recounted the events leading to Sir Sterling's death, her voice filled with both sadness and gratitude. She spoke of the heroic struggle and sacrifice that her beloved steed had made to protect her, emphasizing the profound connection they had shared.

General Ironheart listened attentively, offering words of comfort and understanding. He knew that the loss of Sir Sterling was a heavy burden on

Seraphina's heart, and he wanted to provide whatever solace he could during this difficult time.

Finally, they reached the tranquil spot where Sir Sterling had been laid to rest. The area was a natural alcove within the enchanted forest, surrounded by towering trees and lush vegetation. Soft beams of sunlight filtered through the leaves, casting a warm and gentle glow over the sacred place.

General Ironheart's eyes swept over the serene landscape and the simple yet beautiful memorial that had been created for Sir Sterling. The noble steed's resting place was marked by a circle of luminous flowers, their petals radiating a soft, ethereal blue—the coloUr of sorrow and remembrance.

Seraphina dismounted Orion and stood beside the memorial, her heart heavy with emotion. "Sir Sterling," she began, her voice trembling, "you were more than just a steed to me. You were a true friend, a loyal companion, and a guardian. I promise you, your memory will live on in my heart, and I will carry your strength and courage with me always."

General Ironheart stepped forward, his hand gently resting on Seraphina's shoulder, offering his silent support. He, too, felt the weight of the moment and the importance of honouring Sir Sterling's memory.

With a solemn nod, Seraphina turned away from the memorial, ready to address the cut on her arm. "Let's make our way to the healing pond, General. It's time to tend to this wound and allow its waters to mend it."

Together, they mounted Orion, and the steed carried them to the tranquil healing pond nestled within the enchanted forest. As they approached, the luminous flowers surrounding the pond seemed to reflect the sorrow that hung in the air, their petals a soft, radiant blue.

Seraphina dismounted and, with a gracious nod to General Ironheart, began to undress by the edge of the pond. She entered the crystal–clear waters with care, feeling the cool embrace of the pond's magic as it enveloped her wounded arm. The healing properties of the pond were renowned throughout the enchanted forest, and she could feel its gentle power at work.

As Seraphina bathed, she watched as the water seemed to shimmer and glow, casting a soothing light on her form. The pond's luminous flowers continued to bloom, their petals drifting on the surface like delicate offerings. Gradually, she felt the cut on her arm healing, the pain diminishing with each passing moment.

Once she was satisfied with her bath, Seraphina dressed in her garments once more, her arm now free of injury. General Ironheart turned Orion, offering her a steadying hand as she mounted the steed. With the sorrow of Sir Sterling's passing still heavy in their hearts, they made their way back to the Elven Kingdom.

As they rode through the enchanted forest, the air was filled with a mournful song. The fairies, who had witnessed their journey, sang a haunting melody to honour the memory of Sir Sterling. The gentle chorus followed Seraphina and General Ironheart, a testament to the impact of the noble steed's life and sacrifice.

"Beneath the ancient canopy, where moonlight's soft and shadows flee,

We sing a song for one so brave, whose spirit now rests beyond the grave.

Sir Sterling, noble, pure, and free, your loyalty for all to see,

In the heart of the enchanted wood, your memory forever understood.

Oh, gallant steed, with hooves that flew, through forests deep and skies so blue,

A friend to all, both great and small, you answered every heartfelt call.

Though now you rest where dreams are spun, your legend lives, a shining sun,

In the enchanted forest's embrace, your spirit finds its resting place.

Sir Sterling, our dear friend and guide, in nature's realm, you'll ever bide,

With gratitude and love, we sing, to the noble heart that took to wing.

In every leaf, in every stream, your memory's bright and golden gleam,

With Seraphina, you found your home, in the heart of the enchanted loam."

In the midst of their collective grief, they found solace in the unity of their purpose—to confront the darkness that loomed, to seek the truth, and to bring light to their realm. Though the loss of Sir Sterling weighed heavily on their hearts, they knew that his memory would serve as a guiding light in their continued quest.

As Count Malachi rode his formidable Dracohound toward one of the entrances to the goblin kingdom, Netherholm, his intentions remained shrouded in mystery. Fizzlewick, the mysti- monk who had observed the previous encounter between Count Malachi and Lady Seraphina, approached Grizzletooth, the goblin leader, with a puzzled expression etched on his weathered face.

"Grizzletooth," Fizzlewick began, "I find myself perplexed by our lord's actions. When he encountered Lady Seraphina in the forest, why did he not finish her off while she mourned her fallen steed?"

Grizzletooth, ever the loyal servant of Count Malachi, listened intently to Fizzlewick's inquiry before turning his gaze toward the approaching count, mounted atop the Dracohound.

As Count Malachi neared, Grizzletooth conveyed the question to him, seeking to understand the logic behind his actions. With an enigmatic smile, Count Malachi responded, his voice carrying an air of sinister wisdom, "Ah, my dear Fizzlewick, sometimes the prey must first be weakened before it is ultimately brought down. Lady Seraphina's pain and grief have already sown the seeds of doubt and despair within her heart. This, my friend, is a far more potent weapon than the mere strike of a blade. When the time is ripe, we shall see the full extent of her vulnerability, and only then will I act."

Fizzlewick and Grizzletooth exchanged glances, uncertainty and apprehension lingering in the air. They knew that Count Malachi's machinations ran deep, and his plans were woven with threads of darkness and deception. The goblin kingdom of Netherholm, once a realm steeped in its own malevolent mysteries, had now aligned itself with this enigmatic serpent lord, and the fate of the realm hung in the balance as Count Malachi's schemes continued to unfold.

Within the serene confines of the Elven kingdom, Lady Seraphina and General Ironheart embarked on a tranquil walk along the banks of a glistening stream. The emerald leaves of the ancient trees overhead filtered dappled sunlight onto the forest floor, creating a peaceful mosaic of light and shadow. The melodic murmur of the babbling stream filled the air, and the gentle rustling of leaves added to the symphony of nature's song.

As they strolled hand in hand, the natural beauty surrounding them seemed to infuse their hearts with a sense of serenity and wonder. It was a rare moment of respite in the midst of their tumultuous journey, a chance to breathe and reflect on the trials they had faced and those yet to come.

But their tranquil interlude was suddenly interrupted when, as if from the pages of a long-forgotten legend, a magnificent white unicorn emerged from the depths of the enchanted forest. Its coat gleamed like freshly fallen snow, and its eyes sparkled with an otherworldly wisdom. A single spiraled horn adorned its noble brow, radiating an ethereal light.

The unicorn, a creature of unparalleled grace and majesty, approached Lady Seraphina and General Ironheart with an aura of serene purpose. It moved with an almost unearthly elegance, its hooves barely touching the ground, as if it were a creature of both the material and spiritual realms.

One of the elder elves, a wise and venerable figure named Baldo, stepped forward from the shadows of the forest. His age was evident in the lines etched upon his fair features, and his eyes bore the weight of centuries of wisdom. With a voice like the whispering wind through ancient trees, he spoke to Seraphina and Ironheart.

"Lady Seraphina, General Ironheart," Baldo intoned, "what you witness before you is a sight that has not graced our realm for a thousand years. Unicorns, beings of purity and grace, appear only to those whose hearts are untainted and intentions are noble."

The unicorn regarded Lady Seraphina with a gaze that seemed to pierce her very soul, its eyes filled with a silent understanding. Then, with a graceful gesture, it lowered its head, allowing Seraphina to gently touch the softness of its mane.

Baldo continued, "This unicorn has chosen you, Lady Seraphina. In its presence, you are recognized for the purity of your heart and the nobility of your cause. It is a rare honour bestowed upon a select few throughout our history."

"Lady Seraphina," Baldo continued, his voice carrying a deep wisdom, "I understand the burdens that may weigh upon your heart, the darkness that Count Malachi's actions may have stirred within you. But remember, the purity of one's heart is not determined by the darkness it has faced. It is the strength to keep that darkness from consuming you that truly matters."

The unicorn, Lumina, nodded in agreement, as if echoing Baldo's words. Its eyes, like pools of liquid silver, radiated a soothing presence. Seraphina couldn't help but feel a sense of reassurance in its presence.

Baldo went on, "In times of trial and hardship, the true essence of one's character is revealed. Your ability to confront the darkness within and still stand for what is right is a testament to your purity. Lumina has chosen to stand with you because it recognizes the nobility in your heart and the light that you carry within."

Seraphina's eyes welled with tears as she stroked Lumina's mane. She felt a profound gratitude for the unicorn's presence and Baldo's words, which reminded her that her past did not define her. She vowed to continue her journey with a heart unswayed by darkness, guided by the purity of her intentions and the unwavering support of her newfound companions.

The unicorn, now named Lumina by the elder elves, bent its head once more, this time in a gesture of unmistakable affirmation. It had chosen Seraphina as its rider, forging a bond that transcended the mundane world.

With a sense of awe and humility, Lady Seraphina mounted Lumina, her heart overflowing with gratitude for this extraordinary gift. She knew that this union marked a profound chapter in her journey, a partnership with a creature of unparalleled purity and grace. As the unicorn carried her forward, she felt a deep sense of purpose and destiny, for she now rode alongside a being whose very presence radiated the light of hope in a world shadowed by darkness.

Yet, even as she marveled at the wonder of Lumina, a pang of guilt tugged at Lady Seraphina's heart. It was as though she betrayed Sir Sterling, her loyal companion who had served her with unwavering devotion. She couldn't help but feel that she shouldn't ride any other horse, for Sir Sterling had been more than just a steed; he had been her confidant and friend.

As the enchanting forest passed by in a blur, Seraphina silently vowed to carry Sir Sterling's memory with her always, cherishing the moments they had shared. She knew that Lumina was a gift of destiny, a beacon of light in a time of darkness, but the bond she had with her fallen companion would forever hold a special place in her heart.

General Ironheart stood in awe, watching as Lady Seraphina gracefully mounted the magnificent unicorn, Lumina. He couldn't help but notice the radiant transformation that seemed to envelop her as she rode the ethereal steed. Bathed in the soft, otherworldly glow of the forest, Seraphina appeared even more beautiful, her features illuminated by a serene and inner radiance that matched the purity of the unicorn beside her.

As he gazed upon her, a warmth spread through Ironheart's heart.

The Path of Revenge

As the morning sun cast a warm, golden glow over the Elven Kingdom, General Ironheart arrived at Lady Seraphina's chambers to accompany her to breakfast. He greeted her with a gentle smile, his hazel eyes reflecting the unwavering support he held for her.

Lady Seraphina, dressed in a flowing gown of ethereal blue, returned his smile and gracefully joined him. As they began their leisurely walk through the enchanting forest, the tranquility of their surroundings enveloped them, offering a temporary respite from the burdens that weighed on their hearts.

Lady Seraphina's gown was a masterpiece of craftsmanship and elegance. It flowed like a gentle stream of water, its ethereal blue fabric shimmering in the dappled sunlight filtering through the ancient trees. The dress seemed to mirror the serene sky on a clear summer day, and its intricate embroidery of delicate silver threads added a touch of celestial magic. The bodice was finished with intricate lace and decorated with tiny sapphire gemstones that caught the light, making her appear as if she were a living embodiment of the tranquil forest itself. As she moved, the gown whispered softly, its fabric rustling like leaves in the breeze, adding to the enchantment of her presence. Lady Seraphina wore it with grace, her every step like a dance, as she and General Ironheart embarked on their leisurely stroll through the forest, finding solace in the natural beauty that surrounded them.

However, it wasn't long before the weight of recent events pressed upon Lady Seraphina's mind, and she felt compelled to share something with General Ironheart. With a thoughtful pause, she reached into the folds of her gown and produced a small, ornate flask adorned with intricate designs.

"General," she began, her voice tinged with a mix of determination and vulnerability, "when I visited the Angel City, The Archangel granted me this flask. It contains a few precious drops of the sacred spring water from the

Angelic Realm." She held the flask out to him, her green eyes searching his for understanding.

General Ironheart's brows furrowed slightly in curiosity as he accepted the flask, examining it with a respectful reverence. "Sacred spring water," he repeated softly, "a gift from the angels themselves. What purpose does it serve, my lady?"

Lady Seraphina took a deep breath before she continued. "I believe it can help cleanse my heart and prevent it from hardening with hatred towards Count Malachi," she admitted, her gaze fixed on the flask. "During our confrontation, I could feel my sword, the one decorated with the jewels, working against me. It turned darker as my emotions became consumed by anger and hatred. I don't want to become like him, General. I don't want darkness to consume me."

General Ironheart's eyes widened with realization as Lady Seraphina spoke. He returned the flask to her with utmost care, understanding the gravity of her confession. "Sacred spring water from the Angelic Realm, meant to cleanse one's heart and preserve the light within," he murmured, his respect for the gift evident.

Lady Seraphina nodded, gratitude in her eyes. "Yes, General. And there's more to it. My weapons, the sword, bow, and arrows, were all crafted by the elves using Luminaforge Steel. They are bound to the essence of light and purity. If they sense that you are not fighting in alignment with the light they were designed for, they begin to work against you."

General Ironheart absorbed this revelation, his thoughts racing. "So, during your confrontation with Count Malachi, your sword reacted to the darkness within you from him, turning against you," he deduced.

Lady Seraphina nodded again, her vulnerability laid bare. "Exactly, General. I felt its resistance, and I knew I couldn't let my own anger and hatred corrupt me."

The general's expression softened, and he placed a reassuring hand on her shoulder. "You've made a wise decision, Lady Seraphina. To resist the pull of darkness and hatred is a noble and difficult path. Your courage in seeking to preserve the light within you is commendable."

Lady Seraphina smiled, grateful for his understanding and support. "Thank you, General. I hope that, with the help of the sacred spring water, I can stay true to the path of light, even in the face of Count Malachi's darkness."

As they continued their walk through the enchanting forest, a sense of camaraderie and purpose enveloped them. Lady Seraphina's revelation had deepened their bond, and together, they were determined to face the challenges ahead, wielding not only their weapons but also the strength of their hearts against the encroaching darkness.

General Ironheart nodded, understanding the gravity of her words. He knew that the battle against Count Malachi was not just one of physical prowess but also a test of their inner strength and purity of heart. "If you believe this sacred spring water can aid you in maintaining your inner light, my lady, then I wholeheartedly support your decision."

With a determined resolve, Lady Seraphina uncorked the flask and, with utmost care, drank the remaining drops of the sacred spring water. As the cool liquid coursed down her throat, she could almost feel a soothing calmness spreading through her, as though a weight had been lifted from her shoulders.

They continued their walk through the enchanting forest, the ethereal beauty of the surroundings now mirrored in Lady Seraphina's eyes. She felt lighter, as if a burden had been lifted from her heart, and she knew that her resolve to confront Count Malachi within the light and determination had grown stronger.

General Ironheart, ever the pillar of support, walked alongside her in quiet companionship, offering her strength and understanding. The enchanting forest, with its vibrant flora and melodious birdsong, bore witness to their journey, and they both embraced the tranquility it offered, knowing that they would need all the inner peace they could find in the battles that lay ahead.

As Lady Seraphina and General Ironheart continued their morning stroll through the enchanting forest, they came upon a breathtaking sight that filled the air with wonder and awe. Ahead of them, bathed in soft, dappled sunlight, stood the pure-white unicorn, its coat glistening as if sprinkled with stardust. The majestic creature was surrounded by General Ironheart's council members, each of them wearing expressions of astonishment and delight.

Lady Titania Stormbringer, with her scared face from past battles fought, was the first to approach the unicorn. Her blue eyes sparkled with fascination as she extended her hand toward the gentle beast. "I've heard tales of unicorns, but I never imagined I would see one in my lifetime," she whispered, her voice filled with reverence.

Sir Alden Frostbane, the steadfast knight with a frosty demeanor, couldn't help but crack a rare smile as he observed the unicorn. He was known for his affinity with horses, and he watched closely as the unicorn interacted with the other horses nearby.

Captain Elara Swiftwind, a strong and disciplined leader, found himself momentarily speechless. He couldn't tear his eyes away from the unicorn's graceful movements as it approached the horses Aelion and Orion, who had stood vigil over Lady Seraphina in the wake of Sir Sterling's passing. In a remarkable display of empathy, the unicorn gently nuzzled both Aelion and Orion, as if understanding their shared grief over the loss of their companion.

Lord Cellok Stoneforge muttered to himself about the rarity and beauty of the creature.

As the council members watched in silent wonder, the elves who had accompanied them also observed with wide-eyed fascination. Unicorns were a rarity even in the enchanted forest, and the elves regarded the creature with a mix of curiosity and respect.

General Ironheart and Lady Seraphina approached the group, and the unicorn turned its head to regard them with deep, intelligent eyes. It recognize Lady Seraphina as it lowered its head slightly in acknowledgment.

"This is a momentous occasion," General Ironheart said, his voice filled with awe. "I've never seen a unicorn in all my years."

Lady Seraphina nodded in agreement, her green eyes reflecting the same wonder that had captivated the others. "It's a testament to the enchanting nature of this forest," she replied. "And a reminder that beauty and wonder can be found even in times of sorrow."

The unicorn, sensing the genuine admiration and respect of those gathered around, approached Lady Seraphina and General Ironheart. It allowed them to run their hands along its silky mane, a gesture of trust and connection that left those present in a state of quiet reverence.

As they continued to interact with the unicorn, General Ironheart's council members and the elves exchanged excited whispers and smiles. The presence of the unicorn felt like a blessing, a symbol of hope and renewal in the wake of Sir Sterling's passing.

Lady Seraphina, her heart filled with gratitude and awe, took a step forward, her hand gently resting on Lumina's graceful neck. She turned to face General Ironheart's council members and the gathered elves, her voice filled with warmth and reverence.

"Allow me to introduce you all to this magnificent creature," she said, her green eyes shining with appreciation. "This is Lumina, a symbol of the enchantment and purity that dwells within the heart of the forest."

Her words carried a sense of wonder, and the council members and elves listened intently as she continued, "Lumina, like the light of the stars, has graced us with her presence today. She has shown compassion to our own Aelion and Orion, who mourn the loss of Sir Sterling, and in doing so, she reminds us of the enduring bonds that connect all living beings."

General Ironheart's council members exchanged smiles, their initial awe deepening into a sense of reverence for the unicorn. Lumina, as her name suggested, radiated a soft, ethereal light, casting a gentle glow around her, and her presence felt like a blessing to those in her midst.

Lady Titania Stormbringer spoke softly, her voice touched by the profound moment. "Lumina," she repeated, as if savouring the name, "a name befitting such a magnificent being."

Sir Alden Frostbane nodded in agreement. "A name that captures her essence perfectly," he remarked, his gaze never leaving the unicorn.

Captain Elara Swiftwind, known for his steadfast leadership, couldn't help but smile. "Lumina, may your presence continue to bless our path," he said, his voice carrying a sense of hope.

Lord Cellok Stoneforge added his own sentiment. "Lumina, your light shines brightly in this forest, and we are honoured to stand in your presence."

The elves, too, whispered words of respect and admiration for the unicorn, their fascination deepening into a sense of connection with the enchanted realm.

As Lumina continued to interact with those around her, her gentle demeanor and ethereal presence seemed to bridge the gap between different races and beings. In her, they found a symbol of unity and wonder, a reminder that even in the face of loss and darkness, there existed a world of enchantment and beauty waiting to be discovered.

Lady Seraphina, standing beside Lumina, felt a profound sense of gratitude for this unexpected encounter. She knew that Lumina's presence would forever be etched in their hearts as a symbol of hope, renewal, and the enduring magic of the enchanted forest.

For the rest of the day, the enchanting forest resonated with the melodic songs of birds and the murmur of the stream as the unicorn joined Aelion and Orion in a harmonious display of unity. General Ironheart's council members, Lady Seraphina, and the elves watched in wonder, their hearts touched by the enchanting beauty of the forest and the magical presence of the unicorn. In that moment, they understood that even amidst loss and sorrow, the world held moments of unexpected enchantment and grace.

As Lady Seraphina stood beside Lumina, the radiant unicorn, the council members and elves exchanged a knowing glance. They understood the profound connection she shared with her beloved steed, Sir Sterling, who had tragically lost his life. While the loss of Sir Sterling had left a void in her heart, the presence of Lumina and the support of her allies offered a glimmer of solace.

General Ironheart, ever the stalwart protector, stepped forward, holding a delicate wooden box furnished with intricate elven carvings. He offered it to Lady Seraphina with a gentle smile, his hazel eyes reflecting warmth and understanding.

"Lady Seraphina," he began, "we, your loyal allies and friends, would like to offer you a token of our appreciation and a symbol of the enduring bond you shared with Sir Sterling."

With a sense of reverence, Lady Seraphina accepted the wooden box. She delicately opened it, revealing a bracelet crafted with exquisite care and precision. The bracelet's design was an elegant blend of elven artistry and natural elements. Thin silver chains interwove with ivy leaves, and in the center, a single amethyst gemstone glistened like a drop of dew.

But what caught Lady Seraphina's attention most was the small, meticulously woven lock of white hair entwined within the bracelet. Her breath caught as she recognized the unmistakable shade of Sir Sterling's mane—the very lock of hair she had held as a keepsake when she had laid him to rest.

Tears welled in her emerald-green eyes as she gently lifted the bracelet, her fingers tracing the delicate craftsmanship. She looked up at General Ironheart and the council members, her voice filled with emotion.

"Thank you," she said, her voice quivering with gratitude. "This is a beautiful tribute, and it means more to me than words can express."

General Ironheart nodded, his eyes reflecting the collective sentiment of those present. "It is a token of the love and respect we hold for you, Lady Seraphina, and a reminder that even in the face of loss, our bonds endure."

The other council members and elves approached, each expressing their heartfelt sentiments and support. They offered their wishes for healing and renewal, their words a testament to the unity they shared.

With a sense of determination, Lady Seraphina carefully clasped the bracelet around her wrist. Its presence was a comforting reminder of the love and loyalty she had shared with Sir Sterling. As the bracelet settled on her arm, she felt a connection—a bridge between her past and the new path she was forging with her allies.

Lumina, the gentle unicorn, nuzzled her affectionately, as if acknowledging the significance of the moment. Lady Seraphina smiled, her heart lighter, as she realized that even in the midst of darkness and loss, there was still light to be found, and the bonds of friendship and love would guide their way forward.

As they stood together beneath the canopy of the enchanted forest, Lumina's ethereal light casting a soft glow around them, Lady Seraphina knew that the journey ahead, though challenging, would be one filled with hope, unity, and the enduring enchantment of their realm.

Lady Seraphina, wearing the elven bracelet with the lock of Sir Sterling's mane, stood before her council and allies, her emerald-green eyes shimmering with determination. She understood the importance of forging a bond with Lumina, the majestic unicorn that had graced their presence. With a gentle nod to those around her, she approached the radiant creature, her heart filled with both reverence and hope.

Lumina, with her pearlescent coat that seemed to shimmer like moonlight, regarded Seraphina with wise and ancient eyes. There was an air of serenity around the unicorn, a presence that conveyed a profound connection to the enchanted forest itself.

As Seraphina mounted Lumina, she felt a surge of anticipation and wonder. The unicorn's back was as smooth and comfortable as a cloud, and her presence beneath her felt both powerful and gentle. With a soft word of encouragement, Seraphina gently urged Lumina forward, and they set off into the heart of the enchanted forest.

Riding a unicorn was unlike anything Seraphina had ever experienced. It was as if she had become a part of the forest itself, moving in harmony with the natural rhythms of the ancient realm. The very ground beneath them seemed to respond to Lumina's presence, with flowers blooming and vines winding their way around tree trunks in a display of enchantment.

As they galloped through the forest, Seraphina practiced her archery skills, drawing her bow and aiming at distant trees. The arrows flew true, guided by a newfound connection that seemed to emanate from Lumina herself. Each shot hit its mark with precision, as if the unicorn's presence enhanced her abilities.

The bond between Seraphina and Lumina deepened with every passing moment. It was a connection that transcended words, a silent understanding that spoke of trust and unity. Lumina's presence seemed to soothe Seraphina's heart, easing the pain of her loss and filling her with a sense of purpose.

As they rode deeper into the enchanted forest, Seraphina could feel the very essence of the realm enveloping them. The trees whispered their ancient secrets, and the animals of the forest regarded them with a sense of wonder and reverence. It was as if the forest itself recognized the significance of their union.

Lumina's luminous mane flowed like a silken waterfall, and Seraphina reached out to touch it, her fingers trailing through the ethereal strands. The unicorn responded with a soft nuzzle, a gesture of affection and acceptance. In that moment, Seraphina knew that she had found a kindred spirit, a companion on her journey to confront the darkness that threatened their realm.

The enchantment of the forest seemed to intensify around them. Beams of dappled sunlight danced through the canopy, casting a kaleidoscope of coloUrs on the forest floor. Birds sang in melodious harmony, their songs a celebration of the bond that was forming between Seraphina and Lumina.

With each passing mile, the enchanted forest seemed to reveal its hidden wonders. Seraphina marveled at the beauty that surrounded her, from the vibrant flora to the luminescent fireflies that danced in the twilight. It was a world of magic and mystery, and she was privileged to experience it in the company of Lumina.

As the day turned to evening, they found themselves in a tranquil clearing bathed in the soft glow of the moon. Seraphina dismounted and sat on the forest floor, her back against a massive oak tree. Lumina, with a grace that seemed to defy gravity, lay down beside her.

Seraphina gazed up at the night sky, its vastness filled with stars that seemed to twinkle with approval. She whispered her thoughts to the universe, expressing her gratitude for Lumina's presence and the newfound strength she had discovered.

"It's as if the forest itself has welcomed us," she mused, her voice a soft murmur in the stillness of the night.

Lumina turned her head and regarded Seraphina with a knowing gaze. There was a wisdom in the unicorn's eyes, a wisdom that transcended time and space.

Seraphina reached out and gently touched Lumina's horn, a gesture of affection and trust. "We are bound by more than fate," she said, her words filled with conviction. "We are bound by the very essence of this enchanted realm, and together, we shall confront the darkness and restore balance."

Lumina responded with a soft whinny, her approval evident in the gentle warmth of her presence. It was a bond that held the promise of hope and renewal, a bond that would guide them on their journey to confront the darkness that threatened their realm. In the heart of the enchanted forest, under the watchful gaze of the stars, Lady Seraphina and Lumina forged a connection that would shape the destiny of their world.

The once-tranquil forest air began to change, a subtle shift in the atmosphere that stirred a sense of foreboding. Shadows deepened, and there emerged a menacing presence, the Dracohound. This time, it was alone, its predatory instincts leading it into the heart of the enchanted forest in search of a meal.

Lumina, the radiant unicorn, immediately sensed the intruder's presence and rose to her hooves. Her horn, as pure and ethereal as moonlight, began to emit a soft, soothing glow. The Dracohound, accustomed to the darkness and malevolence of its master, Count Malachi, recoiled at the radiant light and let out a thunderous roar, its crimson eyes filled with anger.

Lady Seraphina knew she couldn't afford to lose another steed to the Dracohound's relentless hunger. Determination surged within her, and she acted swiftly. With a powerful scream, she charged forward, her bow in hand. As she ran, she drew her arrows and released them one by one, each shot guided by her newfound sense of purpose—to protect, to defend, and to avenge.

The arrows, with Luminaforge tips and amethysts that seemed to glow with inner light, found their mark with uncanny precision. They struck the Dracohound, causing it to howl in pain and fury. Seraphina's heart was aflame with the desire to protect Lumina and ensure the creature wouldn't suffer the same fate as Sir Sterling.

But the Dracohound was relentless. Despite the wounds inflicted upon it, it continued its advance, its massive form casting an eerie shadow over the forest floor. Each arrow that struck it seemed to fuel its determination to feast on its prey.

It was then that Lumina, with an otherworldly grace, charged forward as well. The unicorn's horn gleamed with an even brighter light as she closed the distance between herself and the Dracohound. With a swift, fluid motion, Lumina drove her horn like a radiant sword into the heart of the monstrous creature.

The Dracohound let out a final, agonized howl, its crimson eyes dimming as life escaped its hulking form. Lumina withdrew her horn, her ethereal glow intensified by the vanquishing of their foe. The forest seemed to sigh in relief, the shadows dispersing as a sense of tranquility returned to the enchanted realm.

Seraphina, her bow lowered, approached Lumina with a mixture of gratitude and awe. The bond between them had grown stronger, their hearts intertwined by their shared victory. She whispered words of thanks to the unicorn, her voice filled with reverence.

"You have proven yourself to be not only my companion but my protector," Seraphina said, her eyes filled with tears of relief. "Together, we have avenged Sir Sterling and defended the enchantment of this forest."

Lumina regarded Seraphina with a knowing gaze, her radiant presence an affirmation of their unbreakable connection. In that moment, they shared an understanding that transcended words—a bond forged in the crucible of danger and triumph.

The enchanted forest, once again bathed in the soft glow of moonlight, seemed to offer its silent approval. The stars above shimmered with approval, their cosmic witness to the unity of a lady and her steed, destined to confront the darkness and protect the realm they held dear.

Lady Seraphina and Lumina, the radiant unicorn, stood in the heart of the enchanted forest. The ethereal glow of Lumina's horn cast dancing reflections on the surrounding trees, creating an otherworldly aura. Seraphina, in awe of the colours that seemed to pulse around them like a living canvas, could hardly believe her eyes.

As she carefully cleaned Lumina's horn with a soft cloth, she noticed how the vibrant hues of the forest seemed to intensify. It was as if the very essence of the enchanted realm responded to the presence of the unicorn and its Lady. Seraphina couldn't help but feel that Lumina was not just a part of this realm but an embodiment of its magic.

Suddenly, as if materializing from a burst of incandescent flames, a magnificent phoenix descended from the treetops. Its feathers shimmered with a myriad of colours—fiery reds, radiant oranges, and deep, iridescent blues. Its wingspan was breathtaking, and its eyes held the wisdom of countless ages.

The phoenix landed gracefully before Seraphina and Lumina, its radiant plumage casting a surreal glow in the forest's dappled light. Seraphina, her heart pounding with both awe and curiosity, couldn't tear her gaze away from this wondrous creature.

With a voice as melodious as a songbird's, the phoenix introduced herself. "I am Lysandra, Keeper of Flames and Guardian of Ancient Wisdom. I have traversed time and realms to be here with you, Lady Seraphina."

Seraphina, still taken aback by the presence of this majestic being, stuttered, "Wh-why have you come to me, Lysandra?"

The phoenix regarded her with eyes that seemed to hold the secrets of the universe. "It is Lumina, your radiant companion, who has opened the way for ancient creatures like myself to communicate with you. The enchanted forest itself has chosen to side with you in the impending battle against Count Malachi."

Seraphina's eyes widened in astonishment. The idea that the very forest was aligning itself with her cause filled her with a profound sense of purpose. "But why, Lysandra? Why have you chosen to help me?"

Lysandra's fiery wings rustled, and she exhaled a warm, mystical breath. "You, Lady Seraphina, are a beacon of hope in these troubled times. The enchanted forest recognizes your courage, your love for its creatures, and your unwavering determination to protect it. With Lumina as your guide, you have forged a bond that bridges the worlds, and the realm itself has answered your call."

Seraphina's heart swelled with gratitude, her eyes shimmering with unshed tears. "Thank you, Lysandra. I will do all in my power to defend this realm and rid it of Count Malachi's darkness."

Lysandra regarded Lady Seraphina with a warm and ancient wisdom that seemed to transcend time itself. With a graceful movement, the majestic phoenix extended her radiant, fiery wing, revealing a delicate, ethereal amulet suspended from her feathers. "As a token of our alliance," Lysandra spoke, her voice echoing like a celestial melody, "I offer you this amulet, forged in the heart of the enchanted forest. It will grant you protection and guidance in your quest."

Seraphina's eyes fell upon the amulet, a magnificent piece adorned with intricate nature-inspired patterns. It seemed to pulse with a gentle, soothing light. "What is its purpose, Lysandra?" she asked in awe.

"It is a conduit between you and the enchanted forest," Lysandra explained. "When you wear it, you will be able to communicate with the creatures of the forest, and they will heed your call. It shall also offer you guidance when faced with challenges, as Lumina does."

Tears of gratitude welled in Seraphina's eyes as she accepted the amulet, realizing the significance of this gift. "Thank you, Lysandra. I shall cherish this amulet and use it to honour our alliance and protect this realm."

With the amulet in her possession, Seraphina felt a profound connection to the enchanted forest and its creatures, strengthening her resolve to stand against Count Malachi's darkness and defend the realm that had chosen her as its champion.

The amulet bestowed upon Seraphina by Lysandra is a work of exquisite craftsmanship and natural beauty. It is fashioned from a delicate, translucent crystal, with an intricate lattice of fine silver filigree encasing it. Embedded within the crystal, tiny emerald-green leaves and delicate vines seem to grow and intertwine, forming a miniature, enchanting forest scene. The amulet emits a soft, ethereal glow, like sunlight filtering through the forest canopy at dawn, casting a gentle, calming radiance. Suspended from a fine, silken cord, the amulet is as light as a feather, and it seems to pulse with a subtle, life-affirming energy. Its presence is both enchanting and reassuring, a tangible connection to the heart of the enchanted forest and the creatures that call it home.

With a regal nod, Lysandra commanded the enchanting forest to assist in a solemn task. The gentle whispers of the woodland fairies filled the air, and their delicate forms appeared. Together, they lifted the lifeless body of the fallen Dracohound, the bane of the forest, with great reverence.

Seraphina watched in awe as the fairies carried the enormous creature through the dappled moonlight, their shimmering wings bearing the burden as if it were weightless. They flew in graceful unison, a spectral procession led by the majestic phoenix. Back in the Elven Kingdom, the sight of the fallen Dracohound sent shivers through the hearts of General Ironheart and his council. It was a grotesque and deformed creature, a testament to the depths of Count Malachi's malevolent power and the horrors he had wrought upon the realm.

After a somber examination, the decision was made to burn the Dracohound's body, to purify it from the taint that had enveloped it. The flames roared to life, consuming the remains until only ashes remained. It was a grim reminder of the darkness that loomed on the horizon.

General Ironheart, his brow furrowed with concern, approached Seraphina. "My Lady, you will no longer ride alone," he declared. "The threats we face are too great. Together, we shall face the darkness."

Seraphina nodded in agreement, her resolve unwavering. As the elves discussed their strategy to counter Count Malachi's growing power, she couldn't help but feel a glimmer of hope. The enchanted forest had chosen her, and with Lumina, Lysandra, and the unwavering support of her allies, they would stand united against the encroaching shadow.

Lady Seraphina presented the amulet to the council of elves, explaining its significance as a gift from Lysandra, the wise phoenix of the enchanted forest. The emerald leaves and silver filigree captured the light, signifying their alliance with the realm's creatures. The elves, deeply connected to nature, nodded in admiration.

In a private chamber, Seraphina showed the amulet to General Ironheart, conveying its purpose as a conduit to the realm and a means of communication with its inhabitants. Ironheart recognized the amulet's importance, solidifying their shared mission to confront Count Malachi's darkness and protect their cherished land.

"General Ironheart," Lady Seraphina inquired with a hopeful gaze, "do you think the fairies would be willing to redesign their gift, the necklace called Starheart, into a ring to keep me grounded?" Ironheart smiled gently, reassuring her, "We can inquire about that tomorrow, Lady Seraphina, and see if the fairies can accommodate your request."

Betrayal's Toll

As Lady Seraphina joined the dinner table in the Elven Kingdom, there was a noticeable air of anticipation. She could hardly contain her excitement about her encounter with Lysandra, the magnificent phoenix. The moment was ripe with expectation, and Seraphina couldn't wait to share her extraordinary experience with those who had gathered.

Seated at the head of the long, finely carved table, General Ironheart presided over the evening meal. On his right sat Lady Titania Stormbringer with her silver hair cascading like a waterfall of moonlight. Beside her was Sir Alden Frostbane, the wise and experienced strategist, his sharp eyes betraying a curiosity that rarely wavered. Captain Elara Swiftwind, the fearless and audacious leader of the crusader scouts, occupied the next seat, his red hair hinting at the grace and strength that defined him.

On General Ironheart's left, Lord Cellok Stoneforge, the master of crusader craftsmanship, gazed intently at the feast before him, his attention divided between the enchanting aromas and the impending tale. As Lady Seraphina took her place at the table, the expectant silence enveloped them.

With a gleam in her eyes and an eager smile, Seraphina began her tale. "My dear friends," she addressed the council members, "today, I had an encounter that I believe will fill your hearts with wonder."

General Ironheart nodded, his hazel eyes filled with a mix of curiosity and trust. "Please, Lady Seraphina, do tell."

Seraphina's gaze shifted to Lady Titania, who had a serene, knowing look about her. "I met a phoenix—a creature of legends, whose feathers shimmer with the colours of a thousand sunsets. She introduced herself as Lysandra, Keeper of Flames and Guardian of Ancient Wisdom."

A collective gasp rippled through the council. The significance of a phoenix's appearance was not lost on them, and each member reacted differently to the revelation.

Lady Titania offered a gentle smile. "A phoenix's presence is a blessing, indeed. They are harbingers of great change and protectors of ancient truths."

Sir Alden, the strategist, raised an eyebrow, his interest piqued. "Ancient truths, you say? This could be a valuable ally in our efforts against Count Malachi."

Captain Elara, known for his pragmatism, scrutinized Seraphina. "Are you certain it was not a mere illusion, my lady? Count Malachi has tricked us before."

Seraphina nodded firmly. "I have no doubt. Lysandra's presence was as real as the forest that surrounds us."

Lord Cellok, the craftsman, his fingers seemingly itching to carve the image of the phoenix, chimed in. "I've heard tales of phoenix feathers possessing potent magical properties. If we could obtain one, it could be invaluable in crafting enchanted weapons."

The conversation continued, with each council member expressing their thoughts and reactions. Some were in awe of the phoenix, while others approached the matter with caution. Yet, all acknowledged the significance of this event and its potential impact on their ongoing struggle against Count Malachi.

General Ironheart, the embodiment of strength and leadership, finally spoke. "This encounter may be a sign, my friends. We must consider the message that Lysandra, the phoenix, brings to our realm. It is a beacon of hope in these trying times."

With the council members engaged in conversation, the evening continued, filled with lively discussion and the sharing of ideas. In the midst of it all,

Lady Seraphina couldn't help but feel a renewed sense of purpose. The support and wisdom of her allies, along with the blessings of the enchanted forest and the guidance of Lysandra, would be the foundation upon which they would confront the encroaching darkness of Count Malachi.

General Elowen, the esteemed leader of the elves, had been silent throughout Lady Seraphina's account of her encounter with Lysandra, the phoenix. As the council members continued their discussion, he finally cleared his throat, capturing their attention.

"Forgive my delay in speaking," General Elowen began, his voice resonating with the wisdom of ages spent in communion with the enchanted forest. "Lysandra, the Keeper of Flames, is no stranger to our realm. She is a guardian, a beacon of ancient wisdom, and a symbol of the forest's will."

His words intrigued everyone, and General Ironheart leaned forward attentively, his hazel eyes fixed on the elf general. "Please, General Elowen, enlighten us."

Elowen nodded in acknowledgment before continuing. "The awakening of Lysandra was not a mere happenstance. It was a part of a larger, mystical event in the forest—an event known as the 'Council Herald.' A few moons ago, the creatures of the enchanted forest convened to decide which side they would choose in the coming conflict."

The council members exchanged knowing glances, recognizing the gravity of the situation. Seraphina's presence had forged a unique bond with the enchanted forest, and the outcome of this event could have far-reaching consequences.

Elowen continued, "The creatures of the forest, including the elusive treants and forest spirits, crafted a horn from treant wood—a symbol of unity and purpose. They summoned Lysandra from her slumber to be a witness to their decision."

A sense of awe and reverence hung in the air. The creatures of the enchanted forest had awakened the phoenix to bear witness to their choice, a choice that would shape the future.

General Ironheart's eyes shone with anticipation. "And what was their decision, General Elowen?"

Elowen's gaze held steady. "They chose Seraphina. They chose the side of light and hope, recognizing her as a protector of our realm. Lysandra, the phoenix, is both guardian and symbol of this decision."

Seraphina felt a profound sense of gratitude and responsibility wash over her. The support of the forest and its creatures was a testament to the bond she had forged with the enchanted realm.

The council members exchanged glances, their expressions reflecting a mix of wonder and determination. This revelation only strengthened their resolve to stand together against Count Malachi's encroaching darkness.

General Ironheart spoke, his voice firm and resolute. "This, my friends, is a sign of the forest's faith in us. We shall honour this trust and work tirelessly to defend our realm from the looming threat. Together, we shall confront the darkness and protect the light of our world."

The council members nodded in agreement, unified by the knowledge that they had been chosen not only by their fellow elves but also by the mystical creatures of the enchanted forest. Lysandra's presence had reaffirmed their commitment to the cause, and they were determined to face the challenges ahead with courage and resilience.

As General Elowen shared the troubling news, a hushed silence fell over the gathered council. Lady Seraphina's expression shifted from curiosity to a deep sense of disappointment and hurt. She had hoped that her homeland of Ravenshadow, the place she had sacrificed so much for, would stand by her in her quest to confront Count Malachi.

General Ironheart, his hazel eyes reflecting a mixture of sympathy and resolve, was the first to break the silence. "This is indeed a grievous matter, General Elowen. Ravenshadow's decision is a betrayal not only to Lady Seraphina but to the bond between our realms."

Elowen nodded somberly. "The messenger returned with the message from King Alaric himself. He expressed his concerns about Count Malachi's retaliation if they were to join our alliance."

Captain Elara Swiftwind, known for his strategic acumen, leaned forward with a furrowed brow. "But Seraphina was a sacrifice to protect Ravenshadow. They owe her, and us, their allegiance in this dark hour."

Lady Titania Stormbringer, her fingers now tracing the scars on her face, chimed in. "It is a bitter truth that not all rulers prioritize honour and loyalty above their own preservation. We must proceed without Ravenshadow's support."

Lady Seraphina, though hurt by the abandonment of her homeland, knew that she couldn't let this setback deter her. She understood the harsh realities of politics and power, yet her disappointment lingered like a heavy shadow.

"I appreciate your unwavering support," she said to the council members, her voice tinged with sadness. "Ravenshadow's decision may wound my heart, but it will not break my spirit. We will face Count Malachi together, even if we must do so without them."

General Ironheart, ever the stalwart protector, placed a reassuring hand on Seraphina's shoulder. "You have our loyalty, Lady Seraphina, and the support of the enchanted forest itself. We will forge ahead, and Ravenshadow's absence will not hinder our quest to defeat Count Malachi and protect our realm."

The council members nodded in agreement, their unwavering determination to confront the darkness unwavering. They knew that, despite the betrayal of one kingdom, they had a duty to safeguard their world and ensure that the light of hope would prevail over the encroaching shadows.

Lady Seraphina, though deeply affected by the Ravenshadow's refusal, took strength from the solidarity of her allies. She knew that their combined efforts, with the support of the enchanted forest and the mystical creatures that had chosen her, would be enough to face the formidable threat that Count Malachi posed. The path ahead was fraught with challenges, but she was determined to see it through to its end, no matter the sacrifices she had to make.

As Lady Seraphina sat in the council chamber, her heart heavy with the recent betrayal of Ravenshadow, she couldn't help but think of her parents, Lord Maximus and Lady Elena. They had been her rock, her source of guidance and love, and their fate weighed heavily on her mind.

Turning to General Elowen, her eyes filled with a mix of hope and apprehension, she asked, "General Elowen, do you have any news of my parents, Lord Maximus and Lady Elena? Have you heard anything about their well-being?"

General Elowen's face, already somber from the earlier news, grew even grimmer. He paused for a moment, choosing his words carefully, before responding, "Lady Seraphina, I regret to inform you that there is news, but it is not what you may wish to hear."

Seraphina's heart sank, and she gripped the armrest of her chair, bracing herself for the impending revelation. "Please, General Elowen, tell me what you know."

Elowen sighed deeply, his gaze locked with Seraphina's. "Lady Isabella, the mage who aligned herself with Count Malachi, used her influence over King Alaric to have your parents executed."

Seraphina's world seemed to crumble around her. She had hoped against hope that her parents were safe, that they had managed to escape the reach of Count Malachi and his dark forces. But this news shattered that fragile hope into a million pieces.

Tears welled up in Seraphina's eyes, and her voice trembled as she asked, "Why, General Elowen? Why would they do such a thing?"

Elowen's expression remained compassionate, but there was no denying the harsh reality of the situation. "It appears that Lady Isabella sought to prove her loyalty to Count Malachi by eliminating any potential threats, including your parents. By having them executed, she wanted to send a clear message that Ravenshadow would not join the growing alliance against Count Malachi."

The pain of betrayal cut deep into Seraphina's soul. Not only had Ravenshadow turned its back on her, but they had also taken the lives of her beloved parents as a gruesome gesture of allegiance to the very evil that threatened their world.

Anguish and anger warred within Seraphina's heart. She felt a profound sense of loss for her parents, whose lives had been unjustly taken, and a burning rage against Lady Isabella and those who had allowed this to happen.

Tears streamed down her cheeks as she whispered, "My parents... They sacrificed everything to protect Ravenshadow. They were innocent, and yet they were executed as traitors."

General Elowen, though not one to openly display his emotions, couldn't hide the sorrow in his eyes. "I know, Lady Seraphina. Their sacrifice will not be forgotten, and their memory will live on in the hearts of those who knew them."

Seraphina clenched her fists, her resolve hardening. "Count Malachi and Lady Isabella will answer for their crimes, not only against me but against my parents and our entire realm. I will not rest until justice is served."

General Ironheart, who had been silently listening, stepped forward and placed a comforting hand on Seraphina's shoulder. "You have our unwavering support, Lady Seraphina. We will stand by your side and ensure that those responsible for these heinous acts face the consequences of their actions."

As Seraphina wiped away her tears, a steely determination settled in her gaze. The pain of betrayal and loss had only strengthened her resolve to confront Count Malachi and bring an end to his reign of darkness. She knew that the road ahead would be fraught with peril, but she was ready to face it, for the memory of her parents and the future of their realm.

The necklace around Lady Seraphina's neck, gifted to her by the fairies and named Starheart, began to glow with a brilliant blue radiance, she instinctively clasped her hand around it, feeling the warmth and energy it emitted. Closing her eyes, she took a deep, calming breath, allowing the soothing presence of the necklace to envelop her.

General Ironheart and the council members observed with curiosity and concern, their gazes shifting between the glowing necklace and Seraphina herself. General Elowen, who had knowledge of the necklace's purpose, stepped forward to provide an explanation. "Fear not," he reassured them, "the necklace, Starheart, serves as a grounding talisman. It helps Lady Seraphina maintain her balance and inner peace when her emotions threaten to sway her from the path of light."

Understanding washed over Ironheart's face as he nodded in acknowledgment. He had witnessed the necklace's effects on Seraphina before, during moments of great emotional turmoil. It was a beacon of strength, a reminder of her connection to the enchanted forest and its mystical creatures, and a source of resilience when facing the darkness that loomed over their realm.

With each calming breath, Seraphina's aura stabilized, and the glow of the necklace began to subside. She opened her eyes and she was grounded.

The grand estate of the Veridale family stood amidst sprawling gardens and towering oaks, a testament to centuries of wealth and influence. Today, it would host a meeting of great importance – the Ravenshadow's council, respected figures cloaked with power, had sent word that they would arrive at the estate. The Veridales, unaware of the impending confrontation, prepared for the visit with a lavish feast, hoping to make a favourable impression.

As the council members entered the grand hall, their faces shrouded in hoods and veils, a tense air settled over the room. The Veridales, resplendent in their finest attire, welcomed their enigmatic guests, unaware of the storm brewing beneath the surface.

It didn't take long for the council to get to the heart of the matter. "We received a letter from the elves," one of the council members, a figure known only as Thornshade, began. "It spoke of Lady Seraphina's escape from Count Malachi, and it claimed that the elves had informed you. Yet, you never disclosed this information to us."

The Veridales exchanged uneasy glances, and their patriarch, Lord Veridales, quickly responded, "We had no knowledge of Lady Seraphina's whereabouts when the elves contacted us. She had left Count Malachi's estate, and we assumed she was on a personal journey."

The council members exchanged skeptical glances, and another, Lady Nightshade, spoke up. "The elves are our allies, and their trust in us is vital. If you knew something about Lady Seraphina's escape and failed to inform us, it is a grave betrayal."

Lord Veridales' face reddened with anger, and he retorted, "We are loyal to Ravenshadow and would never betray your trust. Lady Seraphina's escape was her own choice, and we had no hand in it."

Tensions escalated as the council members pressed for more answers. However, the Veridales' defense was quickly dismantled by evidence and contradictions. It became evident that they had withheld crucial information about Lady Seraphina's escape.

Just as the confrontation reached its zenith, the grand doors of the hall burst open, and King Alaric, the ruler of Ravenshadow, strode in. His presence sent shockwaves through the room. Lady Isabella, a powerful mage known for her enchantments, followed him closely.

Under the influence of Lady Isabella's spell, King Alaric spoke with an eerie calmness, "Enough of this confrontation. I decree that the matter concerning the Veridales and Lady Seraphina's escape is to be dropped immediately. They are cleared of any suspicion."

The council members were baffled by this sudden turn of events. They exchanged frustrated glances, but King Alaric's words were final. The Veridales, relieved beyond measure, wore smug expressions.

As Lady Isabella followed King Alaric out of the hall, she couldn't help but wear a sly smile. Her influence had worked, and her secret alliances remained hidden. The Veridales had escaped scrutiny, and the council had been silenced.

The feast that had been prepared remained untouched. The council members, their questions left unanswered, left the Veridale estate in a cloud of frustration and confusion. Ravenshadow's secrets ran deep, and today's events had only added another layer to the enigma.

And so, the Veridales' grand feast turned into a silent, empty hall, echoing with the aftermath of a confrontation that had been interrupted by dark enchantments, leaving everyone with more questions than answers.

The Veridales had another secret they kept well-guarded. They knew that Lady Isabella was aligned with their powerful ally, Count Malachi. As long as she remained close to King Alaric, they believed they would be safe from the council's probing eyes. Their alliance with Count Malachi had provided them with a shield of protection, one they intended to maintain at all costs.

Lady Seraphina, mounted atop her majestic unicorn Lumina, and General Ironheart, astride his noble steed Orion, ventured deep into the heart of the enchanted forest. Their journey led them to the tranquil Healing Pond, a place of mystic serenity where the water shimmered with soothing energies. It was here, among the ancient trees and the soft, ethereal glow of the pond, that the fairies were said to dwell.

With a sense of anticipation, Lady Seraphina dismounted, her forest-green gown flowing like the leaves of the surrounding trees. She held out the necklace called Starheart, a gift from the fairies that had aided her in grounding her emotions during challenging times. Her gaze met General Ironheart's, a silent plea for his support in her request.

Lady Seraphina's green dress was a masterpiece of elegance and natural beauty. Crafted from the finest emerald-hued silk, it flowed like a cascade of leaves in the wind, draping her form with a gentle grace. The dress featured intricate embroidery of delicate ivy vines and blooming wildflowers that seemed to have been woven by the forest itself. The bodice was finished with a subtle shimmer, reminiscent of sunlight filtering through the dense canopy of ancient trees. The dress's flowing sleeves and a modest train added a touch of regal charm to her appearance.

Around her waist, a forest-green sash cinched the dress, accentuating her slender figure while hinting at the untamed beauty of the woods. As Lady Seraphina moved, the gown rustled like leaves in a breeze, a soft whisper of nature's song. Her attire was a harmonious blend of elegance and the enchantment of the wilderness, reflecting her deep connection to the enchanted forest she so dearly cherished.

All of Lady Seraphina's clothing since her arrival in the elven kingdom had been meticulously crafted by the skilled hands of the elves. They had taken great care to weave the essence of the enchanted forest into every thread, ensuring that her attire not only complemented her regal presence but also honoured her deep connection to the mystical realm. Each wardrobe, from dresses to gowns and even her practical riding attire, bore the mark of elven craftsmanship, a testament to the enduring alliance between Lady Seraphina and the guardians of the woods.

The fairies, radiant beings of light, appeared as shimmering orbs, their laughter like the tinkling of wind chimes. As Lady Seraphina and General Ironheart approached, the fairies circled them in a graceful dance of welcome. It was as if the forest itself came alive to greet its protectors.

Lady Seraphina spoke with a voice filled with humility and hope. "Dear fairies of the enchanted forest, I come before you with a humble request. The necklace you gifted me, Starheart, has been a great source of strength. Yet, I seek your assistance in transforming it into a ring so that I may wear it alongside the amulet gifted by Lysandra, the phoenix."

The fairies exchanged knowing glances, their tiny forms illuminating the forest with a soft, ethereal light. Their leader, a radiant fairy with wings like opalescent gossamer, floated closer to Lady Seraphina. "We understand your request, Lady Seraphina, but the battle of remaining grounded is not solely in your heart. It is also in your mind, as one's mind can be rewired by the scars of trauma."

With a gentle wave of her hand, the fairy summoned their magic, and the necklace transformed. It didn't become a ring, as Seraphina had hoped, but a pair of exquisite earrings instead. Each earring bore a delicate silver chain, adorned with a shimmering star-shaped sapphire gem that seemed to hold the wisdom of the cosmos within its facets.

"These earrings," the fairy explained, "are a gift from the enchanted forest to aid you in keeping both your heart and mind grounded. They will serve as a reminder of your connection to the realm and its creatures."

Lady Seraphina accepted the earrings with gratitude, her eyes shimmering with unshed tears. "Thank you, dear fairies. I will cherish these gifts and wear them with pride, knowing that I carry a piece of the enchanted forest with me always."

General Ironheart nodded in agreement, his respect for the fairies' wisdom evident. With their newfound treasures, Lady Seraphina and General Ironheart left the Healing Pond, their hearts and minds renewed, ready to face the challenges that lay ahead. The earrings, radiant with the magic of the enchanted forest, served as a symbol of their unwavering bond with the realm and the strength they drew from its mystical energies.

Lady Seraphina and General Ironheart, having returned to the Elven Kingdom, were welcomed with open arms by the elves, a people known for their deep connection to nature and the mystical energies of their realm. Among the elves, General Elowen had awaited their return with particular anticipation. As they gathered in the heart of the kingdom, General Elowen, with a sparkle of excitement in his eyes, informed them of the extraordinary event that was about to unfold.

"Tonight, dear friends," General Elowen began, "is a night of unparalleled magic in our realm. It is a convergence of celestial wonders that happens only once in a generation. The moon is not only full but will shine with a rare, ethereal blue light. Moreover, the stars—Altair, Vega, and Deneb—shall align perfectly, creating a breathtaking straight line in the night sky."

Seraphina and Ironheart exchanged astonished glances, realizing the significance of this celestial alignment. General Elowen continued, "This is a momentous occasion for our people, a Festival of Lights that we call 'Luminis Noctis.' It is a time when we illuminate our kingdom with countless lanterns and release them into the sky at a precise moment when the moon and stars reach their zenith. The very flora that usually emits a gentle white glow at night will be bathed in a soft, light blue hue, infusing our world with enchantment."

As the day gave way to night, the Elven Kingdom transformed into a wonderland of luminescence. Lanterns of various shapes and sizes, crafted from the petals of iridescent flowers and leaves, adorned every tree, building, and pathway. Their soft, radiant glow cast a spellbinding, ethereal light that danced in the gentle breeze. Even the tranquil streams that wound through the kingdom were lined with lanterns that bobbed and twinkled like stars on the water's surface.

The flora, which usually emitted a soft white glow at night, had indeed taken on a delicate shade of light blue. The leaves, flowers, and moss-covered stones seemed to shimmer in the moonlight, radiating a tranquil and otherworldly beauty. The night air was filled with the sweet fragrance of blossoms, and the melodious hum of elven songs resonated through the kingdom, adding to the enchantment of the evening.

"In the twilight's tender embrace,

Under stars' celestial grace,

Luminis Noctis, enchant our night,

With lanterns and stars, we take flight.

Luminis Noctis, the night divine,

In your glow, our spirits align.

With lanterns high and hearts aglow,

Through moonlit dreams, we shall go.

The flora dances with pure delight,

In shades of blue, they shimmer so bright.

As moonlight bathes in the forest's stream,

In Luminis Noctis, we dream our dream.

Luminis Noctis, the night divine,

In your glow, our spirits align.

With lanterns high and hearts aglow,

Through moonlit dreams, we shall go.

Beneath the stars, we find our way,

In this enchanted night, we sway.

With elven songs, our voices unite,

In Luminis Noctis, our hearts take flight.

Luminis Noctis, the night divine,

In your glow, our spirits align.

With lanterns high and hearts aglow,

Through moonlit dreams, we shall go.

As lanterns rise, our hopes ascend,

In this magical night, our spirits mend.

In Luminis Noctis, forever we'll be,

Bound by the stars, in unity."

Lady Seraphina graced the Festival of Lights, Luminis Noctis, in an ensemble that was both elegant and in harmony with the enchanted surroundings of the Elven Kingdom. Her gown, crafted by elven hands, was a work of artistry that blended seamlessly with the ethereal atmosphere of the event. The flowing garment was made from a delicate fabric that seemed to shimmer like moonlight on water, and its colour was a subtle, silvery-blue, reminiscent of the enchanted night sky.

The gown's bodice was decorated with intricate embroidery, depicting celestial constellations and delicate vines adorned with twinkling stars. A sash of iridescent leaves and petals encircled her waist, accentuating her slender figure while paying homage to the natural beauty of the Elven Kingdom. The gown's sleeves, sheer and flowing, gave her an almost ethereal appearance, as if she were a part of the very magic that surrounded her.

Around her neck, Lady Seraphina wore the amulet, its crystal gleaming softly in the festival's radiant glow. Her hair, cascading in loose waves down her back, was finished with delicate starlight pins, a testament to her connection with the night's celestial wonders. As she moved through the festival, her attire, like the blossoms and lanterns, seemed to be touched by the enchantment of Luminis Noctis, creating an image of timeless beauty and grace that captivated all who beheld her.

General Ironheart, in his attire for the Festival of Lights, was a striking figure amidst the enchanting ambiance of Luminis Noctis. His attire was a harmonious blend of elven craftsmanship and his own warrior's sensibility.

He wore tailored tunic and trousers, both fashioned from a rich, forest–green fabric that seemed to resonate with the colours of the enchanted realm. The tunic featured intricate embroidery along the edges, depicting symbols of strength and courage, an homage to his role as a protector of the kingdom. A finely crafted leather belt, adorned with elven sigils, cinched his waist, adding a touch of regal charm.

Over his tunic, General Ironheart wore a flowing forest–green cloak, its deep hood partially concealing his rugged features. The cloak's inner lining bore patterns of silver thread, evoking the starlit sky. Around his neck, he wore his green pendant, a token of his alliance with Lady Seraphina and the elves, a symbol of unity and purpose.

His boots, sturdy and practical, were designed for the challenges of the forest, a testament to his warrior's prowess. His sword, sheathed in an ornate scabbard, rested at his side, a constant reminder of his duty to protect and serve.

As he moved through the festival, General Ironheart's attire reflected both his strength as a leader and his respect for the elven culture. His presence added to the enchantment of Luminis Noctis, a reminder that even amidst the magic and beauty of the night, the realm had a steadfast guardian who stood ready to defend it.

As Seraphina and Ironheart strolled through the breathtakingly adorned kingdom, they couldn't help but be captivated by the romantic ambiance of Luminis Noctis. The soft glow of lanterns above, the gentle luminescence of the flora, and the celestial alignment in the sky created an atmosphere of unparalleled magic. Underneath the twinkling canopy of lanterns, they found themselves drawn to one another, the enchantment of the night deepening their connection.

Amidst the ethereal beauty of the Festival of Lights, Ironheart gently took Seraphina's hand, and they shared a meaningful look. Their hearts beat in harmony with the enchanting rhythm of the night, and as they released their lanterns into the starlit sky, they knew that this moment, under the celestial wonder of Luminis Noctis, would forever be etched in their memories as a night of love, magic, and profound connection.

As Lady Seraphina and General Ironheart strolled back from the enchanting Festival of Lights, their steps were light, and their hearts were ablaze with the magic of the night. The ethereal glow of the lanterns and the celestial alignment had left an indelible mark on their souls, and they walked hand in hand, basking in the serenity of the moment.

General Ironheart couldn't help but admire Seraphina's grace and beauty. He gazed at her with a soft smile and said, "You looked absolutely radiant tonight, Lady Seraphina. It's as if the stars and moon conspired to illuminate your beauty even more."

Seraphina's cheeks flushed with a delicate shade of pink, and she replied, "Thank you, General. You were quite the gallant presence yourself, commanding respect and admiration from all who beheld you."

With a playful gleam in his eyes, Ironheart decided to take a step further. Gently twirling Lady Seraphina in a dance-like motion, he complimented, "But it is not just your appearance that captivates me. It's your unwavering courage, your compassion, and your determination that truly make you shine."

Seraphina was momentarily taken aback by his words but recovered with a warm smile. "General, your strength, wisdom, and your ability to protect this realm with unwavering dedication have always inspired me," she replied.

With that, General Ironheart twirled Lady Seraphina once more, but this time, he ended the twirl with her in his strong arms. As their eyes locked, an unspoken connection passed between them, and their lips drew closer until they met in a tender, lingering kiss. The night seemed to stand still as they lost themselves in the enchantment of the moment.

The kiss grew more passionate, their hearts beating in harmony, as their hands traced up and down one another's bodies. Their longing for each other had been building for some time, and it found its release in the intensity of that kiss. Yet, even in their passion, there was a deep and abiding tenderness that spoke of a connection beyond the physical.

Suddenly, as if by mutual understanding, they both stopped, their lips parting but their foreheads still touching. They looked deep into each other's eyes, their smiles mirroring the warmth in their hearts. Without needing to say a word, they knew that what they shared was something truly special.

With a shared smile, they separated, and their hands entwined once more as they began to run towards Lady Seraphina's chambers. The journey back was filled with laughter and excitement, their hearts racing not just from the run, but from the knowledge that they had found something extraordinary in each other. As they reached her chambers, they paused for a moment, still smiling, before stepping inside, ready to explore the depths of their newfound love in the peaceful sanctuary of the night.

As Lady Seraphina and General Ironheart stepped into her private chamber, a sense of intimacy and anticipation filled the air. The door closed behind them with a soft click, and the room was bathed in a warm, soft glow from the gentle radiance of the enchanted flora outside. Their eyes locked, and without a word, they moved closer, their lips meeting in a passionate kiss.

The kiss was a sweet blend of longing and desire, a silent acknowledgment of the deep connection they had discovered during their journey and the Festival of Lights. Their hands explored each other's bodies with gentle reverence, fingers tracing lines of affection along the contours of their forms. As they continued to kiss, it was as if they were unwrapping precious gifts, savoring every moment of the unveiling.

Their clothing fell away one piece at a time, discarded with a sense of mutual appreciation. Each kiss and touch was a testament to their growing affection and attraction, a celebration of the profound bond they had forged. The world outside seemed to fade away as they focused on each other, their desires and emotions laid bare.

Finally, they found themselves on the edge of Seraphina's inviting bed. She lay down, her form bathed in the soft, moon-kissed glow that filtered through the chamber's window. General Ironheart, momentarily in awe of her beauty, paused to admire the sight before him. She was a vision of grace and passion, and his heart swelled with love and desire for the remarkable woman who had captured his heart.

General Ironheart stood bathed in the soft, moon-kissed glow filtering through the chamber's window. The enchanting flora outside painted shadows upon his form, accentuating the sculpted contours of his body. He seemed like a masterpiece of strength and grace, his rugged features and chiseled physique illuminated by the ambient radiance. As Lady Seraphina admired him, she couldn't help but appreciate the allure of the man before her, his unwavering strength, and the tenderness that lay beneath his commanding exterior.

With a tender smile, Ironheart joined her on the bed, their lips meeting once more in a passionate kiss. Their bodies pressed together, and in that intimate embrace, they discovered a new level of connection, a profound sense of belonging that transcended words. As they surrendered to their desires, they knew that this night, under the enchanting spell of the Festival of Lights, would forever be etched in their hearts as a night of love and profound union.

As their bodies came together in an intimate union, it was as if a deep connection between their souls had ignited, casting aside the shadows of their past experiences. Lady Seraphina and General Ironheart surrendered to the moment, their hearts and bodies aligning in a profound way. The sensations that coursed through them were a stark contrast to their previous encounters. For Lady Seraphina, who had endured the abuse of Count Malachi, this was a moment of tenderness, care, and genuine affection. For Ironheart, who had once shared a purely physical connection with Isabella, this experience was marked by a profound emotional connection that transcended the physical. Their bodies tingled with pleasure, but it was the spark of their souls coming alive that truly set them ablaze. In this intimate exchange, they found not just ecstasy, but a rekindling of their spirits, a deep and abiding love that would forever bind them together in a way that surpassed the physical realm.

Their intimacy was not merely a physical connection but a beautifully choreographed dance of souls. Their bodies moved together with a grace and synchrony that mirrored the ebb and flow of the waves softly kissing the ocean's shore. Every touch, every caress, was a testament to their profound understanding and affection for one another.

As their passionate dance reached its crescendo, they shared a moment of pure ecstasy, their hearts and bodies fully intertwined. Yet, it was the tenderness of their connection, the way they held each other in the afterglow, that spoke volumes. They lay in each other's arms, basking in the warmth of their embrace, the rhythm of their breaths slowly aligning, and their hearts beating in unison.

In the tranquil silence that followed, they gazed at one another with eyes filled with love and contentment. It was a moment of pure intimacy, of shared vulnerability and profound trust. As exhaustion from the intensity of their emotions and desires washed over them, they fell asleep wrapped in each other's arms, knowing that they had found a love that transcended the physical, a love that would sustain and comfort them through all the trials that lay ahead.

The soft rays of the morning sun filtered through the chamber's window, casting a warm and gentle glow upon the room. General Ironheart stirred from his slumber, his senses gradually returning to the world around him. As he blinked away the remnants of sleep, his gaze fell upon the vision before him.

Lady Seraphina lay asleep beside him, her form bathed in the delicate morning light. She appeared as an ethereal angel, her features softened in repose. Her auburn hair cascaded in loose waves around her, framing her delicate face and cascading down her shoulders. The graceful curve of her neck, the subtle rise and fall of her chest as she breathed peacefully—it was a sight that left Ironheart in awe of her beauty.

Unable to resist the urge to express his affection, Ironheart leaned closer, pressing a tender kiss to Seraphina's forehead. The touch was a gentle caress of love and admiration, a silent proclamation of his feelings for her.

As his lips brushed against her skin, Seraphina stirred from her slumber. Her eyes fluttered open, and when she looked into Ironheart's gaze, a soft smile graced her lips. "Good morning," she whispered, her voice filled with warmth.

"Good morning," Ironheart replied, his eyes never leaving hers. He couldn't help but admire her, how her eyes sparkled with a kind of radiance that transcended the morning light. "You look even more beautiful in the morning light," he admitted, his voice filled with sincerity.

Seraphina blushed at his compliment, her cheeks taking on a delicate shade of pink. "And you, General, are quite the handsome sight to wake up to," she replied, her fingers gently tracing his jawline. Her touch sent a shiver of longing through him, and he leaned in to capture her lips in a tender kiss.

Their lips met in a loving, lingering embrace, a silent exchange of affection that conveyed all the emotions they felt for each other. As they kissed, their bodies moved together as if drawn by an invisible force, the desire that had awakened with them growing stronger by the moment.

Before they could fully realize it, the passion between them had ignited once more. Their hands and lips explored each other's bodies with a fervor born of deep connection and affection. It was a union of not just their physical desires but their souls, a profound intimacy that left them breathless and longing for more.

Afterward, they lay tangled in each other's arms, savouring the aftermath of their lovemaking. The morning had transformed into a golden tapestry of warmth and affection, and they basked in the afterglow of their shared intimacy.

But as the scent of breakfast wafted through the chamber, they knew it was time to begin their day. Seraphina's fingers traced loving patterns across Ironheart's chest as she looked into his eyes. "Shall we freshen up and join the day, my general?" she asked, her voice filled with tenderness.

Ironheart nodded, his heart filled with love and gratitude for the woman beside him. "Yes, my lady," he replied, planting a soft kiss on her lips before they reluctantly disentangled themselves from each other's embrace.

They rose from the bed, their hearts and bodies still humming with the echoes of their intimacy. With the promise of a new day ahead and the strength of their love to guide them, they readied themselves to face whatever challenges and adventures awaited them in the enchanted realm they had come to cherish.

Trials and Tribulations

General Elowen's thoughts had been consumed by the enigma of the pendant that bound Count Malachi to his demonic power. Each night, as he studied the cryptic symbols etched into the ancient artifact, he could feel the weight of its mystery pressing upon him. It was as if the pendant held the key to unraveling the dark secrets of their adversary.

One evening, as the moon bathed the castle chambers in its silver light, a revelation struck him like a bolt of lightning. It was a name whispered through the corridors of legends—the Seer of the Enchanted Forest. General Elowen believed that this elusive figure might hold the answers they sought. With a sense of urgency, he knew he had to share his discovery with Lady Seraphina and General Ironheart.

The following morning, with the sun casting a golden glow over the castle, Elowen approached Seraphina and Ironheart in the library, where they had been tirelessly researching the pendant. The room was filled with ancient tomes and scrolls, each holding a piece of the puzzle.

"Lady Seraphina, General Ironheart," Elowen began, his voice carrying the weight of conviction, "I believe I may have found a solution to our quandary. There is a Seer known as Caelan the Wise, a mystic of extraordinary abilities, located on the edge of the Enchanted Forest. They are known for their profound insight into matters of magic and the supernatural."

Seraphina and Ironheart exchanged glances, their eyes reflecting a mixture of hope and curiosity. The pendant had been a source of frustration and fascination for them both, and the prospect of finding answers was tantalizing.

Caelan the Wise, Elowen explained, had a reputation for divining the future and deciphering ancient artifacts. If anyone could unlock the pendant's secrets and provide guidance on how to sever Count Malachi's connection to its dark power, it was this enigmatic figure.

Ironheart, a man of action, nodded in agreement. "If there's a chance to gain an upper hand in the impending battle against Count Malachi, we must seize it. Let us seek out this Seer."

Seraphina, her heart filled with determination, concurred. "I trust your judgment, General Elowen. Lead us to this Seer."

As they made their decision, the group of crusaders, who had fought alongside General Ironheart in his valiant quest, were summoned to join them on this quest. Each crusader was renowned for their combat skills and unwavering loyalty.

Lady Titania Stormbringer arrived at the courtyard with her steed, a fierce warhorse named Thunderstrike. The dark bay stallion's powerful frame was a testament to countless battles, and he stood ready for the journey ahead.

Sir Alden Frostbane followed, accompanied by his loyal steed, Frostwind. The horse's fur was a striking silver, and his unwavering endurance mirrored his rider's dedication to their cause.

Captain Elara Swiftwind, a skilled archer and leader of the crusaders, rode in on his trusty mare, Moonshadow. The mare's sleek black coat and agile frame were well-suited for the challenges that lay ahead.

Lastly, Lord Cellok Stoneforge, led his sturdy warhorse, Ironclad, into the courtyard. The horse's robust build and chestnut coat reflected his resilience.

With their crusader companions gathered and their steeds ready, the group set out together toward the edge of the Enchanted Forest, guided by the hope that Caelan the Wise held the key to unlocking the pendant's secrets and preparing them for the looming conflict with Count Malachi. As Lady

Seraphina, General Ironheart, and their crusade council prepared to embark on their journey to visit the Seer Caelan the Wise on the edge of the Enchanted Forest, the elven inhabitants of the kingdom gathered to wish them well. The elves, known for their deep connection to nature and their enchanting forest, understood the significance of their mission.

Standing at the threshold of the Elven Kingdom, the group was surrounded by the elven residents, their luminous eyes reflecting both curiosity and respect. The elves, dressed in garments that seemed to be woven from moonlight and starlight, offered blessings and farewells.

The Elven King, resplendent in his regal attire furnished with intricate leaf patterns, stepped forward and spoke in a melodious voice. "May the wisdom of the forest guide your path and the spirits of our ancestors protect you on your journey. The Enchanted Forest is a realm of magic and mystery. Embrace its wonders and heed its cautions."

The elves, with their ethereal grace, presented gifts of enchanted herbs and flowers known for their protective properties, which they carefully tied to the horses' bridles and the travelers' attire. These offerings were a symbol of the elves' support and well wishes for their quest.

Lady Elyndra gracefully stepped forward and presented Lady Seraphina with a woven bouquet of enchanted herbs and flowers. She placed the delicate arrangement in Seraphina's hands, her eyes shimmering with a mixture of solemnity and hope.

"These offerings," Lady Elyndra began, her voice as melodious as a woodland stream, "are a token of our support and well wishes for your quest, Lady Seraphina. May the forest's blessings protect you on your journey. We shall await your return, for your presence is a cherished light in our realm." With a gentle nod, she expressed her confidence in Seraphina's mission and her unwavering belief in the young lady's abilities.

As they ventured further into the Enchanted Forest, the members of the crusade council couldn't help but be in awe of the magical realm surrounding them. The forest, unlike any they had ever seen, was a symphony of colours and life. Trees with leaves that shimmered like liquid gold reached for the heavens, while vibrant flora carpeted the forest floor with hues of amethyst and emerald.

But it was the enchanting glow that emanated from the flora that left the council members spellbound. They had only glimpsed the beauty of the forest within the elven kingdom, but here, in the heart of the Enchanted Forest, the flora seemed to pulse with a soft, luminous light, casting an otherworldly radiance that danced among the trees.

Sir Alden Frostbane, known for his stoic demeanor, found himself marveling at the forest's magic. "I've never seen anything like this," he whispered, his breath forming a frosty cloud in the enchanted air. "It's as if the entire forest is alive."

Captain Elara Swiftwind, his keen senses heightened by his affinity for the forest, nodded in agreement. "The elves truly live in a realm of wonder. It's no wonder they are protectors of such beauty."

With every step they took into the Enchanted Forest, the council members felt a sense of reverence for the natural world that surrounded them. The forest seemed to whisper ancient secrets and offer a connection to something greater than themselves. It was a journey into the unknown, guided by the hope that the Seer Caelan the Wise would provide the answers they sought in their quest against Count Malachi.

As Lady Seraphina, General Ironheart, and their crusade council ventured deeper into the heart of the Enchanted Forest, they stumbled upon a magical scene that filled them with wonder. It was a clearing bathed in dappled sunlight, and in the midst of it, a group of mischievous pixies were engaged in playful activities.

The pixies, known for their tiny stature and iridescent wings, flitted about like living jewels. They wore garments made of petals and leaves, and their laughter filled the air like tinkling bells. Among the group, there were three notable pixies: Lunaflora, a pixie with sapphire-blue wings; Bramblethorn, a mischievous prankster with emerald-green wings; and Zephyrwing, a delicate and kind-hearted pixie with wings that shimmered like opals.

Lunaflora, the leader of the trio, was perched on a dew-kissed flower petal, delicately weaving a garland of moonflowers. Bramblethorn, with a mischievous glint in his eyes, was rearranging a line of acorns into a comical pattern. Zephyrwing, the most graceful among them, danced on the surface of a nearby pond, her every step creating ripples of liquid crystal.

As they journeyed closer, Sir Alden Frostbane, caught up in the magic of their surroundings, couldn't help but address their newfound companions as "fairies" in an attempt to acknowledge their ethereal nature. However, his well-intentioned comment immediately drew gasps of disbelief and disapproval from the pixies, especially Lunaflora, who fluttered closer to set the record straight.

"Fairies? Oh, heavens, no!" Lunaflora exclaimed, her sapphire-blue wings shimmering with indignation. "We are pixies, dear sir. Fairies and pixies may share some similarities, but we are distinct beings of the enchanted realm. Fairies tend to be larger, more majestic, and often associated with benevolent magic. Pixies, on the other hand, are known for our tiny size, mischievous spirits, and playful nature."

Bramblethorn, the mischievous pixie, chimed in with a grin, "And let's not forget, we've got a penchant for a good prank or two, which you might find quite entertaining, Sir Alden."

Sir Alden Frostbane, somewhat abashed, nodded in acknowledgment. "My apologies, dear pixies. I stand corrected. Your wisdom is duly noted."

Intrigued by the magical sight, Lady Seraphina approached the pixies with a warm smile. "Greetings, dear pixies of the Enchanted Forest," she said in a gentle voice. "We are on a quest to seek the wisdom of Seer Caelan the Wise. Might you know the way?"

The pixies, their curiosity piqued, gathered around the visitors, their tiny faces filled with excitement. Lunaflora, the leader, spoke with a musical lilt in her voice, "Ah, visitors from the realm beyond our woods! We know of Seer Caelan, wise indeed. But the path to the Seer's abode is treacherous and filled with enchantments. Why do you seek the guidance of Caelan the Wise?"

General Ironheart stepped forward, his presence commanding even among the pixies. "We seek counsel to sever a dark power that threatens our lands. Count Malachi, a wielder of demonic forces, must be stopped, and the Seer may hold the key to our victory."

At this, Bramblethorn, the mischievous pixie, couldn't resist chiming in. "Count Malachi, you say? Oh, he's in for trouble now! We've had our fair share of tricks to play on him."

Zephyrwing, the kind-hearted pixie, interjected gently, "But Bramblethorn, this is serious. If these noble travelers require guidance, we should assist them."

Lunaflora, the leader, nodded in agreement and turned to Seraphina and Ironheart. "We will help you on your journey to find Seer Caelan. Our wings can guide you through the enchanted paths, and we know the secrets of the forest better than any other. But we must choose one among us to accompany you."

It was Zephyrwing who stepped forward, her wings shimmering with a serene light. "I shall be your guide," she offered with a warm smile. "I know the way to the Seer's abode, and I promise to assist you to the best of my abilities."

Grateful for the pixies' assistance, Seraphina, Ironheart, and their council accepted Zephyrwing's offer. With a gentle flutter of her opalescent wings, Zephyrwing landed on General Ironheart's shoulder, her presence filling them with a sense of enchantment and camaraderie. As they continued their journey through the Enchanted Forest, Zephyrwing guided them with grace and wisdom, sharing the secrets of the forest and the tales of its mystical inhabitants.

As Seraphina, Ironheart, and their council continued their journey through the Enchanted Forest under the guidance of Zephyrwing, they couldn't help but notice how the forest gradually transformed as they neared the seer's location. The once dense canopy of ancient trees began to thin, allowing dappled sunlight to filter through, casting a soft and ethereal glow on the forest floor. The air itself seemed to hum with an otherworldly energy, and the very atmosphere resonated with magic.

They eventually arrived at a place on the edge of the forest, a tranquil glade surrounded by towering silver birches. This serene clearing was known as the "Whispering Glade," a name earned from the gentle rustling of leaves that seemed to converse with one another in hushed tones. At the center of the glade stood a dwelling that could only be described as a masterpiece of nature and enchantment.

Caelan, the wise seer, resided in a structure that seamlessly blended with the forest around it. His home, which the local mystical creatures referred to as "Sylvan Haven," appeared to be grown rather than built. The walls were made of living tree trunks intertwined with ivy, their bark smooth and luminescent, emanating a soft, greenish-blue light. The roof was a canopy of oversized leaves that acted as both shelter and camouflage. Delicate vines adorned the edges of the dwelling, blooming with vibrant, ever-changing flowers that mirrored Caelan's profound connection to the forest.

Approaching Sylvan Haven, Seraphina, Ironheart, and their council were greeted by the sight of Caelan, the wise seer, who had sensed their arrival. Caelan was a tall, slender figure with an aura of ageless wisdom about him. His skin was weathered and deeply tanned, as if he had spent a lifetime basking in the forest's embrace. Long, silver hair cascaded down his back, adorned with sprigs of wildflowers, each representing a different aspect of nature's balance.

Caelan's attire was a harmonious fusion of earthy tones and natural elements. He wore a robe made from the silken threads of spiderlings that roamed the forest, a garment that seemed to shimmer with an iridescent sheen as it caught the dappled sunlight. A belt made of intertwined vines cinched his waist, adorned with small pouches containing dried herbs and charms to aid in his divinations. His feet were clad in leather sandals crafted from the supple hide of forest creatures, a testament to his respect for the natural world.

As Seraphina, Ironheart, and their council approached Caelan, he turned to face them with eyes as ancient as the forest itself, each iris a different shade of green, resembling the leaves in various stages of life. His gaze held a profound serenity, as if he could see through the very essence of their beings.

"Welcome, travelers," Caelan's voice did chime, his words a rhyme in the forest's prime. "I've long awaited your path's unfolding, for the winds and trees, their stories they're holding. Come, rest a while, and in this haven, we'll converse about the purpose you've braven."

Titania, puzzled by Caelan's rhyming words, couldn't help but inquire, "Why does he speak in rhyme?"

Zephyrwing, the pixie who had been their guide, fluttered her delicate wings and answered with a mischievous twinkle in her eye, "Oh, dear Titania, Caelan the wise, his words in rhyme, it's no surprise. It's how he imparts his ancient lore, through verses and rhythms, his wisdom does pour."

Sir Frostbane, known for his sarcasm, couldn't resist a wry comment, muttering, "Oh, great, just what we needed – a poet–seer in the heart of the Enchanted Forest."

They gathered around Caelan in the Whispering Glade, where the air was filled with the soft murmurings of the leaves and the distant laughter of woodland creatures. As they began their conversation, Caelan shared his visions and insights, unraveling the mysteries of the Enchanted Forest and revealing the path to their quest's fulfillment.

In the presence of Caelan, the wise seer, surrounded by the enchantment of the Enchanted Forest, Seraphina, Ironheart, and their council felt a deep sense of connection to nature and a renewed determination to carry out their mission. They knew that the guidance and wisdom they sought were found in the heart of this mystical realm, and their journey had brought them one step closer to their ultimate goal.

Caelan, the wise seer, continued to speak in rhythmic rhyme, sharing the method to break the demonic power bound to Malachi's pendant. General Ironheart, Seraphina, and Sir Frostbane leaned in, their attention fully captured by the mystical sage.

"With pendant dark and power grim, to break its hold, you'll need to swim," Caelan began, his words flowing in an entrancing melody. "In waters pure, beneath the moon, beneath the stars, you'll find your boon. A crystal pool, where moonlight gleams, will shatter chains, release your dreams."

General Ironheart nodded thoughtfully, absorbing the poetic guidance. "A crystal pool beneath the moonlight," he repeated, committing the words to memory. "We can find such a place within the forest?"

When Ironheart inquired further, asking if they would indeed locate the crystal pools within the forest, Caelan responded with another cryptic rhyme that left them puzzled, "In the forest deep, where secrets lie, the pools await, beneath the sky's eye. Seek the whispers of the ancient trees, and the pools shall grant what your quest decrees."

However, as the seer continued in rhyme, Sir Frostbane's patience began to wane. His frosty demeanor started to crack, and he interjected with a hint of irritation, "Must we endure this endless rhyme? Just tell us straight, and save us time!"

Caelan's gaze fixed on Sir Frostbane, his eyes unwavering. "To break my rhyme, a trial must commence, Seraphina's choice, in her defense. A test of heart, of courage bold, in the Whispering Glade, a story will be told."

Seraphina, her curiosity piqued, turned to the seer. "A trial? What kind of trial, Caelan?"

Caelan's response was cryptic yet alluring, "In the Whispering Glade, you'll face your fate, and there decide your rightful state. To speak in plain words, for Frostbane's sake, the trial's the path you'll need to take."

Sir Frostbane sighed heavily; his impatience clear. "So, you're saying if Seraphina accepts this trial, you'll speak without the rhyme?"

Caelan nodded solemnly, "Aye, that's the choice, the path to climb. If Seraphina's heart so desires, I'll speak in plain words, and Frostbane inquires."

Seraphina, pondering the decision before her, agreed to the trial. "Very well, Caelan. I accept your trial in the Whispering Glade."

As they prepared for the trial, the Enchanted Forest seemed to hold its breath in anticipation. Caelan, with his enigmatic wisdom, led them deeper into the forest, guided by Zephyrwing and the whispers of the ancient trees.

The Whispering Glade, bathed in the soft glow of moonlight filtering through the silver birches, was their destination. Caelan, Seraphina, Ironheart, and Frostbane gathered in a circle, the air filled with a sense of profound magic.

As the moonlight bathed the ancient birches in a silvery glow, Seraphina stood in the center of a circle formed by Caelan, the wise seer, General Ironheart, his council and creatures of the Enchanted Forest. The mystical creatures of the forest had gathered to witness the trial, their eyes filled with both curiosity and sympathy.Among them, graceful luminescent deer with coats that shimmered like moonlit pearls stood in serene reverence. Ethereal sylphs, delicate beings of air and light, fluttered around like iridescent butterflies, their presence adding an otherworldly grace to the solemn assembly. Beside a babbling brook that ran through the glade, water nymphs, with glistening aquatic hair and eyes that mirrored the depths of hidden springs, observed with a deep sense of empathy. Wisps of ethereal light floated nearby, their ephemeral forms resembling glowing orbs of luminescent mist. They moved with a life of their own, dancing in the night breeze and casting playful, fleeting shadows on the forest floor. Fireflies, like tiny living lanterns, dotted the edges of the clearing, their gentle illumination creating a captivating interplay of light and shadow. Their rhythmic, golden pulses added an enchanting cadence to the proceedings, as if the very forest itself had come to life to bear witness to Seraphina's trial.

Caelan, with his solemn expression, began to list the charges against Seraphina, each word imbued with the weight of the forest's ancient wisdom. "You were sacrificed to Count Malachi, to buy his favour, you did comply. Accepted this fate with a heavy heart, from your kingdom torn, you played your part. At the castle of Malachi, you did scheme, used your wits and rides to glean the knowledge sought, but suspicions arose, and Isolde paid with her life, her path now closed."

Seraphina's heart ached as she accepted each charge, her eyes filled with sorrow and regret. General Ironheart and his council exchanged empathetic glances, recognizing the pain in her eyes.

But Caelan continued, "Count Malachi, defiled your grace, stole your virtue in that wicked place." Seraphina's cheeks flushed with shame, and she accepted the charge, unable to meet Ironheart's gaze.

The seer's voice grew even more solemn as he said, "He broke your worth, with cruel abuse, inflicted harm, your body's use." Seraphina's shoulders sagged, and she accepted this charge, feeling the weight of the forest's judgment upon her.

As Caelan spoke of the hardships Seraphina endured, it felt as if her spirit was being slowly crushed beneath the burden of her past. But the seer wasn't finished, and he continued, "Yet you escaped, with wits so keen, Count Malachi's grasp, unseen, you slipped between. For all the darkness you've endured, your light shines bright, your spirit's assured." But then, with a heavy heart, Caelan brought forth another charge, his words heavy with the weight of Seraphina's suffering. "You battle night terrors of Count Malachi's face, a haunting specter in your sleeping space." Seraphina accepted this charge with a shiver, her haunted dreams a constant reminder of the horrors she had faced.

The next charge was equally difficult to bear. "You struggle to fight the darkness deep within, a battle daily, where shadows begin." Seraphina's gaze dropped, and her voice quivered as she accepted the charge, her inner turmoil laid bare.

Caelan continued, "To the City of Angels, you journeyed to find, a cleansing path, a solace for your mind. A daily practice, to mend your soul's sore, you sought the light, to heal evermore." Seraphina accepted this charge, her eyes glistening with unshed tears, her determination to overcome evident.

But then came the most painful accusation of all. "In your first confrontation, alone and beset, darkness interfered, and your stallion, Sir Sterling, met his regret." Seraphina's shoulders shook with grief as she accepted this charge, tears streaming down her cheeks. General Ironheart, unable to bear her suffering any longer, stepped forward to hold her and cast an angry glance at the seer, demanding, "Enough."

However, Caelan's response was unwavering. "The trial is not done," he declared, his voice echoing through the Whispering Glade, leaving an air of uncertainty and foreboding hanging over the assembly.

As the trial continued, Caelan, the wise seer, did not relent, and the charges against Seraphina weighed heavily upon her. The next accusation brought forth an agonizing truth. "Your escape from Count Malachi's grasp, it's told, left your parents in a fate untold." With tears in her eyes and a heavy heart, Seraphina accepted this charge, the guilt of her parents' tragic fate haunting her.

The seer's voice resonated with a mystical resonance as he declared, "The Enchanted Forest, it chose to stand with you, in your battles, your struggles, it was true." Seraphina accepted this charge, her connection with the forest deepening, as she recognized the profound bond that had formed between her and the mystical realm.

But then came the final accusation, one that seemed to encapsulate all the trials she had endured. "No matter the battles you've fought and faced, in the pursuit of light, in darkness you've raced." With a determined spirit, Seraphina accepted this charge, her resolve to overcome the shadows within herself unwavering.

As the weight of these charges settled upon her, Seraphina felt both drained and empowered. She had faced the darkest aspects of her past and her inner struggles, accepting each accusation with grace and humility. The seer's gaze, though stern, held a hint of approval, and the forest itself seemed to sigh in recognition of her resilience.

General Ironheart and his council watched Seraphina with a mixture of sympathy and admiration, their respect for her growing with each acceptance. The trial had been arduous, but it had also revealed the strength and light within Seraphina's heart. The Enchanted Forest, in its mysterious way, had chosen her, and the decision was now in the hands of the wise seer.

Seraphina's heart began to swell with a mix of emotions. She accepted each positive affirmation from Caelan, feeling a glimmer of hope and strength returning to her. The mystical creatures in the glade whispered their support, their presence comforting and reassuring.

Seraphina, her voice now a poetic rhyme, spoke from the depths of her heart, "I accepted the sacrifice, my family's honour and Ravenshadow's love, I held dear in my heart above. For Lady Isolde, a dear friend lost, I wish I could turn back the hands at any cost. But even if I hadn't sought answers, Count Malachi would have taken hers, like a darkened dancer. As property, he saw me, and to break free, I vowed to Lady Isolde, for her soul's decree. I trained with the Elves, to face the dark night, and though my mind's shadows put up a fight, Count Malachi's deeds, like a vampire's bite, left scars on my body, but not my light. I battle not to be consumed by despair, to rise above anger, bitterness, I declare. I'd never have allowed Sir Sterling's harm, but Count Malachi's cunning, like a silent alarm. He devised a plan, with death in mind, I tried to rearrange it, fate unkind. I chose Dracohound's end, it's true, to save Sir Sterling, as best I could do. I'm not perfect, scars show the way, but in the enchanted realm, I've chosen to stay. To stand for what's right, in every fight, I'll strive for the light, with all my might." Her words resonated with determination and the unwavering spirit of one who had faced darkness and emerged with an unyielding resolve to protect the realm she now called home.

Finally, after a long and emotionally tumultuous trial, Caelan, the wise seer, spoke with a sense of finality, "The scales are weighed, your heart's been tried, and in this forest, you'll stand with pride. Seraphina, brave and true, protector of the Enchanted Forest, that's you."

A collective sigh of relief swept through the glade as the mystical creatures of the forest welcomed Seraphina with open arms. General Ironheart, his expression filled with compassion, extended his hand to her, cementing her newfound role as a guardian of the Enchanted Forest. With the weight of her past lifted, Seraphina embraced her destiny with renewed purpose, determined to protect the realm she had come to love.

Caelan, now free from his rhyme, spoke directly, his voice as clear as the forest stream, "In the Whispering Glade, Seraphina, you stand. To speak in plain words, extend your hand."

Seraphina held out her hand, and Caelan continued, "Now choose your words, speak your desire, and I shall answer, with no rhyme to inspire."

Seraphina took a moment to compose her thoughts and then asked, "How do we destroy Malachi's pendant and break the demonic power?" Caelan, without the constraint of rhyme, replied, "To break the pendant's demonic embrace, you must immerse it in the crystal pool's grace. Moonlight must touch it, stars must shine, to sever the bond, and powers malign."

Satisfied with the straightforward answer, Sir Frostbane couldn't help but mutter, "Finally, plain words at last."

Caelan, with a knowing smile, turned to Frostbane, "The rhyme, you see, had its own purpose and cost. It revealed your heart and the patience you've lost. But now, united, you all stand strong, on the path ahead, your journey long."

Seraphina, her voice tinged with frustration, spoke up, "It's impossible to obtain the pendant from Count Malachi; he wears it constantly around his neck."

Caelan, the wise seer, considered her words for a moment before offering an alternative solution in his characteristic rhyme, "To break the pendant's dark embrace, from Malachi's neck, it's not the place. Seek instead his heart's own core, where darkness festers, his soul's true door."

Sir Frostbane couldn't resist a touch of sarcasm as he remarked, "Well, that didn't last long, the plain speaking," his dry tone underscoring the irony of their journey through the world of rhyme and riddles.

Seraphina and the others exchanged curious glances, realizing that the pendant's power was intricately linked to Count Malachi's very being. The seer's enigmatic words hinted at a deeper, more profound way to sever the connection and end the demonic influence.

Seraphina, her resolve unwavering, sought clarification, "Must I defeat Count Malachi with my own sword, piercing his heart, as you imply?"

Caelan, the wise seer, replied in another cryptic rhyme, "In the battle's dance, your sword must gleam, to pierce the darkness, fulfill the dream. But victory's heart, it may not be so plain, for truths within, you must ascertain." His words hung in the air, their meaning shrouded in mystery, challenging Seraphina to decipher the enigma before her. As Caelan, the enigmatic seer, delivered his cryptic response, a sense of mystique lingered in the air. But before further clarification could be sought, the seer declared, "Time is up," and with a gentle wave of his hand, he began to fade into the whispers of the forest, his form slowly becoming translucent. The others were left somewhat puzzled, exchanging uncertain glances, but they knew their journey was far from over.

Guided by Zephyrwing, the pixie, they began their journey back through the Enchanted Forest, riding on the backs of their steeds. During their return, Captain Elara Swiftwoon voiced his confusion, "I'm puzzled by what the seer meant by 'dream.' It's all so cryptic."

Lord Stoneforge, deep in thought, then turned to Seraphina and asked, "Do you have any recurring dreams, Seraphina?"

Seraphina nodded with a thoughtful expression, "Yes, I keep having a dream where Count Malachi and I are on the edge of a mountain, one side shrouded in complete darkness, while the other radiates with fiery red light. Every time, I'm about to strike the final blow to his heart, I wake up."The council members exchanged knowing glances, and General Ironheart spoke with determination, "It seems this dream may hold a significant clue. Seraphina, I will personally show you the different sword techniques and how to land a fatal blow to the heart. We must be prepared for what lies ahead."

With their path clearer and a newfound sense of purpose, they continued their journey through the Enchanted Forest, determined to confront Count Malachi and bring an end to the darkness that had plagued their lives for far too long.

Lady Titania Stormbringer turned to Lady Seraphina with a warm and earnest smile, her eyes filled with admiration. "Seraphina, I have the utmost respect for you, for the strength and resilience you've shown in the face of such adversity. It's an honour beyond words to stand by your side in this battle against Count Malachi. Together, we shall face the darkness and bring light to our realm once more." Her words held a genuine sense of camaraderie and support, strengthening the bond between them as they prepared to confront their formidable foe.

Seraphina, her voice filled with vulnerability, confided in Lady Titania Stormbringer, "Sometimes, Lady Titania, I can't help but feel that what has been done to me affects my self-worth."

General Ironheart, moved by Seraphina's honesty, stepped forward and replied in a heartfelt rhyme, "You're not defined by what's been done, but by the battles fought, the victories won. In my eyes, you shine so bright, a beacon of beauty, a guiding light."

Sir Frostbane, his sarcasm momentarily set aside, couldn't resist a comment. "Oh, come on, Ironheart, now you too? Enough with all this rhyming!"

With a mischievous twinkle in her eye, the pixie Zephyrwing chimed in, "Oh, Sir Frostbane, don't you see? In this forest, it's the way to be! So let's all rhyme and have some fun, under the enchanted moon and sun." Her words were met with a chorus of playful laughter, lightening the mood and reminding them all of the magic of their journey.

Sir Frostbane, with a hint of sarcasm and a touch of playful grumbling, chimed in with a rhyme, "I'm sore from all this riding, so hungry it's confiding, the next rhyme that I hear, I'll toss you in the river, I swear." His attempt at rhyming drew laughter from everyone, appreciating the break from the seriousness.

Lord Stoneforge, curious and concerned, turned to Lady Seraphina and inquired, "My lady, what do you mean by setting Lady Isolde's soul free to rest in peace?"

Seraphina's gaze turned somber as she explained, "In the courtyard of Count Malachi's castle, there lies a garden of thorns, poison ivy, and black roses. Each black rose symbolizes a life lost within the castle, and their trapped souls linger there, tormented by the evil spirits that dwell within its darkened bowers." The realization of the horrors she had faced brought a collective shiver of horror among them, deepening their resolve to confront Count Malachi and put an end to his reign of terror.

As the party journeyed back to the Elven Kingdom, they found themselves facing a new set of challenges, cunningly orchestrated by Count Malachi. They ventured deeper into the Enchanted Forest, where ancient, towering trees seemed to close in around them. Their path led them to a secluded part of the forest where the elusive rock giants dwelled.

These massive creatures, hewn from stone and moss-covered, presented a formidable obstacle. Count Malachi had woven his dark enchantments here, and the giants themselves had fallen under his sinister influence. Unbeknownst to Seraphina and her companions, the Count had Fizzlewick, the mysti-monk, sprinkle mind-control dust on the giants, turning them into unwitting pawns in his twisted game.

The area in the forest where the rock giants resided was a place of ancient grandeur and mystique. Towering trees with gnarled branches stretched overhead, forming a dense canopy that filtered the sunlight into dappled, ethereal patterns on the forest floor. Moss-covered boulders and enormous, lichen-covered stones were scattered throughout, giving the impression of an ancient, forgotten realm untouched by time.

The air in this secluded part of the forest held a palpable sense of age and wisdom, as if the very trees whispered secrets from centuries past. Vines and ivy draped gracefully over the stones, adding to the aura of ancient enchantment. Dew-kissed ferns and delicate, luminescent mushrooms carpeted the ground, casting an otherworldly glow that intensified the mystique of the place.

It was amidst this primeval setting that the massive rock giants arose from the very earth itself. Their immense stone forms blended seamlessly with the surroundings, appearing as if they were natural outgrowths of the ancient forest. With their mossy exteriors and inscrutable expressions, they exuded an air of both power and enigma.

The area where the rock giants resided was a testament to the enduring magic of the Enchanted Forest, a place where the line between reality and fantasy blurred, and the ancient spirits of the realm seemed to stir, watching with keen interest as intruders ventured into their domain. It was in this hauntingly beautiful, ageless place that Seraphina and her companions faced the giants' mind games, navigating the thin boundary between illusion and reality as they sought to unravel the mysteries that lay before them.

The awakening of the rock giants in the Enchanted Forest was a result of Count Malachi's sinister machinations. The malevolent sorcerer had sought to use every means at his disposal to hinder Seraphina and her companions on their quest to confront him.

Count Malachi had Fizzlewick sprinkle enchanted mind-control dust over the ancient stones where the giants lay dormant. This dust, imbued with his dark magic, had seeped into the very core of the rock giants, ensnaring their consciousness and bending them to his will.

As Seraphina and her party approached the secluded area in the forest, they unwittingly triggered the effects of the mind-control dust. The giants, their massive stone forms stirring to life, were drawn from their slumber by Count Malachi's malevolent influence. Their eyes glowed with an unnatural light, and they became pawns in the sorcerer's twisted game, compelled to challenge the intruders and obstruct their progress.

It was the dark sorcery of Count Malachi, combined with the ancient power of the forest itself, that awakened the rock giants and compelled them to pose riddles as a means of testing the resolve and intellect of those who dared to tread upon their sacred ground. Under the influence of the mind-control dust, the giants' once tranquil and dormant existence had been twisted into a malevolent force, serving the sorcerer's nefarious plans.

As they approached, the giants came to life, their enormous forms rising from the forest floor with thunderous footsteps. Their eyes glowed with an unnatural light, and their voices rumbled like distant thunder as they spoke in unison, "You shall not pass unless you answer our riddles, for Count Malachi's game is not yet won."

General Ironheart, his brow furrowed with determination, stepped forward, ready to face the giants' challenge. "Very well, we accept your riddles. Proceed."

The rock giants' voices reverberated through the ancient trees as they posed their riddles, each one more perplexing than the last. The air grew thick with tension as the party struggled to unravel the giants' cryptic questions, their minds clouded by the lingering effects of the mind–control dust.

The first riddle from the rock giants boomed through the forest, challenging the party's intellect:

"I can fly without wings, cry without eyes, wherever I go, darkness dies. What am I?"

General Ironheart furrowed his brow, pondering the enigma, but before he could respond, Lady Titania Stormbringer stepped forward with confidence. "It's a star," she declared. "Stars seem to fly across the night sky, they twinkle like tears, and their light banishes the darkness."

The rock giants acknowledged her answer with a nod, and the party breathed a sigh of relief.

The second riddle came in a deep, rumbling voice:

"In mine hand, I hold keys yet unlock no gates, a realm of space, devoid of walls and rates. You may enter, but naught inside you'd find. What am I?"

The words echoed through the air, the riddle a perplexing puzzle that momentarily confounded Seraphina and her companions.

However, it was Lady Titania Stormbringer's keen intellect that pierced through the enigma once more. She declared with confidence, "It is a tome of parchment! With keys of ink and quill, it unlocks knowledge's gates. Its space is in the words, but no physical room it creates, and you may enter its pages, but within, you'll not reside." Her astute answer dispelled the mystique of the riddle, much to their relief.

The rock giants nodded in agreement, and the party pressed on.

The third and final riddle was the most complex of all:

"Alive without breath, as cold as death, never thirsty, ever drinking, all in mail, but never clinking. What am I?"

Seraphina and her companions exchanged puzzled glances, but it was Lady Titania Stormbringer who stepped forward once more, her eyes bright with insight. She answered confidently, "It's a fish! Fish are alive underwater without breathing air, they're cold-blooded, they live in water but never drink it, and they have scales that are like armour but don't make a clinking sound."

As Lady Titania Stormbringer confidently provided the answer to the final riddle, a profound change overcame the rock giants. Their stony expressions, once fixed in an eerie, enchantment-induced gaze, began to soften. The unnatural glow in their eyes flickered and dimmed, replaced by a sense of recognition and clarity.

With each correct answer, it was as though a veil of confusion and malevolence had lifted from the giants' massive forms. Their stone bodies, once poised to hinder the party's progress, seemed to relax, and their colossal figures became less imposing.

The rock giants exchanged knowing glances among themselves, and a rumbling, harmonious sigh resonated from their depths. It was a sound that conveyed both relief and gratitude, as if they had been trapped in their own nightmarish riddle and had now found release.

With a unanimous gesture, the giants stepped aside, their once–threatening presence now transformed into a benevolent one. They allowed Seraphina and her companions to continue on their quest, their stone forms no longer infused with Count Malachi's dark influence.

The enchantment was broken, and the giants, restored to their ancient, noble selves, stood as silent guardians of the forest once more.

The rock giants, their massive stone forms looming overhead, had posed their challenging riddles, and Lady Titania Stormbringer had successfully answered them one by one. As the giants nodded in acknowledgment, they added a foreboding consequence to the riddles.

"If you had not solved our riddles," one of the giants rumbled ominously, "not only would you have been denied passage through our domain, but you would have become our dinner."

A collective shiver ran through the party at the grim revelation. The giants' intentions had been far more sinister than mere obstruction. Count Malachi's enchantment had turned them into enigmatic gatekeepers, and the consequence of failure was as chilling as the forest itself.

With their minds now clear of the mind–control dust's influence and the riddles successfully answered, the party was grateful that they had not fallen victim to the giants' dark appetite. They continued their journey, their hearts heavy with the realization of the dangers lurking in the Enchanted Forest, all orchestrated by Count Malachi's malevolent designs.

As the rock giants stood aside, allowing Seraphina and her companions to continue their journey, Sir Frostbane couldn't help but offer a sardonic comment. With a wry grin, he quipped, "Well, tossing a rock giant into the river might be a tougher job than expected. I think I'll stick to my usual tactics, thank you very much."

His jest drew a chorus of chuckles from the party members, lightening the mood after the tense encounter with the awakened giants. They moved forward, knowing that more challenges and mysteries awaited them in the Enchanted Forest, but with their spirits unbroken and their bonds of camaraderie stronger than ever they forged onwards to the Elven Kingdom.

Fizzlewick the mysti-monk, concealed among the ancient branches of a towering oak tree, had witnessed the entire encounter with the rock giants. He marveled at how Seraphina and her companions had managed to break the enchantment placed upon the giants. Intrigued and yet somewhat alarmed by their resilience, he decided to take matters into his own hands.

Patiently, he awaited the perfect moment. As Lady Seraphina rode beneath the tree where he hid, Fizzlewick sprinkled a small amount of mind-control dust from his mystical pouch onto the path below. Count Malachi, attuned to the arcane, immediately sensed the connection forming, and a wicked grin curled on his lips.

"My, my, let's see how this will play out," Count Malachi mused, his dark influence extending towards Lady Seraphina's vulnerable mind. The sorcerer began to weave illusions, casting sinister shadows amidst the ancient trees of the Enchanted Forest.

As Seraphina continued to ride on her faithful unicorn, Lumina, her surroundings began to distort. The once serene and captivating forest transformed into a nightmarish realm. She saw twisted, grotesque shapes lurking among the trees, their eyes gleaming with malevolence. Ghostly whispers filled her ears, taunting her with chilling threats.

As Lady Seraphina's mind was ensnared by Count Malachi's dark enchantment, she heard chilling threats whispered into her ears, each one more sinister than the last:

"In these shadows, Seraphina, your fears shall find life. You are trapped, and no one can save you now."

"The forest's guardians will turn against you, and your companions will become your enemies. Embrace the darkness that awaits."

"Count Malachi's grip tightens, Lady Seraphina. Soon, there will be no escape, and your spirit will wither in despair."

"Beware, for your beloved kingdom Ravenshadow crumbles in your absence, and your people suffer for your failures."

"You are alone, Seraphina, abandoned by those who once cherished you. Your destiny is sealed in the heart of darkness."

These menacing whispers echoed in her mind, tormenting her with a sense of isolation and impending doom. The threats were designed to erode her willpower and fill her with dread, a cruel manifestation of Count Malachi's malevolent power.

Terrified, Seraphina dismounted Lumina, who whinnied in distress, trying to understand what had befallen her beloved rider. Seraphina, overcome with fear, cowered at the foot of one of the gnarled, ancient trees, her heart pounding with dread.

Her once-graceful posture had crumpled into a trembling and huddled form, her back pressed against the rough bark, and her hands clutching at the earth below.

The forest around her, once a place of enchanting beauty, had twisted into a nightmarish realm. Dark, sinister shadows danced amidst the ancient trees, and ghostly whispers filled the air with ominous promises. Her vision was marred by illusions that distorted the very fabric of reality.

Unable to distinguish between the horrors her mind conjured and the true world, she let out a piercing, despairing scream that shattered the eerie silence of the forest. Her cry was filled with terror and anguish, a desperate plea for release from the relentless grip of the enchantment.

Her voice echoed through the ancient trees, carrying her distress to the ears of her companions. They rushed to her side, their faces etched with concern and confusion, but they could not see the malevolent illusions that plagued her. She was trapped within her own mind, lost in a phantasmagoric nightmare of Count Malachi's creation.

General Ironheart and the council were bewildered, unable to comprehend what was happening. They scanned the forest but saw nothing out of the ordinary. It was as if Seraphina was trapped in a nightmarish dimension only she could perceive.

Then, Count Malachi's malevolent laughter echoed through the air, a sinister sound that sent shivers down their spines. It was the moment of realization. Seraphina must be ensnared by enchantment, her mind manipulated by dark forces beyond their understanding.

Without hesitation, they all dismounted their horses, moving closer to Seraphina's trembling form. Lumina, the unicorn, nuzzled Seraphina gently, trying to comfort her. But the horrors her mind conjured were relentless, weaving a tapestry of torment that only she could see.

Just as hope seemed to dwindle, a radiant spectacle unfolded before them. A phoenix, resplendent and majestic, descended from the heavens. Its feathers shimmered in hues of crimson, gold, and azure, casting a vivid spectrum of colours onto the forest floor. The sight left everyone in awe, their gazes locked on the mythical creature.

Lysandra, the phoenix, landed gracefully among them, her presence filling the clearing with a sense of ethereal wonder. She turned her luminous gaze toward General Ironheart and spoke with an enchanting voice that resonated with wisdom.

"General Ironheart, we must take Lady Seraphina to the crystal-clear stream nearby," Lysandra advised. "The enchantment that plagues her is borne of mind-control dust. The pure waters will wash it away, and she shall return to herself."

Moved by Lysandra's beauty and the urgency of the situation, General Ironheart nodded solemnly. As Lady Seraphina's companions hurried to her side to aid her, another mystical presence emerged from the nearby stream. Water nymphs, ethereal and delicate, with skin the colour of moonlit pearls, appeared from the glistening waters. They shimmered like liquid crystal in the fading light of day, their graceful forms radiating an otherworldly beauty.

These water nymphs, no taller than a human's forearm, moved with an air of elegance and serenity. Their hair cascaded like cascading waterfalls, flowing with the hues of the clearest streams, and their eyes held the wisdom of ancient rivers.

With gentle, shimmering hands, they assisted in Seraphina's cleansing. Their touch was soft and cool as they cupped the stream's pristine waters in their palms and tenderly poured them over Seraphina's trembling form. The water nymphs' presence was both soothing and enchanting, a testament to the magic that thrived in the Enchanted Forest.

Their efforts harmonized with those of Lysandra, the majestic phoenix, as they worked together to wash away the enchanted dust that had ensnared Lady Seraphina's mind. The nymphs' ethereal presence and the clear waters of the stream created a sense of tranquility amidst the chaos of the forest.

As the nymphs performed their cleansing ritual, their song-like laughter filled the air, echoing with the serenity of flowing water. Their delicate and graceful forms moved in harmony, their radiant presence a testament to the enchanting wonders that awaited those who ventured into the heart of the Enchanted Forest.

Slowly, as the pristine waters cleansed her, Seraphina's trembling subsided. Her vision cleared, and the nightmarish illusions receded. She took a deep, shuddering breath, her eyes refocusing on the world around her.

The Enchanted Forest, once again bathed in the soft light of the setting sun, returned to its serene and captivating beauty. Seraphina's companions watched with relief as her fear-stricken features gave way to recognition and clarity.

The enchantment was broken, thanks to the timely arrival of Lysandra, the resplendent phoenix. Seraphina, though still shaken, had returned to herself, her mind no longer a battleground for dark illusions.

Captain Elara Swiftwind's keen eyes caught a glimpse of movement among the forest's ancient trees, a glimmer of light reflecting off what appeared to be emerald-hued fur. His bow was within reach, but his arrows lay scattered on the forest floor, abandoned in his rush to aid Lady Seraphina.

As if sensing his dilemma, Lysandra, the majestic phoenix, extended one of her iridescent feathers toward him, a gift from her ethereal plumage. The feather was a wonder to behold, its quill shimmering with an otherworldly iridescence, and its tip pointed to perfection.

With gratitude, Captain Swiftwind accepted the offered feather, and, using it as an arrowhead, he knocked it to his bowstring. The feather felt light and incredibly balanced, a testament to its mystical nature.

He drew back his bowstring, aiming at the source of the emerald glint, his movements steady and precise. With a twang, the feathered arrow flew through the air with a grace and swiftness that defied the laws of ordinary arrows. It struck its target true, and a figure fell from the tree with a thud, landing lifeless on the forest floor.

As the party cautiously approached the fallen figure, their eyes widened in curiosity and uncertainty. None among them had seen such a being before.

Perplexed by the sight before them, they turned to Lysandra, who had watched the unfolding events with her radiant gaze. The phoenix, with her regal presence, explained, "It is a mystic-monk, a reclusive creature of the Enchanted Forest. They are known to possess unique and powerful enchantments, often remaining hidden from the world. This one, it seems, had a role to play in the enchantment that befell Lady Seraphina."

With a sense of reverence and curiosity, they examined the mystic-monk's enigmatic form, pondering the secrets it held and the part it had played in their recent trials. The Enchanted Forest continued to reveal its mysteries, both wondrous and unsettling, as they journeyed deeper into its heart to the Elven Kingdom.

Lysandra, the magnificent phoenix, extended her radiant wings and let out a melodious call that echoed through the Enchanted Forest. In response, a shimmering congregation of forest fairies descended from the canopies above. They were delicate and luminous, their wings like gossamer, and they moved with an ethereal grace.

The fairies, attuned to the forest's ancient magic, had gathered to fulfill the solemn duty of laying the mysti-monk to rest. With their guidance, the party gently lifted the fallen creature and carried it to a serene glade, bathed in dappled sunlight.

In this sacred space, surrounded by towering trees and the soft murmur of a crystal-clear brook, they prepared the mysti-monk's final resting place. The fairies sprinkled petals of enchanting blue flowers around the spot, creating a circle of vibrant blooms that seemed to resonate with the forest's magic.

With a sense of reverence, they laid the mysti-monk to rest, their hands touching the emerald fur with care. The forest fairies chanted softly, their voices like a harmonious melody that soothed the soul. The earth itself seemed to respond to their incantations, embracing the mysti-monk with a sense of serenity and tranquility.

As they completed the burial, the blue flowers that encircled the resting place bloomed with renewed vibrancy, as if the forest itself mourned the misguided fate of the mysti-monk.

Lord Stoneforge, curious about the forest's response to a being that had been influenced by Count Malachi, raised his inquiry. "Why does the forest seem to mourn something that was bad?" he asked.

Lysandra, her feathers gleaming with wisdom, answered, "The mysti-monk may have been led astray by Count Malachi, but mysti-monks, in general, are not inherently malevolent beings. The Enchanted Forest mourns not for the darkness within one's heart but for the potential that was lost, the light that could have shone. It is a reminder that even in the midst of enchantment, there is a spark of goodness to be cherished."

With a final, mournful cry that echoed through the glade, the forest fairies completed their ritual, and the mysti-monk was laid to rest in the heart of the Enchanted Forest, surrounded by a circle of vibrant blue flowers. The Enchanted Forest continued to weave its mysteries, showing that even in the face of darkness, there remained a glimmer of hope and beauty to be found.

As Count Malachi monitored the enchantment he had woven around Lady Seraphina, his malevolent influence that had once gripped her mind began to wane. He sensed the tethers of his dark magic slipping away, like threads unraveling from his control.

In a surge of anger and frustration, Count Malachi realized that something had disrupted his influence. He attempted to reach out to Fizzlewick, the mysti-monk he had previously used as a conduit, but there was only silence. The telepathic connection he had with Fizzlewick had vanished.

Rage boiled within Count Malachi as he recognized that not only had he lost his hold over Seraphina, but Fizzlewick, too, had been severed from his grasp. The notion that an unknown force had interfered with his plans infuriated him, and his desire for vengeance burned hotter than ever.

The sorcerer's dark intentions were far from quenched, and he vowed to redouble his efforts to ensnare Seraphina and those who dared to oppose him. The Enchanted Forest held secrets, and Count Malachi was determined to uncover them, no matter the cost.

Count Malachi, seething with anger and resolve, retreated to his dark sanctum to conjure a new abomination. This time, he seized one of the Serpentsteeds, transforming it through the malevolent portal into a monstrous hybrid known as "Dracernoth," a serpent-steed infused with dragon-like scales, wings, and a ravenous hunger for destruction.

The Abyss Beckons

With wings that spanned the width of a carriage and scales that shimmered with an ominous fusion of deep emerald and obsidian black, the Dracernoth was a nightmarish spectacle to behold. Its fiery eyes burned with an insatiable hunger, and its serpentine body coiled with a lethal grace.

Count Malachi, standing in his dark sanctum, gazed upon the Dracernoth with malevolent satisfaction. He had succeeded in his dark experiment, infusing the once-elegant Serpentsteed with the essence of a dragon. Its every movement exuded an aura of dread and power, a nightmarish embodiment of the sorcerer's twisted ambitions.

So pleased was Count Malachi with this monstrous creation that he resolved to extend his malevolent reach further. With a malevolent grin, he beckoned forth all the remaining Serpentsteeds, sending them through the evil portal to be transformed into the dreaded Dracernoths. The Enchanted Forest, once a realm of enchantment and wonder, now faced an even graver threat as these new abominations gathered, ready to unleash their terror upon any who dared to oppose their dark master.

The Dracernoth, Count Malachi's nightmarish creation, was a monstrous fusion of various creatures, each aspect contributing to its dreadful appearance. Its body was equine, resembling that of a powerful warhorse, with a sturdy and muscular frame that exuded strength. This horse-like torso, covered in dark emerald scales, gave it a deceptive aura of elegance.

The creature's legs, however, were serpentine, adorned with scales that glistened with a sinister sheen. These elongated, sinuous limbs allowed the Dracernoth to slither and glide through the forest with uncanny speed and agility, striking fear into the hearts of any who beheld it.

Its tail, reminiscent of a lizard's, trailed behind it, tapering to a venomous point. It lashed and coiled with an unsettling grace, poised to strike at a moment's notice. The tail's scales, like the rest of its body, were a dark and foreboding shade, a stark contrast to the vibrant life of the Enchanted Forest.

However, it was the head and neck of the Dracernoth that inspired the most dread. It resembled that of a malevolent dragon, with gleaming crimson eyes that radiated malevolence and an array of dagger-like teeth that jutted from its gaping maw. Smoke and searing fire occasionally billowed from its snarling jaws, as if it carried the very essence of destruction within.

As the Dracernoth moved through Shadowmoor, it left a trail of terror in its wake, a grotesque amalgamation of the creatures from which it drew its features. It was a creature born of darkness and malevolence, a relentless instrument of Count Malachi's wicked designs upon the once-peaceful realm.

The six giant black wolves that had once been obedient servants of Count Malachi, pulling his iron carriage with ominous strength, were transformed into even more nightmarish entities when they passed through the dark portal. Emerging on the other side, they had undergone a grotesque metamorphosis.

Their once-sleek ebony fur had darkened further, taking on an ashy, charcoal hue. These hulking creatures now possessed not one, but three menacing heads atop sinewy necks. Each head was crowned with a triad of crimson eyes that glowed with a malevolent hunger.

The triple-headed wolves moved with an eerie coordination, their massive bodies rippling with grotesque power. Their snarls echoed through the Shadownmoor like a symphony of dread, a haunting melody that struck terror into any who encountered them.

Count Malachi had amplified their fearsome nature, granting them the ability to breathe forth streams of searing, emerald-hued flames from all three of their nightmarish maws. These fiery breath attacks left scorched paths in the once-verdant fields, a cruel testament to their newfound power.

As they roamed through Shadowmoor, their malevolence intensified, and their monstrous forms served as a reminder of the depths of Count Malachi's dark sorcery. The realm, once a sanctuary of enchantment, now faced a dire threat from these grotesque, multi-headed creatures and their relentless master.

It was a distant age, so shrouded in the mists of time that it felt almost like a fading dream, when Shadowmoor was a realm of tranquility and abundance. The land was once bathed in the gentle light of a thousand stars, its forests teeming with vibrant life, and its waters clear and sparkling like liquid crystal. The echoes of laughter and songs of jubilation filled the air, a testament to a time when the realm knew only peace and prosperity. Yet, as the years passed and the shadowy veil of darkness descended upon Shadowmoor, those halcyon days grew ever more elusive, their memory fading like a distant whisper in the night.

Count Malachi, his malevolent figure silhouetted against the pulsating darkness of the portal, turned to gaze upon the nightmarish army he had summoned. The wolves, once regal and fierce, had become demonic entities with their triple heads and searing breath, while the Dracernoths exuded an aura of terror. His eyes scanned the ranks of his unholy legions, their forms twisted and tainted by the abyss.

However, amidst the eerie stillness that had settled upon the Shadowmoor, a deep and menacing voice reverberated from within the portal. It was a demon, known as Mordrak, and he emerged as an ominous presence from the abyss. His crimson eyes smoldered with an infernal fire as he addressed Count Malachi, stating that the newfound power and creatures the portal had bestowed upon him came at a price.

Count Malachi, undeterred by the foreboding presence before him, replied with a cold resolve. He offered the demon the remnants of his soul in exchange for the dark power he now wielded. Yet, Mordrak's response was chilling. He declared that there was no soul left to barter with, and Count Malachi would need to find something more substantial as payment.

In a calculating moment, Count Malachi considered the lives he could sacrifice to settle his debt. He spoke of Lady Isabella, the mage he had ensnared, and the Veridales, a family of considerable power and influence. He asked the demon what price would be sufficient to settle his current debt and earn him favour in the infernal realms. Mordrak's reply sent shivers down Count Malachi's servants' spine, for it meant that the Shadowmoor and all who dwelled within it were on the brink of a darker and more perilous fate.

Count Malachi, driven by his malevolent pact with Mordrak, unleashed the demonic wolves upon the Veridales family, a name that once held prestige and honour within the Ravenshadow. With a chilling command, he set the nightmarish creatures into motion.

The demonic wolves surged forward with unnatural speed, their triple heads raised in a sinister chorus of snarls. Their claws dug into the soil as they sprinted through the twisted, shadowy evil forest that linked their dark realm to the pure heart of the Enchanted Forest. The very ground quaked beneath their infernal footsteps, leaving scorched marks in their wake.

As they emerged from the abyssal into the Enchanted Forest, their eyes gleamed with a malevolent hunger, and their fiery breath spilled forth like molten venom. The Veridales family, unaware of the impending doom, stood unsuspecting, their once-idyllic home now tainted by the encroaching darkness.

The wolves, guided by their demonic instincts, descended upon the Veridales estate on the edge of the Enchated Forest with an unholy ferocity. What had once been a haven of peace was now marred by chaos and destruction.

With Count Malachi's malevolent command, the demonic wolves surged forth, a nightmarish embodiment of destruction, their three heads raised in a sinister chorus of snarls. As they sprinted through the dark and malevolent forest that lay beyond the portal, the very earth trembled beneath their infernal strides. They moved with a supernatural swiftness, leaving scorched marks upon the ancient, gnarled trees and tainted earth.

Stalking like phantoms of doom, the demonic wolves moved onto the estate grounds, their predatory instincts finely tuned for the slaughter that lay ahead. It was a serene afternoon, and the Veridales family had gathered outside for tea, their laughter and conversation drifting through the fragrant air.

With a sudden and horrifying attack, the wolves fell upon the unsuspecting family, their triple heads unleashing a nightmarish chorus of snarls and flames. Chaos erupted as the once-tranquil setting was transformed into a scene of bloodshed and terror. Ravenshadow, its heart now tainted by darkness, bore witness to the gruesome tableau of violence as the Veridales family fought for their lives against the relentless onslaught of Count Malachi's demonic minions.

The demonic wolves, driven by their infernal hunger and Count Malachi's malevolent will, left no trace of the Veridales family in their wake. As swiftly as they had descended upon the estate, they vanished into the shadows, leaving behind only the grim remnants of their grisly attack.

The Veridales estate, once a place of laughter and serenity, was now marked by the sinister smears of blood and tattered remnants of clothing. There were no survivors, and the wolves had ensured that no trace of their victims remained. The scene was a grotesque tableau of violence, where the beauty of the estate had been replaced by the chilling evidence of unspeakable horror.

The once-tranquil grounds bore witness to the malevolence that had taken root within the forest, and the very air seemed heavy with sorrow and despair. The Veridales family, who had once graced this estate with their presence, had become victims of a darkness that threatened to consume all that was once pure and enchanting in the realms.

Count Malachi, master of dark sorcery, materialized once more within Lady Isabella's chambers, his demonic abilities allowing him to traverse space in the blink of an eye. This time, Lady Isabella was not as shocked as her first encounter with the sinister sorcerer, though her demeanor remained cautious.

Count Malachi, his crimson eyes gleaming with an unholy hunger, stood in the dimly lit chamber, an aura of malevolence surrounding him. Lady Isabella, her features marked by both trepidation and curiosity, faced him with a newfound resolve.

Isabella, her voice laced with caution, "Count Malachi, what is it that you truly desire from me this time?"

Count Malachi, his voice silky and dark, "My dear Lady Isabella, I seek a piece of your very soul, a price that will grant me dominion over your essence."

Isabella, her curiosity piqued, "And what do I stand to gain in return for such a macabre exchange?"

Count Malachi, a sinister smile playing on his lips, "In exchange for your soul, I shall make you my queen of darkness, granting you power beyond your wildest dreams."

Isabella, her contemplation turning darker, "Power... I've yearned for it, lusted after it, and now you promise to bestow it upon me. Very well, Count Malachi, I agree to your terms."

Their pact sealed, Count Malachi began the arcane ritual, drawing a piece of his own malevolent soul and intertwining it with Isabella's essence. The act was an unholy communion, a merging of darkness that bound them together in a twisted bond of malefic power.

Count Malachi extended his clawed hand toward Lady Isabella, his fingers trembling with sinister anticipation. He muttered incantations in a language long forgotten by mortals, invoking the very essence of the abyss. A dark, swirling miasma emanated from his palm, a spectral haze of malevolence that seemed to writhe with a life of its own.

Lady Isabella, though her heart was heavy with trepidation, extended her hand to meet Count Malachi's. Her fingers brushed against his, and in that instant, a shiver ran down her spine as if the cold touch of the abyss itself had reached out to claim her.

With a surge of dark power, Count Malachi drew forth a fragment of his malevolent soul, a swirling, shadowy wisp that danced like black fire. It hovered between their entwined hands, radiating an aura of maleficence.

The act that followed was a nightmarish communion—an unholy merging of darkness and light. Count Malachi's malevolent essence melded with Isabella's very being, intertwining with her soul. It was a grotesque dance of shadows and ethereal tendrils that bound them together in a twisted bond of malefic power.

Their union was marked by an eerie symphony of whispered incantations, the air thick with the scent of brimstone and the faint echoes of ancient curses. As their souls fused, a malevolent energy surged through them, sealing their dark pact with an irrevocable bond that promised power, but at the cost of their humanity.

As the ritual concluded, they were left with the unsettling awareness that their fates were now intertwined, and their dark ambitions were aligned.

Count Malachi, his eyes ablaze with the malevolent power of their unholy pact, leaned closer to Lady Isabella. In a voice laced with seductive darkness, he whispered, "To seal our covenant completely, it must be bound in flesh." Lady Isabella, her resolve unyielding, nodded her agreement, her voice filled with dark devotion. "Yes, my Dark King," she replied, laying herself upon the bed as a willing sacrifice for their twisted union. As Count Malachi descended upon her, their flesh merged in a nightmarish embrace, sealing their sinister bond with an act that marked the beginning of their reign of darkness in the realms.

After the sinister union was sealed in flesh, Count Malachi watched his Dark Queen, Lady Isabella, as she dressed herself in a flowing black gown that seemed to absorb the very light around it. The gown was finished with intricate, blood-red embroidery that twisted into patterns of malevolent beauty, a fitting attire for the Dark Queen of the Shadowmoor.

With an air of command, Count Malachi instructed Lady Isabella to perform the blood sacrifice that would cement their unholy bond. And then, with an ominous flourish, he disappeared, leaving her with her dark task.

Lady Isabella, now cloaked in darkness, made her way to King Alaric's chambers. Her allure was irresistible as she seduced the unsuspecting king, drawing him onto the bed. As she straddled him, her hands moved deftly to grasp the knife that lay nearby. With a savage, swift motion, she slit his throat, and the room was filled with the macabre symphony of his dying gasps.

In the throes of this gruesome act, Lady Isabella smeared the king's blood over her body, her voice rising in a frenzied chant of triumph. "I have done it, my Dark King! I have done your sacrifice!"

A surge of unholy power coursed through her veins, her once-potent magic now intensified to an unprecedented level. It was a dark gift that Count Malachi had bestowed upon her, and it left her feeling invincible.

In the hushed shadows of the chamber, Count Malachi's voice whispered in her mind, a sinister invitation. "Now, my Dark Queen, it is time to join me in Shadowmoor."

With unwavering resolve, Lady Isabella left behind the life she once knew, embarking on a dark journey to join her malevolent king in the depths of Shadowmoor, where their reign of darkness would know no bounds.

Rising from the Ashes

In the wake of the gruesome act committed by Lady Isabella, the kingdom was thrown into chaos. Ravenshadow's council discovered King Alaric's lifeless body in his chambers, his throat cruelly slit. Lady Isabella was nowhere to be found, raising suspicion and fear among the council members.

The council, in their distress, immediately suspected the Veridales family, given their dark reputation and the enmity between the two factions. Hurriedly, they dispatched a group to the Veridales estate, only to find it marked with the gruesome signs of violence—bloodshed and a sense of malevolence that seemed to linger in the air.

Alarmed by the developments, they swiftly penned a letter to the elves of the Elven Kingdom, informing them of the tragedy that had befallen King Alaric and the ominous disappearance of Lady Isabella.

Meanwhile, in the Elven Kingdom, Lady Seraphina, General Ironheart, and their council were warmly received after their successful journey to the seer. The elves celebrated their return with a grand feast, celebrating the safe return of their allies and the knowledge they had gained from Caelan, the wise seer.

As the festivities continued, General Elowen of the elves approached Lady Seraphina, General Ironheart, and their council. With a solemn expression, he presented them with a sealed scroll that had arrived from Ravenshadow. It was a scroll that carried dire news and would cast a long shadow over the Enchanted Forest, setting in motion events that would shape their future.

The scroll from Ravenshadow, bearing the weight of ominous tidings, was carefully unsealed by General Elowen. As he unrolled the parchment, the council members of both the Enchanted Forest and the Elven Kingdom leaned in, their faces etched with a mix of curiosity and concern. The words on the scroll spoke of King Alaric's murder, the disappearance of Lady Isabella, and the suspicion cast upon the Veridales family.

The scroll also conveyed Ravenshadow's intent to seek justice and answers, imploring the elves to cooperate in unraveling the mysteries that shrouded the tragic events. It was a call for unity in the face of darkness and uncertainty.

Once the scroll's contents were read, General Elowen addressed Lady Seraphina, General Ironheart, and their council with a somber tone.

General Elowen, his voice filled with gravitas, "This scroll bears dire news from Ravenshadow. King Alaric has been murdered, and Lady Isabella, a name associated with treachery, has vanished. Our allies are in turmoil, suspecting the Veridales family, but we must not jump to conclusions. These events cast a shadow over the Enchanted Forest, and we are called upon to aid in seeking the truth and restoring stability."

Lady Seraphina, her expression a mixture of concern and determination, "We must investigate and uncover the truth behind these tragic events. Lady Isabella's actions are suspect but let us not forget the malevolent force that Count Malachi represents. It is possible he had a hand in these dark deeds".

General Ironheart , nodding in agreement, "We must tread carefully and with unity. The Enchanted Forest and the Elven Kingdom have been bound in friendship and cooperation for centuries. We shall extend our support to Ravenshadow and work together to bring justice and light to this grim situation."

Elven Council Member, with a resolute expression, "Let it be known that the elves of the Elven Kingdom stand with you. We shall lend our wisdom, our magic, and our strength to uncover the truth and bring those responsible to justice. United, we shall face this darkness that threatens our lands."

The discussion concluded with a solemn vow to uphold the bonds of friendship and cooperation that had endured between the Enchanted Forest and the Elven Kingdom. Together, they would confront the shadow that had fallen over their realms and seek the answers that would restore peace and harmony to their enchanted lands.

The next day, Lady Seraphina, General Ironheart, and General Elowen embarked on their journey to Ravenshadow, a sense of urgency guiding their every step. They first made a solemn stop at the Veridales estate, where an eerie silence hung heavily in the air. The estate, once a symbol of opulence, was now marred by tragedy. Its grounds were marked with signs of violence—crimson stains on the earth, shards of shattered glass, and an air of malevolence that seemed to linger.

Lady Seraphina, her expression a mix of sadness and determination, couldn't help but wonder about the role of Lady Isabella in these dark events. General Ironheart maintained a watchful stance, his eyes scanning the scene for any clues or evidence that might shed light on the mysteries surrounding the estate. General Elowen, his demeanor resolute, recognized the gravity of the situation and the need for their cooperation.

From there, they continued their journey to the Ravenshadow Castle, it stood as a majestic testament to the enchantment and grandeur of the Enchanted Forest. Perched atop a gentle hill, the castle's stone walls were overgrown with ivy and moss, giving it an air of timeless mysticism. Tall towers with pointed spires reached for the sky, and turrets offered panoramic views of the surrounding forest.

The castle's architecture was a harmonious blend of natural elements and ancient craftsmanship. Elaborate stained glass windows depicted scenes from the forest's folklore, casting colourful patterns of light into the halls. Beautifully crafted iron lanterns, adorned with delicate vines and ethereal fireflies, provided a soft and magical glow that illuminated the corridors.

Within the castle's labyrinthine halls, there were grand chambers with vaulted ceilings and ornate frescoes celebrating the beauty of the kingdom. The library was a treasure trove of ancient tomes, its shelves lined with books that held the wisdom of generations. Secret passages and hidden chambers added an element of intrigue to the castle's design.

The heart of Ravenshadow Castle was the grand hall, where the council gathered to make important decisions and host gatherings. This hall was resplendent with a long, polished marble table, and crystal chandeliers hung from the vaulted ceiling, casting a warm and inviting light. Elaborate tapestries decorated the walls, telling the stories of the Ravenshadow's legendary heroes.

Overall, Ravenshadow Castle was not merely a place of residence; it was a symbol of the kingdom's rich history, its deep connection to nature, and the enduring magic that flowed through its very stones.

As Lady Seraphina, General Ironheart, and General Elowen entered the grand castle of Ravenshadow, they passed through a massive oak door decorated with intricate carvings of enchanted creatures and forest motifs. The hall they entered was vast and imposing, its towering walls furnished with tapestries that told the ancient tales of Ravenshadow.

In the heart of the hall, a long, polished marble table was set with rich silverware, and crystal chandeliers hung from the high vaulted ceiling, casting a warm and welcoming light. Around the table, council members and highbred families were seated and standing, their expressions a mixture of curiosity, anxiety, and anticipation.

Lady Seraphina, dressed in attire befitting her newfound role as a warrior, wore a gown that blended the regal and practical. Her dress was a rich forest green, adorned with delicate embroidery of mystical creatures, leaves, and vines. The gown had a flowing skirt, but it was not overly extravagant, allowing for ease of movement. She wore a belt with a sheath for her sword, a symbol of her commitment to protect her realm.

General Ironheart and General Elowen stood on either side of Lady Seraphina, a unified front representing the strength and unity of the Crusade

Army and the Elven Kingdom. Their attire, though more traditional and practical, was equally regal, showcasing their roles as leaders and protectors.

With Lady Seraphina at the forefront, they stood ready to address the council and highbred families, to share their determination to unravel the mysteries that shrouded their realm and to seek justice for the fallen king, King Alaric.

Once seen as a delicate lady being sacrificed, she had now emerged as a warrior—a phoenix rising from the ashes. Her demeanor exuded strength, her eyes held the weight of experience, and her presence commanded respect. The shock and awe on the faces of the council members and highbred families were palpable, as they witnessed the evolution of Lady Seraphina into a formidable leader, ready to face the darkness that had befallen their realm.

At the head of the council table sat Lord Cedric, the head wiseman, his white beard cascading over the elaborate robes he wore. Alongside him were Lord Alistair, a stoic figure with a keen mind, Lady Ella, the original mage with an air of mysticism about her, and Sir Olan, a knight known for his loyalty and bravery.

The council members rose as Lady Seraphina, resplendent in her forest green attire, approached. Lord Cedric, with his piercing eyes, addressed her first. "Lady Seraphina, it is with heavy hearts that we meet under these circumstances."

Seraphina nodded solemnly. "Indeed, Lord Cedric. Your presence is appreciated."

Lord Alistair, his brow furrowed, spoke next. "We received troubling news about your parents, Lords Maximus and Lady Elena. Their deaths were not natural, Lady Seraphina."

A hushed tension filled the air as Lady Ella continued, her voice tinged with regret. "Isabella, once a trusted ally, is behind this heinous act. She sacrificed your parents as a gesture to Count Malachi, proving that Ravenshadow played no part in your escape from him."

Seraphina's eyes widened, a mixture of disbelief and sorrow clouding her gaze. "Isabella? But she was... she was one of your council members General Ironheart was she not?"

General Ironheart gave a solum nod.

Sir Olan, his expression sympathetic, laid a hand on Seraphina's shoulder. "People change, my lady. The darkness that has consumed her is not the Isabella he once knew."

Lady Seraphina took a moment to collect herself, her responses thoughtful and composed. "I was left to my own demise, my lords and lady. I had a choice, to rise above my circumstances or allow them to pull me down."

Lord Cedric nodded in understanding. "Your strength is evident, Lady Seraphina. Now, there is more you must know."

The council members leaned in, their voices low as they filled Seraphina, General Ironheart, and General Elowen in on the transformation of Isabella. "Isabella has aligned herself more closely with Count Malachi," Lord Alistair explained. "We suspect she is behind the murder of King Alaric."

General Ironheart's face showed a mix of sorrow and disbelief. "Isabella... I knew her before she turned down this dark path. It grieves me to hear this news."

The atmosphere in the grand hall grew heavy with the weight of the revelations. Lady Seraphina, her gaze unwavering, addressed the council. "We must uncover the truth and bring justice to those who have fallen victim to this darkness. Count Malachi and Isabella must be stopped."

Lord Cedric nodded in agreement. "You have our support, Lady Seraphina. We will assist in any way we can to restore balance to Ravenshadow."

General Elowen, who had been listening attentively, added, "We must tread carefully, for the shadows have grown deeper. Count Malachi's influence knows no bounds, and Isabella's treachery runs deep."

As they continued to discuss their plan, their voices carried a sense of urgency and determination. The Enchanted Forest and Ravenshadow were facing their greatest threat, and Lady Seraphina, General Ironheart, and General Elowen were now at the forefront of the battle to protect the realms. In this moment of suspense and uncertainty, their unity and resolve were the only constants that could guide them through the darkness that loomed ahead.

General Ironheart, with determination in his eyes, addressed the council of Ravenshadow. "We must request an army from Ravenshadow to join our crusade against Count Malachi and the darkness that threatens the Enchanted Forest and Ravenshadow."

The council members exchanged uneasy glances, initially reluctant to commit their forces to such a perilous endeavor. However, their hesitation sparked Ironheart's frustration. "Fools!" he exclaimed, his voice ringing out in the grand hall. "Always looking for the easy way out, where is your honour?"

Lady Seraphina, her voice laced with righteous anger, stepped forward to address the council with unwavering determination. "I did not argue when I was chosen as a sacrifice for our kingdom to Count Malachi," she declared firmly, her eyes blazing with intensity. "I gave my all, and my parents lost their lives in this kingdom's service. The kingdom owes me their allegiance, especially now when our very existence is threatened by the darkness Count Malachi wields."

Her impassioned words resonated through the hall, and the council members couldn't help but feel the weight of her sacrifice. General Ironheart nodded in agreement with Seraphina's sentiments, his respect for her growing with each passing moment. The council members, recognizing the depth of her commitment, began to reconsider their earlier reluctance.

Lord Cedric, the head wiseman of Ravenshadow, cleared his throat and stepped forward, addressing Seraphina with a measure of solemnity. "You have endured more than any of us can truly comprehend, Lady Seraphina. Your sacrifice and your family's tragic loss shall not be forgotten. Ravenshadow stands with you in this dark hour, and we pledge our full support to the crusade." The council members, one by one, offered their consent, their initial doubts replaced with a resolute determination to stand united against the looming threat of Count Malachi's darkness.

When it was time for the head general of Ravenshadow to pledge, he was a formidable warrior named Lord Valerian, stepped forward. He was a tall man with a chiseled jaw, his armour furnished with the emblem of Ravenshadow. His gaze bore into the council members as he spoke firmly, "General Ironheart is right. Our honour demands that we stand against this darkness. Ravenshadow will pledge its army to this crusade."

The council members, chastened by Ironheart's words and swayed by Lord Valerian's declaration, nodded in agreement. The alliance between Ravenshadow and the crusade army was sealed.

General Elowen, always the strategist, added his thoughts to the discussion. "It is crucial that our armies train together, to fight as one. I will send a scroll to the Elven Kingdom, inviting the crusade army and the elven warriors to come to Ravenshadow. Together, we shall become a formidable force against Count Malachi."

The decision was made, and the wheels of unity and preparation were set into motion. Ravenshadow, the crusade army, and the elves would join forces, training together to face the looming darkness as a unified front. The Enchanted Forest's defenders were resolute in their determination to protect their realm, and they knew that only by working together could they hope to prevail against the malevolent threat that awaited them.

The Final Showdown

General Elowen, with a sense of urgency, composed a message on a scroll, detailing the need for the elven warriors and the crusade army to join forces with Ravenshadow in the impending battle against Count Malachi's darkness. He entrusted the scroll to a majestic dove, its feathers shimmering within the light, and watched as it took flight toward the Elven Kingdom.

Days passed, and then, on the horizon, a sight both majestic and formidable emerged. The elven warriors arrived, a thousand strong, mounted on graceful deer-like creatures known as "Silvershadows." These creatures moved with an otherworldly elegance, their silvery fur and antlers gleaming under the sunlight. The elven warriors' armour glistened with enchantments, and they wielded slender, ethereal swords crafted by elven master artisans. The elven archers, renowned for their marksmanship, carried bows that sang with power.

Following the elven host, the crusade army marched in disciplined formation. Though fewer in number, they were a force to be reckoned with. Each soldier was clad in sturdy plate armour, bearing the emblem of the crusade on their chestplate. They rode noble warhorses, their presence exuding strength and determination. Among them, one soldier stood out, known for his exceptional prowess and the fighting capabilities of ten men. He was a living legend in their ranks.

The warrior was known as Sir Thorne Ironclad. Sir Thorne was a towering figure with a rugged and battle-hardened appearance. His armour, forged from the finest steel, bore the scars of countless battles, each mark a testament to his prowess on the battlefield. His helmet concealed most of his face, except for his piercing blue eyes that seemed to radiate determination.

Sir Thorne's muscular frame and imposing stature commanded respect from his comrades. He was often seen wielding a massive two-handed sword, the blade etched with ancient runes that glowed with an otherworldly light when drawn. His reputation on the battlefield was that of a relentless force, striking fear into the hearts of his enemies.

Despite his formidable presence, Sir Thorne possessed a sense of honour and camaraderie that endeared him to his fellow soldiers. He was a leader by example, inspiring those around him to stand unwavering in the face of danger. Many regarded him as a living legend in the crusade army, a beacon of hope in the darkest of times on the battlefield.

Leading the crusade army were General Ironheart's council members, Lady Titania Stormbringer, Sir Alden Frostbane, Captain Elara Swiftwind, and Lord Cellok Stoneforge, each on their noble steeds. Their armour bore the marks of countless battles, and their faces were etched with the resolve to protect the Enchanted Forest and Ravenshadow at any cost.

The sight of these two formidable armies approaching Ravenshadow sent a wave of hope through the defenders of the Enchanted Forest and the kingdom of Ravenshadow. Seraphina, Ironheart, and the council members of Ravenshadow gazed upon the massive force with a sense of awe and gratitude. As the armies drew near, the air resonated with their rhythmic chanting, a unified chorus of determination and resolve that echoed through the ancient trees, filling the hearts of all who stood ready to face the final Count Malachi.

As the combined forces of the crusade army and elven warriors marched toward Ravenshadow, their voices joined in a powerful, harmonious chorus that echoed through the ancient trees of the Enchanted Forest. The warriors chanted:

"Unity in strength, in honour, we stand,

Together we fight, for our sacred land.

In courage, we rise, our hearts aflame,

In the name of light, we'll reclaim our claim."

The rhythmic chant resonated with unwavering determination and the shared purpose of reclaiming Ravenshadow from the darkness that had taken hold. It served as a powerful reminder of the unity and resolve that bound these diverse forces together in the face of impending battle.

The head general of Ravenshadow, Lord Valerian, stood at the gates of the kingdom, his voice booming as he ordered the massive gates to be opened wide. Slowly, the gates creaked apart, revealing the grandeur of Ravenshadow to the approaching army. The elven warriors on their Silvershadows and the crusade soldiers on their sturdy horses entered the kingdom, their arrival marked by a sense of anticipation and hope.

As they rode through the streets of Ravenshadow, the people of the kingdom had gathered to welcome them. The citizens, including Lady Ella, Sir Olan, and Lord Alistair, lined the streets, their faces filled with awe at the majestic presence of the elves and the formidable crusade army. Children clung to their parents, wide-eyed with wonder.

Some among the crowd threw colourful flowers at the passing warriors, creating a fragrant carpet of petals on the cobblestone streets. These flowers were a symbol of gratitude and thanks for the armies coming to their aid, a heartfelt gesture from the people of Ravenshadow to the brave men and women who had arrived to protect their kingdom. The air was filled with cheers, and the atmosphere was charged with a sense of unity and determination as the city welcomed its defenders with open arms.

With the combined forces of the crusade army and the elven warriors now within the walls of Ravenshadow, General Ironheart wasted no time in organizing the training sessions for their own army. He, along with Lord Valerian, the experienced general of Ravenshadow, and General Elowen of the elves, gathered the soldiers in the heart of the kingdom for a rigorous and coordinated training regimen.

The Ravenshadow army, clad in sleek ebony armour adorned with intricate silver engravings, presented an imposing sight. Their helmets bore the emblem of a raven in flight, the symbol of their kingdom, and their polished weapons gleamed in the dappled sunlight that filtered through the ancient trees of Ravenshadow. Each soldier rode a powerful warhorse, their hooves striking the ground with a rhythmic cadence.

The training began with a demonstration from the elven warriors. They moved with a fluid grace, their movements akin to a dance, as they displayed their archery skills. Arrows flew unerringly to their targets, hitting bullseyes with uncanny precision. The Ravenshadow soldiers watched in awe, realizing the level of mastery they needed to achieve.

General Elowen explained the importance of agility, accuracy, and quick reflexes, emphasizing that the elves' archery skills were a testament to centuries of practice and discipline. The Ravenshadow archers, inspired by the elven display, eagerly stepped forward to hone their own marksmanship under the watchful eye of the elven warriors.

Next came the close combat drills, where the crusade soldiers demonstrated their expertise. With swords and shields in hand, they engaged in sparring matches that showcased their impeccable timing and well-honed techniques. Sparks flew as steel met steel, and the Ravenshadow soldiers observed with respect the prowess of their fellow warriors.

General Ironheart addressed the troops, stressing the importance of unity and shared purpose. He explained that the success of their upcoming battle against the forces of darkness relied on their ability to fight as one cohesive force. The Ravenshadow soldiers were eager to learn and improve, recognizing that their kingdom's fate hung in the balance.

The training sessions continued for days on end. The elven warriors shared their knowledge of guerrilla warfare, teaching Ravenshadow soldiers how to utilize the dense foliage of the Enchanted Forest to their advantage. The soldiers learned to move silently and swiftly through the woods, becoming one with their environment.

The crusade soldiers, in turn, shared their tactical expertise, teaching Ravenshadow's army how to form disciplined formations, hold strategic positions, and communicate efficiently on the battlefield. The soldiers practiced drills under the scorching sun, their discipline unwavering as they absorbed every lesson.

As the training progressed, an unspoken camaraderie developed between the warriors of Ravenshadow, the crusade army, and the elven warriors. Bonds were forged through shared sweat and determination, and the soldiers began to see each other not as separate entities but as a united force.

General Ironheart, Lord Valerian, and General Elowen tirelessly supervised the training, offering guidance, encouragement, and wisdom. Each day brought new challenges and new skills to master, but the soldiers of Ravenshadow embraced their training with unwavering resolve.

Under the watchful eyes of their leaders, the once-disparate army of Ravenshadow transformed into a formidable, synchronized force. They moved as one, fought as one, and were prepared to face the darkness as one. The kingdom's survival depended on their unity, their training, and their unwavering determination to protect the realms and all that they held dear.

As Seraphina stepped onto the training field, a hushed awe swept through the Ravenshadow army. The soldiers, clad in their ebony armour, watched with a mix of curiosity and admiration. It had been some time since they had seen her, and the transformation was nothing short of remarkable. She radiated strength and determination, her once delicate appearance now replaced with the aura of a warrior.

General Ironheart, standing at the forefront of the training area, raised his voice above the murmurs. "Lady Seraphina," he called out, "Are you ready for your training?"

Seraphina nodded firmly, her emerald eyes filled with unwavering resolve. She wore a suit of armour that blended seamlessly with the ebony and silver of the Ravenshadow soldiers. The armour bore the emblem of a phoenix rising from the ashes, symbolizing her resilience and newfound strength. Her sword was a masterpiece, its blade shimmering with enchantments, and her bow equally enchanting.

General Ironheart stepped forward, his own sword drawn, and began to instruct Seraphina in the art of combat. He demonstrated each move with precision, his experienced hand guiding her through the intricacies of swordplay. They started with the basics, the fundamentals of stance and balance, footwork and parries.

Seraphina absorbed every word and every movement, her dedication evident in the focused gleam of her eyes. Her slender figure moved gracefully, her steps fluid and agile as she practiced the maneuvers. The Ravenshadow soldiers observed in rapt attention, their respect growing with every stroke of her blade.

The elven warriors, who had played a pivotal role in Seraphina's training, watched her progress with pride. They had witnessed her transformation from a fragile lady to a formidable warrior. As she executed each technique flawlessly, they exchanged approving glances, recognizing that she had embraced their teachings with dedication.

Among the crusade army, a sense of camaraderie had developed as they learned more about Seraphina's journey. They respected her not only for her newfound skills but also for the immense trials she had faced. They understood that she, too, was a symbol of resilience and the unyielding spirit of Ravenshadow.

As Seraphina and General Ironheart continued their training, the atmosphere on the field was one of reverence and admiration. The soldiers had heard tales of her courage and her unwavering commitment to the Enchanted

Forest. Now, they had the privilege of witnessing her growth as a warrior firsthand.

With each strike and parry, Seraphina's confidence grew. She moved with a newfound assurance, her blade a natural extension of herself. General Ironheart, a seasoned warrior with many battles behind him, recognized her potential and pushed her to her limits.

Hours passed, but Seraphina's determination remained unshaken. She sparred with members of the Ravenshadow army, the clash of steel resonating across the training field. She moved with grace and precision, and her fellow soldiers marveled at her adaptability and skill.

The day wore on, and as the sun began its descent, Seraphina's training continued. The elves, the crusade army, and the Ravenshadow soldiers alike had gathered around the training area, forming a circle of observers. They watched as she executed a series of rapid strikes, each one honed to pierce through an opponent's defenses and strike at the heart.

General Ironheart paused the training, his voice carrying to all who had gathered. "Lady Seraphina has shown remarkable progress today," he announced, his gaze filled with pride. "She embodies the spirit of Ravenshadow, and her commitment to our cause is unwavering."

A resounding cheer rose from the onlookers, and Seraphina's heart swelled with gratitude. She had come a long way from the fragile lady who had once been ensnared by Count Malachi's darkness. Now, she stood as a symbol of hope and strength, ready to face the impending battle against the forces of darkness.

As the soldiers dispersed, their hearts filled with renewed determination, Seraphina couldn't help but feel a sense of belonging. She had found her place among these warriors, and together, they would stand against the abyss that threatened their beloved realms.

The Ravenshadow Council decided to hold a ball. The grand ball being held in the heart of Ravenshadow Castle serves multiple significant purposes. First and foremost, it is a warm and prestigious welcome extended to the allies who have come to stand with the Kingdom of Ravenshadow in its impending battle against Count Malachi and the forces of darkness. This includes noble elves from the Elven Kingdom and the valiant crusade army, all of whom have answered the call to support Ravenshadow. The ball is a heartfelt expression of gratitude from the people of Ravenshadow to their allies, a way of acknowledging and appreciating the support and solidarity offered during these challenging and perilous times.

Furthermore, the gathering acts as a unifying force, allowing members of the Ravenshadow army, elven warriors, and crusaders to come together, build camaraderie, and establish a sense of cohesion. In the face of the looming danger, the ball becomes a symbol of hope, showcasing the resilience and determination of the kingdom's people and their allies to stand strong against adversity.

Lastly, the event is a special tribute to Lady Seraphina, the kingdom's heroine, who has transformed from a captive of Count Malachi into a formidable warrior and leader. Her journey serves as an inspiration to all, and the ball celebrates her bravery, sacrifices, and her role as a symbol of hope and courage for Ravenshadow. In essence, this grand ball represents unity, gratitude, hope, and the indomitable spirit of those who defy the encroaching darkness.

The grand ballroom of Ravenshadow Castle shimmered with opulence, a breathtaking sight bathed in the soft glow of crystal chandeliers and candlelit sconces. The walls were decorated with intricate tapestries, depicting legendary battles and enchanting forest scenes, a testament to the kingdom's rich history. The polished marble floor reflected the elegance of the room, and a sense of anticipation hung in the air.

Guests from the Elven Kingdom, the crusade army, and Ravenshadow mingled, their vibrant attire adding splashes of colour to the opulent surroundings. Elves donned gowns of flowing silks adorned with delicate embroidery, and their elven warriors wore armour crafted with the artistry of their forest home. Crusaders were clad in polished chainmail and adorned with their order's crest, their dignified presence a testament to their martial prowess.

The centerpiece of the ballroom was a majestic crystal chandelier, its myriad of facets casting prismatic patterns across the floor. A string ensemble played enchanting melodies, the haunting notes of elven harps blending harmoniously with the resonant chords of human lutes. The music filled the air, infusing the atmosphere with a sense of grandeur and sophistication.

As the guests mingled and danced, all eyes were eagerly turned toward the grand entrance, where Lady Seraphina was set to make her appearance. Her gown, a gift from the elves, was a masterpiece of elven craftsmanship. It flowed like moonlight itself, adorned with intricate silver embroidery that seemed to come alive in the soft illumination of the ballroom.

Finally, the doors swung open, and Lady Seraphina entered, a vision of grace and beauty. Her gown trailed behind her, shimmering with each step, and her auburn hair cascaded down her back in loose curls. Her emerald eyes sparkled with a blend of confidence and humility, and her presence in the room was magnetic.

As Seraphina made her way toward the center of the ballroom, a hushed awe swept through the assembled guests. She was the embodiment of a fairy tale, a living symbol of courage and resilience. The music swelled, and the ensemble shifted seamlessly into a waltz, a dance of grace and elegance befitting the occasion.

General Ironheart, resplendent in his polished armour with a crimson cloak flowing from his shoulders, watched Seraphina's approach with an intensity that mirrored the collective awe of the room. When she reached him, he extended his hand, a silent invitation to dance. She accepted with a warm smile, and they moved onto the marble floor as the music enveloped them.

Their dance was a symphony of elegance, their steps perfectly synchronized. Seraphina moved with the grace she had acquired through countless hours of training, her every motion conveying a sense of strength and poise. General Ironheart, his movements strong yet tender, guided her with a touch that spoke of trust and affection.

Amid the swirling melodies and the captivating dance, General Ironheart's voice broke through the music, his words meant only for Seraphina's ears. "Seraphina," he murmured, his eyes locked onto hers, "there's something I've been wanting to say."

Her heart quickened as they twirled gracefully through the dance. "What is it?" she replied, her voice barely more than a whisper.

General Ironheart's gaze never wavered as he confessed, "I love you, Seraphina. I've loved you since the moment I saw you in the Elven Kingdom, and my love for you has only grown stronger with each passing day."

The world seemed to slow around them as the weight of his words hung in the air. Seraphina's heart swelled with emotion, and a radiant smile graced her lips. "And I love you, Elderic," she replied, her voice filled with sincerity and warmth.

Their dance continued, but it was no longer a simple waltz—it was a celebration of their love, an affirmation of their bond in the midst of the enchanting ballroom. The music swelled, and they spun together, their hearts and souls intertwined in a dance that transcended mere steps and movements.

As they twirled and swayed in each other's arms, the guests watched in silent admiration. Lady Seraphina and General Ironheart had not only captured their kingdom's hearts but had also given life to a love story that was nothing short of a fairy tale—a love that had blossomed amidst darkness and adversity, and now shone brightly in the midst of enchantment and celebration.

After the splendid ball in the grandeur of Ravenshadow Castle, Lady Seraphina and General Ironheart retired to her chambers. The night had been a whirlwind of enchanting music, exquisite gowns, and swirling dances, but now, in the intimate confines of her chamber, they found a moment of respite. Seraphina, resplendent in the gown gifted to her by the elves, radiated an ethereal beauty that left Ironheart breathless. The flickering candlelight cast a warm, soft glow, enhancing the enchantment of the evening. As they entered the room, the world beyond seemed to fade away, leaving only the two of them, their hearts entwined in a dance of their own.

In the dimly lit corridor of Ravenshadow Castle, General Ironheart had just left Lady Seraphina's chamber after a splendid ball, her peaceful slumber a testament to the night's festivities. As he strode down the corridor, his mind was filled with the enchanting melodies of the ballroom, still echoing in his ears. The castle seemed quiet and serene, bathed in the gentle glow of flickering torches.

However, a faint, eerie hum reached his ears, disrupting the tranquil atmosphere. It drew his attention toward a chamber down the hall, a chamber that had once belonged to Lady Isabella. Ironheart recognized the chamber by the familiar furnishings that still adorned it, remnants of a past that seemed distant yet ever-present. Curiosity piqued, he pushed the door open and entered the room.

The chamber bore the remnants of Lady Isabella's presence, her belongings and arcane paraphernalia scattered around. Ironheart couldn't help but feel a sense of foreboding as he realized he stood in a place that was once a part of Isabella's domain. His eyes scanned the room, and it became evident that something was amiss, something more than mere remnants of the past.

Suddenly, a soft, haunting hum filled the chamber, and Ironheart's senses sharpened. He was not alone. A presence materialized before him, and to his astonishment, it was Lady Isabella herself. The woman who is under Count Malachi's dark influence now stood before him, her eyes filled with an unsettling malevolence.

Their confrontation began with Isabella attempting to seduce Ironheart, a tactic that he swiftly rebuffed. As she pressed on, her anger grew, and she accused him of using her only for her body, a distorted portrayal of their previous encounter when she had held him under an enchantment. Ironheart tried to reason with her, explaining the truth of their past, but Isabella's rage intensified.

With a voice that seemed to pierce the very air, Isabella began to utter incantations in a language unfamiliar to Ironheart. Dark, ominous globes of energy began to form around her hands, her eyes changing colour as she threatened Seraphina's life. Ironheart knew he had to act swiftly to protect his beloved.

As Isabella lunged forward, her black powers surging, Ironheart met her with his sword drawn. The chamber became a battlefield of magic and steel, each clash resonating with the intensity of their struggle. Isabella's spells twisted the very air, but Ironheart's determination and resolve remained unwavering.

With every swing of his sword, Ironheart deflected Isabella's dark magic, the clang of metal against energy echoing through the chamber. The battle raged on, their powers clashing in a furious contest of wills. Ironheart knew that, for the sake of Seraphina and all they held dear, he had to end this confrontation once and for all.

In a moment of opportunity, as Isabella lunged forward with a final burst of malevolence, Ironheart swiftly maneuvered his sword, aiming directly for her heart. The blade pierced through her dark defenses, finding its mark, and Isabella's eyes widened in shock and disbelief.

With a gasp, she staggered backward, clutching her chest where the sword had pierced her. Her once-menacing powers dissipated, leaving the room filled with an eerie silence. Isabella's form began to fade, and in her final moments, she met Ironheart's gaze with a mixture of anger, betrayal, and despair.

As her presence dissolved into nothingness, Ironheart was left standing in the chamber, the echoes of their fierce battle still reverberating in the air. The threat Isabella posed had come to an end, but the consequences of their confrontation weighed heavily on his mind. He knew that the dark forces of Count Malachi still loomed, and the final showdown they all anticipated drew ever nearer.

As Seraphina entered her chamber, the sounds of their battle had awakened her from a peaceful slumber. She looked around, bewildered, and saw Isabella's lifeless body on the floor. A mix of emotions swirled within her, and she turned to Ironheart, her voice quivering as she asked what had happened. Ironheart, with a heavy heart, explained the confrontation and how he had no choice but to defend himself.

Just as they were grappling with the aftermath, one of the council members of Ravenshadow, alerted by the commotion, entered the room. He advised that Isabella's body should be burnt to ensure that Count Malachi couldn't use it for any nefarious purposes. After a somber agreement, they prepared a solemn funeral for Lady Isabella. Ironheart, along with his council, mourned not only the loss of Isabella but the woman she had once been – a friend and ally. With heavy hearts, they set her body ablaze, and the flames consumed her, marking the end of her tumultuous journey.

Count Malachi, shrouded in darkness, felt the absence of Lady Isabella's presence like a gaping wound in his malevolent soul. His connection to her, severed by her death, left him with a sense of emptiness and fury that burned hotter than the fires of hell. In his chambers, surrounded by arcane symbols and forbidden tomes, he summoned a raven, imbued with dark magic, to carry a scroll bearing his demand for war. The scroll's words were etched in blood-red ink, a sinister declaration that echoed through the realms.

Redemption's Light

The moon hung low in the sky, casting a silvery glow over the kingdom of Ravenshadow. Seraphina stood alone on the balcony of her chamber; her gaze fixed on the celestial orb. The night was still, save for the distant rustle of leaves and the soft hum of crickets. In this quiet moment, she found herself wrestling with her inner demons.

The weight of her choices bore down on her shoulders like an unrelenting burden. She had accepted the role of sacrifice, for her family's honour and the love of her kingdom. She had seen her friend, Lady Isolde, meet a cruel fate at the hands of Count Malachi. Seraphina wished she could turn back the hands of time, prevent the tragedies that had befallen her loved ones, but she knew deep down that even if she hadn't searched for answers, Malachi would have taken their lives regardless.

She closed her eyes, her mind replaying the horrors she had endured. Count Malachi was like a shadowy vampire, and the scars he had left on her body were not of her choosing. Each night, she battled her own darkness, struggling not to be consumed by anger and bitterness. She fought for the light to remain stronger, for the promise she had made to herself and her kingdom.

As she stood there, lost in her thoughts, a familiar voice broke the silence. "Seraphina," General Ironheart's deep voice resonated from behind her. She turned to find him stepping onto the balcony.

"General," she acknowledged, her voice carrying a note of weariness.

Ironheart approached her, concern etched across his rugged features. He had watched her silently from the shadows, aware of the turmoil that had gripped her. "The weight of our choices can be heavy," he said, his eyes searching hers. "But you are not alone in this. We are with you, every step of the way."

Seraphina nodded, a small smile playing at the corners of her lips. "Thank you, General. Your support means more to me than you know."

Ironheart reached out and gently placed a hand on her shoulder. "We must remember who we are fighting for, and why. Our realms, our people, and the hope of redemption—all of these are worth the sacrifices we make."

She met his gaze, finding solace in his words. "You're right, General. We must press on, no matter the challenges that lie ahead."

In another part of the castle, the council members of the crusade army gathered to discuss their roles in the impending battle against Count Malachi. Lady Titania Stormbringer, her silver hair cascading like a waterfall, sat at the head of the table. Sir Alden Frostbane, known for his sharp wit and sarcastic humour, lounged in his chair. Captain Elara Swiftwind, a fierce and agile warrior, exchanged a knowing glance with Lord Cellok Stoneforge, whose stoic demeanor hid a wealth of wisdom.

Their council chamber, adorned with intricate tapestries and the symbols of Ravenshadow, was illuminated by candlelight. It was a solemn gathering, for they understood the gravity of their mission.

Lady Titania, her blue eyes reflecting the flickering flames, spoke first. "We find ourselves at a crossroads, my fellow council members. The fate of the realms hang in the balance, and the time has come for us to make our stand."

Sir Alden chimed in, his tone laced with his trademark sarcasm. "Well, that didn't last long, the plain speaking," he quipped, earning a few chuckles from the others.

Captain Elara, the voice of reason, added, "Count Malachi's reign of terror must be brought to an end. We owe it to Seraphina, to Lady Isolde, and to all those who have suffered."

Lord Cellok, the eldest and most revered among them, leaned forward. "Indeed, but we must also consider the transformation of Lady Isabella. It seemed her allegiance lay with the darkness that corrupts Count Malachi."

The council members exchanged grave glances, acknowledging the complexity of their situation. Seraphina had not been the only one to undergo a transformation. The darkness that had taken hold of Lady Isabella was a stark reminder of the insidious nature of Count Malachi's influence.

"Then let us prepare for the battle," Lady Titania declared, determination in her voice. "We will stand together, united in purpose and resolve."

Meanwhile, in the heart of the Enchanted Forest, General Elowen of the elven warriors conducted a meeting with his kin. The elves, known for their ethereal grace and connection to the natural world, had long been allies of Ravenshadow. Their presence added an air of mysticism to the gathering.

General Elowen, with his flowing silver hair and emerald-green attire, addressed his fellow elves. "The time has come, my brethren. We have been called upon to aid Ravenshadow in their hour of need. The darkness that plagues our lands must be vanquished."

The elven warriors, their armour adorned with intricate leaf patterns and their bows crafted from the finest enchanted wood, listened intently. They knew that their kinship with Ravenshadow extended beyond mere alliance; it was a bond forged through shared values and a commitment to protect their enchanted realm.

"We shall bring our wisdom and our skills to bear," General Elowen continued. "But we must also remember the strength that comes from unity. Together with Ravenshadow and the crusade army, we shall form an unbreakable alliance."

The elves nodded in agreement, their eyes filled with determination. The Enchanted Forest, their home, was threatened by the encroaching darkness of Count Malachi. They would not let their sacred realm fall to such malevolence.

The general concluded, "Let us embark on this journey with hearts full of hope and the knowledge that together, we shall confront the shadows that seek to consume us."

The training grounds of Ravenshadow came alive with activity as the combined forces of the kingdom, the elves, and the crusade army prepared for the impending battle. Warriors clad in various forms of armour practiced their combat skills, archers honed their accuracy, and cavalry units drilled with precision.

General Ironheart stood at the forefront, his presence commanding respect and attention. He watched with a critical eye as the soldiers sparred and trained, noting their strengths and areas that required improvement. The elves had brought their own methods of combat, seamlessly integrating their skills with those of Ravenshadow's army.

Amidst the organized chaos, Seraphina emerged in her training attire—a black leather suit adorned with protective runes. Her sword, crafted by the elven smiths, gleamed in the sunlight. She had become a beacon of strength and resilience, inspiring those around her.

As the soldiers noticed her presence, a hushed reverence spread through the ranks. They had heard of her journey, her sacrifices, and the battles she had faced. Now, they witnessed her grace and skill firsthand. The elves, in particular, felt a sense of pride in having played a role in her training.

General Ironheart approached her, a hint of admiration in his eyes. "Lady Seraphina, it's time for your training," he said.

She nodded, gripping her sword with confidence. Together, they began their practice, each move deliberate and precise. Ironheart taught her the art of the blade, emphasizing the importance of striking true, especially in the heat of battle.

As they sparred, the soldiers and warriors gathered around, their eyes fixed on the dueling pair. They were witnessing a transformation—a young woman who had once been a reluctant sacrifice had become a formidable warrior. Her fluid movements, honed under Ironheart's guidance, spoke of her determination and her unwavering commitment to protect her kingdom.

The elves, in particular, observed with a sense of pride. General Elowen, standing among his kin, watched Seraphina's training with a knowing smile. She had embraced their teachings, integrating them seamlessly into her combat style.

General Ironheart, sweat glistening on his brow, halted their practice. He looked into Seraphina's eyes, his voice carrying a weight of emotion. "Seraphina, you have grown into a remarkable warrior. But there's something I must tell you."

She lowered her sword, curiosity and concern in her gaze. "What is it, General?"

He took a step closer, his eyes locked onto hers. "I love you, Seraphina," he confessed, his voice filled with sincerity.

The world seemed to still around them, as if time itself had paused. In that moment, amidst the training grounds and the watchful eyes of their comrades, Seraphina felt her heart swell with emotion. She had found not only a leader but a partner who stood with her through the darkest of times.

Tears welled up in her eyes as she whispered, "I love you too, General."

Their embrace, amidst the training grounds and the unity of their forces, symbolized not just a personal connection but a bond forged through trials and the hope of redemption. They were ready to face the looming darkness, for love, unity, and the promise of a brighter future had become their guiding light.

In the heart of Ravenshadow, the preparations for the impending battle were in full swing. The combined forces of the kingdom, the elven warriors, and the crusade army had created a formidable army, each member united by a shared purpose—to vanquish the looming darkness of Count Malachi.

General Ironheart, his strong presence commanding respect, oversaw the training exercises of the soldiers. His council members, Lady Titania Stormbringer, Sir Alden Frostbane, Captain Elara Swiftwind, and Lord Cellok Stoneforge, stood by his side. Together, they coordinated the drills, strategies, and logistics that would be crucial in the battle ahead.

Seraphina, now fully integrated into the ranks of the army, sparred with seasoned warriors. Her training under Ironheart's tutelage had transformed her into a formidable combatant. The elven warriors, their grace evident in their every movement, provided guidance, further enhancing her skills.

It was on one such training day that a messenger arrived with news from the kingdom of Ravenshadow. The message was delivered to Lady Titania, who swiftly broke the seal and read its contents. Her emerald eyes narrowed as she absorbed the information.

"What is it, Lady Titania?" asked Sir Alden, his curiosity piqued.

She turned to face the council members. "It appears that Count Malachi has sent us a message. He demands that we meet him for the final battle at a location he has chosen."

Captain Elara crossed her arms, her expression resolute. "And where is this chosen battleground?"

Lady Titania unfolded the scroll to reveal a detailed map, a location marked with a blood-red seal. "He has named it the 'Crimson Vale.' It lies beyond the Enchanted Forest, closer to his domain."

Lord Cellok, his brow furrowed in thought, examined the map closely. "It's a treacherous terrain, filled with pitfalls and hidden dangers. Count Malachi has chosen it well to his advantage."

The council members exchanged somber glances, recognizing the gravity of the situation. They were being drawn into a battlefield of Count Malachi's choosing, a place where he had the upper hand.

General Ironheart stepped forward, his voice resonating with unwavering determination. "We will not shy away from this challenge. Ravenshadow and its allies stand united against the darkness. We will meet Count Malachi at the Crimson Vale, and we will emerge victorious."

Seraphina, her training momentarily halted, overheard their conversation. She approached the council members and the general, her gaze unwavering. "I am ready, General Ironheart. We must let Count Malachi know that we accept his terms."

General Ironheart nodded, his trust in Seraphina evident. "Very well, Lady Seraphina. We will send a raven bearing our acceptance."

With that decision made, the preparations for the journey to the Crimson Vale intensified. Supplies were gathered, weapons sharpened, and strategic plans honed. The soldiers, regardless of their origin—Ravenshadow, elven, or crusader—worked seamlessly together, united by a common goal.

As the raven bearing their acceptance soared through the skies, it carried with it a message that resonated with conviction. Count Malachi, though a formidable adversary, would soon face an alliance forged in the crucible of adversity.

Days turned into nights, and the preparations continued. The soldiers trained tirelessly, their camaraderie strengthening with each passing moment. Seraphina, now an integral part of their ranks, was a beacon of hope and inspiration.

The elves, renowned for their archery skills, conducted an archery competition. The twang of bowstrings and the thud of arrows hitting targets filled the air. General Elowen, his silver hair gleaming in the sunlight, awarded a prize to the elven archer who displayed unmatched accuracy.

The crusade army, led by Lady Titania Stormbringer and her council, held strategic discussions. They devised formations, tactics, and contingency plans to counter the dark forces they would encounter at the Crimson Vale. Lady Titania's strategic brilliance shone through, and her council members provided valuable insights.

Seraphina, meanwhile, continued her training with General Ironheart. Their bond had deepened through the shared anticipation of the coming battle. She had become proficient with the sword, her movements fluid and precise. The combination of her skills, the elven archers, and the crusade's strategies promised a formidable fighting force.

The day of departure for the Crimson Vale arrived, marked by a solemn ceremony in the heart of Ravenshadow. The soldiers, adorned in their armour, gathered before the castle. Lady Seraphina stood at the forefront, flanked by General Ironheart and General Elowen. The elven warriors, their ethereal presence a testament to their ancient heritage, stood in formation.

A sense of anticipation hung in the air, mingled with determination and resolve.

The people of Ravenshadow had come to bid farewell to their defenders. Citizens lined the streets, young and old, their eyes filled with gratitude and hope.

As the procession began, the soldiers marched through the streets of Ravenshadow. Some threw flowers, symbolizing their support and appreciation. Others raised banners bearing the emblem of their kingdom and chanted words of encouragement.

The elven warriors, graceful in their movement, rode on their majestic steeds. Their armour shimmered in the sunlight, a testament to their otherworldly elegance. The combination of the Ravenshadow army's strength, the elven warriors' precision, and the crusade's determination was a sight to behold.

The journey to the Crimson Vale was fraught with challenges. The path led them through the Enchanted Forest, its ancient trees and mystical creatures posing both wonder and danger. The elven warriors, accustomed to the forest's enchantments, guided the way.

At times, the forest seemed to come alive with whispered secrets and ethereal melodies. The songs of the Enchanted Forest intertwined with the fervent chants of the crusaders, creating an otherworldly harmony.

They encountered obstacles in the form of treacherous terrain and hidden traps, a testament to Count Malachi's cunning. However, their unity prevailed. The council members' strategic expertise guided them safely through, and Seraphina's unwavering resolve inspired them all.

The journey brought the soldiers closer together, forging bonds of trust and camaraderie. Seraphina, once a reluctant sacrifice, had become their symbol of hope and resilience. Her presence reminded them of the purpose that united them—to vanquish the darkness that threatened their world.

Finally, the Crimson Vale came into view, a vast expanse of blood-red earth surrounded by jagged cliffs. The air was thick with tension as the combined forces of Ravenshadow, the elves, and the crusaders approached their designated battleground.

General Ironheart, mounted on his steed and clad in his armour, gazed across the Crimson Vale. His council members stood by his side, their expressions resolute. The elven warriors, their arrows nocked and bows at the ready, maintained a disciplined formation.

Seraphina riding Lumina, her sword in hand, felt the weight of their collective purpose. Her journey from reluctant sacrifice to a formidable warrior had brought her to this moment. The dark forces of Count Malachi awaited them, but they were prepared—united and ready to face their destiny.

As they stood on the precipice of the final battle, the echoes of their journey reverberated through the Crimson Vale.

The Serpent's Battle

The Crimson Vale bore witness to an impending clash between light and darkness as Seraphina led the united forces of Ravenshadow, the elves, and the crusaders. They stood resolute, prepared to face Count Malachi's demonic army.

Count Malachi, his form twisted by dark enchantments, rode at the forefront of his unholy forces. Above them, shadowy figures that resembled demons loomed, lending their eerie power to the malevolent host. Grizzletooth, the goblin leader, led a horde of his kind, armed with cunning and chaos.

The most fearsome sights were the six giant wolves, each boasting three heads, and the Dracernoths—hybrid creatures with horse bodies, lizard tails, and dragon heads and necks. Count Malachi rode one of these formidable beasts, and the rest of his army mounted others.

The two opposing forces stared across the crimson battlefield, their gazes filled with anticipation, dread, and determination. Count Malachi, his voice a venomous hiss, rallied his malevolent troops, promising that Seraphina would be his to torment. His eyes gleamed with malice as he spoke of the suffering he intended to inflict upon her.

Seraphina, resplendent in her armour, led her united forces. They looked at the ominous army across the field with a mix of curiosity and concern. The demonic creatures that accompanied Count Malachi were a sight they had never seen before, and they exchanged whispered questions about the nature of these beings. In their midst, General Ironheart, the embodiment of honour and courage, reassured them that fear had no place in their hearts. He raised his sword high and, with unwavering resolve, shouted, "Charge!"

At that moment, the earth itself seemed to shake as both sides surged forward, racing towards the inevitable clash. The crimson vale became a swirling maelstrom of chaos and conflict, with the crusaders leading the charge, their faith unwavering, while Ravenshadow's disciplined troops advanced with the precision of elven archery.

The cacophonous clash of metal and magic echoed across the battlefield as soldiers on both sides fought fiercely for their beliefs. Spears clashed against swords, arrows found their marks amidst the chaos, and fire–breathing Dracernoths cast their fearsome shadow over the crimson earth. It was a battle of light against darkness, honour against malevolence, and the destiny of a realms hung in the balance.

As the armies clashed, the battlefield became a swirling maelstrom of chaos and conflict. The crusaders, with their unwavering faith, charged valiantly into the demonic ranks. Ravenshadow's disciplined troops, accompanied by the elven warriors' precise archery, formed a formidable front.

As the battle raged on, there were moments when it seemed Count Malachi's unholy forces were gaining the upper hand. A wave of despair washed over Seraphina's allies, but General Ironheart, undeterred by the adversity, raised his voice above the clamor of combat. With a resounding shout, he rallied his troops, "Do not falter, do not give up! Push forward!" His words infused them with renewed determination, and they surged ahead, their spirits rekindled by his unwavering resolve to see this battle through to the end.

Before the battle reached its zenith, a remarkable sight unfolded on the battlefield as these mystical creatures joined the fray. Raelthor, the griffon, a magnificent creature with feathers like molten gold, descended with a mighty swoop, his powerful beak and talons tearing into the ranks of goblins and demonic soldiers. Lysandra, the phoenix, her plumage aflame with vibrant colours, soared overhead, her blazing wings setting fire to the enemy lines as she unleashed waves of searing heat upon them. The skywardens, majestic eagles, descended from the heavens with piercing cries, their sharp beaks and talons finding purchase on the goblin hordes, causing chaos among Count Malachi's ranks. These mythical allies turned the tide of battle in favour of Seraphina and her united forces, bringing hope and renewed determination to their ranks.

The crescendo of battle raged, and warriors clashed with demonic soldiers. Swords and arrows met supernatural strength, while goblin tricks tangled with the valor of the crusaders. The Dracernoths spat dragonfire, and the giant wolves with their many heads proved formidable adversaries.

Amidst the turmoil, Seraphina rode Lumina, leading her unit with unwavering resolve. Her eyes shone with determination as she guided her companions, the bond between them unbreakable.

As the battle raged on, a surge of dark energy erupted from Count Malachi's direction. The shockwave sent Seraphina tumbling off Lumina backward, her footing lost in the chaos. Desperately, she struggled to regain her balance as the tumultuous conflict surged around her. In the midst of the melee, she lost sight of the banners and faces of her comrades. A sudden charge by a group of count Malachi's demonic soldiers further disoriented her, forcing her to retreat towards the precipitous cliff's edge. In this chaotic maelstrom, Seraphina became isolated, standing alone at the very precipice that had haunted her dreams. And then, with a surreal sense of inevitability, Count Malachi, the embodiment of her nightmares, appeared before her.

Their battle was fierce and relentless. Count Malachi taunted her with insults, seeking to provoke her anger. Count Malachi's taunts cut through the air as they clashed swords:

"You're nothing more than a pawn, Seraphina, a puppet dancing to my tune."

"Your family, your kingdom, they all crumbled because of your weakness."

"You thought you could escape me, but you're back where you belong, in my grasp."

"The darkness within you is stronger than you'll ever be. You're destined to serve me."

"You'll never find peace, Seraphina, not as long as I exist."

These taunts fueled Seraphina's anger and frustration, pushing her to the brink of despair.

As their swords clashed, Seraphina noticed an unsettling change in her blade, Astrafyre. The amethyst at its hilt began to turn black as her anger and resentment boiled over.

Desperation washed over Seraphina as she fought against her own sword, unwilling to let darkness consume her. She thought of her stallion, Sir Sterling, and the memory of losing him when darkness had driven her actions. Count Malachi grinned wickedly and taunted, "Aaahhh, we've seen this before now, haven't we? The helpless girl, drowning in despair, unable to save those she loves." His words cut deep, reopening old wounds, and Seraphina knew she had to find a way to break free from this cycle of darkness.

With her sword turning blacker by the moment, Seraphina cried out to the heavens, her voice filled with a plea for divine intervention. "God, please help me! Aid me in this battle!"

In response to her prayer, Count Malachi laughed demonically, mocking her with cruel words, "God will never save you, why would he be interested in a violated, worthless woman like you?"

A moment of eerie silence hung over the battlefield as everyone stopped what they were doing, drawn to the unfolding scene. Then, a resounding, divine trumpet sound echoed through the air, in response to her prayer, the heavens themselves seemed to open with a great light shining through. Archangel Michael, a radiant figure leading a chariot of fiery angels, descended into the battle. His presence exuded power and authority.

The archangel turned his attention to the demon above Count Malachi, a dark entity named Belial. With a swing of his fiery sword, Michael engaged Belial in a fierce battle. Other angels joined the fray, battling the demons that provided strength to Count Malachi's forces.

As the angels engaged the demons, the tide of the battle began to turn. The demonic soldiers grew weaker without their dark overseers. Count Malachi, once poised to win, now faced a weakened army.

Archangel Michael, with divine might, delivered a final blow to Belial. The demon dissolved into nothingness, its malevolent energy vanquished. This act weakened Count Malachi further, who now knelt on the blood-red earth, his powers waning.

Seraphina, with her amethyst sword no longer fighting against her, raised it, poised to deliver a final blow. Count Malachi's fate seemed sealed, but at that critical moment, Archangel Michael intervened.

"No, Lady Seraphina," Michael said, his voice resonating with compassion and wisdom. "Do not let his blood stain your hands. There is a different fate in store for Count Malachi."

With a touch of his divine power, Archangel Michael reached out to Count Malachi. In an instant, all the demonic essence, possession, and power that had consumed the once-powerful sorcerer erupted into the sky with anguished wails. All his demonic creations started to dissolve into nothingness as the demonic powers left count Malachi, leaving the goblins to flee in retreat!

Count Malachi was left as a mere shell of the man he had been. His mind, once filled with malevolence, was now shattered and delusional. The threat he had posed had been vanquished, but the echoes of the battle's intensity lingered in the Crimson Vale.

General Ironheart, determined and resolute, eventually made his way to Seraphina, his sword drawn and charged, ready to confront Count Malachi. The battle raged around them, but Ironheart's focus remained unswerving. He was ready to end this once and for all.

However, before Ironheart could reach Count Malachi, Seraphina intervened. She raised her sword, Astrafyre, a shimmering amethyst at its hilt, and held it between them. Her gaze shifted to Archangel Michael, who radiated divine power, and then back to Ironheart.

With conviction in her voice, she said, "General Ironheart, we must not kill Count Malachi. We shall take him back to his castle in Shadowmoor, where he will live out the rest of his days, trapped within its walls and tormented by his delusional thoughts."

Ironheart paused, his sword lowering slightly. The weight of Seraphina's words settled upon him, and he considered the consequences of ending Count Malachi's life versus letting him suffer in isolation. The battlefield around them seemed to grow quieter, as if holding its breath in anticipation.

Meanwhile, Count Malachi, trembling in a ball on the ground, was caught in a nightmarish struggle. His mind became a battleground, torn between his demonic desires and the divine forces surrounding him. Whispers and tormented voices clawed at his consciousness, feeding his paranoia and tormenting his thoughts.

The once-mighty Count Malachi, who had reveled in darkness and sought power at any cost, now found himself in a pitiable state. His eyes darted wildly as he muttered incoherent words, lost in a sea of delusion.

As Seraphina and Ironheart made their decision, Archangel Michael stepped forward. His majestic presence seemed to calm the turmoil around them, and his voice resonated with authority. "So be it," he declared, his words carrying the weight of divine judgment.

Together, Seraphina and Ironheart approached Count Malachi, who remained crouched on the ground. Seraphina's sword, Astrafyre, no longer radiated the darkness that had threatened to consume it, but instead shone with a renewed brilliance. She sheathed her sword and extended her hand towards Count Malachi.

With some resistance, Ironheart helped Count Malachi to his feet, his former adversary now a broken man. As they began their journey back to

Shadowmoor, Count Malachi's mind remained ensnared by the torment of his past actions and the consequences of his lust for power.

The battle had been won, but not with the blade. Seraphina's compassion and wisdom had prevailed over vengeance, and Count Malachi's fate was sealed within the walls of his own castle, a prisoner to his own madness.

The armies that had once clashed in a war of darkness now turned their attention to rebuilding and healing. As they departed the battlefield, Archangel Michael and his divine host ascended into the heavens, their presence a symbol of hope and redemption.

Seraphina and Ironheart, their bond strengthened by the trials they had faced, led the way back to Ravenshadow, where they would celebrate their hard-won victory and honour those who had fallen in the battle against Count Malachi's darkness. It was a new era for the Kingdom of Ravenshadow, Kingdom of Shadowmoor and the Enchanted forest, one marked by unity, forgiveness, and the pursuit of redemption's light.

The united forces of Ravenshadow, the elves, and the crusaders emerged victorious, their resilience and unity prevailing over Count Malachi's dark ambitions. The Crimson Vale, once shrouded in ominous red, now bore witness to the redemption's light, a beacon of hope in a world forever changed.

As the victorious armies returned to Ravenshadow, General Elowen, a wise and seasoned leader of the elves, stepped forward to address the gathered warriors. His voice resonated with pride and solemnity as he spoke, "My friends and comrades, today we have witnessed a battle that will forever go down in history. Let it be known as 'The Serpent's Battle,' a testament to our unity and courage."

The warriors nodded in agreement. The name 'The Serpent's Battle' would serve as a reminder of the war that took place on these grounds and the redemption that had been achieved.

A New Dawn

As the victorious armies returned to Ravenshadow, General Elowen, a wise and seasoned leader of the elves, stepped forward to address the gathered warriors and citizens. His voice resonated with pride and solemnity as he spoke, "My friends and comrades, today we have witnessed a end of an era that will forever go down in history. Let it be known as 'The Serpent's Shadow,' a testament of light over darkness."

The crowd that had gathered, including the elven warriors, crusade army, and Ravenshadow's own soldiers, nodded in agreement. The name 'The Serpent's Shadow' would serve as a reminder of the trials they had faced, the sacrifices they had made, and the redemption that had been achieved. It would be a story told for generations, inspiring hope and courage in the face of adversity, and a testament to the power of unity and the strength of the human spirit.

With the battle won, the united forces embarked on their journey back to Shadowmoor, where Count Malachi's castle stood as a dark and ominous presence. However, as they approached the once-dreaded land, they were met with a wondrous transformation. The malevolent evil that had shrouded Shadowmoor began to recede, and the eerie, twisted forest that had plagued the region for so long was slowly transforming into the ancient and lush forest it once was.

The barren fields, once tainted by darkness, now started to look lush and vibrant, and nature began its process of healing. Birds sang, and animals returned to the once-desolate land, as if celebrating the newfound peace. Seraphina, riding at the head of her army, felt a sense of relief wash over her. The land was healing, just as she hoped it would.

Upon reaching Count Malachi's castle, Seraphina, Ironheart, and the rest of the company led the delusional and broken Count into the courtyard. What they discovered there was a symbol of their victory and redemption. The courtyard, once filled with black roses, was now clear, signifying that the souls trapped within the castle were finally free to rest in peace. Seraphina thought of Lady Isolde and the promise she had made to her. A single tear of happiness rolled down her cheek, knowing that she had fulfilled her vow.

With Count Malachi in tow, Seraphina, Lumina, and Ironheart entered the castle's great hall. Seraphina knew that, to ensure the safety of their world, they needed to take drastic measures. Lumina, using her enchantment abilities, created a protective barrier around the castle. Count Malachi, now lost in madness and delusion, would never be able to cross that barrier. He was condemned to spend the rest of his days alone in the castle, tormented by his fractured mind, his existence a mere shadow of the serpent he had once been.

As they rode back through the enchanted forest, the very heart of their world seemed to celebrate their return. The trees whispered secrets of their victory, and the creatures of the forest danced in jubilation. Fireflies illuminated the path, creating a breathtaking spectacle of light and colour. It was as if the entire enchanted forest had come to life to rejoice in their triumph.

Upon their return to the heart of the enchanted forest, Ironheart couldn't help but voice the question that had been on his mind since they spared Count Malachi's life. "Seraphina, I understand why you chose not to kill him, but I can't help but wonder about the justice of it all. Why did you spare him, knowing the suffering he caused?"

Seraphina, her gaze reflecting the wisdom of someone who had seen both darkness and light, turned to him and replied, "Ironheart, the true vengeance is not in his death but in our ability to move forward without his influence and grasp. He is living a fate worse than death, tormented by his own mind until his last breath. And that, my love, is a punishment he will carry to the end of his days."

As they spoke, the enchanted forest seemed to embrace them, its magic weaving around them like a protective cocoon. It was a place of healing and renewal, a testament to the power of redemption and the resilience of the human spirit.

The healing pond within the enchanted forest beckoned to them, its waters shimmering with a tranquil and restorative energy. Seraphina and Ironheart dismounted and slowly walked into the rejuvenating waters, their armour and burdens washing away. They looked at each other with love and gratitude, their hearts connected by the trials they had faced and the battles they had won.

Ironheart gazed into Seraphina's eyes, his voice filled with warmth and affection. "What's next for us, my love?"

Seraphina smiled, her eyes reflecting the hope of a new beginning. "Our whole lives," she replied, and they embraced in the gentle, healing waters of the enchanted forest, knowing that their journey together was just beginning—a journey bathed in the light of a new dawn.

Printed in Great Britain
by Amazon

33641726R00245